BULLET

BULLET

LAURELL K. HAMILTON

BERKLEY BOOKS, NEW YORK

A BERKLEY BOOK
Published by the Penguin Group
Penguin Group (USA) Inc.
375 Hudson Street, New York, New York 10014, USA
Penguin Group (Canada), 90 Eglinton Avenue East, Suite 700, Toronto, Ontario M4P 2Y3, Canada
(a division of Pearson Penguin Canada Inc.)
Penguin Books Ltd., 80 Strand, London WC2R 0RL, England
Penguin Group Ireland, 25 St. Stephen's Green, Dublin 2, Ireland (a division of Penguin Books Ltd.)
Penguin Group (Australia), 250 Camberwell Road, Camberwell, Victoria 3124, Australia
(a division of Pearson Australia Group Pty. Ltd.)
Penguin Books India Pvt. Ltd., 11 Community Centre, Panchsheel Park, New Delhi—110 017, India
Penguin Group (NZ), 67 Apollo Drive, Rosedale, North Shore 0632, New Zealand
(a division of Pearson New Zealand Ltd.)
Penguin Books (South Africa) (Pty.) Ltd., 24 Sturdee Avenue, Rosebank, Johannesburg 2196,
South Africa
Penguin Books Ltd., Registered Offices: 80 Strand, London WC2R 0RL, England

This book is an original publication of The Berkley Publishing Group.

This is a work of fiction. Names, characters, places, and incidents either are the product of the author's imagination or are used fictitiously, and any resemblance to actual persons, living or dead, business establishments, events, or locales is entirely coincidental. The publisher does not have any control over and does not assume any responsibility for author or third-party websites or their content.

First edition: June 2010

Library of Congress Cataloging-in-Publication Data

Hamilton, Laurell K.
    Bullet / Laurell K. Hamilton.
        p.   cm.
    ISBN 978-0-425-23433-4
    1. Blake Anita (Fictitious character—Fiction.   2. Vampires—Fiction.   3. Werewolves—Fiction.
4. Serial murderers—Fiction.   5. Attempted assassination—Fiction.   6. Saint Louis (Mo.)—Fiction.
I. Title.
    PS3558 A443357B85   2010
    813'.54—dc22   2010009928

PRINTED IN THE UNITED STATES OF AMERICA

10   9   8   7   6   5   4   3   2   1

One mustn't look at the abyss, because there is at the bottom an inexpressible charm which attracts us.

—Gustave Flaubert

To Jonathon, who has stood at my side and looked into the abyss and found both charm, attraction, and love, for we are not made up only of our light and happiness but also of darkness and sorrow. To deny the darkness of yourself is to deny half of who you are, and when you love, truly love, you need to love the whole person not just the part that smiles and waves, but the part that thinks murderous thoughts and knows that pain is both pleasure and temptation, but still thinks puppies are really cute.

Acknowledgments

Carri, who took point on this one, and stayed at my side during some pretty rough weather. I keep waiting for her to rethink that *I'll quit work when you do*, because apparently I never quit. Wendi and Daven, who let me retreat to their house and lick my wounds. To my daughter, Trinity, who is now old enough to tell me, "Mom, maybe you need a vacation." Out of the mouths of babes . . . To Pili, who helps nourish us with food, friendship, and just being herself. To the rest of the crew, Mary, Sherry, and Teresa: Thanks for staying at your posts under fire. Shawn, who keeps the home fires burning from a few states away. I'm hoping for quieter times soon, but I can't promise. To my writing group, who have seen some of the battles: Tom Drennan, Deborah Millitello, Marella Sands, Sharon Shinn, and Mark Sumner.

1

I WAS WORMING my way through a mass of parents and children with a tiny clown hat clutched in one hand. In my navy blue skirt suit I looked like a dozen other mothers who had had to come straight from work to the dance recital. My hair was a little curly and a little too black for all the blond mothers, but no one gave me a second glance. The one saving grace as I threaded my way through the crowd of parents, aunts, uncles, grandparents, and siblings was that I wasn't one of the parents. I was just here as moral support and last-minute costume rescuer. It was just Monica Vespucci's style to leave part of her son's costume at her house and need an emergency save. Micah and I had been running late with client meetings so we got to ride to the rescue, and now since the vast majority of the performers were female I was the only one safe to go backstage without scandalizing the mothers. What did little girls who only had male relatives do at things like this? My dad would have been at a loss.

A little girl and her mother damn near knocked me down the stairs in their rush to get up past me. The little girl was knocked into me so that my suit jacket pushed back and she was staring at my holstered gun and U.S. Marshal badge. The child's eyes went big as she met my eyes. The mother never noticed, dragging the silent child up the stairs. I let them get ahead of me, the little girl's huge, dark eyes following me until the crowd hid her from sight. She couldn't have been more than five. I wondered if she'd even try to tell her mother she'd seen a woman with a gun and a badge.

I started pushing my way up the stairs, keeping the hand with the clown hat in it close to my jacket so I wouldn't flash the gun by accident anymore. I was going to try to keep my occupation a secret from the screaming children and their frantic mothers. They didn't need to know that I hunted bad little vampires and wereanimals for the preternatural branch of the U.S. Marshals Service. They certainly didn't need to know that I raised zombies as my day job. I blended in as long as no one figured out who I was.

I got to the upper hallway and there was one lone male over the age of twelve being herded by his mother. She had an almost embarrassed look on her face, as if apologizing for not having a girl. I knew there were more men up here, because some of them were mine, but they were safely away from the estrogen-rich room of little girls.

Monica's son was under five, so he didn't count as male yet. He was just a generic child. Now if I could only find the generic child, hand his mother the hat, and flee to our seats where everyone was waiting for me, I'd count it as a win, though knowing Monica she'd need something else. I didn't like her at all. But her husband had been one of Jean-Claude's vampires who died sort of in the line of duty, so Jean-Claude made sure that he and others stood in for her lost husband. It was honorable, I even approved of it, but I avoided Monica when I could. She'd betrayed me and a shared friend to some bad vampires once. She'd apologized, and she depended on Jean-Claude's people for emergency babysitting and things like tonight. She'd been bad because the old Master of the City had been bad; now that we had a good Master of the City, Jean-Claude, she was good. Sure, and the Easter Bunny is a friend of mine.

The fact that I had a key to her house in case of emergencies still bugged me, but Jean-Claude was right; someone who could go out in the daylight needed to have the key. He also knew that no matter how much I disliked Monica, I'd do the right thing. He was right, damn it. A herd of pink, sequined little girls barreled past me. I hugged the wall and let the teachers chase them down. There were so many reasons I didn't have children yet.

I heard my name squealed out, in that high-pitched generic toddler voice, "'Nita, 'Nita!" I had no idea why, but just lately Matthew, Monica's son, had taken a liking to me.

He came rushing at me in his bright multicolored clown outfit with the little balls on the front that matched the ones on the hat. His hair was a deep auburn like his mother's, but there was something about his three-year-old face that made me think of his dead father. Robert hadn't been my favorite vampire, but he'd been handsome and Matthew was a cute kid. He came running with his arms up and launched himself at me. He was not big for his age but it was still startling. I caught him and swept him up in my arms because to do anything else would have either knocked me flat or been churlish.

He put those little hands on my shoulders and leaned in for a kiss. I offered a cheek, but he touched my face and shook his head, very solemn. "I'm a big boy now, 'Nita. I kiss like a big boy now." Cheek kisses had been fine until about two weeks ago, and now Matthew was very certain that cheek kisses were baby kisses. It made me wonder if Monica was being overly friendly with the new boyfriend in front of the kid. It was Monica; there would be a boyfriend.

I'd told Monica about it and she thought it was cute. Matthew puckered up and planted one on my mouth, which meant he was wearing my very red lipstick. "Now you've got my lipstick on you, and that's more big girl than big boy," I said, as I looked around for some Kleenex or something to wipe his mouth with. I was also looking for his mother. Where was Monica?

"It *is* big boy if it's *your* lipstick."

I frowned at that tiny face just inches from mine. "What do you mean, it's big boy if it's mine?"

"All the big boys kiss you, 'Nita."

I had a sinking feeling that maybe it wasn't just Monica and a boyfriend in front of Matthew that were giving him ideas. "Where is your mother?" I said, and began searching the room for her a little desperately.

She finally separated herself from the mass of women and girls of various ages and came toward us beaming. It creeped me out a little that Monica seemed to think I didn't hold a grudge about her betraying me five years ago. I did hold a grudge and I didn't trust her. She seemed unaware of that.

She had Matthew's curly auburn hair, cut shorter and more styled, but her face was thinner, more of a sharp triangle, as if she'd lost weight since I saw her last. Once upon a time you could have asked if she was feeling all right, but now women dieted for no reason at all. Monica was shorter than I was by a few inches, and I was five-three. She was still in her skirt suit, too, but her blouse was white, and mine was blue.

Matthew kept his arms around my neck while she used a wet wipe on his mouth. Then she put a paler shade of lip gloss on his lips, though they didn't seem to need any to me. She took the hat from me and put it over his curls. If he'd been any older the outfit would have been embarrassing to any boy I'd ever met, but at three it was actually . . . cute. I would not admit it out loud, but it was.

"Thank you so much, Anita," Monica said. "I can't believe I forgot it."

I could, but I just smiled and kept quiet. Quiet usually worked better between Monica and me. A mass of little girls dressed in the girl version of his outfit bounced up, and he wiggled to be put down. I did so, happily.

Monica watched him run away with the others in his class with that proverbial mother's look: pride, love, and almost possession. I never doubted that she loved her little boy. It was one of the reasons I was nice to her.

She turned to me, still smiling. "I'm so glad the recital is tonight so I can concentrate on the business tomorrow."

I nodded, and tried to make my escape. Monica was apparently a better lawyer than she was a human being, or at least Jean-Claude trusted her to do up the contracts that might, or might not, be getting signed tomorrow. I trusted Jean-Claude to be a good businessman.

"Agreed," I said, and tried to slip away.

She grabbed my arm. I don't like to be touched by people that I'm not close to. I stiffened under her hand, but she didn't seem to notice. She leaned in and whispered, "If I was being offered a seventeen-year-old boy toy I'd be more excited, Anita."

Matthew was out of sight so I let my eyes show just how happy that comment made me. Monica let go of my arm, her eyes a little wide, face surprised. "Oh, come on, Anita, what woman wouldn't be flattered?"

"First, I haven't agreed to letting him stay in St. Louis when they bring him in from Vegas tomorrow. Second, don't ever call him a boy toy again."

"Touchy," she said, and then her face softened and her eyes glittered with some thought that I knew I wasn't going to like. "Defensive of him already, Anita. My, my, he must be better in bed than I remember at that age."

I leaned in and hissed in her ear. "We were all mind-raped by one of the scariest vampires to ever exist, Monica. She used me to feed on his power as a weretiger. She used me, and him, and all the other tigers in a bid to survive even if it meant destroying all of us. You tell me, what part of that was a good thing?" I had grabbed her arm somewhere in all that.

She spoke low. "You're hurting me."

I let go of her, and stepped back. She looked up at me, and I think for a moment let herself see me, really see me. She was angry, and for just a moment I knew that she didn't like me any more than I liked her, not really. Then I watched a different look cross her face, one that most men would have thought was a good look, but a woman knows when another woman is about to drive the blade home.

"Funny how it's never your fault when you have to have sex with all these men, Anita," and with that she walked away. She walked away with the proverbial knife stuck deep and hard right through my heart. Nothing cuts deeper than when another person says exactly what you're afraid to say out loud. Hell, Matthew had said it, too, in his way. *All the big boys kiss you, 'Nita.*

I fled the laughing costumed children and Monica's knowing eyes. I waved at Matthew as he called my name, all lined up with the little girls in his class. I wanted to be in my seat so I could see him; he'd go on second. Yeah, that was it, I hurried to my seat to make sure I'd see his performance, but I knew that wasn't the truth. I ran toward my seat and the men waiting for me, because part of me believed that Monica was right and all my words were just a case of the lady protesting too much.

2

I GOT BACK to the foot of the stairs and the still-crowded lobby. I scanned the crowd for Micah, but since he was my size neither of us could see the other over the crowd. The people parted and I could see him about halfway across the room, talking with a family I didn't recognize. He was smiling, face alight with good humor. He laughed, head back, soundless to me over the murmur of the crowd. The crowd closed again and just like that I couldn't see him. I started easing my way toward him. The crush cleared and I could see him again. He was one of those rare men who could look delicate, until you took in the wide shoulders tapering down to a slender waist. He was built like a swimmer, though his sports were jogging and weight lifting like most of the wereanimals I knew. His suits all had to be tailored-down athletic cuts. Italian suits seemed to fit best. American suits were mostly shaped like boxes and looked terrible on short men with muscles. Though Micah went for strength, not bulk. Micah's suit fit him perfectly, and I caught several women giving him covert glances as they hurried past with their families. I had to smile because I knew he looked even better out of the suit than in it. A man looked at his ass as he went past. Micah got that a lot, too. I think it was being short and pretty, because I could call him handsome if he wanted, but he was too pretty for words like *handsome*. It was also the nearly waist-length hair. Curly, and that rich, deep brown that said it might have been paler when he was little. His hair was almost as curly as mine and spilled down his back to the envy of many a woman. My own hair was almost to my waist, because he wanted to cut his hair and I didn't want him to. I wanted to take a few inches off my hair and he didn't want me to. So he'd made me a deal. If I cut my hair, he got to cut his. We had a stalemate, and my hair hadn't been this long since junior high.

He turned his face toward me as if he'd felt me looking, and I could finally see all that delicate line of face, maybe a little long through the jaw for perfection, but that one line was all that saved him from looking like a beautiful woman instead of a man. Elementary school must have been hell, because short and pretty men don't usually fare well. He told me that his eyes had originally been brown, but I'd never seen those eyes, the ones he was born with. He'd come to me with leopard eyes trapped forever in those dark lashes, chartreuse eyes green and yellow depending on what color he wore near his face or how the light caught them. Most of the time he wore sunglasses to hide the eyes, but wearing them after dark sometimes attracted more attention than what they hid, and it amazed him how many people could look him in the eyes and only remark, "What beautiful eyes." Or, "What a great shade of green," and never make the connection.

Nathaniel would say, "People see what they want to see, or what their minds tell them they should see most of the time."

Micah gave me the smile that was all for me. It was made up of love, lust, and just that connection we had had from almost the moment we'd met. He was my Nimir-Raj, my leopard king, and I was his Nimir-Ra, leopard queen. Though I didn't shapeshift to anything, I still somehow held a piece of leopard inside me, and that piece had seemed to know him. Micah had never questioned it, and I had done something unprecedented: I'd let him move in with me. We were two years and still counting; two years and still happy with each other. It was a record for me.

Usually by now I'd wrecked it somehow, or the man had done something I could point at and go *See, see I knew it wouldn't work*. Micah had managed to walk the maze that was my heart and not get caught in any of the traps. He said his good-byes to the people and came to me.

He smiled, the edge of his mouth quirking up like it did sometimes, his eyes shining as if laughter were just a thought away. "What are you looking at?" he asked, voice low.

I smiled back because I couldn't help it. "You."

Our hands reached for each other at the same time, our fingers just finding each other, entwining, playing along the touch and feel of each other. I'd had one friend say that we could get more out of just holding hands than some couples got out of kissing. But we did that, too, leaning in and being careful of the lipstick. Micah went through most nights with a touch of my lipstick on his mouth. He didn't seem to mind.

"Who was that?" I asked as we turned and began to make our way hand in hand with the last of the crowd toward the auditorium.

"One of the families in our support group," he said.

Micah was the head/spokesperson for the Coalition for Better Understanding Between Human and Lycanthrope Communities. It was affectionately known as the Furry Coalition. The Coalition helped new shapeshifters adjust to the change in lifestyle, and kept them from shifting early outside safe houses. A new shifter was unpredictable. It could take months of full moons before they were in control enough to be trustworthy without older, more experienced shifters riding herd on them. And yes, unpredictable meant they were consumed by a craving for flesh, and fresh was better. They also blacked out and had few memories of what they'd done. Most newbies passed out after shifting back to human form, so they needed to be either in a safe place or where someone could get them under some literal cover.

Micah and some of the other local leaders had come up with an idea for a family support group, where the members of the families that weren't shapeshifters could talk freely about their parents, siblings, or even grandparents. It was legal to be a shapeshifter in the United States now, but discrimination still occurred. There were entire professions where failing one blood test would get you excluded forever. Military, police, food industry, medical care—it was hard to keep a job if you were a teacher of children and the parents found out you turned into the big bad wolf once a month. That kind of discrimination was illegal, but hard to prove. It was one of the reasons that Richard Zeeman, junior high science teacher and local Ulfric, wolf king, wouldn't be here tonight sitting on the other side of Jean-Claude. Richard was technically Jean-Claude's wolf to call, as I was his human servant. We were a triumvirate of power and should both have been here at his side, but Richard wouldn't risk being outed and losing his job. That, and Richard really hated being a werewolf, but that was a problem for later. For right this moment, nobody who had come with Jean-Claude had a problem being exactly who and what they were.

Most of the seats were already full, and it was Asher's hair that I spotted first, gleaming golden under the lights. I wasn't kidding about the gold. He wasn't blond; his hair was as close to true gold and still a natural color as any person I'd ever met. Of course, once I'd found Asher, Jean-Claude was at his side. Jean-Claude's black hair curled over the seat back, inches longer than Asher's, which was just past shoulder length. Jean-Claude had grown his hair out because I seemed to like more hair on my men. Asher had informed me, "It takes energy for a vampire to grow his hair longer than it was when he died. I don't have that kind of energy to spare." Which implied that Jean-Claude did, and that had been interesting to know.

There was another blond on his other side. J.J., Jason's current girl-friend, had traveled from New York so she could watch him onstage. They'd gone to school together and known each other a little during college. They'd met again at a friend's bachelorette party, and now here she was coming to see him onstage. He'd traveled to see her onstage with the New York City Ballet three times. This would be her third trip to St. Louis in as many months. It was as serious as I'd ever seen Jason over anyone.

He'd been almost embarrassed when J.J. said she'd come out for the recital. He'd said, "It's just amateur stuff. You do the real deal." I don't know what she'd said, because I'd left him to finish the phone conversation in private, but whatever she'd said, there she sat looking pale and beautiful, her long, straight blond hair in a neat braid down the graceful curve of neck and shoulders. Her dress was a pink that was almost white, with thin spaghetti straps. She was like most ballet dancers, honed down to muscle and grace so she could wear the filmy dress with nothing much under it and have it look great. I'd have looked like I was in desperate need of a bra. My curves only honed down so far.

Jean-Claude and Asher stood before we'd actually come up to the aisle. They turned without looking around, as if they'd sensed us, and maybe they had. Or at least Jean-Claude had.

Another man stood up in the row in back of them, and only then did I realize it was Truth. He'd combed his shoulder-length hair back in a tight, neat ponytail, and he was completely clean-shaven. Truth's face was trapped in that not-quite-beard stubble because that's how he'd looked when he died. Shaving meant that he might not be able to grow it back even if he wanted to. He was wearing a nice suit, too. If his hair hadn't still been its usual brown I might have thought it was his brother, Wicked.

I stood there staring up into his face, stunned. I wanted to ask, *Where are your boots? Where's your leather?* But that seemed the wrong thing to say.

Micah leaned in and said, "Say something to him."

"Um, you look nice," I said, and it was hopelessly inadequate. I tried again. "I guess I've just never seen you cleaned up like this. You look great."

He tugged on the front of the suit jacket. "I borrowed it from Wicked. He's in the row ahead of them."

Micah mercifully turned me away, so I moved up to Asher and Jean-Claude, who were still standing. Truth always looked like a mix between an outlaw biker and a medieval forest ranger. He was here as security. Had Jean-Claude insisted he get neatened up?

Wicked gave a small nod and a smile from the row in front of them. He looked, more than ever, like his brother's twin, though I knew they had been born a year apart as humans. His hair was straight and blond, thicker-textured than his brother's slight wave of brown. They both had the same blue-gray eyes, and now that Truth's chin was bare, the same deep dimple in their chin was very clear.

Asher took my hand in his and I was suddenly looking up at someone who made both Wicked and Truth look too manly, too modern-day handsome in comparison. Asher was almost as broad of shoulder as the brothers, but that face. The mass of wavy gold hair, the eyes so pale a blue, like ice given life and color, in a rim of darker lashes and brow. But it was the face that was always breathtaking. It was a beauty to make angels weep, or want to trade sides. He was just simply one of the most gorgeous people I'd ever seen. He thought his face was ruined because holy-water scars traced the right side of all that beauty. But they only went about halfway up, and the perfect curve of mouth was untouched. It was almost as if the inquisitioner who had tried to burn the devil out of him had flinched at the ruin of that face.

I knew the scars continued down the right side of his chest to trace the edge of his hip and thigh. He managed the Circus of the Damned and was the masked ringmaster, so he could be beautiful and mysterious and not show everyone the scars. For him to come out in public like this was a good sign. Though he was a master at using shadow, darkness, his hair, so that people around him would probably never see the scars if he didn't wish them to. He was wearing a soft blue silk shirt with a high, soft collar pierced by a stickpin that held a pale blue diamond almost the color of his eyes. Jean-Claude and I had bought it for him just this year. Admittedly, most of the money for the stone had come from Jean-Claude. I made good money, but the diamond was almost as big as my thumbnail.

Seeing him wearing it so that it attracted attention to his face made me feel that every penny had been well spent. I smiled up at him and went on tiptoe so his six foot one didn't have to bend down too far.

From the waist down he was wearing dark brown leather and boots that came up to his knees. The fact that I hadn't looked below the waist until he kissed me said something about just how nice the upper bits were, because it was all nice. I also knew that Jean-Claude had dressed him for tonight. Asher was more suits, unless he was dressing for a fetish event and then leather worked dandy, just not this kind of leather.

It was more a cheek press than a kiss, to save him from wearing my lipstick, but it made me think of what Matthew had said, about everyone kissing me. I'd had sex with every vampire waiting for me. It wasn't a comfy thought.

Asher whispered, "What has put a frown on that lovely face?"

"Something Matthew said backstage," I whispered back.

"Precocious indeed if he can make you that unhappy."

I gave him a look, and he passed my hand over to Jean-Claude. He was wearing a white shirt that was almost identical to the blue one that Asher wore, but he'd put a short black velvet jacket over his, and the stickpin through his cravat was an antique cameo. It had been one of the first Christmas presents I'd ever gotten for him. It was nice, but not even close to the same kind of nice as Asher's diamond. It made me think I needed to go shopping.

Jean-Claude's black leather pants looked poured on, and his boots rose up over his thighs like a second skin. I didn't have to see the back of the boots to know they laced all the way up his leg. I liked these boots and had seen them with and without pants. I stumbled as he drew me closer, thinking too hard about the boots and nothing else on him, and then there was the moment when I had to look up, had to see that face. He and I had been a couple on and off for five years, almost six now, and I kept waiting for a moment when I could see him and not feel like there had to be some mistake. Someone this beautiful couldn't possibly be in love with me when he had an entire planet of people to choose from. I cleaned up well, but Jean-Claude made me feel like I'd sneaked into the Louvre and stolen a masterpiece off the wall so I could roll around on it naked.

His eyes were a midnight blue so dark that a shade more would have made them look black, but they never did. His eyes were the darkest true blue I'd ever seen, as Asher's were the palest. The head of their bloodline, their *sourdre de sang*, literally "fountain of blood," had a thing for blue eyes and had collected different colors of blue-eyed and beautiful men. She'd had centuries to find them, and I had two of her most amazing right here.

She'd thrown Asher away when he was scarred, and Jean-Claude had fled from her. Now he was his own *sourdre de sang*, the first new master of his own bloodline to appear in a thousand years.

He leaned down and laid a gentle kiss on my lips. I kissed him back, letting my body fall in against his, and his arms encircled me and it was like breathing, as if I'd been holding my breath until we kissed.

He pulled away with my lipstick on his lips, but it was a good color for him. He smiled down at me, his eyes sparkling as if he was on the verge of laughter. "*Ma petite*." That was all, just my nickname, but it seemed to hold years of *I love you*s.

The lights flashed. It was the signal to get to our seats before the curtain went up. J.J. was standing so that Jean-Claude could help me into the seat beside him where she'd been sitting. She smiled and said hi. I told her I was glad she could make it. "I wouldn't have missed seeing Jason dance again," she said, and her face lit up as she said his name. She was pretty, always, but in that moment she was beautiful. She had the same spring-blue eyes that Jason had. They both had the soft good looks that sometimes goes with blond, blue-eyed coloring. They looked enough alike to be siblings, but then they shared a common great-great-grandfather. A lot of the kids from their school looked like siblings. Apparently Great-Great-Granddad had been a busy boy.

Something made me turn and look back to Micah and Asher at the head of the aisle. Asher had tried to give Micah the same greeting he'd given me, but Micah had pulled away. Asher sat down laughing as Micah eased past Jean-Claude and me to sit on my other side by J.J. Jean-Claude patted Micah's back, as if saying, *It's all right*. In private Jean-Claude and Micah greeted each other pretty intimately, but Micah had made it clear that he wasn't food for everyone. Asher had taken it as a challenge to see if he could seduce Micah, and when that hadn't worked, he seemed intent on embarrassing him. I loved Asher, but he had a sadistic streak in him that I wasn't always crazy about.

If he didn't stop pushing, he was going to be on Micah's shit list permanently. I wasn't sure what to do about the rising tension between the two men, but something was going to have to be done before Asher pushed my Nimir-Raj far enough to do something unpleasant. Micah and Jean-Claude had tried to rip each other's throats out the first time they'd met. If Jean-Claude and I couldn't get Asher to tone it down, Micah would take care of it; we just might not like how he did it. He wasn't homophobic, he just didn't want to donate blood to Asher, and the other man seemed to have taken the rejection badly.

Micah was tense beside me, his face striving for neutral but showing anger if you knew where to look for it. I covered his hand with mine. He was stiff and unyielding and then he relaxed into my hand. He finally gave me a small smile, but his reaction in public let me know that Asher was very close to pushing him too far.

I glanced at Jean-Claude to see if he'd seen it. He was watching the stage as if nothing untoward had happened. Had he not noticed, or was he trying to ignore the problem for a little longer? I needed some backup here, not the old ostrich-hiding-in-the-sand routine. But if Jean-Claude had a soft spot, it was Asher, and okay, maybe me. We both got away with things that he probably should have put a stop to long before he did.

Wicked was looking at me. He'd seen and understood the problem. Both the problem between Asher and Micah, and the fact that Jean-Claude seemed to be ignoring it. I was pretty sure that Wicked and Truth would back my play if I could come up with one that wouldn't destroy our happy little apple cart.

The trouble was, in vampire land I was Jean-Claude's human servant, and Asher was a master vampire with enough power to have his own territory. He stayed as Jean-Claude's second-in-command because he loved us and didn't want to be without, but it meant that my position of authority was a little shaky.

I was a vampire executioner, but I wouldn't kill Asher, and he knew that. So my threat was gone. I was a necromancer and could control the undead, not just zombies, but lots of undead, including some vampires. But I knew that if I got out my major mojo and controlled Asher like that he'd never forgive me. And once I had that much control over someone, sometimes it didn't go away, and that had become completely disturbing to me.

Monica came hurrying up the opposite side of the aisle. The one that made more people have to move their legs or stand up. The side that was farthest away from all of us who were supposed to be part of her group. It was very Monica. She'd apparently made a serious play for Asher and been rebuffed. She'd given him a wide-ish berth since then.

She smiled and waved at all of us as she sat down beside J.J. There was still one seat saved with us.

The lights flashed again and Vivian was at the head of the aisle by Asher. He and Jean-Claude stood, so I did, too. Micah was already on his feet. Vivian was petite enough that we probably could have stayed in our seats, but the older vampires often reacted to women as if bustles had never gone out of fashion, and if they could be gentlemen then so could I.

She brushed past me with a hurried, "Sorry I'm late."

"You're not late," Micah said.

I added, "You're just on time." That earned me a small smile. Nothing could really make Vivian less than beautiful, but there was tightness around her eyes and mouth, worry lines on that beautiful skin. Her skin was that shade of coffee with enough cream to make it almost white. She was technically African American, but it was by way of Ireland, and that showed a lot from the thick, nearly straight hair to the pale gray-blue eyes. She was one of the wereleopards in our pard. I'd had to rescue her from a very bad man once. He had done terrible things to her. I'd killed him in the end, but revenge only makes things all better in the movies. In real life, once the villain is dead the trauma lives on inside the victims.

She was here to watch her live-in boyfriend, Stephen, onstage. She spoke to J.J. as she sat down on the other side of Monica. Vivian slipped her coat off, and the moment I saw the dress I knew why she was running late. She'd gone home from her job as administrative assistant at an insurance agency to change. The dress was a little slip of nothing, black with a beading of bronze and gold beads so that it shimmered as she moved. Seeing J.J. and Vivian in their party dresses made me half wish I'd changed for the show, but I'd have been truly late. I could have taken something to work to change into, but in all honesty it hadn't occurred to me until just that moment. Oh, well.

Micah leaned in and whispered, "You look great."

I whispered back, "Was it that obvious?"

"To me," he said, and squeezed my hand. I squeezed back and we shared that smile that was mainly just for us. Nathaniel was the only one who got to share that smile sometimes, and he wasn't here because he was going to be onstage.

Jean-Claude's hand touched the edge of mine, and I took the hint, leaning my head against his shoulder and taking his hand. He had been a ladies' man for centuries and he swore that I was the first woman to make him feel a bit insecure. I tended to be hard on the egos of a certain kind of men. The ones who normally swept women off their feet had never moved me much, because I'd always felt that if they swept me off my feet they'd practiced on a lot of women before me, and would practice more with women after me. I'd rarely been wrong on that. Besides, the normal sweep-you-off-your-feet tricks often left me puzzled. I still wasn't sure if I should apologize to Jean-Claude for throwing his game off this badly, or take a certain pride in it.

There was a part of me that still believed if I'd fallen into his arms easily he'd have wooed me, won me, and left me for other game by now. Was that unfair, my own insecurities talking, or just truth?

His hand was warm in mine. That meant he'd fed on someone. It had been a willing blood donor. Women, especially, lined up to feed him. In fact, one of the reasons I'd spent the last few weeks going through a stack of photographs and DVDs with some help from the other men had been that we needed more regular food. Other vampire and wereanimal groups across the country had sent in applications for some of their people to join us. The DVDs had been everything from flat-out porn to strangely awkward dating tapes. It was like the old idea of an arranged marriage, though this was more an arranged mistress, sort of. The groups hoped it would give them a stronger tie to our power base, and it might.

They'd been sending candidates to Jean-Claude for a while, and he had politely turned them all down. This last batch came addressed to me, personally. They seemed to feel that Jean-Claude had turned everyone down for fear of pissing me off, and there might be something to that, so I'd sat down and watched. I'd had Nathaniel and Micah help some, and Jason, but none of the vampires. I hadn't done that on purpose, but . . .

Who had Jean-Claude fed on? For a second I wanted to ask, and then I let it go. I didn't really want to know. Taking blood was entirely too close to foreplay for the vampires of his bloodline. Of course, he shared me with a lot of other men, so my being jealous of him taking blood from some other woman seemed childish and unfair. But just because it's childish and unfair doesn't mean it isn't the way I felt. Stupid, but true.

The lights went down and I was saved from having to think too hard as the curtain rose. I got to sit in the dark holding the hands of two of the men I loved most. It wasn't a bad way to start the weekend. I noticed Monica watching us. Was it envy on her face, or anger? I turned back to the stage and left Monica to get her face back to its usual polite I-like-you expression. Usually I liked the truth from everyone around me, but I'd make an exception for her. I knew not to trust her, so she could pretend to like me, and I'd pretend to like her. It wasn't friendship, but it was an understanding.

The music came up; I hugged Micah and Jean-Claude to me, and watched Asher holding Jean-Claude's other hand. Even in the Bible Belt, when the lights dimmed you could still hold hands.

3

THE FIRST GROUP out was the two-year-old class. Five little girls in pink tights with sparkly itty-bitty tutus walked onstage holding hands in a line. The audience did a group "Awww." They were almost illegally cute. The dance teacher was at the front of the stage, visible to the audience and the wide-eyed little girls.

The Dance of the Sugar Plum Fairy from Tchaikovsky's *Nutcracker* filled the air. It was one of the few classical pieces I knew well enough to name. The teacher began to move her arms. Most of the tiny girls followed her, but one of them just stared off at the audience with huge, fear-filled eyes. Were the toddlers good? No. But at that age it's not about being a prodigy, it's about showing up and being too cute for words. I wasn't much for babies, older was definitely better, but even I couldn't deny they were nearly painfully adorable.

Micah began to rub his thumb over my hand. Jean-Claude was still against my other hand. The tots trooped off, holding hands again, to rousing applause, and then it was Matthew's turn. I heard Monica tell J.J., "Usually they have to combine the two- and three-year-olds, but they had enough this year to have two classes." Interesting, but my hearing it meant Monica was talking too loud. She had a certain desire to be noticed.

The little girls I'd seen earlier in their clown tutus came trooping out, with Matthew in the middle in his boy costume. They were holding hands just like the last group, and the dance instructor was at the bottom of the stage visible to the children and the audience. I wondered how old you'd have to be for the teacher to hide.

The music was still from the *Nutcracker*, but it was one of the songs for the dolls that danced in the first act. I couldn't remember which dance this was, just vaguely where it came from in the ballet. Little arms went up in near unison, and then they danced. Not all the girls danced, they moved, but Matthew and two of the little girls danced. It wasn't smooth, or perfect, but it was real. They did what the teacher did with smiling faces, but as they continued Matthew lost his smile, his concentration visible on his small face. I watched him do some of the moves I'd seen him practice at our house, with Nathaniel and Jason working on his moves with him.

I leaned into Micah and whispered, "Is it stupid to say he's good?"

Jean-Claude leaned into us and whispered, "*Non, ma petite*, he has a certain flair, does Matthew."

The music stopped, and the children took hands and bowed. The applause was a little more heartfelt this time, or so it seemed to me. It's not every day you see someone that young display the beginnings of true talent. When they were offstage Asher leaned over all of us to speak to Monica. "He is good, your boy."

She beamed at him, and she had every right to be proud. Micah congratulated her, too. J.J. said, "For three he's amazing."

I spoke in her and Monica's direction. "I hope that Jason and Nathaniel got to see it; I've been watching them work with him."

"Matthew has really enjoyed his time with his uncles," Monica said.

I pulled back a little, because I didn't like the whole *Uncle Nathaniel* and *Uncle Jason* thing, and I had put a stop to *Aunt Anita*. Matthew had given us his own version of nicknames; Natty, Jason-Jason, and 'Nita for me. Jean-Claude was more Gene-Clod. Asher was the closest to getting his whole name. We'd been seeing a lot of Matthew lately.

The music came back up and the next group of little girls, slightly older, came out. And there was a lot of that in the next hour and change. Older girls, sometimes the same girls, because we got to see them do ballet, jazz, and modern, even a couple of tap dances. I liked dance, and it was no reflection on the kids, but my will to live began to seep away by about the fifth group of sequined children.

I had been warned that the dance school didn't allow anyone to grab their kids and leave until every last student had had their chance onstage. I just hadn't understood what that meant.

In between acts I leaned over J.J. to Monica and asked, "How long is the show?"

"Last year it was four hours," she said.

I gave her wide, horror-filled eyes. She giggled. I sat back in my seat and exchanged a look with Micah. He said, "Nathaniel and Jason will be up soon."

Wicked leaned back from the seat in front of us and whispered, "Did you say four hours?"

I nodded. He looked pained as he turned back to give his attention to the stage, though I knew as security he was actually aware of a lot more than the performance. He'd be aware of things that I would miss, and so would Truth behind us.

Jean-Claude raised my hand up and laid a kiss on the back of it. He was smiling at me in that trying-not-to-laugh way. I glared at him and then caught Asher giving me the same look. I rolled my eyes at both of them and settled back in my seat.

I fell into a sort of daze, and then Micah raised the open program in his other hand in front of my face. I had to blink to read it. Jason Schuyler was listed as accompanying senior student Alicia Snyder. He'd said that the men were really just mobile props so the senior girls could have a wider choice of dances for their last hurrah before going off to college. "We're just there to make the girls look good, and tote and fetch them."

When I'd asked, "Then why do it?" he'd looked at me as if I'd said something silly. Jason had been in dance and theater all the way into college; apparently it was just some sort of dance thing that I wasn't going to understand, but it made sense to him and to the other men that he'd talked into doing it. It had been Jean-Claude and Jason's idea to make the exotic dancers at Guilty Pleasures, and the less exotic dancers at Danse Macabre, two of Jean-Claude's clubs, learn to really dance. Jason and Nathaniel had been working with them and the teachers at the school all summer. It was the most men that the senior girls had ever had access to for partners, and most of them had taken our men up on the offer.

The ballerina with Jason was actually shorter than he was, and since he was only an inch taller than me, she was tiny in her black proverbial ballerina outfit with white tights and a flash of sparkle in her bound hair. He'd tied his own longish blond hair back in a tight, smooth ponytail so that it gave the illusion of being short. He wore an outfit that matched hers and I realized I'd never seen Jason in black before. They both looked elegant. Jason was usually smiling, joking, and one of my best friends. He was a lover as well. He was cute and even handsome, but I'd never realized that he could be elegant and beautiful. The music began and I saw instantly why she'd wanted him to partner her. I knew Jason moved well, even danced well, and I'd seen some of the practices, but I hadn't seen much of him with the girl. I'd never seen him move like this in dance.

He had the grace both of his years of dance training and of being a werewolf. All the wereanimals moved well, as if it came with the disease in their veins. He didn't have a lot to do but hold her en pointe and help her twirl and do some lifts, and finally lift her completely over his head one-handed and carry her rainbowed body across the stage to bring her in a heart-stopping drop to be caught an inch above the floor with her body still graceful and taut in his arms.

The last move made the entire audience gasp. There was a moment of dead silence and then thunderous applause. J.J. leaned over and said, "That moment of silence is worth more than the applause afterward. It means you've nailed it." She was clapping as she spoke, and when the audience actually rose to their feet we joined them.

The girl curtseyed and was given a bouquet of roses by one of the earlier students still in costume. They kissed cheeks and then the ballerina took two of the long-stemmed roses out of her bouquet and handed them to Jason. He came forward, took the roses, kissed her hand, and then she insisted on bringing him forward so they bowed together. I didn't need anyone to explain to me that Alicia was showing that she knew she could not have wowed the audience without Jason's help.

He was beaming, eyes glowing, even as his chest still rose and fell from the effort of lifting and throwing her, and making it all look pretty and effortless.

J.J. said, "I don't envy who goes next."

I agreed and was glad it was a senior girl by herself. I didn't want to see one of our own guys compete with what we'd just seen. It seemed like a damned hard act to follow.

The senior girl was good, but she wasn't as good, and I sympathized that here at her last performance she had to know she wasn't going to nail it. I think that would feel bad.

But the next senior girl had Nathaniel Graison listed as her partner, and I actually found myself leaning forward on my seat. It was no longer about just the performance but how Nathaniel would feel after seeing Jason onstage. They were best friends and not competitive in that typical guy way, but still, Nathaniel was my other live-in sweetie and I was a little worried. Nathaniel, unlike Jason, had never been in dance class other than with Jason taking him. He'd been on the streets before age ten, and it had gone downhill from there. Nathaniel had been a prostitute, porn star, still was an exotic dancer, so he'd performed before, but not like this.

Micah's hand was tense in mine, and we exchanged a glance. Micah said out loud, "He'll be fine." But simply by his saying that, I knew he was worried, too. I realized it was more than just being in love with Nathaniel; because of his horrendous childhood we felt almost parentally anxious. It sounded stupid, but he'd never had a chance to be one of the little toddlers in their costumes seeing the parents smile. He'd missed so much as a child, and in a way this was him trying to experience some of what he'd missed. He hadn't expressed any stage fright about tonight. It was all just my nerves and Micah's apparently.

Nathaniel entered the stage hand in hand with his ballerina. The girl wore a filmy white gown around her white leotard so that it had the look of white and silver rags, elegant rags, and moved around her as though it were breathing. He wore white tights but his shirt was of rougher material and loose around his upper body, even open at the neck. His shoulders looked amazingly broad, and the rest of him looked even better in the white tights, but that might have just been me. His ankle-length auburn hair was up in a bun at the nape of his neck. The ballerina's blond hair was cut short and flattened around her face like lace. From this far out in the audience his lavender eyes looked blue.

The music began and though it was ballet it was a very different kind. Jason and his ballerina had been about physical movement in space; they'd been flashy and technically great, but now we saw the difference. This ballerina and Nathaniel told a story. I didn't know the music and didn't need to, because they told the story with their bodies, their faces, and their hands. It was graceful and beautiful and they acted. It wasn't just dance, it was theatre.

It was a tale of lovers lost and found, and of some great tragedy. Nathaniel held her, but it was soft holding, as if their bodies melted into each other, and their gaze made the audience watch their hands as they rose above their heads so that those entwining arms, hands, fingers, seemed terribly important.

I'd known Nathaniel could dance, but as I hadn't known Jason could be elegant, I hadn't realized Nathaniel could do this. It was both amazing and wonderful, and made me feel the loss of what he might have been in his life if things had been different. Of course, he was only twenty-two. It wasn't like it was too late for him to change jobs. But it felt odd thinking that, as if Nathaniel not working at Guilty Pleasures would change things, as if the man I was watching swoon and dance onstage would be someone else if he did this every night.

He lay down on the stage and his hair began to unroll from the bun, but it was too sudden a change and I realized as she collapsed on top of him that the hair was part of the show, the emotion. His hair spilled out around them across the pale wood stage and something about the lights hitting it, or the color of gel used, turned all that auburn hair to red so it was as if they both lay in a pool of thick blood. She made one last futile gesture with her pale arms, and again something about the lighting put her in a pale, white glow so she looked almost translucent. It was a neat trick with the lights, her glowing and ethereal while Nathaniel lay in the richer reds so it was all death and violence and transcendence and beautiful.

There was another of those breathless silences as the lights faded so we wouldn't see them leave the stage. And then the audience was on its feet again, and it was wonderful.

"Oh my God," I said, as I stood there and clapped along with everyone else. Micah beside me was shaking his head. I wondered if he'd been thinking the same things that I'd been thinking.

Jean-Claude beside me said, "Our kitten has become a cat."

I leaned around Micah to J.J. "Tell me if I'm just in love with him, or was that amazing."

She nodded. "That was really good. With more time and work it could be amazing."

Another bouquet of roses was brought out for the ballerina. She tore her bouquet in half and handed it to Nathaniel, and made him bow with her.

Monica leaned around J.J. and said, low, but not so low that J.J. wouldn't hear, "And to think you get to take that home and play with it."

I must have turned pretty abruptly, and what I was about to say wasn't friendly, but Micah grabbed my arm and blocked my view of her. The look on his face was enough. It made me count to ten. But while I counted J.J. said, "You're going to take that from her?"

I looked at Micah. He said, "No, but easy."

I nodded. Jean-Claude leaned in to it all and said, "Is something wrong?"

I leaned over everyone. "Nathaniel is not an *it*, okay."

She made a little push-away gesture, but there was something in her face that let me know she'd baited me. The only question was, why?

Vivian on the other side of her had been utterly quiet through all of it. She was standing and applauding, but she wasn't looking at us. It was almost like she wasn't really here.

I reached past Monica and touched Vivian's arm. She startled and turned wide eyes to me. She was a wereleopard—you didn't sneak up on them—but I'd genuinely startled her. What was she thinking about so hard?

Asher said something to Jean-Claude. I caught enough of it to know it was French and that was all, but whatever he said, Jean-Claude looked less happy than I did about Monica. I watched Asher's face as he looked at the other man, and I knew that look. It was the same look he'd had when he tried to kiss Micah tonight. What the hell was wrong with Asher tonight? He could be pushy and a pain in the ass, but he usually had a reason that I could figure out. Tonight I was lost.

The next senior girl was Stephen's ballerina. I wondered how they'd top or even come close to what Nathaniel and his had done. But lucky for everyone concerned, it was a jazzy tap dance to some older Broadway musical number. The girl and Stephen were both in fedoras, white dress shirts with rolled-up sleeves, loose collars, unbuttoned vests, and belted dress slacks. Both of them had hair past their shoulders; his was curly and blond, hers was curly and brown. His suit pieces were black and hers were thin navy pinstripes.

The number was funny, with sliding pratfalls across the stage. They slid from one corner of the stage to the other, passing each other by inches. It was athletic, fun, and so different from the other two numbers that it worked.

They ended with her jumping into Stephen's arms and him carrying her offstage. The applause was immediate this time with laughter mixed in; we'd needed something light after the sadness of the last number.

"Very Gene Kelly," Micah said.

I said, "I didn't even know Stephen could tap-dance."

Vivian said, "He learned for the show."

"Wow," I said, "that's quick."

Vivian smiled and a look of quiet pride crossed her face, the most positive emotion I'd seen on her face all night. Stephen and the senior girl were taking their bows, and he had a handful of roses from her bouquet. Vivian beamed up at him and you didn't have to know a thing about them to see that she loved him.

The stage cleared, the music changed, and this was the one that had made Jason nervous. He and the last senior were about to dance a number that he'd choreographed for them. He did a lot of the choreography at Guilty Pleasures, but he'd said, "It's not the same, Anita. Customers don't really care if we dance, not really, they want to see skin. This is different." I'd never seen him nervous like that about performing in public before. It had been both endearing and a little nervous-making.

I CAUGHT J.J. smiling and running her finger over his name where it was written in the program. It was a wistful smile, as if she were thinking of things that might have been.

She and Jason were both only twenty-three, but that smile was sad like doors had been closed, choices made, and no turning back. Or maybe I was being overly romantic. Nah, not me, not romantic. Every man in my life would say that wasn't my gig.

The ballerina entered to a dim stage at a run. She was dressed in a silky white nightgown, and her face, her body, everything telegraphed fear. But like in any good horror movie the scary thing is never behind you if that's where you're looking.

Jason jumped from the ceiling. I knew he had to have been on the catwalk, but it looked like he simply jumped from the sky and landed on feet and hands in front of her. Her scream as she turned and saw him cut through the sudden silence of the audience. There was still no music, as he stood, slowly, dressed in only close-fitting tights so that the muscles in his upper body writhed and molded as he came to his feet. His hair was loose, a fall of yellow around his shoulders, half hiding his face. He stood there muscled, beautiful, feral, and as she radiated fear, he gave off waves of predator.

The girl turned and ran. Jason was a blur of movement and was just suddenly in front of her. She gave another scream, but it was almost drowned by the gasp from the audience.

Music came up slowly, as she began to run around the stage and he was always there, always ahead of her. I knew he was a werewolf. I knew he could move faster than any human, but I'd never seen him do it, not Jason.

He always seemed more human than most, but on that stage, in this moment, he stopped pretending. He was a muscled blur, hair flying around him as he moved.

The girl fell to the middle of the stage at last. Her thin chest was rising and falling so hard I could see it. She held an arm out as if to ward him off, as he stalked around her.

I heard J.J.'s breath go out in a long shudder. I looked away from the stage to her for a moment. Her face was intent and raw with some emotion that I couldn't define.

Micah touched my hand and I looked back to find that Jason and the girl were dancing. It was as if he'd watched a cat play with a mouse and choreographed it, except that this cat was thinking more sex than food.

The girl played the virgin victim, slender arms rising and falling, hiding her face, her body leaning away, only to find his arm, his chest, his body there to catch and hold her, and then as the music grew she melded into his body and they danced. They danced, they moved, and he showed what his body was capable of and she held her own. There weren't many human dancers that could have kept up, and fewer still who were seniors in high school. I didn't have to know more about dance than I did to realize I was seeing something special, someone special. Hell, two someones. It was almost hard for me to watch and think, *That's Jason, that's our Jason.*

The music changed, subtly at first, and then it was Jason who was pulling away, the girl who was reaching out to him. I thought it was a seduction finished until I realized that Jason was running now and the girl was just suddenly there. It wasn't superhuman speed that put her always in front of him, but him looking back, him reluctant. They turned the seducer into the victim and gradually it was Jason who projected fear, and the girl who began to stalk him.

The music built and built as they danced around each other on the stage, and then he fell. It was one of those graceful falls where he caught himself, his hair trailing down so his face was completely hidden, and his strong muscled arm reached outward as if to ward off a blow, as she crept closer.

Her hand closed on his, and it was as if the world narrowed down to their fingers interlacing. He collapsed onto the stage, his arm at a harsh angle as she held his hand and turned to look out at the audience. Her face was clear and clean, eyes defiant, so straight, so tall, so in control with him crouched at her feet. She jerked on his arm as if pulling it behind his back, and he was on his knees, spine bowed as if in pain. She let go of his hand abruptly so that he half fell, and then she began to walk offstage. Two spotlights held on them as she moved away, the lights growing dimmer as she moved proud and brave. Jason collapsed in the light and began to weep, great, silent racking sobs that made his whole body rise and fall with it as her breath had at the beginning of the dance.

The lights were almost gray, almost out, as she stopped at the very edge of the stage to look back, and he came to his knees, one leg outstretched, one arm reaching out to her, the other arm across his face as if to hide his tears. There was a moment where they froze like that and the music stopped. The girl turned and left the stage, and Jason fell into a heap in the middle of it, and the light left.

The silence this time was longer, and I swear I heard several people inhale as if they'd been holding their breaths. Jason and the girl came to the center of the stage and took each other's hands still in silence, and it was only as they moved toward the front of the stage that the audience reacted. The crowd rose in a thunderous mass, calling "Bravo," and just screaming as if they were at a rock concert instead of a dance recital.

We clapped until our hands were sore. Micah hugged J.J. and I realized she was crying. I hugged her, too. Jean-Claude's arm went around my shoulders and I turned to find a kiss waiting for me. He spoke above the dying rumble of the crowd. "They are all growing up, our young men."

I could only nod. I'd known Jason and Nathaniel since they were nineteen, and the boys I'd met were not the men I'd seen tonight. I wasn't sure if *growing up* was the right term, maybe more growing into themselves.

Asher was already sitting down. I looked at him and saw the shine of pinkish tears on his face. I moved past Jean-Claude to lean over him. He wiped at the tears as if he didn't want me to see, but he took the kiss I offered, though his heart wasn't in it. I asked, "Are you all right?"

"I didn't know our little wolf could be that beautiful," he said.

"Me either," I said. But looking into his face I wasn't sure I meant the same thing he had meant. It was one of those moments when the same words can mean so many things. I knew I was missing something, but I was so puzzled I couldn't even figure out what questions to ask to get past Asher's mood. Something was up, something serious and emotional, and I didn't know what that something was.

The audience started moving toward the stage. The parents of the smallest dancers apparently could get their children directly from the stage. Monica came back to us with Matthew in her arms.

J.J. had found Jason and was being introduced to his dance partner. The girl was obviously excited to meet J.J., who had done what the girl dreamed of doing. J.J. was a professional dancer in one of the top dance companies in the United States and maybe the world. Most dancers would never make that cut.

Micah and I moved forward hand in hand to find Nathaniel. Vivian was just suddenly behind us as if nervous to be in the crowd by herself. I offered her my other hand and she took it with a grateful little smile. Vivian was usually pretty nervous, but I hadn't realized she didn't like crowds. Had she never liked crowds, or was it new? She was one of our wereleopards. I should know these things.

Wicked was suddenly with us. "You shouldn't make us split the security, Anita."

I glanced back but was too short to see Truth with Jean-Claude and Asher. "Sorry," I said.

Micah held a hand up and I knew he'd seen Nathaniel, or Stephen. Wicked helped us get through the crowd and there they were. Stephen came off the stage to hug and kiss Vivian. He was as downright happy as I'd ever seen him. Then Nathaniel was there and it was my turn to be hugged. He lifted me off my feet and spun me. It made me laugh out loud. He was just so full of himself, and he should have been.

He kissed me while he was still holding me above him, so that I slid down his body still locked in the kiss, held in his arms. He got me to my feet, breathless from his attentions.

Micah clapped him on the shoulder and was suddenly getting a full-body hug. There was a moment when Micah hesitated and then he just went with it. You saw hugs like it on every sports field in the world, but when the hug broke Nathaniel kissed him, and that you didn't see so much in sports. In private, they had kissed, but never in public. There was a moment when Nathaniel looked startled, and I think he was going to apologize, but Micah shook his head and put a hand on the back of the other man's neck and leaned in and kissed him back, softly and thoroughly. Micah pulled back smiling and Nathaniel looked a little dazed, and then that smile came back, the one he'd leapt off the stage with, so happy that it just beamed off him.

I put my arms around them both and held them. Something behind me made me turn. I found Jean-Claude and Asher standing with Truth beside them. Jean-Claude's face was beautiful and unreadable, the face he used when he was hiding what he was thinking, but Asher's face made up for it. Anger, no, rage. Something had made Asher absolutely furious.

I went back to hugging my men and enjoying this moment, but I knew now the moment would pass and I'd have to deal with that look on Asher's face. Some moments are perfect, and then someone comes along and fucks it up. Ain't it always the way.

4

JEAN-CLAUDE AND ASHER took the limo with Wicked and Truth and went ahead to Circus of the Damned. Why didn't we keep security? One, our car wouldn't hold that many people. Two, I was armed and had three wereanimals with me. I felt pretty secure.

Jean-Claude said he'd have a light repast prepared. He actually said that. He only talked like that when he was trying to hide emotions, thoughts, whatever. Was it cowardly to let him drive away with Asher, knowing they'd be fighting all the way home? Maybe, but I was hoping it wasn't my fight. One of the serious downsides to sleeping with this many men was the emotional upkeep.

J.J., Micah, Vivian, and I waited for the men to change. Stephen could have gone home in his outfit, but Nathaniel and Jason weren't really street safe. We'd gotten away with a guy-on-guy kiss and not gotten any negative reactions, but I think we all felt that wearing nothing but tights home would be pushing it in the buckle of the Bible Belt.

All three of them went to find the showers, and the rest of us wandered into the lobby to wait for them. We found the only bench and there was only room for three of us, and none of us were large people. Small bench. Micah insisted on standing, and I let him since I was still in three-inch heels from work. When he wore heels I'd let him sit.

J.J. and Vivian looked even more delicate and lovely in their gauzy dresses. J.J.'s looked almost like she could have worn it onstage in some of the numbers we'd seen tonight. Vivian's was a little heavier with the shiny beading on it, but they both looked like the fair maidens ready to greet their knights who had fought the good fight. I looked like what I was, someone who had hurried out of work to make the event.

Micah leaned against the wall beside me. I took his hand in mine, and just that made me feel better. He was in his work clothes, too, after all, and I thought he looked great.

J.J. didn't sit long before she had to get up and begin to pace. It wasn't really pacing, it was more like she was humming in her head, but her idea of humming needed physical movement. She almost danced as she moved, tracing some shape with her flat slippers and her pink dress. She wasn't that much taller than me, but she seemed much taller, longer, leaner, all graceful lines, like someone should have been painting her.

Vivian moved a little closer to me on the bench. She was a wereanimal, and our leopard, and when wereanimals feel low they like touch. It's comforting. I took the hint and held my other hand out to her. She accepted my hand with a little smile and took it as an invitation to sidle close enough for our hips to touch. There was a time when that would have weirded me out, but I knew Vivian didn't mean to encroach on my personal space. She just needed touch.

I raised my arm and let her cuddle under it so that my arm was across her slender shoulders. Sitting down I was taller through the torso than she was, so I could actually keep my arm around her and have her tucked underneath. I felt very guy all of a sudden, but the fact that she cuddled in against me in public meant that for Vivian, something was wrong.

Micah's hand squeezed mine and I looked up to meet his gaze. I knew that look. I sighed and hugged Vivian, putting my cheek against her hair. "What's wrong, Vivian?"

She straightened up and started to pull away. I tightened my arm around her and made it another hug. "Its okay, Vivian, just talk to us."

Micah said, "We are your Nimir-Raj and your Nimir-Ra, and your friends. Tell us."

She took a breath that made her shoulders shake. She huddled around herself, and I just drew her in against me. Her arms slid around my waist, hesitating at the feeling of the gun holster, but she finished the gesture and laid her head in the hollow of my shoulder. Whatever it was had to be bad for this level of public display, because Vivian was a very private person.

"The weretigers got Gina through three full moons without her shifting. She's still pregnant."

I frowned and looked up at Micah. He raised eyebrows as if to say he didn't understand, either.

"Yes, Crispin and Domino are helping Gina control her beast so she doesn't shapeshift and lose the baby," I said.

Vivian clung tighter to me. Her body started to tremble, just a fine shaking. I let go of Micah's hand and put both arms around her. Her voice was small and squeezed tight as she said, "Shapeshifters can get pregnant, but we can't keep a baby to term. The shift is too violent and we miscarry."

"That's why the weretigers are trying to teach some of us how to do what they've done for centuries, so we can help the women in our animal groups have children." When Crispin and Domino had come to live in St. Louis, we thought we'd just gained some new willing blood donors, a new dancer for Guilty Pleasures in Crispin, and a new security person in Domino, but the tigers had spilled one of their clan's big secrets. The weretigers were the only animal group that could breed true. They had what they called purebloods, who were born with hair and eyes the color they would be when they took tiger shape, but they didn't shapeshift until they hit puberty. These purebloods themselves didn't shift into a normal orange and black tiger, but their victims did, usually. I hadn't even known that the tigers bred true until I had to go meet with them in Vegas, but no one outside the tigers had known that they could calm a woman's beast. The men were trained from childhood to work with their mates and help them get through an entire pregnancy without shapeshifting, so they didn't miscarry. Crispin had quieted Gina's beast the first time without realizing that it was a big surprise to the rest of us. We were now at three months and counting; if we made one more month it would be longer than any lycanthrope female on record outside of the weretigers. The tigers were freaked out that their psychic ability worked on any other wereanimal. One of the reasons a group of them was visiting us tomorrow was to discuss the implications of Gina's pregnancy and what her potential breeding success could do to the entire weretiger culture.

Vivian buried her head tighter against me, so her voice was muffled. "I'd accepted that Stephen and I would never have children, that we couldn't, that I couldn't have children."

"We are going to get Gina through this with her baby," Micah said, and he sounded so sure. I wasn't that sure, because not only did Crispin or Domino have to be with her every full moon, but someone had to be able to run to her side if she called for help. It wasn't just a full moon that could make your beast rise; strong emotion, pain, lots of things could trigger that response.

I was one of the people trying to learn how to do what Crispin and Domino did so effortlessly. I wasn't making much progress, maybe because my beasts were trapped in my human body and I couldn't give them animal shape. Micah was learning, though, and he was good at it. Crispin thought he'd have it down cold in a few more days. All of us who were learning how to calm Gina's beast were on speed dial for her, so that if she felt herself starting to lose control we could come running. The two tigers were really hoping some of the other dominants of the animal groups learned the skill soon, so they'd have more backup.

The shaking got worse as Vivian clung to me. "If Gina has her baby, I want one, too."

I laid my cheek against her hair. "Then you can be next."

She shook her head. "Stephen doesn't want to."

"What?" I asked.

She raised her face from my shoulder. Her lipstick and eye shadow were smeared across that perfect skin. "He says with his background he doesn't want children. He's afraid he'll be like his father."

"Stephen could never be like his father," I said. Stephen and his twin, Gregory, had been sexually abused by their father for most of their lives until they left home. The father kept trying to apologize to them as part of his twelve-step program. They wanted nothing to do with him, and his insistence on trying to make amends for their nightmare childhood just seemed to me to be another way of putting his need for the apology above their need to be left the fuck alone.

"I told him that, but he's afraid. He worked with Matthew some on his dance and it brought back horrible memories. Stephen's been having the worst nightmares. His therapist says its a good sign, that things get worse so they can get better."

It sounded like something a therapist would say, but out loud I tried to be more helpful. "Stephen is not his father."

"That's what his therapist says, but he's scared." She swallowed hard enough for me to hear it. It sounded painful, as if she were trying to swallow something that hurt. "I want children, Anita. I want them, and if Stephen doesn't then I'd have to lose him to have children. I don't want to lose him. I love him, and I know he loves me."

I didn't know what to say, but luckily Micah did. He came and crouched in front of her, putting a hand on her knee. "We've got six more months before Gina has her baby. That's a long time in therapy. Six months can change everything if Stephen works on his issues."

"But what if he doesn't work it out?"

Micah gave her that patient it-will-be-all-right look. I put my face back against her hair as she looked at him. I had no comforting face to give her, so I'd just cuddle.

"It'll work out," he said, patting her knee in a sort of fatherly way. As Nimir-Raj he was supposed to be a combination of father figure, big brother, and boyfriend, but without the sex.

"How can you be so sure?" But I heard the note in her voice; she wanted to believe his surety, his face, his touch.

Micah smiled at her and there was that certainty in him that I'd seen almost from the beginning. He projected utter confidence that what he said, would be. "I know Stephen, and I know you, and I know you love each other. You've gone through a lot together; you'll make it through this, too."

"You sound so certain." Her voice was still breathy, but hopeful now, too.

He smiled wider. "I am."

I could not have said that, because I was always willing to believe someone would screw up. And because I couldn't add my certainty to his, I kissed the top of her head where she'd cuddled into the bend of my shoulder.

Monica was suddenly in front of us. I looked up and my face was already set to warn her off, and Micah stood up I think ready for the same thing, but the look on her face wasn't mean. I'd never seen her look kind before.

She called to J.J. "Can you keep Matthew occupied for a few minutes?"

J.J. glided over to us and got the little boy chasing her. I must have looked surprised, because Monica said, "I was married to a century-old vampire. I know what it's like to want a baby and believe you'll never have one. You know how rare it is for one of the older vampires to father a child."

I did know. I could only nod.

Micah moved out of the way as Monica took his place kneeling in front of Vivian. "Let me take you to the ladies' room so we can fix your makeup before Stephen gets back."

Vivian blinked at her and then nodded wordlessly. "I don't want Stephen to know I told anyone."

"I won't tell him," she said, and she held out her hand. Vivian looked at Micah, who nodded, then at me, and I nodded, too. She went with Monica, and we trusted Monica not to fuck this up. It was a little like sending your daughter off with the mean girl from school and trusting her not to be mean, but strangely, I did.

Micah sat down beside me, and his hand found mine. We sat there and watched J.J. dart around the lobby while Matthew chased her. He was squealing and happy about it, but something about the game reminded me of Jason and his ballerina's last number. Was I looking for similarities, or was the little boy really imitating Uncle Jason?

As he often did, Micah spoke as if he'd read my mind. "When I was Matthew's age I begged for a little holster and gun set with plastic badge."

"Because your dad was a sheriff?"

He nodded. "He wasn't sheriff when I was three, but he was in law enforcement and I wanted to be just like him."

"It's not just me, then; Matthew is trying to imitate some of the dancing he saw tonight."

Micah watched the toddler chase the lithe, graceful dancer. "He's started trying to figure out what it means to be a boy. He's imitating the men he sees."

I told him what Matthew had said about how all the big boys kissed me. Micah hugged me, and I realized it was the same way I'd hugged Vivian. It made me sit up straighter and even pull away a little.

"What's wrong?" he asked.

"I'm just wondering what Matthew's learning and how it will affect him later."

"But why did you pull away?"

I took in a deep breath and said, "Because I won't let myself huddle like Vivian."

He smiled and drew me in so he could kiss me on the forehead. "You will never huddle like Vivian, Anita."

I hugged him, pulled him close, and wasn't so sure. I wanted to ask him, did he want children. He'd had a vasectomy years ago so that a very evil shapeshifter couldn't use him to get the women of their animal group pregnant. The bad guy had liked them pregnant and liked the pain and sorrow of the miscarriages. He had been one of the most twisted people I'd ever met, and I never regretted killing him.

I couldn't have Micah's biological child, but we'd been sharing a bed and a home with Nathaniel for two years. Did they want children? If I'd really been as brave as everyone thought I was, I would have asked, but I didn't ask, because I didn't want to know. I was afraid I already knew the answer.

5

AN HOUR LATER five of us were walking through the big dungeon door at the bottom of the long stairs leading from the upper parts of Circus of the Damned, where there was a permanent carnival midway and circus ring, plus a freak show that held mostly mythological creatures, to the quiet underground that was the lair of the Master of the City of St. Louis. The first time I'd come through that big, scary door, Jean-Claude had only been one of the master's minions. I'd killed her to save my life and others, but I'd opened the way for Jean-Claude to be the new master. Talk about your unintended consequences.

We closed and locked the door behind us and were in an open space bordered by huge gauzy curtains that ran from the floor to vanish into the darkness of the ceiling. When I called this the underground I wasn't joking. It had been carved out of existing caverns under the city, and to add a homey touch the curtains were the walls of the living room.

Jason and J.J. were hand in hand ahead of us as he parted the curtains, hitting the opening out of long habit. If it was new to you, the "door" was nearly impossible to find the first time. They went through laughing, looking at each other in a way I never thought I'd see Jason look at anyone.

We came behind them, my hand in Nathaniel's and my arm through Micah's. We almost ran into Jason and J.J. just inside the curtains. Something about the way they were standing made me drop the men's hands and go for my gun. Maybe I was overreacting, but a lot of our enemies are faster than human. You don't get a second chance to draw your gun against that kind of speed. I used Jason and J.J. to hide my hands as I tried to see around to what had made them stop, and I could see Jason's tension level go through the roof. I knew rationally that he'd have yelled a warning if it was a gun situation, but a gun was what I had.

When I could see around them it didn't make sense. Wicked and Truth were standing with our other black-shirted security guards, but they were all standing in the middle of the room with Jean-Claude and Asher on opposite sides of the group. It looked for the entire world as if the guards were trying to keep the two vampires apart. What the hell?

I stepped out with the gun pointed at the floor. "What's going on?" I asked.

Some of them looked at me, but most of them looked at one of the two master vampires, waiting for them to answer me. I turned to Claudia, the only female guard we had, and the only woman I'd ever known who was over six feet tall. She came toward me, her long black hair in its tight ponytail moving as she stepped to the edge of the group.

"We thought they were going to fight."

"Fight about what?" I asked, and put my gun up. I wasn't going to shoot either of them, and they would know that. Unless you're willing to use it, a gun is just a useless piece of metal. I put my useless piece in its holster.

"I'm not entirely sure," she said.

"One of you talk to me," I said.

"We will not come to blows," Jean-Claude said, and he backed away from the cluster of bodyguards to sit on the big white couch on the far side of the room. He let himself fall into it in that graceful I-don't-care way, but he ended up looking like he was waiting for some passing photographer to snap a picture of him. He was always beautiful, but this level of care and control over how he looked was usually reserved for guests, and hostile guests at that.

"What happened?" I asked.

Asher backed up to the white loveseat with its gold and silver cushions. He put his arms on the back of the loveseat, careless, but in his own way just as posed as Jean-Claude. Asher's gold hair spilled over the scarred side of his face so that he sat there like some fallen angel, perfect and coldly beautiful.

"What is wrong with you guys? What's happened?"

"Nothing's happened," Asher said, "and that is precisely the problem."

We all stood in the white and gold room, and I had no idea what was going on. The bodyguards were huddled between the faux fireplace and the two chairs, the silver by the faux fireplace and the gold with its white cushions by us at the end of the room between the couch and loveseat.

The huge glass-and-metal coffee table in the center of everything had food on it, but it was also forcing the guards to move around it, having to be careful of the food and the vampires. It seemed like you shouldn't have to tiptoe around refreshments when you're standing between two master vampires, but sometimes you end up between the cutlets and the cutlery, with nowhere safe to stand.

I frowned from one to the other of them and finally turned to the guards. Claudia and her fellow wererat Fredo looked at me. The two newer guards were both werehyenas, one tall and blond, the other a little shorter with skin a few shades darker than Vivian's, hair tight and curly to his head. They were both looking at Asher. Wicked looked from one to the other of the vampires, but Truth looked at me. I said, "Truth, report."

The dark-haired vampire stepped away from the T-shirted security and faced me. "Asher is threatening to take his werehyenas and find another city."

I looked at Asher. "What? Why?"

Micah moved up beside me. "Narcissus's werehyenas are the third most powerful animal group in this city. He wouldn't leave and start over."

"He would, for me," Asher said.

"Have you made him your animal to call?" Micah asked.

Asher scowled at Micah, and his ice-blue eyes flashed with a hint of glow, a hint of vampire power. "I do not have to answer your question, cat."

"Fine, then answer it for me," I said.

He gave me an unfriendly look. "No, no I have not done what Narcissus so terribly wants. I have not made him my animal to call, but if I would, and if I would come to his bed as he wants, then he is willing to leave St. Louis and go where I go."

I didn't know what to say to that. Micah said, "Narcissus must love you a great deal to be willing to leave a safe city and fight for control somewhere else."

Asher laughed, and as Jean-Claude's laughter could be sensual and sexy, Asher's laugh held sorrow as if the light dimmed. My heart hurt for a moment. "I'm not certain Narcissus is capable of truly loving anyone, but he wants me. He wants me badly enough that he would destroy everything he has built if only I will be his in every way."

The conversation had the feel of something that had been talked about a lot, but it was totally news to me. I looked at Jean-Claude and said what I was thinking. "How long have you known about Narcissus's offer?"

"Long enough," he said.

"And you were going to mention this when?"

"He couldn't tell you," Asher said, "because that would have forced him to tell you the reason I want to leave, and that is a conversation he does not want to have, is it, *mon bellot*? Ah, but then you are not my pretty one, are you, not anymore?"

"What's that supposed to mean?" I asked.

"It means that if I cannot be loved, then I want the respect due me as a master vampire with his own animal to call."

"I'm still lost here, guys, explain," I said.

"I want a formal greeting," Asher said.

"We are all friends here, *mon ami*," Jean-Claude said.

"No, no we are not all friends here," Asher said. "I am either a master vampire or your second-in-command or I am not. If I am all those things, then it is within my rights to demand a formal greeting from everyone in the room."

"I don't think this is J.J.'s business," Jason said.

We all looked at him. I wasn't sure what I would have said, but Jean-Claude said, "You are quite right. She is your guest and this does not concern her."

"I'll be right back after I get her settled," he said, and he led her away to the other side of the curtains and the hallway beyond. She was asking him questions as they walked, her voice low and serious. He just shook his head.

"What do you mean, you want a formal greeting from everyone in the room? That's what we have to do for out-of-town guests or other dominants and masters. We don't do that to each other."

Asher looked at me and with the hair fallen over one half of his face, and all that blue silk, he was all beautiful arrogance, but I knew that was one of the emotions he hid behind. He'd come to us with that as his shield when he was afraid something would hurt too much.

It made me look over the guards' heads to the painting above the mantel that the whole room had been designed around. It was a picture of Jean-Claude and Asher, and their dead Julianna, back when everyone dressed like they'd stepped out of Dumas's *Three Musketeers*.

The Asher in the painting was all gold and white perfection with Juliana sitting in front of him, and Jean-Claude behind them both, in his signature black and white even then. The Asher in that painting was unscarred, and the artist had captured the arrogance I was looking at now.

"When you say everyone in the room? Do you actually mean everyone?" I asked.

"I do," he said.

"Jean-Claude?" I said.

"We are an informal lot here, but he is within his rights as a master to be greeted formally at every entrance," Jean-Claude said.

"The formal greeting is a kind of pissing contest," I said. "We don't have to do that with just each other."

"I thought we did not," he said, and his face was empty, telling me nothing. Shit.

I turned back to Asher. "You're seriously going to make all of us do this."

"Yes," he said.

"Why?" I asked.

"Because I can."

I stared at him for a moment, and then said, "Fine, fine, how do we do this?"

"Whoever sees me as dominant to them can greet me, and whoever feels they are dominant or equal to me, well, we shall see."

"See what?" I asked.

Micah answered, "See who offers up their flesh and blood."

"The greeting is just a formality," I said. "The submissive offers up a blood point, the vampire or wereanimal sniffs or kisses it, and we move on."

"That is not always the case, *ma petite*," Jean-Claude said.

"What else is there?" I asked.

"You know that some vampires use it as a way of trying their power one against the other."

"Yes, I've seen that."

"The ritual is an offering of blood. The dominant, or master, is within his rights to take what is offered. That is how it was originally done centuries ago. The master would pick one of the offerings and feed, and by offering to be submissive to him you give him the right to choose to feed."

"That is not how we've done it when we've had visiting masters from out of town," I said.

"Asher is invoking his rights, and that is within his rights." Jean-Claude motioned and the guards moved so the two vampires could see each other. "Isn't that what you mean to do?"

"Yes," he said, and there was nothing pleasant in his voice.

"I feel like we've stepped into a fight that I don't know anything about. If we're offering up our flesh and blood, then I want to know why."

"You only offer it up if you see me as dominant to you, Anita, and you don't."

I frowned at him, then turned back to Jean-Claude. "Help me out here. What does that mean?"

"He means that you only offer blood point to him if you see yourself as lesser than Asher. If you don't think he is your superior, then you don't offer blood, and you could insist he offer flesh or blood to you."

I shook my head and turned to Micah and Nathaniel. "Is this a surprise to both of you, too?"

They both nodded, but Micah said, "Asher has been getting pushier."

"Like trying to steal a kiss at the recital," I said.

Micah nodded.

I took a deep breath, let it out slow, and said, "Asher, don't do this, just talk to me."

"Your master has forbidden me to bring up certain topics. He has left me few avenues to demonstrate my displeasure, but the ways he has left open to me I will now take. I want to know where everyone in this room stands. I want to know where I stand with everyone in this room, and I want to know now."

"Jean-Claude, just tell him he can talk to me about whatever it is. If we start this kind of dominance thing with our own people, it's going to go all pear-shaped."

"Guards, leave us."

"I'm not sure that's a good idea," Truth said.

"I am sure," Claudia said, "it's a bad idea."

"We need to discuss some very personal issues. You are not privy to them, now go."

Claudia and Truth looked at me. Fredo and Wicked kept the vampires in their line of sight, which wasn't easy since they were across from each other, but the men managed.

"Don't look at her," Asher said. "Your master has told you to leave. Didn't you hear him?"

"He's not my master," Claudia said. "I just work here."

"He is ours," Wicked said.

"No," Truth said, "he's not."

The brothers looked at each other and then both of them looked at me. I got a hint of maybe what Asher was meaning. "If Jean-Claude says go, go. We'll be all right."

"Bad idea," Claudia said.

"Very bad idea," Fredo said.

"I trust Jean-Claude and I trust Asher."

That earned me a look from Asher that wasn't arrogant or hostile. It was almost a pained look, and then he was back to being gorgeous and unreadable.

The guards started to move toward the curtains in the direction that Jason and J.J. had gone. Asher called out, "Perses, Dares, I want you to stay."

The two werehyenas hesitated. It was the shorter, dark one, Perses, who said, "We're hired to guard Jean-Claude and his people."

"I'm not talking about who signs your paychecks," Asher said. "I'm talking about who is your master in this room."

"Don't do this," Micah said, and that one sentence let me know he'd seen some danger that I was still oblivious to.

"Will you come over here and offer up your neck to me, leopard king?" Asher asked.

Nathaniel moved in front of Micah. "I will."

"And you are tasty, *mon minet*, but I know you will not fight me. You and I have no quarrel about dominance."

Micah took his arm and pulled him back. "This isn't about sex; it's about power, Nathaniel. He wants me to acknowledge him as more powerful."

"There were other things I wanted from you, Micah, but wasn't it Machiavelli who said, 'It is better to be loved than feared, but if you cannot be loved, then fear will do.' Well, you don't love me, so I will settle."

"You are not doing all this just because I don't like boys," Micah said.

Asher laughed again, and this one hurt, as if the sound of it had bits of glass to rend the skin. It was an illusion, a vampire power, and I should have been proof against it; that I wasn't meant that Asher had grown in power since last he'd tried shit like this.

"When I believed that I let it go, but I saw you tonight at the dance. I saw you with your kitten, and you like him well enough."

"Wait, are you doing all this because you think Micah is . . . doing Nathaniel, but not you? That's such a girl reason for a fight."

"No, it's not," Asher said. "It's a very male reason for a fight. A man's ego can only take so much rejection, Anita."

"Oh my God," Micah said.

Again he was ahead of me. "What? What did you figure out that I haven't?"

Micah looked at Jean-Claude. "You sleep in the same bed with him almost every night. We find you naked together dead to the world during the day when none of us are with you. Are you really telling me that you and he aren't—"

"Aren't what?" I asked.

Nathaniel answered, "Lovers."

"What?" I asked.

"They aren't lovers."

"Who aren't lovers?"

"Jean-Claude and Asher," Nathaniel said.

I turned and looked at Jean-Claude. I just looked at him. "Are you telling me that even when I'm not with you, you're still not . . ."

"No, he's not," Asher said, "and when I say *not*, I mean not *anything*. He thinks that if you came into the room and caught us doing it, it would distress you." Since that could be a long list, I just stared at Asher.

Asher laughed, and this one was almost ordinary. "Look at their faces, Jean-Claude; our nearest and dearest all thought we were together as of old."

I turned to Jean-Claude. "Are you saying that you've had him in our bed, in your bed, naked all this time and you still haven't . . . been, oh, hell, you aren't completely lovers?"

"And what would you have done if you walked in on us being lovers, *ma petite*?"

"I'd have been a lot less upset than if I caught you with another woman," I said.

"But you would be upset," he said.

"I don't know, I . . . we do Asher together. We've all been in the bed together, the five of us, in various ways. I mean . . . I honestly thought you were saving the more intimate stuff for when I wasn't there."

"You have taught me to fear your moral compass, *ma petite*. I never wish to be on the wrong side of it again."

"But it's Asher, it's him, you love him, you have loved him for centuries."

"He loves you more," Asher said. "He loves you enough to have refused me again and again, to have stopped my touch, my body, and if you attract one more mostly heterosexual man to our little group I am going to do something violent," Asher said. Then he laughed again, and it held sorrow and something bitter in it. "But wait, I've decided to do something violent tonight." He looked at the guards who were frozen by the curtains trying to pretend they weren't listening. "Perses, Dares, come stand by me."

The two werehyenas looked at each other, and then the blond said, "We'd rather just leave you two to discuss things. This sounds more personal than bodyguard."

"I don't want you to leave. I want to make my point and the two of you will help me do that." He held out his arm and called them to him. He called them the way Jean-Claude could call wolves and I could call so many animals. He opened up his power and it filled the room like something cool and thick. I felt it touch me as it flowed by, almost like I should have been able to wrap it in my hands. He called the werehyenas and they simply turned and went to him. They took up posts behind the loveseat, at Asher's back. They faced the room like that, and it was very clear that the two werehyenas were with Asher, and not us.

"Don't do this," Micah said.

"There are no leopards here to help you, little king. There are no wolves to aid Jean-Claude, and the rats belong to no one. I am the only master in this room who has help at hand."

"Not true," Micah said.

"Do you mean our kitten? I don't think you want to risk him against me."

"I'm not talking about me at all," Micah said. He looked at me.

I shook my head. "Don't make me do this."

"He's setting up the rules, not me," Micah said.

"If you mean Anita, then save your breath, leopard. She and I established that she'd bow to me long ago."

I looked at the vampire. "What does that mean exactly?"

"You let me dominate you in the bedroom along with our kitten."

"In the bedroom is different."

"You once let me feed until I almost drained you dry. You and I both know that I stopped myself from killing you; you would have let me do it, and enjoyed it right up until the moment you died."

He was talking about the last time we'd been alone and he'd fed from me. His vampire power was to make his bite orgasmic, and it was, and what he'd just said was absolutely right. In that one moment I wouldn't have fought to live; it had felt too good to stop. He and I had never told anyone the entire truth of it before. We'd simply avoided being alone together for feedings.

"Don't push me, Asher."

"Or what? You'll kill me? I don't think so."

"Just as you won't kill us," Jean-Claude said, softly, "and if death is off the table, then what is left to prove?"

"That I have grown too powerful to be your second. I need a territory of my own and lovers who aren't ashamed of me."

"We aren't ashamed of you."

"The men are, and he"—he pointed at Jean-Claude—"says he refuses my body because you would reject him if you saw us together. I told him you were with him and Augustine, Master of Chicago, and you did not turn from what happened, or from Jean-Claude. But it was when I saw your cats kissing in public that I knew that Jean-Claude had lied. You have no problem sharing yourself with men who are sharing each other; it is Jean-Claude who doesn't want to be with me again. You are his excuse to keep me from that last part of him."

"I don't know what you thought you saw at the recital," Micah said.

"I saw two men who love each other and aren't afraid to show it in public. Don't deny it."

"I had no intention of denying how I feel about Nathaniel." Nathaniel laid his head on Micah's shoulder, and Micah reached a hand up to touch the taller man's face. It always seemed odd that Nathaniel was taller than Micah, but dominance isn't always about height.

"Please, can the guards go for the rest of this discussion?" I asked.

"See, you are embarrassed by me."

"I'm embarrassed in general."

"I am not."

I met his too-calm, too-arrogant face, and said, "Fine, fucking fine, let's do this." I turned to Jean-Claude. "Are you telling me that you haven't been his lover because you thought I'd leave you?"

"You've gone away for months for much lesser offenses of your small-town morality."

"That was a while ago, Jean-Claude, give me some credit here. If you and Asher want to be together . . ."

"Be lovers," Asher said.

I gave him an unfriendly look, but turned back to Jean-Claude. "Fine, if you and Asher want to be lovers when I'm not in the bed, that's okay with me."

"*Non, ma petite, non.*"

"It is you who is afraid of being with me," Asher said. "I cannot live like this, and eventually I will give in to Narcissus if I have no one else to turn to."

"If I say I'm fine with it, then why not?" I asked.

"Asher assumes that Micah and Nathaniel are doing what I will not; are they lovers?"

I wanted to squirm and fought not to. "Why don't you ask them—they're standing right here."

He looked at the men. "Are you lovers?"

Nathaniel said yes, and Micah said no, at the same time. Asher laughed, and this laugh held humor. "How can you not know?"

"Micah loves me. He takes care of me. We sleep nude in the bed even if Anita is out of town. I clean his house, I fix his meals. We touch each other in private. We just don't do certain things."

"You don't sodomize each other," Asher offered.

"Yeah," Nathaniel said, and he almost smiled, but not like he was happy. "We don't do that."

"It's not to every man's taste. Even those who like men are not always sodomites," Jean-Claude said.

"But Micah doesn't think you are lovers, do you, Micah?" Asher asked. I realized that Asher wasn't just going to try to tear down what he and Jean-Claude and I had; he was going to try to tear down everyone.

Micah took a deep breath and let it out in a loud rush. "I guess I thought that if we weren't fucking each other, we weren't lovers."

"So Nathaniel is trapped as I am trapped, wanting, but never having."

Nathaniel said, "I think I like girls a little better than you do, so it's not as big an issue for me."

"If Micah would fuck you in the ass, would you say no?"

I so wanted out of this conversation, but it was like a car accident: Once you started spinning you could only wait and see what you hit.

"No," Nathaniel said.

"Liar," Asher said.

Nathaniel started to smile, fought it off, and said, "You've seen him nude. I've never had anyone that large do anal sex on me. I think it might hurt."

"You are a pain slut. You like hurt," Asher said.

"In most ways, yes, but I was raped as a kid, so I like anal sometimes and I miss it, but I don't like it to hurt. Hurting like that is a trigger event. It throws me back into being raped." He shook his head, a little too rapidly. "I think if I'd been treated better, then I probably would like it, but I wasn't, and we do together almost everything that I want to do."

Asher said, "I am sorry, Nathaniel; in my own hurt feelings I forgot that other people have been hurt, too. But I will not let even your sad story stop this conversation. We will have it out, and then when I am rejected one last time I will go and stay with Narcissus until arrangements can be made for us to leave."

"The werehyenas are a third, or more, of the security for Jean-Claude," Micah said.

"Not my problem," Asher said.

"You'd really cut our manpower that badly, knowing that there are masters out there who would see that as weakness and try to kill us?" I asked.

"I cannot stay here and have my heart broken over and over, Anita. I will go mad. Either I must be someone's lover, or I must go."

"Wait," I said, "you're my lover. You're my lover in every way that any other man has been. I haven't denied you any part of me."

He looked at me, and I gave him a look back. "Oh, come on, just because I don't like anal. No one else gets to do that, either."

"It's not you he wants," Micah said.

Asher looked at him. "Are you saying it's you I'm pining over?"

"You said that Jean-Claude loved Anita better than you; well, don't you love Jean-Claude better than you love Anita?"

Asher looked at Micah, and finally he nodded. "Touché, Nimir-Raj. I have loved Jean-Claude for centuries, so yes. Did you know that I chose Julianna as my human servant because I feared I was losing Jean-Claude's love?"

Jean-Claude said something rapid in French. He was sitting forward and looked startled at last.

Asher went on. "I never told you because it was too pathetic. You know I like women, but I like men more. Didn't you ever puzzle at why I chose to tie myself to a woman as my human servant?"

"You loved her," Jean-Claude said.

"Eventually, but I chose her for you. I knew what you liked and I shopped with an eye for keeping you, not for satisfying myself, and it worked. It worked better than I could have dreamed. I should have realized that I had set myself up for the two people I loved most in the world to love each other more than they loved me."

Jean-Claude made as if to reach out to the other man, and then let his hand fall back. "We did not mean to hurt you."

"You never mean to hurt me, Jean-Claude, but you do seem to keep doing it." He turned back to us. "What does Micah deny you, Nathaniel? What do you want him to do that he will not?"

Nathaniel looked at Micah, who just nodded. No one looked at me; in that moment it was just the men. "I'd like him to go down on me and do me by hand."

"You are denied everything I am denied; how can you be happy?"

"I just am," Nathaniel said.

"He's not denied everything," Micah said.

"I have heard the truth," Asher said.

That first roll of power trickled off of Micah's skin. His beast peeking out with his anger. "He said he wanted me to go down on him and do him by hand."

"*Exactement.*"

"You only hear what you want to hear tonight, Asher. Let's just say I can prove that Nathaniel really does have absolutely no gag reflex."

There was a moment of thunderous silence. Micah glared at Asher. Nathaniel looked pleased and tried not to. I had no safe place to look and no idea what expression to wear.

"Was Anita with you?" Jean-Claude asked.

"Yes," Micah said.

"*Ma petite.*"

I didn't want to look at him.

"*Ma petite*, look at me."

I've turned and faced men with guns when it took less courage than to meet Jean-Claude's eyes in that moment. "This is a recent change?"

I nodded.

"What did you think? How did you feel about it?"

I so did not want to discuss this in front of people, but damn it, if I was really all right with it, why was it embarrassing? Damn it. "Without the *ardeur* I have a gag reflex, and Micah . . ."

"Is *bien outillé*, well hung, *oui*," Jean-Claude said.

"Yes, so one afternoon we took turns going down on Micah." I said it fast as if that made it sound more ladylike, but some things just aren't ladylike and sucking a man's dick is one of them. I loved doing it, but . . . Oh, hell. I was blushing so hard I was light-headed. I thought I'd stopped blushing like that, damn it.

Micah and Nathaniel each touched an arm, which meant I looked as shaky as I felt.

"And have you done it since?" Jean-Claude asked.

I swallowed and concentrated. I would not faint. I never fainted. Fuck. I kept a good hold on both their arms and said, "Not the taking turns part, but Nathaniel going down on Micah, yes."

"And you are all right with it?"

"Jesus, Jean-Claude, I'm not the small-town virgin that you found years ago. Give me some credit for being a little more open-minded. The three of us have shared a bed for over two years."

"You are right, *ma petite*; I remembered you as of old and didn't trust you."

"So, you would be all right with Jean-Claude and me being lovers."

"Yes."

"Would you be all right in bed with us while we touched?" Jean-Claude asked.

"Depends on the touch, but I like men. When you and I did Augustine together, I learned I liked seeing men kiss each other, and I love watching Nathaniel and Micah together. I love . . . Look, don't blame this mess on me. I didn't keep you from Asher; you decided that on your own."

"I thought it was you I was protecting, but Asher is right, it was me." He looked at the other man. "You almost consumed me once before Julianna. It wasn't that you were a man that had made me withdraw, it was that your power works on vampires, too. You were very close to making me your slave, and if I wasn't willing to be Belle Morte's slave, then I wouldn't be yours."

"So another man brought in would have worked as well?" Asher asked.

Jean-Claude smiled and shook his head. "No, you chose well for my heart. Julianna was everything I could have dreamed of in a woman at that time."

"You don't have to add the *at that time* for my benefit, Jean-Claude. I know you loved her; hell, I've felt the memories."

"The person who loved Julianna died when she died."

"We all died that day," Asher said.

"Yes," Jean-Claude said.

The silence sat for a minute full of old sorrow and older loss. Then Micah said, "But if Anita were with you, would you want to be Asher's lover?"

Jean-Claude looked at Micah, then at me, and finally he looked directly across the room at Asher. "Yes."

"Just empty words," Asher said, "to save your hyenas and your power base."

Jean-Claude stood up and held his hand out to me. "*Ma petite.*" I admit I hesitated, but I went and took his hand. Then Jean-Claude turned and held out his hand to the other vampire.

Asher said, "You mean now?"

"You say words are empty. Let me show you actions."

I looked from one to the other of them, and fought a sudden panicking feeling in my stomach. It wasn't that I didn't want to, but it was all moving a little too fast for me and I had a niggling feeling that I was missing something.

Asher stood up. The werehyenas behind him asked, "What do you want us to do?"

"Whatever you were doing. Do your jobs." He went to Jean-Claude's outstretched hand without a backward glance at the two shapeshifters, and that was why Asher would probably never have his own territory. It wasn't lack of power, but lack of wanting power. He would always let his heart overrule his head, and Masters of the City don't survive long making decisions like that.

Jean-Claude led us toward the curtains. The guards standing there scattered as if we'd shouted *Boo.* Jason was on the other side of them. He raised eyebrows, and just his expression let me know he'd heard and knew what was happening. I reached out my free hand and he gave me his. The moment I touched him his power flared over me like heat in a summer meadow. It felt so good, and then I smelled trees, leaves, forest, and I knew that there were more wolves just outside the big dungeon door.

Jean-Claude, Jason, and I all turned toward the far curtains as Jamil and Shang-Da swept through them. They were both tall and muscular, Jamil with his long cornrows and tailored suit, Shang-Da the tallest Chinese man I'd ever met, hair cut skater straight, his black trench coat flaring around him showing glimpses of the guns underneath. The moment I saw both of them I knew who was coming next, and there he was, Richard, our Ulfric, our wolf king. He was dressed in blue jeans with a leather and denim jacket open over a bloodred T-shirt. His shoulder-length hair fell in foaming waves, a brown shot full of gold and red highlights. He swept in with his guards on either side, and it was like my heart stopped for a moment. Nothing would ever make Richard less than handsome, from the short brown boots peeking out from the jeans to the poured-on jeans and everything I knew lay in them, to the upper body that he'd hit the gym hard enough to make even wider, even more impressive, and then the face. Once I'd thought I'd marry him, and even now my heart and libido leapt up, but my mind went, *No, whatever he wants, no*. Once it goes to hell, no one can cut you up like the love of your life. Fuck.

6

SHANG-DA STAYED BY the two werehyenas near the loveseat, his trench coat swept back to show the weapons more clearly. What was going on? Jamil stayed at his Ulfric's side, and there was something way too formal, too dangerous, about all of it for our normally less-than-action-oriented Richard.

The guards by us fanned out and looked a little uncertain. They'd picked up on the urgency, too.

"Richard, what has happened?" Jean-Claude asked.

"I'm in time, so nothing yet," he said.

Truth and Wicked moved in front of him and Jamil. "You're moving like you have a purpose, Ulfric," Truth said. "What is that purpose?"

He let them stop him. "I'm here to complete Jean-Claude's triumvirate of power."

"I expected you tomorrow for the weretigers," Jean-Claude said, "but tonight is a surprise."

"Did I interrupt something?"

"Yes," Asher said, and that one word was very unhappy.

"Then I am just in time."

Micah came to me with Nathaniel literally in his hand. Micah offered me his free hand, and I let go of Jason to take it. Micah and Nathaniel were the ones who had held me the most when Richard cut me up. Since he'd left Jean-Claude when he left me, it had seemed wrong to cry on Jean-Claude's shoulder.

"Who did you bring the guards for, Richard?" Jean-Claude asked.

"Hopefully, no one, but Anita is always complaining I'm not cautious enough; I'm trying to change that."

"Truth, Wicked, enough."

The vampires looked at me, and I nodded. Only then did they move aside.

Micah squeezed my hand, and I leaned in against him with Jean-Claude's hand still in mine. Richard looked at Micah. "I guess I've earned that look, Nimir-Raj, Micah."

"What do you want?" Micah asked.

"To help. I swear to you, I'm here to make things better instead of worse."

"That would be a change," Micah said.

There was a flash of anger across Richard's handsome face, and then he nodded. "I deserved that." He looked at me then and said, "Anita, I don't know what to say to you."

I sighed. "You said you came here to make things better; do that, make them better, and we'll go from there." I met the perfect brown of his eyes, and he nodded.

He turned to Jean-Claude. "I don't know what to say to you either, Jean-Claude."

"Start with what you are doing here, Richard," he said.

Richard moved into the group of us. Asher actually moved a little closer to Jean-Claude, as if he would block the other man. Normally that would have been enough to stop Richard in his tracks, but tonight he kept coming. He swept his hair to one side to expose the long, smooth, muscled line of his neck. "First, I would greet the Master of the City."

I felt Jean-Claude go very still beside me, sinking into that stillness that the old vampires could do. It proved that he was as unsure of what was happening as I was, and that he didn't trust this new, more cooperative Richard. We were both expecting him to come in and try, but in the end he would leave us more hurt than when we started, and he would fail us at the critical moment. He had taught us that.

Jean-Claude let go of both my hand and Asher's. He would take the greeting offered—the very kind of greeting that Asher had been trying to force on all of us just minutes ago. It was an almost surreal turn of events, because Richard didn't offer this greeting to anyone, or never had before, not willingly.

Jean-Claude put his hands on the other man's shoulders to steady himself, and leaned in and laid the barest of kisses on the other man's neck. Then he leaned back and studied Richard. "Why are you here?"

"I would stand at your side tonight as I will tomorrow. You need your wolf tonight, Jean-Claude."

"We do not need you tonight, Ulfric," Asher said, and he came up behind Jean-Claude, sliding his arms around the other man's waist and putting his face next to Jean-Claude's. Asher hid his scars with his hair, but the face that showed was arrogant, sensual, and possessive.

I expected Richard to react with disgust, or anger, and he wasn't comfortable with it, but he said, "Oh, I think Jean-Claude does, and Anita does. I think they need me a lot tonight."

"They've agreed to bed me tonight, Ulfric. Jean-Claude and I will be lovers tonight with nothing denied us." He smiled, most unpleasantly, at the other man.

Richard smiled back, and his held anger as Asher's held cruelty. Really, when you came down to it, they could both be pretty unpleasant. I'd never thought of it that way before, but it was true.

Richard had swallowed his power back as he came through the door, being polite to shield. Now the first trickle of warm, vibrating power flowed over us. I shivered where it touched, clutching at Micah's hand. Jean-Claude didn't so much shiver as just smooth the lapels of his jacket, but it was a nervous gesture, I knew that.

"I won't offer sex to you, Asher, but other than that, I wouldn't miss it."

"Richard," I said, "you don't mean that."

He looked at me and held his hand out to me. "If you and Jean-Claude are going to do it, then I do mean it."

I stared at his hand. "What are you offering?" I asked.

"Take my hand, Anita, please, for power, for shared power let Jean-Claude's triumvirate be everything it was meant to be tonight while he embraces Asher."

Micah squeezed my hand. I looked at him, and his eyes told me, *Do it.* I trusted him, and so I reached out. The moment Richard's hand touched mine, the power rushed over my skin like a warm bath that raised every hair on my head. My head went back, eyes closed, and the power hit Micah's hand in mine and kept spilling into Nathaniel. Leopard was my animal to call, and Nathaniel was to me what Richard was to Jean-Claude. The last time we'd tried to combine my triumvirate with Jean-Claude's, Richard hadn't cooperated.

Jean-Claude's hand touched my shoulder, and the power spread to him.

He moved his hand to the side of my face, and bare skin was always better. It was like the power was a deep, still pool of water, and that last touch was a huge rock. The water crashed upward, spilled outward, and the rings of power went out and out and out.

Someone whispered, "Oh, my God," and it was none of us who were touching because we had no words yet. Jason wasn't touching us, but I felt the power stagger him, and he reached out, put his hand on my back so he could become part of that circuit. It was like throwing another, smaller boulder into the waters before they'd settled from the first. I felt Wicked and Truth when the power hit them, because they were ours, and Jamil was Richard's wolf, and his body reacted to the power, and then the were-rats resonated with the power because we'd fed on them through their rat king, so we knew the taste of the wererats and it was good, and then Shang-Da grabbed the back of the loveseat; I felt his hand close on the cloth to steady him. And finally the power found Asher, because all the vampires in this city were ours, but he must have moved away from us to be near Shang-Da. We felt him touch the werehyenas and he was protected from us, from the spill of our power, our heat, our warmth, our mix of death and life. He and his hyenas were like boulders in the wash of it, standing firm and not being swept along.

I heard one of the werehyenas say, "We need to go, Asher."

I had to blink to clear my vision, almost like you do after really good sex where the orgasm leaves you blind and unable to focus. But it wasn't sex, it was pure power.

Asher spoke into the stunned silence. "You've been holding back on us, Ulfric."

Richard's hand tightened on mine and on Jean-Claude's, and for a moment I couldn't tell which hand was mine, or if they both were. We'd had moments of this kind of sharing before, and always Richard or I panicked and broke the power, but there wasn't enough of me solid to be afraid, and Richard was exhilarated as if it had worked even better than he'd planned.

It was his voice, hoarse, raw from the power, that answered for us. "I could say the same for you, Asher."

I could see again, but I was staring at Richard's chest so all I could see was his red shirt with its frame of jean jacket. Jean-Claude's voice came even and unruffled, but I could feel the fierce joy in him. This was the power he'd bound Richard and me to him for; this was why he had locked us into our little three-way of hate, for this possibility. He said, "Why did you cut yourself off from our power, Asher?"

"Anita on her own made a slave out of a dominant werelion, her Nicky. The three of you together would be powerful enough, but with her leopard to call and her Nimir-Raj, I fear my poor heart will be enslaved."

"We would never do that to you," I said. Richard moved into the curve of Jean-Claude's arm, and there was a moment when the vampire wasn't touching me. It changed how the power felt, but it didn't break the bond; we both belonged to Jean-Claude and to touch one was to touch the other.

I could see Asher and his hyenas now by the loveseat, near the curtains with the door just on the other side. He was watching us, face empty and unreadable, but his being over there so far away spoke more than any look could have.

"Unless you tried to do it to us first," Richard said. He squeezed my hand tight and drew Jean-Claude closer to him. The other man moved so he could put his arms around both our waists as he stood between us. I kept my hand in Micah's, and Jason moved to touch me and Jean-Claude.

"You know something, *mon ami*; share it with us," Jean-Claude said.

"Narcissus has been bragging that his master was going to roll mine and then the werehyenas would own St. Louis."

"Narcissus wants that, true," Asher said, "but I did not agree to do it."

"My information says differently, and I believed it enough to drive down here tonight with Shang-Da and Jamil. I believed it enough that I'm sleeping over, if they'll have me."

"And if I said I would bed the three of you, how long would it take for your newfound resolution to crumble?" Asher asked.

"If my choice is between opening a vein to you with Jean-Claude and Anita, or making that sadistic bastard Narcissus the animal king of St. Louis, I'll donate the blood."

Asher came around the loveseat with the hyenas hand in hand with him, as if he wasn't sure what would happen if he let them go, but he stalked toward us putting that grace, that raw sexuality that he held inside him into every step. "I've wanted your neck under my mouth from the moment I saw you, Richard."

"I know." I could feel his pulse try to speed, feel his heart as he concentrated to slow it down so his pulse would stay quiet. Fear meant food to vampires and wereanimals, and Richard hadn't come tonight to be food. He might donate blood, but it wouldn't be as submissive anything. If your hamburger could bite back, that seemed to be what he had in mind.

Asher stopped moving forward and studied us. "Is it just the three of you, or the five, no, six of you?"

"I can't speak for anyone else but myself," Richard said, "but I stand with Jean-Claude and Anita."

"The leopards will do what their Nimir-Ra needs them to do," Micah said.

Jason said, "I'm Anita's wolf to call; that means where I sleep tonight is up to her."

"Jean-Claude and I can fuck and then drink from each of you in turn and fuck some more. It would be enough power to keep us going until dawn crashed the party," Asher said. He fought for control and finally lost. His face showed an almost exquisite pain. He wanted what we were offering. I saw his hands tighten on the werehyenas. They seemed bespelled by him, but I realized they were still enough themselves to have given him their non-gun hands just in case.

Shang-Da was trailing behind them, as if he expected them to need the weapons. For Richard to be here like this, and Shang-Da to be acting like that, would take more than just rumors of Narcissus bragging. The moment I had that thought, it wasn't just a thought, it was more like knowledge. Pictures, images, sensations, memories, and Richard had heard that Asher had a human servant in mind. Narcissus wanted him to make a triumvirate of power like we had made. If they could pull it off, and if they chose well for their human servant, the balance of power in St. Louis could shift and not in our favor. We'd been so worried about out-of-town vampires trying to move in on our power structure that we hadn't noticed a much closer problem.

The rush of shared knowledge left me shaken, and I fought to hide my face by cuddling closer to Richard, burying my face against his chest. But of course, that was too close for other things. You'd think being able to share thoughts would bring us so close that nothing could make it worse, but burying my face against his bloodred T-shirt, I could smell his skin just underneath. The scent of him tightened things low in my body, and bound this tight I couldn't hide it. Not from Richard, and not from Micah, who held my other hand, and through him, Nathaniel. Jason knew, too, but that didn't bother me nearly as much. Jean-Claude knew, but he'd known that from the beginning and used it to bind Richard and me to him.

I was left staring up into Richard's face from inches away, with the look in his eyes that let me know he wanted me, too. We always wanted each other; sex had never been our problem area.

I turned from Richard's eyes to Micah and Nathaniel beside him. I started to say something, but Micah said, "It's all right."

Nathaniel nodded.

Asher took a deep, shaking breath and let it out slow, but it shook on the way out, too. "As you don't trust me or Narcissus, I don't trust you, Ulfric. This is too good to be true, and that means it is a trap. A lovely trap, but a trap nonetheless."

Richard looked out at the vampire. "No trap, just us."

"I would bargain for only you and Anita with Jean-Claude and me tonight."

"I would add one more wereanimal to come after you have fed on both Anita and me."

"Why?" Asher asked.

"You'll only feed on us after you've had sex once apiece; if we have more food waiting, you can fuck again."

"Bold, Ulfric, very bold; what happened to our homophobic wolf?"

"I'm donating blood, not sex."

"Won't it bother you to watch Jean-Claude and me together?"

"We'll see, won't we?"

"Do you really think your nerves can take being in bed with all four of us? You usually protect your virtue from me as if you were an untouched maiden and I the lecherous villain."

"By your standards that's exactly what I am. Remember that I share some of Jean-Claude's memories. You love being the first man to seduce a straight man. The more macho and homophobic the better, because every time you won the game you knew it was because no one was as beautiful as you."

"That was long ago, Ulfric; I am no longer the perfect beauty I was then."

"Beautiful enough to make Jean-Claude and Anita afraid of being alone with you individually, because they love you. That gives a vampire with your abilities a big edge in who's going to be dominant in bed."

"You'll truly let me take blood from you tonight?" Asher asked.

"Do you understand what he'll do to you, Richard?" Jason asked. "His bite is amazing, more orgasmic than Jean-Claude's."

Richard's pulse got away from him then and pushed at the side of his throat. "So I've heard."

"I can taste your pulse, Ulfric; I frighten you."

"A little."

"So arrogant, Ulfric; you think you are proof against me? I would enjoy proving you wrong."

"You can try," he said.

Asher rubbed his thumbs along the knuckles of the two guards. It seemed to help him focus. "But you're not certain you will win this battle of wills. I can feel your doubt. So why would you risk your handsome flesh with me?"

"Anita and Jean-Claude love you; that gives you an edge. But you love them, too, so that balances out. I don't even like you, and you don't like me."

"So it is a stalemate," Asher said.

"No, because we have one thing you don't."

"And that would be what?"

"You want me."

"Oh, that is arrogant," Asher said.

"You don't want me because you like me. You want me because I belong to Jean-Claude and because part of you believes that I'm a greater threat to his affections for you than Anita is. She's just a girl, and what really scares you is that he'll find another man to love. You worried about Micah and Nathaniel, but you've been in the bed with them and him and Anita. I'm the only one you haven't seen with him. Until you see us together you'll never be sure."

"I have never said that."

"Not in words, but you're more jealous of me, because I won't share him with you the way Micah, Nathaniel, and Jason do. Tonight I'm offering to share, and you want that."

It was a challenge, and Richard knew his audience. Asher did want what was on the table, and he wouldn't want to back down from the challenge, especially since it was Richard throwing the gauntlet down. It was a trap, not one we'd spring on purpose, but could Asher really sink fang into Richard for the first time and resist trying his vampire wiles on him? It would almost be too tempting to resist.

"Come home with us, Asher. Let us go back to Narcissus," Perses said.

"This is a one-night-only offer, Asher," Richard said.

Asher licked his lips and said, "This could wait until after the weretigers arrive and go again to Las Vegas."

"No," Richard said, "tonight, now, or never." Richard met Asher's gaze full on; with me and Jean-Claude touching him he was proof against the master vampire's gaze.

"Don't do it," the other hyena said.

"Let go of everyone but the three of you," Asher said.

Jean-Claude thought at us. Micah squeezed my hand tight, and then he let me pull away. Jason let his hands fall and he stepped back. It was just Richard and us now, but the power was still amazing, a warm rush of magic just waiting for us to decide what to do with it.

"Don't," the werehyena said.

"I am master, not you," Asher said, and he pulled away from them. He stood there, alone, and again I knew why he was not master of his own city. Not because he wouldn't be powerful enough, but because he let his heart, or his desire, overrule his common sense. You can look out of control and even be crazy as hell—I'd met a few Masters of the City that were—but in the end they were all about survival. But Asher came to us. He stopped a few feet away as if he'd gotten to the edge of something. I think it was the edge of our power.

"I want this," he said, and his voice was already hoarse with the beginnings of need.

"If we are with you tonight, you must give your word that you will not take the werehyenas to another city until we have enough other guards to replace them," Jean-Claude said.

"And if I refuse?"

"Then you can go to Narcissus for tonight and the three of us will go to my bedroom without you." He drew me in against his body and ran a hand through the waves of Richard's hair, but it was Asher he looked at; we were just props for the game.

Asher's breath went out in a long shudder, and then he simply walked past us toward the far curtains. He parted them, then hesitated in the opening with the stone hallway framed behind him.

"Are you coming, or has your nerve broken already, Ulfric?"

Richard squeezed my hand, then let go of it, and of Jean-Claude's. The link was immediately not as great. It was like being suddenly less warm, as if a cloud had crossed the sun. Richard went to Micah and Nathaniel, leaned close, and whispered something to them. Micah nodded, and then Richard offered first Micah and then Nathaniel his hand. They shook hands, and Richard came back to us. His face was strangely peaceful, but his pulse couldn't lie. It was jumping in the side of his neck. For all his brave talk, he was afraid of Asher.

Jean-Claude offered his hand to him, and Richard took it. He started to reach out to me, then hesitated and looked back at the other man. It made Jean-Claude smile and then reach his hand out to me. I went to him, and he led us by the hands to Asher at the curtains.

Jamil said, "What do you want us to do, Ulfric?"

"Have guards outside the door, and if we call for help, do your jobs."

Wicked said, "Anita, Jean-Claude, this is a bad idea."

I nodded. "Yep."

"Why do it then?" Truth asked.

I couldn't explain and I couldn't share the mind-to-mind with them, so all I could say was, "It'll be all right."

"Don't lie to a liar, Anita," Wicked said.

Jean-Claude said, "Enough. If we're doing this, I want enough hours between now and dawn to enjoy it."

It was Claudia who said, "We have to tell Rafael."

"Do that," Jean-Claude said.

"He knows I'm here," Richard said. "I went to your king for advice."

"Rafael did not tell you to come here and bugger him," Fredo said, pointing a thumb at Asher.

Richard smiled and said, "He knows why I'm here and what I'm planning to do, I promise you."

The wererats exchanged looks, but the promise got them. "Mysterious shit bugs me," Fredo said.

Jason gave a small salute as we moved through the drapes and followed Asher down the hallway. Was it wrong to think that Asher's ass looked really good in his leather pants as he walked ahead of us up the hallway, or was it just true?

7

THE BED WAS done in red and black tonight. Jean-Claude changed all the bedding including the bed curtains between different color combinations. I'd never seen it being changed. I'd just come into the room and it would be blue, or red, or black, or even gold and silver, and various combinations of all the above. It was like magic: always fresh, clean sheets, always impeccably made.

Asher had stopped halfway between the door and the bed. He turned back, staring at us, his ice-blue eyes framed by all that golden hair. The look on his face was eager, but there was that edge of cruelty that I hated in him. I knew that whatever he was about to say, or do, would be unpleasant. He'd said he wanted this, but he was about to do something to wreck it.

"I want to see you nude," he said, and his voice held an echo of what Jean-Claude's could, as if the last word caressed down the body in a shivering line.

I waited for Jean-Claude to say something, do something, help. But it was Richard who said, "You're angry, Asher. You say you want me, all of us, but now you're angry and you're going to sabotage it."

I could feel a sort of sadness from Richard, not upset, just a deep, almost calm sadness.

I felt Jean-Claude's hand in mine, but he started to shield, to cut down the connection between us. I think he was afraid of what was going to happen. We were standing in the bedroom with the two men in our lives most likely to fuck up a good thing.

"What do you know about what I will do, Ulfric?" Asher asked, and his voice already held that edge of derision that he could do so well.

"It's what I would have done a few months ago."

"I am not you, wolf."

"I came here to make things better, not worse, Asher. So I'll tell you all a story."

"Is it a long story?" Asher said, voice thick with scorn.

"A little," Richard said.

"Then we should all sit down." Asher went to the bed and laid himself down in the middle of all the black and red pillows. His hair spilled out like a gilt-edged frame of foaming gold. His scarred cheek was pressed against the pillows so that he was once again that perfect face that had helped Belle Morte nearly rule Europe centuries ago. The blue of his shirt gleamed, the sapphire-and-diamond pin at his throat catching the light as he patted the bed beside him and said, "Come, Ulfric, sit beside me. I won't bite . . . yet." He smiled at Richard and made it everything a heterosexual man never wants to see on another man's face.

Richard laughed. I jumped and Jean-Claude went even more still beside me, as if should I let go of his hand he would simply vanish in plain sight. Most vampires couldn't really do that, but the old ones could be so still that you were forced to remember this was not a truly living being, but something else. Live human beings didn't ever feel like this with their hands in mine. Moments like this were one of the reasons I'd been able to resist his charms for so long. His hand was still wrapped around mine, but it was like holding a "living" mannequin.

I pulled at my hand, and he let me go. He knew how I felt about moments like this, and I also knew that it was his way of protecting himself from what was about to happen. The two men he was probably more attracted to than any others were about to tear us all apart again. Fuck.

"And what have I done to amuse you, Ulfric?" There was no teasing now, but the beginnings of anger made Asher's eyes gleam.

Richard started for the bed, taking his jean jacket off as he moved, so that by the time he got to the bed his upper body was painted against the red of his shirt. He'd been keeping up with his gym time. I knew that because it was one of the few places I'd seen him since summer. When you can bench-press a small car, as he could, you couldn't really get a challenging workout at a normal gym. Thanks to Jean-Claude's vampire marks I was stronger than I should have been, too. Micah, Jason, and Nathaniel had been taking me to the gym that was designed for that.

Richard threw his jacket on the foot of the bed and stood there looking down at Asher. He looked back, his face locked in an arrogant mask that meant whatever he was thinking was something he didn't want to share. I knew part of it; no one who was moved by a handsome man could gaze up at Richard and not want him.

I looked at Jean-Claude. He was more unreadable than Asher. There would be no help from him, and I had no clue what to do.

Richard turned back and held his hand out to us. "Are you joining us?" He was smiling and he didn't look angry.

I shrugged and walked toward the bed. I knew I wasn't going to stay frozen by the door like a scared rabbit. If it was all going to go down in flames, the least I could do was run into the smoking building and try to salvage something. I let Richard take my hand and help me onto the bed. It was tall enough that in hose I tended to slide off the black satin coverlet.

We crawled onto the bed, and Richard used his hand in mine to direct me onto the side of Asher closest to the door, while he crawled around Asher's legs so he could lean into the pillows on the other side. I sat there, a little stiffly, and had a moment to share a look with Asher. He let me see that he was wondering what the hell was going on, too. Glad it wasn't just me.

I took a deep breath, let it out slow, and lay back on the pillows still fully clothed including heels and my weapons, so not exactly comfortable, but so far we weren't completely fucked. It was a record for the four of us alone in a room.

Jean-Claude looked at us. For a moment he was that almost two-dimensional stillness, and then he took a step and from one moment to the other it was as if he came to life. It was like the difference between a photograph and film. He had that easy smile on his face, and was all ease and grace. He walked toward us as he'd probably walked into a thousand rooms over the years, smiling, pleasant, beautiful, and still hiding what he was feeling just as surely.

He stopped by the bedpost, his hands stroking the black and red curtains. He looked at us all and shook his head. "Too good to be true," he said.

Richard nodded. "I've been a bastard and I'm sorry."

We all looked at him, including Asher. It startled him enough that he didn't even worry about how his hair fell so that his scars were bare to the soft glow of the bedside lamps.

"The apology is a wondrous thing, *mon ami*, but forgive this old vampire if he asks, what exactly are you sorry for?"

"What he said," I said.

"When you and I first met, Anita, I'd just gotten away from Raina and Gabriel."

"The vampires still speak of Raina, the old Lupa of your pack, and Gabriel, the ex-leader of the wereleopards. They make some of Belle Morte's court sound kind, and they are not kind," Asher said.

Richard nodded. "They were both true sexual sadists."

"In that real serial-killer sort of way," I added.

Asher turned his head to look at me. "I heard you killed them both while they were trying to make a rape-and-snuff film starring you and Gabriel. I thought the story had grown in the telling."

I shook my head. "I don't know if the details have grown, but the basics are true." I shivered. Gabriel and Raina had been the couple from hell, and it had been part luck that helped me kill them and save the others. I had some scars from Gabriel that I'd have for the rest of my life.

Asher reached out and took my hand in his. "I am glad you killed them."

"We all are," Richard said.

"They are not a loss," Jean-Claude said.

"Like I said, when I met Anita I'd just gotten away from them. They'd tried to make me into a more dominant version of Nathaniel, just another pet."

"They never understood that you would never be that," Jean-Claude said.

Richard nodded and said, "I fought high enough in the pack structure to have more choices, and I beat the shit out of Gabriel one night. But that didn't stop Raina from trying to hurt me in other ways. She made our Ulfric, Marcus, give me to Jean-Claude. I had fought my way into dominance enough to stay out of the beds of people I didn't want to sleep with, and then they give me to a vampire whose power is all about sex. Raina told me that you'd seduce me eventually and she'd get to watch us together."

"I was Master of the City by then, Richard; I would not have let her do that to me, or to you."

Richard sat up, drawing his knees in, his strong, summer-tanned arms hugging them to his chest, making the muscles in his arms work. "I know that now, but she'd been my Lupa for six years. I believed her. So I looked at Jean-Claude as just one more person who was trying to corrupt me. I

realize that he was just as trapped as I was, but I couldn't see that then."
His eyes looked haunted.

I sat up, still holding Asher's hand, and reached across him to touch
Richard's arm. That made him smile, but he turned those serious, haunted
eyes to Jean-Claude. "You were the only one left of the three of them.
Almost every time I looked at you I thought of them. Then I blamed you
for stealing Anita away from me. I know now that I drove her to you. I
made her watch me eat Marcus." He sat up a little straighter as if he'd realized he was hunching. He held my hand against his arm and looked at me.
"I did everything I could to make sure the first time you saw me shift to
animal form that it was frightening and terrible. I am sorry about that."

"You hate being a werewolf. You wanted me to hate it, too."

He nodded. "I did, I just didn't realize that's what I was doing at the
time."

"Your doctor must be very open-minded," Jean-Claude said.

Richard looked at him. "My therapist, yes, she is open-minded. We
didn't really make a lot of progress until Anita was able to take back her
anger this past summer."

One of the things about being a triumvirate of power is that you share
parts of yourself and not just power. I'd gotten the *ardeur* and a craving for
blood from Jean-Claude. From Richard I'd gotten his beast and a taste for
flesh. Jean-Claude had gotten a certain ruthlessness from me; I wasn't sure
what he'd gotten from Richard, or what Richard had gotten from him, but
what Richard got from me was my rage.

I'd gained the ability to feed on anger, the way Jean-Claude could feed
on lust. I could feed on sex, but found it harder to feed on the "emotion"
of lust. Anger, though, I understood that. That had been my emotion of
choice for years. Last summer I figured out how to call my rage back home
from Richard. It was the one thing we'd shared with each other that one of
us knew how to feed on. The other hungers were literally hungers for flesh,
blood, and sex. You can feed a hunger, but you can't feed *on* a hunger.

I took my hand back and Richard let me. I settled back on my side
of Asher. The vampire continued to hold my hand while we watched
Richard.

"I hadn't understood how much the rage kept me from forgiving anyone, or working my issues, until Anita fed off it and took it back. The anger
was almost like another beast inside me, but full moon didn't bring any
relief. It's a horrible way to live, Anita."

I shrugged. "You get used to it."

He shook his head, sending his hair sliding across his shoulders. "I didn't. It was killing me. I had my own problems with self-loathing, but the anger made it all worse."

"I'm sorry about that," I said. I almost didn't want to say anything else, but I knew now that every time we left things unsaid between us, it came back and bit us down the road. "The anger is gone, Richard, I get that," I said, "but the self-loathing was all you. You hated being a werewolf. You broke up with me because I was more at home with the monsters than you were."

"My turn to apologize again," Richard said. His arms loosened and he sat back against the pillows. "I can't stop being a werewolf. It's like trying to stop being human. It is what I am. I could give up being Ulfric, but I'd still have to belong to the pack, and being king is better than being a follower. I learned that the hard way. I am Jean-Claude's animal to call, and the third leg of the triumvirate of power that allows him to run the city and have enough power to keep everyone safe." He looked at Jean-Claude now. "You are a good Master of the City, Jean-Claude. I didn't realize that the Master of the City is like the boss of a business. If the boss is a crazy bitch, then she hires more crazy people, and she keeps everybody else crazy. Nikolaos was that kind of Master of the City. Anita killed her to save all of us, but it was you that took control of the city and made everything work better than it had ever worked. You had managed all the vampire businesses in town for years. You'd been the financial leader all along."

"Thank you, *mon ami*."

"No, all of the wereanimal leaders think things are a thousand times better with you in charge."

Jean-Claude bowed just from the neck. "I have done my best."

"You have, you really have, and so has Anita. The only one that hasn't helped secure our base of power is me. I've spent the last few years alternating tightening my grip on the wolves like a tyrant, and letting go of so much control I was practically forcing some of my dominant wolves to challenge me for leadership. I've apologized to Sylvie for that. She's my second-in-command, and she's earned it putting up with me."

I hadn't seen him in nearly four months, and now he was sitting there saying things I'd given up on hearing. It was all too good to be true. I must have tensed, because Asher began to stroke the back of my hand with his other hand as he held me.

"I have longed for you to understand some of this, Richard," Jean-Claude said, "but I admit I had given up."

"Some of the other wereanimal leaders had an intervention, I guess you could call it. They told me that I was endangering them all. That by crippling the best Master of the City they'd ever had, I was hurting everyone. I reminded Rafael that his biggest taboo for all his wererats had been that they didn't feed Nikolaos, so how could he let his rats be food for you."

Richard looked down, not meeting anyone's eyes. "Rafael said, 'Nikolaos demanded I give her my people. Jean-Claude never asked, I offered, because every animal group that gets close to Jean-Claude and Anita gains in power. They do not steal power away; they help everyone grow more powerful.' I thought about what he said, and it was true. You both help everyone around you be better. I tried to think if I'd helped anyone be better, or stronger, in the last few years, and you know what?"

He hesitated, so I said, "What?"

He gave me a quick smile. "I helped the kids I taught, but other than my job I hadn't helped anyone, not even me."

"This is wonderful, *mon ami*," Jean-Claude said, "but I have to ask. Why are you here tonight? Why have you come?"

"Rafael told me he'd offer up his own body and blood in my place if he could help make St. Louis a safer place for his people. I know that the swan king, Donovan Reece, is already feeding Anita on a regular basis, and his swans are now doing blood donations to the vampires. Micah and his leopards are with Anita, and through her, with you. Everyone is trying to build us into a unit with you as its head, except me."

"Grand talk, Ulfric," Asher said, "but talk is very cheap, so I've found."

Richard looked at the vampire. "I'm working my issues, Asher; you need to do the same."

"What does that mean?" he asked.

"It means you're pissed. You want Jean-Claude to love only you, and he doesn't. I wanted Anita to love only me and for us both to stop being part of the monsters. Neither of us is getting what we wanted. We need to make the best of what we have."

"*Mon Dieu*, you sound too good to be true, Ulfric, and too boring."

I drew my hand out of Asher's. He looked at me then. "You wanted Richard for you to touch, but it's like you're angry that you can't be here alone with Jean-Claude, or Jean-Claude and me. You're so angry and so conflicted that you're going to pick at us all until something breaks. You do that when you're angry; you always did."

He sat up. "So, because I have not spent the last four months in therapy I am to be cast out of the bed. Well, while you were doing therapy I was here doing my part as his *témoin*, his second-in-command."

"I know that, Asher, and I'm sorry that I wasn't here to help," Richard said.

Asher started to push himself out from between us and move for the side of the bed. Richard grabbed his arm. "Let go of me, wolf," Asher hissed.

"I thought you wanted me to touch you."

That stopped the vampire and made him turn to look at the other man. He made sure his hair hid the one side of his face as they looked at each other. "I do."

"Then where are you going?"

Asher looked at Richard's hand where it still held his arm. He relaxed slightly, but said, "Did your therapist put you on drugs? Is that why this new calm?"

Richard smiled. "No, nothing much works for werewolves. Our body processes them too fast."

"Then you cannot mean this, and if you run away from Anita, who you love, and Jean-Claude, who you feel truly drawn to, you will not be able to tolerate my touch."

"There are limits to what you can do to me, and with me, that's true, but I share some of Jean-Claude's emotions and memories. I remember loving you, Asher, and I still have a body that could do it."

I stared at Richard, and then at the look on Asher's face. I'd never seen the vampire so surprised. He laughed, a wild, abrupt sound. "Are you offering what Jean-Claude has denied me?"

Richard smiled. "I think that would be pushing my newfound resolutions, but I am offering to try. You are powerful enough to have your own territory now with Narcissus; by staying here you make Jean-Claude stronger, which makes us all safer."

"And what are you willing to do to make me stay, Richard?" There was derision in his voice again.

Richard pulled him backward with that one hand on his arm. Asher let himself be pulled. Richard settled back against the pillows and drew the other man's back in against his chest. He had his legs to one side so Asher was against only his chest, but it was more touch than I'd ever seen him do with any other man but Jean-Claude. Richard wrapped those strong arms around the vampire and held him. "I'm a shapeshifter; we like to sleep in big puppy piles."

Asher stroked his fingers down Richard's bare arms. Richard settled back deeper against the pillows, cuddling the other man closer to him. Asher bent his head and laid a kiss against that tanned, muscular arm.

"No biting, not yet, remember," Richard said, but he raised the arm that Asher wasn't kissing and stroked his hand through the other man's hair.

I looked at Jean-Claude and he looked at me. I held my arm out toward him. "Pinch me, because this has to be a dream."

Jean-Claude nodded. "You have read my mind, *ma petite*."

Asher rubbed his cheek against Richard's arm like a cat scent-marking. "Come into the pool, Jean-Claude, it is warm and smells so good."

"Don't just look at us—come cuddle," Richard said.

"Sorry, Richard, I just don't quite trust the change," I said.

"You mean you don't trust me," he said.

Asher was petting his arm with his hands and small kisses. "Don't the Americans have a saying, 'Do not look a gift horse in the mouth'?"

"Yeah," I said.

"Then what are you waiting for, Anita, unless you do not want either of us?" He looked at me over Richard's arm, giving me the weight of those beautiful eyes. Did I want both of them? Yes, yes I did.

I looked back at Jean-Claude, who was still standing beside the bed watching them. I held a hand out to Jean-Claude. "If you trust it, so will I."

"Trust," Jean-Claude whispered.

"When I realized how stupid I'd been toward both of you I thought about sending flowers, but didn't think there were enough roses in the world to make up for what I'd almost done to all of us." He rose up, and Asher made a small protesting noise as he took his arm back. Richard took hold of his T-shirt and pulled it over his head in one smooth movement. "I thought you'd like this better than flowers."

Asher hesitated, looking back at him. Richard drew him in against his chest, as he had before. Asher turned and laid a tentative hand on his bare side. Richard held his hands out, one to me and one toward Jean-Claude.

"I can always call a florist if you'd prefer that." His words were joking, but his face was so serious. "But I was hoping that this would say, *I screwed up and I'm sorry* better than anything else."

Jean-Claude said, "If you mean this, then it will."

"If you don't mean it," I said, "and you bail again on us, then that's it, Richard. I can't let you keep cutting us up like this."

Asher laid his head on the other man's bare stomach, his arm hugging all that bare flesh. "Oh, for the love of God, stop talking and join us. He won't get out of his pants for just me."

I laughed, I couldn't help it. Richard didn't laugh. He ran his hand through the other man's hair and grabbed a handful of it, jerking his head back. I had a moment to see Asher's face. I knew that look, the wide, almost unfocused eyes, the slightly parted lips. I'd seen it on Nathaniel's face often enough, and caught it on mine in the mirror a time or two. That look said that Asher had gone from dominant to submissive, switched over by the pain, the suddenness, and the strength in Richard's hand.

Richard used Asher's hair as a handle to move the other man so they looked at each other. I saw the muscles in his forearm tighten. Asher made a small sound, and though pain caused it, it wasn't a pain sound. It was a good sound. One I'd heard Jean-Claude drive from Asher more than once, one that Nathaniel and I had gotten from him when we worked as a unit.

"I'm a dominant; I don't bottom to anyone, so if anyone is losing their pants it's not me." Richard dragged the man a little upward using that painful, pleasurable grip on his hair. Richard lowered his own face a little toward the vampire and said, "I am not food. I am not prey. I am the Ulfric of the Thronnos Rokke Clan, and the next time you forget that, I will hurt you." He whispered the last almost into the other man's lips, close enough to kiss. I watched him use all that beauty on Asher as he had, in different ways, with me over the years. Beauty can be a weapon as devastating as any gun.

Richard sat back up and let go of Asher so abruptly he fell into the other man's lap. Asher lay there passive, his face to one side lost in the tangle of his own golden hair. Richard looked at Jean-Claude and me. "I haven't just been running from being a werewolf or Jean-Claude's animal to call. If pain and pleasure didn't move me, Raina could never have seduced me. I blamed her for me being a pervert, but she didn't invent this part of me, she just unleashed it." He laid his big hand on Asher's head and stroked his hair. The other man shivered under that small touch. "I don't want to have sex with Asher, but causing him pain appeals to me. Making him want me, and denying him what he wants, that appeals to me, too." He laid his head back against the back of the bed and closed his eyes; when he opened them they had gone to a dark amber. "It appeals to me a lot."

Just the look in his eyes made me shiver. Jean-Claude touched my arm and I jumped. "*Ma petite*, shall we join them?"

I just nodded, because saying *Wow* out loud just didn't sound cool enough for what was lying in the bed looking at us with wolf amber eyes.

8

ASHER LOST HIS pants and everything else, though there was a moment when he hesitated on his shirt, because the most severe scars were on his chest and stomach on the one side, and his hair wasn't long enough to be used as a shield as he did for his face. Jean-Claude and I had done our reassuring months ago. It was Richard with his perfect upper body that made Asher embarrassed, shy, some word that I never thought to use for him in any circumstance.

Jean-Claude and I looked at each other, and we were both wondering how to get the two men to work the issue, when Richard said, "Jean-Claude told you to strip; do it."

Asher scowled at him, holding his unbuttoned shirt closed. "He told me to undress, actually."

Richard opened his mouth to say something harsh, I think, but something made him look at Jean-Claude. More than a look passed between them. I think Jean-Claude whispered in his head as he could mine. Whatever was said softened Richard's face. He turned to Asher. "You didn't get to see the scars from the silver bullets that nearly killed me last summer." He traced that broad, untouched spill of muscle. "This half was a mass of scars. I thought it was permanent. It usually is if it scars at all. I didn't think of myself as vain, but I didn't like the scars. I didn't like being less than perfect. When Jean-Claude started using energy to heal his own wounds, I learned how to heal mine. He let me take enough energy from the triumvirate to put me back to this." He spread his hands, framing all that nice smooth skin.

I'd known they used energy from our power as a unit to heal themselves—it was one of the serious perks to having the vampire marks—but I hadn't realized that if we hadn't had enough power, there would be three men in the room with serious scars on all that creamy and tanned goodness, respectively.

"I had no triumvirate to turn to," Asher said, holding his shirt tight, voice sullen.

Richard went to him. "I've tried nice, but sympathy just makes you angry. I understand that, so let me try something else." He moved in a blur, his hand grabbing a handful of Asher's hair, the other hand going around the man's waist, jerking him against Richard. It was sudden, violent, but with that edge of kissing closeness again. Asher's anger seemed to float away on the strength of Richard's hands.

Richard stared into those pale blue eyes from inches away and snarled, "I want you naked. I want to see it all. I want you tied up and naked, and if you make me tell you to strip again I'll rip your clothes off your back." He almost threw Asher away from him and walked away.

Asher staggered, caught the bed to steady himself. When he could stand steady, his shirt went on the floor and the rest of his clothes followed. There was something about Richard wanting to see him nude and tied up that reassured him, made him feel desired. There was no more hesitating.

We tied Asher on his knees to one side of the bed, centered between the bedposts. He was near enough to the edge of the bed that if we wanted to we could have his legs off the side, but we started with him comfortable, kneeling. The bed was the same bed, but the frame had been changed since last we had Richard with us. The frame was metal and custom built so that there were distinct places for attaching things all over the frame. It had originally been done so that Asher could teach me to top Nathaniel, but that meant that all of us had experienced the bed on both sides. The rule was you never try something on your submissive that you hadn't tried on your own body first. There had been a few things that Nathaniel wanted that I couldn't, or wouldn't, try on myself because the pain level was too high and I didn't heal like he did, but Asher had taken more than one for the team in that area, until even he had called *no mas*, and Nathaniel had still not gone to his limit on pain with us. Frankly, Nathaniel's limits in this area still scared me, even as they intrigued me.

Jean-Claude had gotten out the toy trunk—not toy box, *trunk*. It was one of those huge old-fashioned steamer trunks big enough to hide a body in. We'd moved it permanently into the bedroom about a month ago rather than having to get a few toys and carry them in; it had been a tacit acknowledgment of what we were doing in the bed and with each other. I had never dreamed that Richard would be on his knees digging around in the toys. I'd known he liked this kind of sex; he was right: Raina hadn't created the need, she'd just let it out of its box. That he'd gotten comfortable enough with himself to admit it out loud to us was nothing short of miraculous. If miracles were things you thought you'd never see, like the St. Louis Rams winning the Super Bowl, or ice skating in hell.

Jean-Claude had simply taken off his shirt, and he was in leather pants and boots, very BDSM. With Asher tied up nude, my little businessy skirt outfit looked so out of place, but Jean-Claude had a fix for that. It was a leather dress, short but with a full skirt, and it belted at the waist; it looked like June Cleaver does bondage. I went into the bathroom to change with a pair of stiletto heels in hand. The shoes I'd worn before, but the dress was new. But the true beauty of the dress didn't hit me until I put it on and started playing with the heavy zipper that went all the way down the front of it. The upper part of the dress was tight enough through the chest that it held me in place without a bra even when the zipper was nearly halfway down. My breasts stayed mounded, and no matter how I moved they weren't going to fall out by accident. No, I'd have to lower the zipper and let them out. Or I could zip the dress all the way up and show no cleavage at all. It was a nice dress. I played with the zipper until my breasts looked like they were spilling out, or would at any moment, but I knew they were solid in place—well, as solid as real breasts get. I caught a glimpse of myself in the bathroom mirror as I moved for the door, and it stopped me. I wasn't into breasts, but the sight of my own chest in that dress with the wide leather belt making my waist look even tinier in all that leather with the full skirt was eye-catching. Okay, it made even me think, *Wow, look at all that creamy goodness*. It wasn't something I was used to thinking about my own breasts.

When I stepped out in the dress, Jean-Claude let me see on his face exactly how much he liked the view. "*Mon Dieu, ma petite.*" He grabbed Asher's hair and turned him so he could see me. The angle was painful, but as he had with Richard, Asher didn't respond like it hurt. Jean-Claude put their faces together and said, "Look at her, Asher. Look at her and know that you don't get to touch her tonight." He let go of that golden hair and walked toward me, leaving Asher hanging there as if he didn't matter. I knew it was part of the game, and I trusted Jean-Claude to know what kind of submissive Asher was, but if I was the one tied up, humiliation or taunt-ing would throw me out of bottom and right back in my fuck-you-and-you-don't-get-to-fuck-me attitude.

Jean-Claude came to me and offered his hand. The stilettos were four inches. I looked fabulous in them, but as my sexy meter went up, my graceful meter went down, or that's how it felt. He'd assured me if I'd only wear them enough to practice, I'd get better at it. Sure.

With his hand to steady me I felt pretty secure in them. The floggers and some whips were laid out by the bed in neat rows. I caught a glimpse of Richard at the end of the bed, hidden by the belted bed curtains.

"They aren't going to fit," Richard said.

Jean-Claude had fetched a pair of leather pants that had fit Richard. I realized that they must have been the same ones I'd seen him wear more than once. But that had been over a year ago, and apparently it wasn't just his arms that had gotten bigger from the weight lifting.

Jean-Claude led me around the foot of the bed. Richard was leaning against it, his body bent almost double as he pulled the last of the leather over his ankle and foot. He'd tied his hair back in a ponytail so he was one long curve of smooth, summer-tanned skin from his neck to midthigh.

He shook his head and said, "There's no way. I've put on too much muscle." Then he looked up and saw me in the dress, and if Jean-Claude's face had been everything I wanted to see, Richard's was both better and worse. He slid off the bed to land heavily on the floor. He sat there with the leather pants in his lap and stared at me as if I'd hit him between the eyes with a hammer. *Gob-smacked*, Byron, one of our newer British vamps, would have called it. If I'd had any doubts about the outfit, Richard took care of them.

Then Richard rallied and grabbed on to the bed to stand. He was still holding the pants in one hand in front of his body, but he stood every inch of that six foot one inch, shoulders back, face set in that arrogant model look. Most of the time I wasn't sure he knew just how handsome he was, but then he'd get that look on his face, and I knew he understood exactly how amazing he looked. With most of his legs showing I could see the extra muscle that had kept him out of the pants. Then he dropped the pants and let me see all of him. He let me see that it wasn't just his face that had reacted to the sight of me in the dress.

My hand tightened on Jean-Claude's, because I was suddenly not steady enough in the stiletto heels. I couldn't see my face, but I suspected that it was my turn to look like the handsome hammer had got me between the eyes, my turn to be gob-smacked. He'd had that effect on me almost from the first moment I saw him, which had been nude in a bed, come to think of it. I had never asked what he had been doing in that bed with a female shapeshifter. I'd always assumed they'd just passed out changing from animal to human form—most shifters were nearly comatose for hours after shifting back—and someone had put them between the sheets to sleep it off. Staring at him standing there, I realized that assumption had probably been naïve.

"Your face," Richard said, "for a moment it was exactly what I wanted to see, and then you started thinking about something else. You didn't see me anymore. What . . . who were you thinking about while you looked at me?" His face was still almost impossibly handsome; without the hair, the cheekbones that had helped give him the darker skin tone sculpted his face to painful perfection, but the anger was there too now, and that wasn't attractive. Of all the men in my life, only he'd ever used his rage against me.

"*Ma petite*," Jean-Claude said, and his nickname for me was enough. He meant for me to try to fix this. I understood. This was the closest we'd ever gotten with our Richard to something workable. The moment I thought *our Richard*, I knew it wasn't my thought. I'd ceased to think of him as mine, but that was okay; we needed this to work the way kids need their fighting parents to make up before the divorce splits the family and the possessions. The problem with the three of us was that the "possessions" included people. More than any child, the vampires and werewolves and other shapeshifters in this city were possessions. We needed to grow up and fix this.

"You, Richard. I was thinking about the first time I saw you. You were in Jean-Claude's bed in the offices at the Circus of the Damned with the woman shapeshifter beside the bed. You were both nude, and I never asked what you were doing in the bed with a naked woman in the room. I never asked how you ended up there like that."

The anger began to seep away, leaving his face confused, more real somehow. "What do you want me to say about it?"

"I don't know. I was just thinking that I never questioned it. I never asked if you and Rashada were lovers. You asked me out the same night, so I assumed you weren't dating anyone else. Was I naïve, Richard? Was I just that naïve then?"

His face softened, and he smiled. He came to us then, not angry, or arrogant, but gently. I was able to watch his face as he moved instead of staring lower. Point for me, but honestly the look on his face in that moment meant more to me than seeing him nude.

He touched my face, and his skin was warmer than it should have been. A warmth to cuddle against on a cold night, and I moved my face against that touch, and he turned his hand so that I could lay the side of my face in the warm cup of it.

"We both were," he said softly, and I realized his other hand had reached past me. I turned my head, and his hand was big enough that my face still rested against it when I could see that he was touching Jean-Claude's hair.

Richard drew us in toward him until our faces were close together. They had to bend down to touch their faces to mine. Jean-Claude's and my hair mingled, all black curls, so that it was hard to tell whose hair was whose. Richard's hands were on the back of our heads, fingers worked through the curls so I could feel them on the back of my skull. His fingers moved against my skin as if he were massaging. I knew he was doing the same to Jean-Claude. I could have had the tactile memory to go with it, truly felt what Jean-Claude was feeling, but he knew that freaked me out, so we'd been working on me simply knowing without the whole show. I just knew what Richard was doing.

He pressed our faces together and whispered, "If we'd known what would happen, would we have run from each other?"

I didn't know what to say to that, but Jean-Claude did. "Ask, rather, *mon ami*, if we would all be alive now, if we had not had each other to turn to in times of trouble? Ask how many of our vampires and wolves would be dead, or trapped by sadistic masters?"

"Not just my wolves," Richard said. "Anita and Micah have helped a lot of the shapeshifters in town." I heard his breath go out in a long sigh. He moved his head enough to lay his lips on my forehead. It was almost too soft to be called a kiss. "If you want to keep Asher as your second, your *témoin*, and keep the werehyenas in town, we have to tame him."

"*Oui*," Jean-Claude said.

"Define *tame*," I said.

Richard laughed, pulling back enough to look at both of us, but longer at me. "That suspicious tone in your voice, it's so you, Anita, so very you."

I frowned at him, one hand on my hip, the other still on Jean-Claude's hand. "I'm still me, Richard. How else would I sound?"

"How can I love you and still want to do such terrible things to you and with you? How can it be okay with you that I like what I like?"

Jean-Claude went very still beside me. "I don't want to have this talk again, Richard," I said.

"Me, either," he said. He looked at Jean-Claude. "I want to have sex with Anita. I'm willing to touch you and be touched. I want to torment Asher with the fact that he can't have me." A look went through those chocolate-brown eyes and they suddenly looked darker. "I want to watch his face while Anita goes down on me, and I go down on Anita. I want him to watch you fuck Anita, and think he's not getting you. I want to cause him pain while you do it, and know that he'll enjoy the pain, too." That dark look in his eyes became fierce, not anger, but fierceness. "The thought excites me."

His words made me glance down, and his body was responding to the thought. I flicked my eyes back up to his face and found him looking at me. He'd noticed what I'd done, or maybe he'd sensed it the way I'd sensed when he'd petted Jean-Claude's hair.

"Do you want me?"

"What?" I asked.

"Do you want me, Anita?"

I didn't know what to say to that, either. I opened my mouth, closed it. Jean-Claude said, "Truth, *ma petite*, the truth."

I said the only truth I'd had since almost the first time I saw Richard. "Yes."

He smiled, but it held that fierceness that I wasn't sure I understood. "Good," he said, "because I've missed you." He moved so fast, I made that girl-scream squeal. He was just suddenly holding me around the waist. My pulse was in my throat, thudding against my skin. My feet were dangling above the ground and I was looking into his eyes from inches away. My hands were on his arms, but not in a useful way.

"That scared you." He leaned his face in against mine, not quite touching, and sniffed the air above my skin. The gesture made the hair on the back of my neck stand up. "Your skin smells so good because you're afraid of me, Anita. I like it, do you understand that?"

I had to swallow to whisper, "Yes."

"I want you afraid; do you understand that?"

"It's that chase-the-prey thing, I get it," and again my voice was a whisper.

A low growl trickled out from between those soft, human lips. My pulse sped up again, as if I'd choke on it. "Do you trust me?" he whispered, but his voice held that same edge of growl, as if his voice were deepening.

I swallowed twice. I didn't trust my voice, and knew that the real answer was maybe, but Jean-Claude was there and I trusted him to see that things didn't get out of control. So I nodded yes.

"Good," he said again. I felt his muscles tense, and then I was airborne and falling toward the bed.

9

I HIT THE bed, hands slapping against it to take the impact, but the bed was soft enough that it wasn't an impact; it was just startling as hell. If it had been a real emergency I'd have had time to sit up, to scramble for something, but it wasn't that kind of emergency, so I lay there on the bed trying to breathe past the nearly painful beat of my pulse in my throat. I was staring up at Asher's body. There wasn't time to admire the view as he looked down at me, because the bed moved and I started to sit up, and Richard was there.

He dropped the full weight of his body on me and kissed me at the same time. I was suddenly trapped underneath him, and almost choking on his kiss. It was too fierce, too much, and I wasn't there yet. I pushed at him, fought against the kiss, finally grabbed his ponytail and was able to use it to lever him away from my mouth. My teeth were gritted as I said, "You haven't done enough for me yet, Richard."

He stared down at me, and I saw the thought go through his eyes that he was probably big enough to force me. He was bigger than I was, and I was unarmed; only trust had let him get to this point with me. Trust in him and trust in Jean-Claude. The fact that I felt that thought cross all the way through him gave me a glimpse into some of the demons he'd been fighting. It wasn't just being a werewolf, or being Jean-Claude's wolf to call, that haunted Richard. There were parts of him that would have been there even if he'd been as human as he wanted to be. I watched that part slide through his true-brown eyes and felt that shiver of fear trail over my skin again.

He moved down and though the hold on his ponytail had kept him from my face, it didn't stop him from sliding down. When he had enough slack he kissed my upper chest, gently, very gently. He kissed his way down the exposed line of my breasts with the zipper and the leather framing them, but each kiss was ever so gentle. I let his hair slip through my fingers as he kissed his way down my body through the leather. He laid his head on my lap through the soft leather of the dress, and just the weight of him there made me close my eyes and shudder. When I opened them my head must have gone back because I was staring up the line of Asher's body. He met my gaze, and there was in his eyes something so not submissive, or even bottom. The look he gave was most definitely dominant. Asher was a bottom and he was a better submissive than I would ever be, because he was the one who explained to me that I was never a submissive. I was a dominant who sometimes bottomed, but it's not the same thing as a true switch to submissive. Asher could be submissive and things that just pissed me off excited him, but it was a thin line for him. He could switch in the middle of a scene faster than anyone else I'd ever seen. One minute the lamb and the next the lion. I was looking at the lion now. His gaze went down the line of my body to Richard, and I was almost certain that it wasn't me that had switched him to predator. It was the sight of Richard's nude body lying there so close, but still so far away.

I felt Richard raise his head. The movement made me turn to him. He was on his elbows with the hem of the dress in his hands. He was smiling at me, but it was the kind of smile that a man gives you when he is certain of you, certain that there will be only yes, and not no. It had been months since I'd seen him, and that part of me that was always poking at things, demanding, complaining, thought, *He hasn't earned that look.*

Jean-Claude was suddenly there, leaning around Asher's legs, touching my hair, my face, so that I looked up at him. I gazed up into those midnight-blue eyes so dark that a few shades darker and the blue would have been lost to a black, but they were forever the blue of the sky just as the light begins to leave, but darkness is still a few breaths away. I stared up into those eyes and felt him whisper through my mind, as his hands cradled my face. "You can be right, or you can be happy. Look into my face and tell me you do not want him and I will stop this. We will find some other way to seal our triumvirate. But say you do not want him and it ends."

He slid onto the bed, and my head was propped on the leather of his thigh as his other hand moved down my bare arm. He turned me so I could gaze down my body at Richard. He was still propped on his arms, the hem of my dress in his hands. He was watching me, and though his face was still eager, there was wariness around those true-brown eyes. We had taught each other caution of each other.

Richard began, very slowly, to unzip the double zipper at the bottom of the dress. He watched my face as he did it, as if waiting for me to protest. I thought about it, I really did. I wasn't sure I wanted to rake this mess up again. My life worked without him in it.

Jean-Claude breathed through me again. "Do you want him to stop?"

The answer was yes, and no, and that had been Richard and me from the beginning almost. Yes, and no; no and yes, until we both almost went mad with it. Yes and no.

Richard spread the unzipped dress open and lowered his face toward me, his eyes still on my face, still waiting for me to say something. Jean-Claude's hands continued to soothe down my bare arms. I realized they were both treating me as the one most likely to blow this. It was almost as if they'd discussed it, but Jean-Claude had been surprised tonight, too, hadn't he? The moment I thought that, I tensed.

Richard kissed the edge of my thigh, still watching my face. Jean-Claude leaned over me and whispered, "I swear to you that I did not know he would come tonight, but I do want this, *ma petite*, I do want this more cooperative Richard. It is sex tonight, not a change in our living arrangements. It is sex and magic, nothing more."

There was a time when that would have pissed me off, but that was before Micah and Nathaniel. Before we'd made some peace with Jean-Claude, before so much, and now his words made me relax a little.

Richard kissed up the inside of my thigh, still gazing at my face, still being cautious. I let out a breath I hadn't known I was holding, some tension went away, and when I relaxed so did he. He smiled at me, his hands sliding along my legs, so he could put his hands on the outside of them, his arms underneath my legs. He lowered his eyes as he kissed my thigh. He startled, his fingers digging in just a little, but not like he did it on purpose.

He looked up the line of my body at me. "You're not wearing anything under the dress," he said, voice a little strained.

The look on his face made me smile. I couldn't help it. He looked so startled. I said, "No, I'm not."

He finally smiled back at me and lowered his face, and he wasn't trying to look at my eyes anymore. Jean-Claude relaxed against me, as if even he had been holding the breath that he didn't always need to take.

"Were you really afraid I'd fuck this up?" I asked, sliding my head against his thigh so I could see his face. His face was unreadable and pleasant, but he said, "Yes."

Richard licked the hollow of my thigh and didn't stop until he licked between my legs. The sensation of it closed my eyes, caught my breath in my throat. He licked in long, slow strokes around the edges of me, coming over that one small spot at the end of every stroke. He made his strokes smaller, more circular, and my breathing changed, speeding up with my heartbeat.

Jean-Claude moved underneath my head. It made me open my eyes and look at him. He was smiling at me as he slid pillows underneath my head. "I cannot leave our Asher neglected." He bent and kissed me as he slid off the bed. The movement pulled my gaze to the man bound to the side of the bed so close to us, but almost forgotten. I caught Asher's look, and it was still that predatory look, but with more anger to it. I had forgotten him, and that was probably truer than was pretty to think of between us all.

Richard put his mouth around me and began to suck, and suddenly all my attention was staring down my body at the man between my legs. His brown eyes were turned up so that he was staring at my face as he sucked me. There was a darkness, a fierceness, a possessiveness in that look. It wasn't possession of me by Richard, it was a man's pleasure in *I'm making her do that. I'm bringing her pleasure. She's making those sounds because of me.* It was all there in his eyes, as he licked and sucked me over that edge of pleasure that bowed my spine, threw my head backward into the pillows, my hands scrambling for something to hold on to, as the feel of his mouth brought me in wordless, ragged screams.

He sucked me until I lay limp against the bed, boneless with the pleasure of it. He licked one more time, and it made me cry out.

"I love that," he said, voice deeper.

I forced myself to focus on his face, but the world was soft and edged with afterglow. I heard the soft slap of a flogger and knew that it had to be Jean-Claude working with Asher, but it was beyond me to turn my head enough to see. All my scrambling in the pillows during the orgasm had spilled me to one side of the mounded pillows so that they hid the other two men. I managed to say, "What?" My voice sounded thick.

"You just enjoy sex so much once you let yourself go. I love watching you." His face glistened in the lights. His finger pressed into my thighs, and it was too much so soon; it threw me back against the pillows in a small aftershock. He laughed that dark, deep-edged laugh that men only have in those moments. It's a good sound.

He dug his fingers in harder, spreading my legs a little wider. It made me cry out, and he gave that dark chuckle again. The sound of the flogger was harder, meatier, and there were small protesting sounds, and it wasn't me.

Richard let go of my legs, his arms sliding out from under me. I felt the bed move and waited for him to move closer to me, but heard him say, "Jean-Claude, trade me."

That made me open my eyes and look at him. He was kneeling between my legs, and the front of his body was long, thick, and more than ready. I reached a hand out, rising up off the bed, but he moved back out of reach, laughing. "You do that and I won't do anything but you."

"Do me," I said voice languorous with afterglow.

He shook his head.

"Trade me in what manner, Richard?" Jean-Claude asked.

"I know how to use a flogger."

"I have him in the headspace we need, *mon ami*. I would not lose ground, not even for so sweet an offer."

That made me crawl out from between the pillows so I could see what was going on. Asher was still tied up, but his face was slack, lips half-parted, eyes unfocused. It was close to the look I was fighting off my own face. But his wasn't orgasm because he was smooth, and erect, and as perfect as the rest of him. He would have argued that because one line of scar traced the edge of his testicles, but it was just something extra to run my tongue over, an added texture, not a blemish.

Jean-Claude wrapped his arm around him from the back. He was still in the leather pants, but just being held close to him made Asher's eyes roll back into his head. He had waited a long time for Jean-Claude to touch him. It was ironic that Asher's power made those nearest and dearest to him afraid to be alone with him physically, but he'd almost killed me, and he'd nearly possessed Jean-Claude in that demonic way. We had a right to be cautious of him, but seeing him there with such reaction to such an innocent touch from Jean-Claude made me realize just how much he needed and wasn't getting.

"It's not just about the pain, Richard," Jean-Claude said.

"I know that," Richard said, and he moved across the bed on his knees, still perfectly nude, though his body was less erect, but even less erect he was still very male as he moved toward the other men. He got close enough to grab Asher's chin, making him look into his eyes. "You enjoyed watching me go down on her, didn't you?"

Asher spoke just above a whisper, "Yes."

"I have some of Jean-Claude's memories. I know that you enjoyed watching other men have sex with your women." Then, still holding Asher's chin in his hand, he leaned in and kissed him. It was a soft kiss, almost innocent, and he kept a lot of distance between their bodies, but the look on Asher's face when Richard drew back from it wasn't innocent. It was expectant, surprised, happy, and then wary.

"Can you taste her on my mouth?" Richard asked.

"Yes," Asher said, and his voice was that same breathy whisper.

Richard slid off the bed, and Jean-Claude moved back for him to move behind Asher. I lay on the bed watching the show, because that's what it was. Richard did understand BDSM; at its best it's a performance, showmanship counts. Richard moved in behind Asher. He ran his hands down the man's back. "Nice pattern."

"Thank you," Jean-Claude said. He moved in closer to the two men, and I got to see the three of them standing there, two of them nude, Jean-Claude just in the leather pants and boots, and for a minute I didn't care about love, or how much my life worked or didn't; all I could think of was that they were all so beautiful.

Richard ran his hands over the marks on Asher's back again, and it was probably just as well that Richard couldn't see the look on Asher's face, because just that small touch made him close his eyes and fight not to overreact to the touch, but I knew when someone was trying to be still under someone's touch.

Apparently I wasn't the only one, because Richard leaned his face next to Asher's and said, "You liked me touching you, didn't you?"

Asher didn't answer. I think he was afraid of what the other man would hear in his voice. He was having enough trouble controlling his face and body. Vampires over two hundred can control everything. The fact that Asher was fighting so hard to stay in some control said just how much the attention from Jean-Claude and now Richard meant to him.

Richard's arm slid around Asher's waist, as he slid his other arm around his shoulder. I sat up, because if Richard was as close to Asher as I thought,

I wanted to see it. I wanted to see the lines of their bodies pressed against each other. I crawled over the bed, and didn't care if it was ungraceful.

I half-stepped and half-fell off the bed, and Richard's tanned, muscled body was pressed against the back of Asher's pale one so that there was nothing but the line of their bodies like two perfect pieces of some light and dark puzzle.

Jean-Claude was watching them, too, and his face was stricken, that was the only word for it. It was a look made up of want, and surprise, and the same thing I'd felt just a moment before, that they were simply beautiful.

Richard's voice fell into that moment. "Tell me you like me pressed up against you, Asher?"

Asher's breath came out in a shaking sound, not word, or breath, or scream, but it seemed to hold all the longing you would ever want to hear in a lover's voice.

"Good," Richard said, and he stepped back from the other man. "Now I'm going to beat you while Jean-Claude fucks Anita and you get to watch, and then I'm going to fuck her while Jean-Claude fucks you."

I would have protested, or complained, but honestly, it worked for me.

10

JEAN-CLAUDE ROSE ABOVE me, nude and perfect, his body moving in and out of me as he held himself above me on his arms. One, he knew I loved watching him go in and out of my body. Two, he was too tall for traditional missionary, or I was too short. His hair spilled over one shoulder in a mass of thick, black curls. I stared down the line of our bodies watching all that pale perfection work in and out of my body. Just the sight of it made me cry out, like a preview of the orgasm to come. A cry from the side of the bed echoed mine and made me turn my head to see Asher, his head thrown back, body spasming in the chains. His body jerked with each heavy blow of the flogger, and then the sound of the flogger sped up until it was one continuous sound and Asher couldn't react to each individual blow, his body shivering under it all, his eyes fluttering back.

Jean-Claude shoved himself hard and complete inside me, making me cry out and turn back to him, eyes wide. He held my gaze and began to work faster, deeper, lifting with his hips at the top of each stroke so he was touching everything that made me orgasm from intercourse. The men in my bed were all good, but Jean-Claude could hit not just one spot, but all of them. I felt that wonderful heaviness begin between my legs and knew I was close. The flogging stopped and it made me turn to see, even as Jean-Claude brought me closer to that edge of pleasure. Richard had wrapped himself against Asher's back again. His tan looked so dark against the paleness of Asher's body.

I felt Jean-Claude's body lose some of that smooth rhythm. It made me look up at him but he was looking at the other men, and the sight of them had made him miss a step. Then he was looking down at me again, and one moment we were gazing into each other's faces and the next the orgasm took me. It rolled over me, through me, in a wave of warmth and pleasure that made me grab Jean-Claude's arms, holding on as the sensation of it tore screams from my throat, clawed my nails down his arms, as if I were trying to anchor myself to something solid while the world exploded in white-edged pleasure and my body tried to become the fierce joy of it all. I didn't exactly pass out, but I wasn't aware of everything either, and when I could see again, be aware of all of me again, Jean-Claude was smiling down at me.

I smiled back and took my nails out of his arms. I'd left red lines, some with blood in them, from about his mid-upper arm to almost his wrists. Once I would have apologized for it, but I knew he enjoyed the marks, both the pain/pleasure of it and that he could drive me to pleasure deep enough to bleed him. Most of the men in my life took it as high praise.

He drew himself out of me and that made me writhe under him, another smaller orgasm just from that alone. When I could make my eyes focus again he was gone and Richard was above me on all fours, not touching me yet, but looking down at me. His hair was still back in its tight ponytail, leaving his face clean and almost heartrendingly handsome. I looked down the line of his body, but didn't get as far as normal, because his chest and stomach were striped with blood. For a moment I thought it was his blood then realized it had to be Asher's. It takes a lot of force to draw blood with a flogger, or one that was corded, or had metal bits. I knew we had both in the toy chest, but hadn't realized Richard had brought it out to play.

He leaned just his face down to mine, keeping his body off mine. He kissed me and I could still taste the edge of my own body on his mouth, but there was also a taste of other lips, and I knew that I'd missed at least another kiss or two between him and Asher. I felt a little regret at that and hoped I'd get a chance to see it again. Nothing was ever certain with Richard, so I kissed him with tongue, and lips and teeth, and he responded in kind, collapsing on top of me, our mouths locked and eager around each other. The sensation of his body on top of mine made me cry out and writhe underneath him, but the height difference was too great for the angle that we were kissing, and the best I could grind against was higher up his body than what I wanted to touch. He pulled away from the kiss with my lower lip between his teeth. It made me cry out half in protest and half in pleasure, that edge of good and bad so intermingled that I couldn't have told you which side the kiss had ended on. Then I felt that warm roll of power and it caressed things deeper in my body than bone and muscle. It caressed along that part of me that was wolf, and I felt/saw the wolf that was that part of my beast open her eyes. She was mostly cream with black markings around her face and ruff so that she looked at a glance like a big husky dog, but once you saw her eyes like amber glass you knew it wasn't a dog.

"Richard," I said, but when I saw his eyes they were wolf amber. His wolf's eyes were staring at me from that handsome, human face. Maybe I'd spent too much time staring into Micah's leopard eyes in his own human face, but the wolf eyes didn't frighten me the way they had the last time he'd been above me like that.

My wolf started trotting up that long metaphysical pathway that seemed to be inside me, but I knew it was just the way my human mind coped with the beast. I knew in reason that it wasn't a real path, or real trees that rose above the wolf, but it was what my mind had made to help us all stay sane.

"You'll bring my wolf, Richard."

"No," he said, "I won't, I promise, but I want you to bring mine."

I blinked up at him. "What?"

A sound made us both turn and look at the side of the bed. Jean-Claude was standing behind Asher, and I knew he wasn't having sex with him, the angle wasn't right, but I couldn't see what he was doing to make Asher close his eyes, face nearly slack with pleasure.

My wolf started to trot, that ground-eating movement that wolves can keep up for miles. Wolves, like early humans, will just walk prey into the ground until they're exhausted and ripe for the kill. The trouble was that it was my body that the she-wolf would try to eat her way out of; I couldn't shapeshift, and when one of the beasts wanted out they treated my body like a trap that they needed to dig their way out of.

"Richard, you're bringing my wolf."

He stared down at me with those amber eyes and I felt his power again, but it was different than I remembered it. His power could sting, or prickle like electricity, but this was just a warm wash of power, gentle but powerful like a curl of warm ocean water rolling through me. His power touched the wolf in me, and she slowed. The only image my mind could form was the wolf being petted, soothed. She lay down beside the path in among the tall, unreal trees, content with the roll of his energy over her.

"I've been practicing helping Gina's beast not to rise so she can keep the baby. Your weretigers tell me I'm a natural at it."

"I didn't know you were helping."

"If our women could have children, that would be a wonderful thing. How could I not help?"

I thought of a lot of things to say, the mildest of which was that something being a good thing hadn't been enough if it meant he had to use his beast to do it, but out loud I said, "Yes, it would be."

Asher cried out, and we both turned again. Jean-Claude had given the chains more slack and was up behind him on the bed, with both of them on their knees. Jean-Claude's legs and hips were moving, and I knew that he was finally doing what Asher had wanted for so long.

"Jean-Claude's ahead of us. I want to catch up."

"Are you asking if I'm okay with it?"

"Yes."

I thought about it, but with the weight of him pinning me to the bed, and my hands tracing the smooth skin and muscle of his back, all I could say was, "We need a condom."

He smiled, and it was a version of the smile that had once melted me into my socks, and out of them. "Are they still in the same place?"

I nodded. "Yes."

He raised enough of him that I could see his body was hard and eager against the front of him. "Wait right there," he said.

I waited right there.

11

RICHARD WAS ABOVE me, holding himself on his arms, his lower body pushing in and out of me. I realized it was the same position that Jean-Claude had used, but then they were both too tall for straight missionary, or I was too short.

I watched his body work in and out of mine. He was wide, and straight, and long, and beautiful, and the feel of him between my legs was amazing. I turned my head to the side to scream my pleasure, and I was suddenly looking at the other men.

The chains were looser now, letting Asher's body drape forward so that I had both of their bodies in profile, all pale muscled grace. Jean-Claude's body was pushing its way into Asher while the other man jerked at the chains, his body reacting to the thick, muscled push of Jean-Claude's. His hair had fallen over his face, so that both of their faces were hidden by the fall of their own hair, one black, and the other gold.

Richard shoved himself into me in one deep thrust that made me cry out and look up at him. I had a moment to see my face looking up at his, as if I were using his eyes. My eyes were wide, mouth open in a little *O* of surprise, and I watched pain and pleasure fight across my face. The moment passed and I was staring up into his face again. He looked pleased, eager, with an edge of concern in eyes that had gone back to human brown.

My voice came out breathless. "Without the *ardeur*, that may hurt eventually."

"Every other woman I've been with except one would say it hurts the first time."

"With the right prep it's okay to be that deep," I said.

"You orgasm from it," he said, and began to work his way in and out of me again, faster than he had been before, but not as deep as he could be, at first.

"With the right prep," I said.

He used more hip action, lifting his body up more so that I could see just the line of him in and out of me, moving faster, getting a little deeper with each thrust, until he came to the end of me again, but gentler, so that it was more a touch. The warm weight of orgasm began to build between my legs, deep in my body. The width of him rubbed the sweet spot just inside me, and the head of him began to touch as deep as he could, like a caress, but a little more each time.

He started to lose his rhythm, head bowing down, shoulders rounding. I grabbed his arms, holding on as the pleasure built, warm, weight, almost . . . almost, and I was saying it, over and over, with my breath, "Almost, almost, almost . . ."

He fought his body to find that rhythm again, and I was staring into his eyes, watching them lose focus. I watched them swim to wolf amber, and I heard Asher cry out. It turned my head and made me watch him struggle in the chains as his body rode the pleasure.

Jean-Claude's hips were still moving, his hand wrapped in Asher's hair, the other curved under his shoulder across his chest. I saw Jean-Claude hesitate, and a shudder rolled up his body as he fought to make this moment last.

Then Richard brought me screaming, bucking underneath him. I felt his arms tremble under my hands as he fought to keep going just that little bit longer. Asher and I screamed together, and only then did they both lose their control, did they both thrust one last time as deep and firm as they could. Our screams echoed each other and the *ardeur* was just suddenly there on the three of us that carried it. We fed. We fed on the feel of our bodies buried inside each other. We fed on the release of emotion as we finally owned how we felt about each other; there was a moment of honesty so raw that it was like pain, and then there was nothing but joyous release, as if the world were suddenly golden, and edged with white haze, and it all felt good. I felt the chains on my wrists, and my nails gliding down Richard's arms, and the men inside us both. For one moment it was all one, none, everything in one huge mix of pain, pleasure, confusion. There was nothing but the pleasure of it shared, taken back and forth. I'd shared moments like this with Richard and Jean-Claude, but never during sex, and never with Asher. It was as if all the boundaries fell down, all the shields that kept us safe from one another were just gone. We should have been afraid, but in that moment there was no room for anything but pleasure. It just felt too good to be afraid of it.

And then we smelled flowers, flowers that weren't in the room. Roses, and jasmine, and Jean-Claude fought to get us back in control, fought to master us and himself and the pleasure, but it was too late; we were wide open, defenseless, and he and Asher knew now that it had been no accident.

Belle Morte, Beautiful Death's voice echoed through us. "I told you they could not resist each other forever."

12

WE WERE STILL in the bedroom under the Circus. We were still in the bed, still wedded to each other's bodies, but I knew we could all see Belle Morte in our heads like a bad dream. She was dressed in gold, a deep rich satin that made her pale brown eyes look even more amber than they were, but I had Richard's wolf amber to compare with and I knew that try as she might her eyes were not truly anything but brown. Her brunette hair was curled in careful ringlets on top of her head, to cascade around her oval face. It looked complicated and not touchable, as if she'd yell at you if you messed it up.

She spread her arms wide, chin coming up. "I am Belle Morte, I am Beautiful Death, gaze upon me, desire me, but come to me, my petite ones, and I will give you all you desire."

I had a flash of memories of Jean-Claude and Asher and a speech like this for both of them separately. I saw her offer herself to others in front of them, countless others. But none of us wanted her, none of us were tempted, that had so not been the case the last time she'd visited us. Then I'd known that Jean-Claude would always love her; he could run away from her, but he could never be free of her. Now the three of us who had been touched by her didn't want to be touched again, and Richard was the difference. He hadn't been there through any of the other times, and now he was our rock in the tide of temptation, because he wasn't tempted.

Jean-Claude took Richard's lack of interest and built on it so we could all stare at her with cold eyes. We could pull ourselves apart from each other so that Richard lay beside me, holding me, and Jean-Claude could hug Asher and reach up to undo one wrist from the chains. In a way, we ignored her, though it was like ignoring a leopard that just happened to be walking through your living room. Maybe if you ignored it the cat would keep moving, but then again, maybe it would stop and want a snack.

Rejection wasn't something that Belle Morte had dealt with much in the last two thousand years. She didn't deal well with it. Her anger filled her eyes with pale, brown fire, like staring at the sun through dark glass, but as the sun can burn skin if magnified through glass, so could Belle's power if you dared reject her.

Belle tried to flood us with the *ardeur*, but it was too well fed. We were sated. She held her hand out to the darkened room. I caught shadows and realized the only light was torchlight. Where was she? "Lust is no longer my only weapon, Jean-Claude. Feel my new power and learn to fear me again." The scent of roses was thicker, but underneath that was the scent of jasmine, and that had never been Belle's perfume.

A fresh thrill of fear painted my skin in cold goose bumps. Jasmine was the scent of the Mother of All Darkness, but she was dead, her body destroyed by the mercenaries the Vampire Council had hired to do the job. I'd heard her last scream in my mind from thousands of miles away. She was gone, so why did Belle Morte smell of roses and jasmine?

Jean-Claude had used Richard and his connection to the wolves to help us, but Belle's animals were all cats. I smelled leopard. The leopard inside me woke and began to pad up that long path in my head. My beast liked the scent of the leopard touching Belle, and we liked Belle. For the first time she tried to call me as if I were just another wereleopard and she my master. "You are still warm, Anita. Jean-Claude can cut your vampire away from me, but he doesn't hold leopard, and you don't know enough to fight me."

I thought about my leopards, Micah and Nathaniel, and I knew they were coming. I reached out and tasted Damian's power. I called him to me. Belle had opened us too wide and I could feel so many people. It was as if she'd peeled away my shields, like breaking into a house by tearing down an entire wall. I couldn't keep her out, but I was suddenly sensing people that I'd never been able to sense before. I knew that Rafael, the wererat king, was sitting at a table at a restaurant with others of his rodere, his animal group. I knew that the swan king was in St. Louis visiting our local swanmanes. It was as if anyone I had ever fed the *ardeur* on was suddenly clear in my mind. Face after face, body after body, and I realized that Belle was shifting through them like shuffling a deck of cards.

"You have done my bloodline proud, Anita; look at all of them, taste them, feel them," she said.

Jean-Claude undid Asher's other wrist, and Richard went to him, helped him hold the other man, who was still too lost in afterglow. The moment that Richard wasn't touching me, the leopard inside me started to run. It would hit the surface of me and burst on my skin in a rush of pain and damage. Belle laughed that musical, slithering, seductive, frightening laugh.

Then Jean-Claude touched Richard's skin, even a small brush and he thrust that coolness, that calmness that Richard had learned from the tigers into my leopard, and my beast did slow, but she was still walking toward the light with a sense of purpose. Jean-Claude and Richard carried Asher back to me, laid him on one side of me, and Richard laid down on the other. Asher slid down on the bed so he could cuddle his head against my shoulder, his arm around my waist. Asher was still boneless and fighting back to full awareness; as he'd said, he didn't have a triumvirate so he didn't have the energy we did to fight her. He needed a werehyena, which was his animal to call. I thought it to Nathaniel and Micah, and more-distant Damian.

Jean-Claude lay on the other side of Asher, but he put an arm across the bed, and Richard and he clasped wrists, and Jean-Claude put a hand across Asher to take my hand in his. The moment we touched we were more solid. The shadowy torch-lit room was foggy around the edges, beginning to recede like a bad dream.

Then the scent of evil flowers was stronger, like we were bathing in jasmine perfume, but underneath was heat, dry grass, and then lion. The scene in my mind came into focus again like crystal, all hard edges and unbelievably brilliant in color the way dreams so seldom are. She stood there pushing lion and leopard at us and we had only wolf touching us. It wasn't enough.

She smiled, and the scent of roses and jasmine grew stronger. Jean-Claude said, "Belle, what have you done?"

"The roses are your scent, but jasmine is Marmee Noir," I said.

Jean-Claude said again, "What have you done, Belle?"

"She was the Mother of us all. If we had let her power die with her, we would all have died," Belle Morte said.

"That is a lie," Jean-Claude said, "a lie to keep us from attacking those that made us."

"We were not willing to take that chance," she said, and I felt her power reaching out to us, almost visible like some evil fog. I didn't know what she meant to do with it, but if she had truly swallowed some of the Mother of All Darkness, then I didn't want any of that power to touch us. But it was as if the mist were a trick, a sleight of hand to keep me looking in the wrong direction, because her power was just suddenly there, against my body. I could feel a claw digging under my ribs. It tore a gasp of pain from me, and blood began to spill down the front of my body. Belle had never been able to cut from a distance with her animals. But it was more than that; it was as if the invisible claw were a hand being held out to my leopard, saying, *Come, take my hand, let me free you*, and no matter how much control I thought I had on the beasts inside me, they all wanted out. They were all frustrated with this human body that would not let them come out and play.

"Here, kitty, kitty," Belle said, and then she called it in French, but the language didn't matter, only the power. I writhed and fought not to scream.

Richard put his hand on my stomach and I felt that soothing power again. He stroked my leopard as he'd petted the wolf before. The leopard snarled at him, but it stopped racing for the surface. It circled, snarling in frustration. My leopard was stopped, but Belle wasn't. She clawed at my skin, and faint red lines appeared across my stomach.

"I am not so easily stopped now, necromancer. I have the power of the Mother of us all in me, and you cannot stand against it."

The door opened and Nathaniel, Micah, and Damian were there with one of our new female vampires holding Damian's hand. Her name was Cardinal after her red curls, though they were more gold-red than Damian's; nothing was quite as bloodred as his long straight hair, just as his eyes were the green of a cat's eyes, inhumanly beautiful, though I knew that the eyes were the color he'd had in life. He was almost six feet tall, which made Cardinal very tall for a woman in the century she'd died in, thin and small breasted, boyishly hipped under her silk robe. In her day she'd have been too thin, but now she looked like a model.

Micah and Nathaniel reached the bed first and just climbed onto it. Micah was wearing purple silk boxers, but Nathaniel was nude, which meant they'd been in bed sleeping, or trying to; most of the wereanimals wore nothing to bed if I didn't make them. Lately I'd stopped insisting on it. It was only the group leaders who seemed to throw something on for walking around in the Circus.

I held my hand out and Nathaniel touched me first. The power flared like a warm wind over my skin. The moment his power touched mine the claws hurt a little less, but Nathaniel flinched and I saw red lines appear on his skin. He was sharing the damage but not stopping it. Micah knelt by my legs, putting his hand on Nathaniel's shoulder and my thigh. His power was like a soothing wash of water, a calm deep pool, and his beast swirled up through his body and crossed that barrier into me. There was a moment of feeling his beast slide into me and then I could feel it rubbing its silken fur against my side. I could feel our beasts greeting each other with that long sinuous cat rub from cheek to hip, and at the same time it felt as if the fur was rubbing along the inside of my human body, so there was a moment of disorientation, of being my leopard, his leopard, and me at the same time. The two leopards turned as one, snarling, at the power that was trying to dig its way into us.

Micah and I had been enough to chase Belle out once before. She hadn't been prepared for us to be a true Nimir-Ra and Nimir-Raj. With Nathaniel as my leopard to call, we were enough. We pushed her back. The scent of jasmine and roses began to fade.

"Not this time, Anita," Belle said, and I smelled sun on dry grass, and a beating, pulsing heat, and there were bigger claws pushing at my stomach. The lioness looked up from deep inside me and began her walk up the road. "You have no lion to call yet, and you have not joined yourself to the local Rex. You cannot win this. I will bring your beast and make you my animal to call, Anita."

I thought lion and I felt two of them, distant but reacting. One was Haven, our local Rex, and the other was Nicky, who was something less than an animal to call, and something more. He was a Bride, my Bride. It didn't mean marriage; it meant I'd rolled his mind so completely that he was worse than a slave. I'd meant to roll him, but the results were frightening even to me. To Nicky I said, *Come,* but to Haven I said, *Don't.* The local Rex was off my feeding schedule for starting a fight with Nathaniel and Micah one morning, and for "marrying" a female werelion and lying to her and me that she was his Regina. It had been a ploy to make me jealous; when it hadn't worked he'd annulled the marriage and sent her packing. It was like he was stuck in a sitcom mentality and didn't know how to behave in the real world. He projected the thought that he was coming. I thought back, *No, don't.* I had a werelion closer; I didn't need two.

Damian stood beside the bed in a new silk robe that was almost the same green as his eyes, with Cardinal pulling on his hand. He turned to her and I heard him say, "You've seen Belle's court. Do you want her in charge here, too?"

She blinked big blue eyes, shook her head over and over, but she let go of his pale hand and let him crawl onto the bed. He had the palest skin of any of the vampires in our kiss, our group, because in life he'd probably been paler, too. Damian lay down, putting his upper body across my bare legs, and the moment that he and Nathaniel touched me, while Jean-Claude and Richard touched me, it was as if we were a wind, a storm edge that forced back whatever Belle was trying to do. Damian was my vampire servant, an impossibility, but through him and Nathaniel I had my own triumvirate. I was the equivalent of the master vampire for them, and Jean-Claude still had his triumvirate with Richard and me. Triumvirates of power were rare among vampires; to have two that we could draw on was unheard of. Belle's image began to grow dim again.

"I told you it would take more of us," said a man's voice from Belle's vision. I smelled the grass and heat of lion, and the thick pine of forest and the musk of wolf, and rain and jungle, thick and exotic and leopard. I knew who it was before the vision cleared and the Master of Beasts stood with Belle Morte. He was one of the darkest-complected vampires I'd ever met, pale with death, but he'd been dark enough in life that he could only be so pale. He was Indian, as in the country, not Native American. He wore what I used to think of as harem pants with a matching sparkly vest over a silk shirt. It would have looked like a cheap costume except that the sparkle on his clothes wasn't sequins but real small jewels sewn in patterns. He was another Vampire Council member. He'd actually come to St. Louis once and tried to take over, or at least torment us. We'd killed his son, who he'd brought with him, for raping and torturing some of our people. It didn't surprise me that he'd be willing to help Belle possess us. It only surprised me that he hadn't tried to do something to us sooner.

He could call almost every kind of wereanimal, and he had three of them clustered around him now. He smiled out at us. It was a very unpleasant smile. "Jean-Claude, Master of the City of St. Louis, greetings from the Council on High. We have come to tame you tonight as I have tamed all my beasts." Except for his wife, who had been a wererat and given him his now deceased son, he ruled by fear and power, as Belle ruled by seduction, power, and fear.

"We are not so easily tamed as all that," Jean-Claude said, and he settled back against the bed with all of us clustered around him, touching and being touched. I felt him think that the sight would bother Padma, Master of Beasts, because his line of vampire didn't use sex as their tools. Nothing we would be willing to do would scandalize Belle Morte.

"You say that, but you have two triumvirates of power in your bed. We are still using only our beasts to call, and yet the vision remains even," Padma said, and I knew before he called them who would come to his hands. Captain Thomas Carswell was still dressed in a version of the British uniform he'd worn when he was a soldier for Queen Victoria in the 1800s. His dark gold hair was still cut short and neat, but the brownish mustache that curled across his upper lip and up to meet his sideburns always made me unable to really see his face. Still, you had to admire a man who had worn the same look for more than a century. He was Padma's human servant, but the only time I'd seen them in person, well, it hadn't been a love match between him and his master. In fact neither he nor Gideon, Padma's animal to call, liked their master very much. Gideon's hair was still somewhere between brown and blond, but it was longer than last time, shoulder length now, thick and straight with an edge of wave to it as if the longer it got the more it would wave. His eyes were still yellow with orange pinwheels, tiger eyes. I knew he had kitty-cat fangs upper and lower in his mouth. His master had forced him to stay in tiger form too long and now Gideon didn't come completely back.

The more vampires I met, the better a master Jean-Claude seemed in comparison.

Padma made a gesture, and first Gideon touched his shoulder, still standing behind him, and then Thomas raised a slow hand. He said, "If I had a choice, I would not help him do this."

"I believe that," I said, and then there was no air for talking. There was nothing but power. Padma was the storm now, a hot wind blowing out of the edge of a painful hell to make Damian, Nathaniel, and me scream. Micah reached out to the other leopards in the city and fed that power into us. There was a moment where I could draw a breath, but it was as if every beast inside me were trying to come to the surface at once. Padma was muttering in French under his breath. I couldn't understand the words, but my beasts could and they clawed and fought inside me like a crowd with one narrow door and a fire behind them, except that the door they fought at was the inside of my body. I screamed, and then Micah was there, and Richard's wolf, and they chased back two of the beasts, soothed and calmed them with what we'd learned from the weretigers. They should have been able to calm them all regardless of beastie form, or that was what we'd discovered was possible, but it was as if the tigress and lioness inside me spoke a different language that none of us could speak. Padma spoke it.

I reached out for tiger and found Crispin curled in bed with Gina and her boyfriend. I felt him look up, and felt Domino farther away with Nicky, and knew that Domino was already hurrying this way with the werelion.

The only good thing was that I was the only one writhing in pain. Padma's attack was narrowly focused on me. His voice came through the pain. "I control all the beasts you carry, Anita; I am the perfect weapon against you."

There were no claw marks on the outside of my skin; this was different power, and it was my skin that pushed out as if things were fighting to get out through my body. I watched a claw stretch up against my skin like some horrible baby caught inside me. It felt like the claws were ripping up things that no hand should have ever been able to touch with my skin still intact, and I screamed. The pain had to come out somehow, and my body couldn't free the beasts clawing inside me.

Crispin was suddenly above me, pale blue tiger eyes wide. He'd been born with the eyes of his beast. His short, curly white hair stayed the color of his tiger form as his eyes never changed. I hadn't heard or felt him come into the room; the pain was too much, it was eating the world. He held my face between his big hands and forced me to look at him. He was my white tiger to call, and he'd been trained since puberty to help the women of the white tiger clan not to shapeshift while they were pregnant.

He soothed the beasts, all of them, and I was left breathing too hard, lying on the bed staring into the calm of his pale blue eyes. He smiled down at me. "Better," he said.

I swallowed and realized my throat was raw from screaming. "Better," I whispered.

The image of Belle and Padma blurred, as if I were staring at it through a pane of frosted glass. The big bad vampires were growing dim again. Belle's voice came. "Together, Padma."

And the lioness inside me was suddenly flinging herself against my body as if she were trying to use her shoulder to smash through a door, but the door was me. The impact made my body rise on the bed as if I'd honestly been smashed into. Hands were everywhere holding me down, trying to soothe, but there was no lion, and with both Padma and Belle's energy I needed a match to their power.

I heard Nicky's voice before I saw him. "Anita, I'm here, I'm here!" He was stripping out of his clothes as he came, handing his guns to Domino, who was right behind him. Crispin rolled off me so Nicky could press his naked upper body against mine. His blond hair was cut longer on top so that a long fall of it hid most of the right side of his face like some anime character's haircut. It was only as he lay above me so the hair fell forward that I could see the scars where his eye had once been. It was just a slick rush of scars. His one brown eye stared down at me.

"Give me your beast, Anita," he said. He kissed me as if he'd crawl inside my mouth, and I kissed him back and stopped trying to control my lioness. I released my control and let all that heat, all that power, go into Nicky. I'd learned how to be gentler when I brought their beasts, but there was no time for gentle, there was just Padma's lion and mine thrusting upward, spilling into Nicky's mouth, clawing out of my body and into his. There was no sense of Belle's lioness. There was a moment when the pain ate the world in black-edged fog, and I could feel huge claws piercing my stomach and into Nicky's like some macabre conjoined twin, and then Nicky's body exploded, one second human, the next a lionman above me. That thick, warm liquid that always happened when they shifted to animal form was everywhere. I blinked it out of my eyelashes, but I was still too hurt to wipe it away.

Nathaniel's hand cleaned the worst of it off my face, as Nicky's strangely dry body collapsed on top of me in a spill of thick golden fur. The animal form rose out of all the mess and liquid, but the fur was never wet. His mane was coarser fur tickling along my face in a pale brown-and-gold ruff.

His voice came breathless with the pain of such a violent change, but he gasped it out. "See . . . you should . . . keep me beside . . . you always." He managed to raise his head enough that I could see his face, a strange mixture of lion and human, but the eyes were a deep rich gold with an edge of orange around the pupil.

"I need my lion," I said, and my own voice was breathy and pain-filled as if I'd run a very long way and it had all hurt.

"You need . . . me," he said, and that was the worst thing about what I'd done to Nicky; he would have stayed glued to my side if I'd allowed it. He seemed to have almost no will of his own. That was why he was called my Bride, like those pitiful women in the Dracula movies, the Brides of Dracula. The movies showed them as baby vampires, and some vampires could do that to other vampires, but my ability went past species barriers. Theoretically, anyone I could attract could be made into a Bride. Nicky had been a sociopathic assassin, and now he did what I told him.

I said the only thing I could think to say. "Thank you, Nicky."

He smiled, and it was his human smile caught in the half-man face. A shining smile, excited that he'd pleased me.

"I tasted the white tiger when he touched you," Padma said, "so I will not try white, but there are other colors of tiger, Anita."

"Gideon is a standard-issue weretiger," I said, and my voice was steady. Good, I was tired of sounding afraid.

"True enough, but then I didn't have a lion when I helped her call your lion, did I?"

I lay there on the ruined silk sheets with the clear, thick liquid over us like someone had smeared the bed with thin Karo syrup, and tried to think past the fading pain.

"She is my human servant," Jean-Claude said. "It is against all our laws to try to steal her away from me. We are not allowed to break the link between vampire and servants, or animals to call."

"Just as we are supposed to kill all baby necromancers," Belle said, "because if we do not, they become something that can control us. You should have told us the moment she created a vampire servant, Jean-Claude. You should have told us when she gained the ability to call all manner of beasts."

"Did you think you could hide her growing powers forever?" Padma asked.

"She is my human servant. You all agreed not to kill her just because she was a necromancer," Jean-Claude said.

"She killed the Father of the Day, Jean-Claude," Belle said. "Did you think we would not feel both his regaining his power and then his death?"

"If she can kill one of the greatest of us, then we must either tame her and you, or destroy you all," Padma said.

"Where is the rest of the council? Why are you hidden away for this attack?" Jean-Claude said. "They don't know you are doing this, do they?"

The two vampires lied well, but Jean-Claude said, "You would not be deep into the catacombs doing this if you weren't hiding. You are trying to destroy my human servant and attacking another master, and both are crimes among us. Even the council is not above the law."

"She has the powers of two bloodlines, Jean-Claude; don't you see that we must tame her?" Padma said.

"She carries the power of Belle's line," Jean-Claude said.

"She calls beasts like she is one of mine, Jean-Claude. Don't you understand yet how dangerous she is to us all? She gains power from every vampire that attacks her. She touched me once, used her ties to wolf once against me, felt me call beast once, and now she is able to call beasts as I do."

"I was attacked by a panwere," I said.

"And why was he attracted to your city, Anita? Why did he attack your people? He was drawn to you, necromancer."

Funny, it had never occurred to me that my ability to call animals came from the Master of Beasts. I'd blamed it all on Chimera, a panwere who cut me up and gave me the same kind of lycanthropy he'd had, one that adapted to any beast that bled me.

"You're giving me too much credit," I said.

"The Mother of All Darkness wanted Anita, wanted to possess her body," Jean-Claude said. "You ate some of her power, and now you are obsessed with Anita, too. The Mother would defy the council, but the two of you would never do anything so rash. What you are doing could turn the rest of the council against you and your people. It would be civil war among the vampires. Why would you risk all that when we are in America? We are not trying to take anything from you. Why would you risk so much when we are no threat to Europe?"

"The American vampires petitioned the council for permission to kill you, Jean-Claude," Belle said.

Padma said, "They do not need to know that."

"If the council had agreed to our destruction, you would not be doing this behind the other council members' backs," Jean-Claude said.

"Why do they want us dead?" I asked.

"They fear you," Belle said.

"Belle Morte, do not answer their questions."

Something passed over her face, some thought, some idea.

It was Jean-Claude who put the pieces together. "Who among the council voted in our favor?"

Belle simply answered, "The Dragon, the Traveller, and me." She put her hands over her mouth.

I felt Jean-Claude settling in against the bed, felt some tension in him ease. "Padma wishes us dead, but you want to save us, don't you?"

She just stared at him with her hands across her lovely mouth. I realized she was fighting not to answer his questions. What was going on?

Asher stirred and said, "Do you miss Jean-Claude and me, Belle Morte?"

She couldn't leave that alone. "If I had missed you, Asher, I could have had you again any time in the last century. I do not bed the ugly."

Jean-Claude and I moved toward Asher as a unit, and I realized that it was Jean-Claude's thought first, but it didn't matter; I agreed with it. We wrapped ourselves around Asher, his body slick with the thick lubricant that Nicky had gotten on us all. We held him and stared up at the vision of Belle Morte.

"Do you miss being with both of us together?" Jean-Claude asked.

She struggled not to answer. It showed on her face, but in the end she said, "Yes." Then she was angry, so angry, her rage filled her eyes with brown fire, and she threw power into me again. "If I cannot tame you, I will destroy you."

The claws struck, raising fresh welts on my stomach, but then Jean-Claude was there, his power, no, our power, spilling over all of us. He drew the power of both triumvirates to him and used it to shield us.

"Thank you, Padma, for showing us how to control the triumvirates better."

"I did not show you."

"Anita is my human servant. I have been able to gain vampire powers simply by having them used against us. Until now the power did not stay with me, but I think this time it will. I think you have shown me how to do what I've been wanting to do, to bind multiple triumvirates into one thing, one power. Thank you."

Belle Morte screamed, "No!" She thrust that power and there was no lust to it; it was all about anger, rage, and underneath that was pain. I, we, tasted her regret like something bitter and sweet on our tongues. I reached out to all that anger without thinking about it. It was like seeing something shiny and just reaching for it. I felt Jean-Claude at my back, but it was Damian's hard-won control that steadied us. I reached out and siphoned off Belle's rage, because I could eat anger. That was my ability, not Jean-Claude's and not one of Belle's, either.

I felt Nathaniel so calm, Damian cold and controlled, and Richard more fearful but determined not to be the weak link, and beyond that was Jean-Claude more certain, more sure, more master than ever before. He let me reach out to all that angry power and eat it. I drew off that anger and we all fed on it, because Jean-Claude understood how to share the energy between all of us. In that moment I realized that it wasn't my triumvirate and his, but ours, and he knew how to drive the metaphysical car better than I did. I was okay with riding shotgun on this one, as long as I got to shoot Belle Morte.

Her rage wakened my own, that deep pool of anger that I'd carried for so many years. It liked Belle's anger, liked the taste of it, and we drank it, her, down.

She fell to the floor. "No," she said, "this cannot be."

"The piece of the Mother you took into yourself wants Anita," Jean-Claude said, "and that piece is controlling you both. She is not dead, she lives in you. Did the rest of the council take her power into themselves?"

"Yes," Belle said, before she could stop herself.

"Then you are all poisoned with her evil." I felt his fear then, and we all shared it.

"You should have let her die," I said.

"She offered her power to us like a dark wind," Padma said, and he looked lost.

"Oh my God," I said, "she really has possessed you."

Then both the vampires stared at me. "But it's you she wants, necromancer." They spoke in unison. The smell of jasmine was everywhere, and the scent of a rain that had fallen on earth thousands of years ago. It was the scent of the Mother of All Darkness. Marmee Noir wasn't dead; she was in all of them.

They stared at me and said in that echo, "The Lover of Death would feed on your fear, necromancer. But these two bodies cannot, more's the pity. We would enjoy the taste of how much you fear us."

"Do you control Padma and Belle more completely than the rest?"

They both answered, "They are the youngest on the council, the farthest away from me in time."

"They aren't as powerful as the others," Jean-Claude said.

"He hates you for destroying his son; it opened him to me. She wants you; her anger and regret opened her to me. The Lover of Death feels nothing for you, except that your death would be wise. But he hungers for slaughter and deaths to feed upon, and this new, more modern council controls him. I've promised him death, death as he hasn't seen it in centuries if he will be my horse to ride. The Dragon feels nothing for you, except curiosity. The Traveller knows what is happening, and he hides from me. He has one body and if it is destroyed he is no more, but my soul fills many bodies now. You would have to kill all of them to destroy me."

"A separable soul," Jean-Claude said.

"Yes," she said, "and even the death of all the council will not find all of me." They looked at me, and said, "Thank you for killing the Father of the Day; he was the only one who could have challenged me."

"I didn't do it to help you," I said.

"But it did help me, Anita, so much more than you will ever know."

"You ate his power when he died," I said.

The two vampires nodded.

"Belle Morte," Jean-Claude said, "you must fight her."

"She cannot," the vampires said together.

I felt Jean-Claude open the *ardeur* and thrust it into Belle Morte. Belle's head went back, her spine bowing, and when she looked up her eyes were their human brown. "She doesn't understand the *ardeur*, but she understands lust, Jean-Claude."

Then Belle's eyes were drowned in power darker than her own, her eyes like a sea of night sky, and I'd seen those eyes before, and not from the Mother. Belle and Padma spoke in unison. "Lust we know of old, Anita. Remember what we did in your Las Vegas with the weretigers? I can raise the *ardeur* and drown you all in it for hours until the sun does rise and my power grows by every tick of your clocks."

Richard's fingers dug into my shoulder, and I realized that as each man had come into the room he'd been pushed farther away from me, no, not pushed, had moved farther away from me. He understood it was a choice now, because I felt him understand that as his thoughts touched me. Fear ran through Jean-Claude like cold water, and I was feeling almost nothing yet, shoving my emotions away as I did in a crisis. Only Richard, of the three of us, was calm, no, Micah, I could feel him, calm, too, and Nathaniel beyond him. Micah was calm because he was almost always that way, and we got a glimpse of the years and the work that had gone into that calm. He was like a deep, still pool where all the trouble could go. Nathaniel was calm because he honestly believed that I would not fail him, that I would find a way. His unshakable faith had saved us before, but as always it frightened me, too, my fear that I would fail him, and his deep, abiding belief that I wouldn't. And then there was Richard, calm at last, and his was like Micah's, a calm built of work, therapy, effort; he'd built his calm the way he built his muscles, one weight at a time.

I felt Richard's version of the *ardeur* for only the second time ever. It was about possession, but not demonic, just about till death do us part, belonging to you and no other. Once upon a time that had been my heart's desire, but by the time the *ardeur* had risen in me, I needed more help in my life than any one person could give, so the *ardeur* had given me Micah, and Nathaniel, and finally made me someone who could be with Jean-Claude.

I reached out to Jason, because I knew he was still in the room somewhere even though my vision was drowning in the sight of Belle and Padma in that dark room so far away. Jason's hand met mine, as if he'd sensed what I needed. The last time I'd faced Richard's rice-and-roses *ardeur*, it had been Jason's fear of being consumed by a single person that had helped me fight it off. I had a moment to doubt, to wonder if J.J. had made him change his mind, but she hadn't. One of the reasons he and J.J. were working better for each other than anyone else ever had was that they didn't want monogamy, but they did want to belong to each other, to be special, just not in that burn-your-bridges kind of way.

But Richard didn't throw his wedding-veil *ardeur* into me; he aimed it at that distant room. He aimed it at Belle Morte. In all the centuries of the *ardeur*, some had tried to trap Belle in love. Augustine of Chicago had done that, and Jean-Claude and Asher had been her obsessions, but no one had offered this, only Richard. Only he could have turned something that was meant to feed on lust and make it about fiftieth wedding anniversaries and make it sound like a good idea.

He lay on the bed, curling himself around Jean-Claude, Asher, and me, and sent the thought out that you could have this forever, and with the offer to Belle it meant forever. It was that kind of love, and Belle didn't understand it, and if she had no clue, Marmee Noir was lost.

Belle looked at us with her own brown eyes. "Richard," she said, and she'd never said his name with that kind of heat behind it. He stared up at her through that long line of vision and let her see him lying there nude. It was no small promise, what he offered. "Belle," he whispered back. She smiled at him, but spoke to Jean-Claude. "I keep calling you foolish, but you find strength where I have only found weakness. Any power the Mother possesses is hers to command. She feeds on negative emotions, follows them into your mind and heart."

Padma was behind her with a sword in his hands. His eyes were black fire, not his color, not his eyes. I cried out, reached toward them. I wasn't sure if I screamed or if it was Jean-Claude. We cried, "Behind you, Belle!"

We felt her *ardeur* drown Padma. He fell to his knees, overwhelmed by too much desire. I watched Gideon and Thomas hesitate. They hated Padma and they understood now that having him dead might be better. But when he ordered them to help him, they had no choice. Belle picked up her skirts and ran. They let her run, and I knew Padma would make them pay for it later. She said, "Save yourself if you can, Jean-Claude. Contact the Traveller if you can find him. Maybe he can help you. Run if you can. Hide if you can. We are not descended from the Darkness, re-member that." Then it was as if someone had turned off the picture. We were all suddenly lying on the bed with just ourselves and no sense of Belle, or Padma, or Mommie Dearest. The world didn't smell like flowers anymore.

We all just lay there in a silence so thick I could hear the blood in my own head. Into the silence, I heard myself say, "Motherfucker."

"*Exactement, ma petite, exactement,*" Jean-Claude said.

13

IF I HAD ever wanted to give in to hysterics, it was then. How do you fight something with no body to kill? How do you fight something that can possess the most powerful vampires in the world and use them like puppets? How the fuck does anyone fight something like that?

I think we were all lying there thinking about the same thing when someone's cell phone rang. It was playing the theme to the old Mike Hammer show. Nathaniel spilled off the bed and started rummaging in the clothes on the floor. "It's the ring tone for Max, the Master of Las Vegas," he said.

"On your phone?" I asked.

"On yours," he said, and raised my phone from the mess of clothes. He opened it and said, "This is Anita's phone, Max, just hang a minute." He handed it toward me. I mouthed, "The theme to Mike Hammer?" He wiggled the phone at me and frowned. I took the phone, but we were so going to have to talk about what new ring tones he'd put on my phone. I'd just gotten "Wild Boys" off it as my main ring tone and put it to a default peal of church bells.

"Max?" I said, and made it more question than statement. Nicky was still mostly on top of me, not recovered from my forcing his beast. Violent change hurt. I took the phone as I lay wedged between Jean-Claude and Asher.

"Anita, what the fuck are you guys doing tonight?" His voice was an unhappy bass growl. He was a big man to go with the voice, almost totally bald in that I've-lost-my-hair kind of way, not a fashion-statement way. He was built big and solid like an old-time linebacker. If you didn't know what you were looking at you might say fat, but it wasn't; the muscle just hid itself, but it was there.

"Well, hello to you, too, Max," I said, and my voice was unhappy, ready to be grumpy right back to him. It made me feel a little better that I could be grumpy about a rude tone of voice. If I could still be pissy about small things, then maybe the world hadn't ended because the Mother of All Darkness was still "alive."

"Bibi woke up screaming about the dark trying to eat her. She made me call you, Anita, said you and Jean-Claude would know what was happening to her. Do you—know, I mean?" His voice was uncertain now. He'd started life as a mob boss and never lost the job even after death; in fact, he was one of the reasons that Vegas was still an old-fashioned mob town in spite of new blood from Ukraine and other places east. But he loved his wife and he was worried about his little tiger queen.

"Yeah, I know what's happened, though when Bibiana calms down I'd love to hear exactly what the dark did to try to eat her."

"The dark can't be who it used to be, Anita. You told me the Mother of All Darkness was dead. You told me you felt her die when they blew up her body." He was angry now; better angry at me than worried about his wife. Better to blame me than admit he might be scared.

"I told you what I believed at the time, Max. We got our first visit from Mommie Dearest since the bombing tonight, too. Trust me, it wasn't just Bibiana who had a rough night."

"It's been almost a year, Anita. Why now? How?" He cursed under his breath and then said, "What happened to you tonight, Anita?"

I looked the few inches that brought me to Jean-Claude's face. We were all still piled on the bed with the thick goop from Nicky's too-rapid shapeshift beginning to dry in our hair and on our skin. I thought, "What do I say?"

His answer breathed through my mind, "Tell him the truth. He is our ally."

I told Max an abbreviated version of what had happened. Jean-Claude told the others to go and clean up before the gunk dried. Most of the men looked to me to see if I wanted them to go. Honestly, I wanted some hand holding. Jean-Claude sat beside me while I talked to one of his strongest allies, and the men I most wanted to stay and hold me sat on the ruined silk sheets around us, and didn't obey Jean-Claude. I didn't know what to do about it, but I did know that I felt better with Nathaniel, Damian, and Micah near me. Jason had gone to clean up and check on J.J., which was good. Cardinal tried to get Damian to leave, too, but he wanted to know what we were going to do about Mommie Dearest and the council. He was vampire enough to need to know that before he died for the day. Cardinal was woman enough to need her boyfriend farther away from me.

Richard kissed me on the forehead and whispered, "I'll clean up while you do the vampire politics."

I wanted to say more, even though I was still telling Max how deep the shit was, but it felt wrong to let him leave after everything without more good-bye. Jean-Claude must have thought so, too, because he did leave the bed to walk Richard to the door. Micah kissed my cheek and followed them, which surprised me. Jean-Claude might be trying for a last hug, but that was never what Micah and Richard were to each other. Asher stayed by my side, but his face had a listening look. The wereanimals and vampires on the bed could probably hear everything on both ends of the phone. They might be staying to cuddle, but they were also staying to listen.

I finished listing the disaster, and Max said, "Motherfucker."

"That's what I said."

"Bibi insisted that everyone that was coming to St. Louis leave early. Victor, Cyn, Rick, and the others are in the air and headed your way."

"Max, no insult to your people but we have bigger fish to fry than cementing some sort of arranged marriage treaty between your people and Jean-Claude's."

"Bibi says that our only hope to defeat the Dark is to have another Master of Tigers, another Father of the Day."

"I appreciate the vote of confidence for Jean-Claude, but tiger isn't his animal to call and the only vampire we have who's able to walk in the day isn't a master of anything."

"Your vampire servant, Damian, right, he's your day walker?"

"Yeah."

"And who made him a day walker? It wasn't Jean-Claude, no offense to your Master of the City; it was you that made a weak vampire able to do one of the rarest feats among us bloodsuckers."

"Yeah, but . . ."

"We're not sending our boys to Jean-Claude, Anita. We're sending them to you. Though Auggie of Chicago says we should send him some of our women, something about maybe he'd inherit your power to call tiger like you inherited his ability to call wolf."

"What?" I asked.

There was noise on the other end of the phone. Cloth moving and Max saying, "You okay to do this, Bibi?"

A moment later Chang-Bibi of the White Tiger Clan was on the phone, so I guess she was okay to do this. Or Max couldn't stop her from taking the phone. Sometimes he loved his wife a little too much.

"Anita," and her voice was tear-filled, almost hiccupy with emotion. Since she was one of the scariest weretigers I'd ever met, that was not comforting.

"Hey, Bibiana, I mean, Chang-Bibi."

"It is too late for titles between us, Anita." She took a shaky breath and said, "You must embrace my tigers when they arrive. You must bring the tigers with you into their full power."

"I know that you wanted that, but the other tiger clans don't want you favored above everyone else."

"All their Changs have had the same nightmare that I had, Anita. They have seen the Darkness, and they remember in the heart of them when she tried to rule us all. The Father of the Day, he saved us. He controlled us and kept her from harnessing all the power of the tigers. She only defeated him by destroying the last golden queen."

"How do you know all that now? You didn't know it before."

"It was legend, fairy tales, Anita. I didn't believe in stories of the Living Dark, a dark Goddess, and a God of Living Light, who created our people. Who believes such things?"

She had me there. I mean, I know as a good little Christian I should really buy all that Old Testament stuff, but I thought of it as representative stories trying to explain why a God of Love would make a world where people suffered so much.

"But now you believe," I said.

"What choice do I have?" She sounded bitter.

"What did you dream?" I asked.

"No, to talk of such things gives them power, but it was only the Light, the God, that kept us from her power the first time. It was the combined power of all the tiger clans that gave him the power to keep her from conquering the world."

"Look, Bibiana, we're all shook, but being able to call a little electricity and fire isn't going to defeat Mommie Dearest."

"You have only seen what the weaker of my clan can do, Anita. You haven't even seen what Domino's black tiger side is capable of, but if the

Master of Tigers and the Consuming Darkness are real, then the powers that our clans once had must be true, too."

"Bibiana, come on," I said.

"The red tiger you slept with can call fire to his hand, he's a pyrokinetic. They exist even today among the humans."

"Fine, I'll give you that, but white tiger is all metals, and it seems to be basically really uber–static electricity. It's not a weapon."

"Black tiger is water, Anita. The human body is made up mostly of water."

"What are you saying?" I asked.

"I'm saying you have only begun to touch the surface of what we are capable of if you give us back all our powers."

"Cynric hasn't gotten any new powers."

"He's young and you only slept with him once, Anita."

"Once was plenty," I said.

"Blue tiger is the power of air. Legend says that Blue could raise storms and make them obey their will. The golden tigers controlled earth and all energies upon it."

"What does that mean?"

"They could make the very ground obey their will."

"You mean earthquakes?" I didn't even try to keep the disbelief out of my voice.

"One of the council members that Jean-Claude defeated in St. Louis was called the Earthmover, Anita; what do you think he did?"

I licked my lips; I didn't have a good answer, because she was right. The only thing that had kept the duel from turning St. Louis into a pile of rubble was the Earthmover giving his word of honor that he wouldn't use that particular power to defeat Jean-Claude. He'd actually won the duel, but he'd made the mistake of breaking my vampire marks to Jean-Claude and making me belong to his vampire lieutenant. His mistake had been thinking I'd put a stake through Jean-Claude's heart and not risk my own death killing them. They had misjudged me.

"Okay, say that Cynric could call storms, I'm not sure how I feel about a seventeen-year-old with that kind of power in my city."

"But it won't be his power, Anita, it will come to you. If you raise it in the tigers it will come to you, and you will be too powerful for the Darkness to eat."

"I'm not a vampire, Bibiana."

"But you are, you just don't drink blood, Anita. The time for pretty lies is past. The hour is late, Anita, and the Darkness is coming. If you do not save us she will possess all the tigers, including you, and once she has a golden queen—you—as her vessel, she will destroy us all."

"I am not a weretiger. I can't shift."

"Yellow was meant to be our ruler over all, a sort of High Queen. Some say that the power to move the ground is only to the Yellow. We won't know for certain until you bring more of us into our full power."

"Bibiana, this is all speculation. You don't know that any of this is possible."

"Do not doubt it, Anita. You must believe. It must be real. You must be able to harness the power of all the clans. You must."

"I don't must," I said.

"Yes, you must, because if you fail us, the Darkness will rise up and consume the world. It was she who destroyed the yellow tigers so long ago. It was the Darkness who whispered evil in the ear of the First Emperor. She knew once we lost the golden, that the Master of Tigers wouldn't have enough power to stand against her. She crushed him, and nearly destroyed us as a people of any color."

"Do you know how she ended up in the . . . coma in the caverns?" Because that had been where her body lay, in a cavern where only torch-light touched. The vampire council had tried to abandon her a few times when world wars forced them to move countries, but there had been a compulsion that wouldn't let them leave her body behind. But none of the vampires knew why she had fallen into the "sleep." They only knew one night she had not woken. For over a thousand years she'd slept, until now.

"If all the legend is true, then it was her own guards that did it. Those who the vampires are not allowed to name. She let some of them keep their golden tigers as animal to call, because she believed them to be totally loyal to her."

"How did they make her sleep?"

"The story speaks of a spell and a sacrifice of lives. They meant to slay her, but they could not."

"Would not, as in pity moved them, or could not, as in she couldn't die?"

"They couldn't figure out how to kill her permanently. They tied her to the body she last inhabited and left her there."

"Why would the guards tell the tigers?"

"So that if they were all lost, there would be some memory of what happened and what would be needed to defeat her."

"Bibiana, I can't be some sort of weretiger savior."

"Not savior, Anita, master. You must be the Mistress of Tigers. You must be the daywalking vampire who defeats the night once and for all."

I asked what I'd been thinking since it happened. "Does your legend tell how to kill the Darkness, or how to put her back to sleep?"

"The guards that have no name still exist; ask them."

I nodded, and glanced at the bedside table. In the top drawer was my cross and a very ancient piece of metal. The Nameless Vampire Guards were the Harlequin. They'd given me the charm the first time the Mother of All Darkness had messed with me. It was supposed to keep her out of my head and my body. It worked, but it had to be cleansed and recharged periodically, like a gun that needed reloading. My cross just worked, but then it was about faith, and the charm with its imprint of a many-headed tiger on it was magic, not faith. The more witches I knew, the more I realized that there was a difference.

The Harlequin were so scary that simply mentioning them by name could bring them to your door with permission to kill you. They were the elite among vampires, strong enough to have territories of their own, or even be council members, but choosing to cut all ties to their bloodlines and be a combination spy, police, and execution service for the vampire community. Supposedly only the council could set them in motion, but was that still true, or had the Mother of All Darkness already taken back her guards? If she had, we were cooked, done; it was finished before it began. Mommie Dearest was still weak, weaker than she'd been before the council hired mercenaries to blow her to kingdom come. In the past she'd possessed me directly and more easily. Maybe the loss of her body hadn't destroyed her completely, but it had weakened her. She needed the other vampires to talk to us, possess us. If there was a way to destroy her once and for all, we had to do it fast.

"Anita, are you there?"

"I'm sorry, Bibiana, you've just given me a lot to process. I'm thinking."

"Do not think too long, Anita. I will contact the other queens of the clans. I will urge them to send people to you. Our only hope lies in a swift rise to power."

"I haven't agreed to all this, you know that."

"I know, and I know that you are skeptical by nature, but there is no time, Anita. Our time to hesitate has been lost. We have only action before us, and I pray that it is swift action on your part."

"So I what, fuck everyone into their next power level like some pornographic computer game?" I made sure my voice held all the scorn I could manage. I was good at scorn, it was one of my best things. Nathaniel and Damian touched me at the same time, soothing me with their hands and their nearness. Asher put his head in my lap, as if I weren't covered in gunk. With all the terrible things that had happened, he seemed determined to concentrate on the good things. It wasn't like him to be cheerful, but it was like him to be sensual.

Bibiana made a clucking noise at me. "Make all the jokes you wish, but do what we need you to do, or the next time the Dark visits our dreams she will begin to possess the queens of the clans."

"She can't possess anybody who isn't a vampire," I said.

"Why, because the council member known as the Traveller is so limited?" It was Bibiana's turn to sound scornful.

"Yes," I said, my voice no longer so certain.

She laughed, but it was a harsh sound. "You still do not understand what she is; she is one of the first. She has powers that the others mimic, but none of them hold the same level of ability. They are all but pale imitations of her. She can and will possess someone who is not a vampire if it serves her purpose."

"Humans?" I asked.

"I don't believe so. I believe it is vampires and werecats. Her animals to call and her people are all steeds for her to ride if we allow her to grow powerful enough."

"A lot of this is guesswork, Bibiana."

"If Adam and Eve suddenly walked in your door, would you not have to believe in the serpent?"

"What?" I asked.

"This is a story as old to the tigers as the Garden of Eden is to the humans. We believed our story was a metaphor, too, but when the evil from that story turns out to be real, then the story is simply true, Anita. The story is true, and you must process, or whatever word you choose, that fact immediately, and act upon that truth. You must do this for us, Anita, or she will take the vampires one by one, and then she will move against the tigers and take them, too, and when she has that much power to wield she will rise up and cover the world in Darkness. Do you not understand that?"

"Every creation story has an end-of-the-world clause, Bibiana. It's usually just stories of floods or earthquakes that were local to the original people. Disasters that seemed world-destroying, but if you traveled a hundred miles it wasn't."

"You have felt her power, Anita. You have felt that she does not love, or care; she is an intellect and a nearly pure sociopath. She cares only for her own pain; all else is just toys for her to use, not real people, real beings. Do you really believe that she will stop with the destruction of just the vampires?"

I let the silence build as the tight, cold lump in my stomach grew and spread in chills over my skin. "No."

"Then stop trying to throw logic at nightmares. Sometimes the monsters are real, Anita. Sometimes they're real and the only way to defeat them is to be the bigger monster."

"Wait, if I could do all you said, why would I be the bigger monster?"

"Do you really believe that you could hold all that power and resist the temptation to use it?"

"Yes."

"Anita." She said my name the way my stepmother had said it when I was about fifteen.

"Don't you want me to use the power if I could get it? Isn't that the point?"

"Yes, but I'm not just trusting you with the power, Anita. I trust that once you've used it to defeat the Dark, you won't turn all that light and power against us. I'm trusting in your sense of honor and morality as much as I'm trusting in your psychic abilities."

"You've only met me once. That's a lot of trust."

"I put my son, and Cynric, the only known blue tiger in existence, and some of our most powerful weretigers on a plane this morning. If I didn't have faith in you, would I send you such precious things?"

I didn't know what to say to that. Arguing that she was wrong seemed ungrateful; *thank you* seemed inadequate. What do you say when someone trusts you like that?

"I'll do my best not to hurt anyone."

"See, Anita, not that you will do your best, but that you will do your best not to hurt anyone. You believe your moral compass is broken because of the sex, but I believe if you can get past the idea of it being a sin, your moral compass points true north."

"Don't put all your faith in me, Bibiana."

"Where else can I put it?"

And to that, there really wasn't anything else to say. It wasn't that I minded so much trying to save the world, but the idea that if I failed there was no backup plan . . . We needed a backup plan.

14

I'D BARELY GOTTEN off the phone from Vegas before my cell phone started playing the theme song to *The Sopranos*. I looked at Nathaniel. He said, "Augustine, Master of Chicago."

"Because he's a mob boss," I said.

Nathaniel nodded.

I answered my phone. I was actually getting chilled sitting here with the congealing shapeshifter goo on me, and tried to draw some of the now-ruined silk around me. The men responded by wrapping themselves closer around me, even Asher spilling more across my lap, so I was forced to put an arm around him to keep him from falling. I answered, "Hey, Auggie."

"I was visited by someone you assured me was dead." He wasn't his usual teasing self. He usually played it very casual. This was a much more serious voice, and word choice. It was the voice he used when he didn't care that I knew he'd seen Rome at its height.

"It was a surprise to us, too," I said, my voice a little less happy, too. The wet silk was not warm enough to cuddle in, so I stopped trying.

Damian, Nathaniel, and Asher held me closer. Nicky, in his soft, lion-man fur, came to wrap himself around us all as if he were trying to be everyone's fur coat. I half-expected one of the other men to protest, but they didn't. Jean-Claude, Micah, and Richard were still by the door talking. Domino was still inside the door like the guard he was, but Crispin had gone to clean up.

"If Jean-Claude is supposed to be our de facto leader in the U.S., it shouldn't have come as a surprise," Auggie said.

"She was blown up, Auggie; that should be dead." Nicky hugged us all a little tighter, and I forced myself to relax in everyone's arms so

Nicky would relax, too. My relaxing seemed to release some tension in him, because he sighed and rubbed his face against my hair and Nathaniel's cheek. Like most wereanimals Nicky liked to cuddle, and it wasn't about sex any more than a pile of kittens sleeping together was about sex.

"Well, I guess it wasn't," and Auggie sounded angry.

I realized he was doing one of my tricks, hiding his fear with anger; thinking that helped me not be angry. "Look, Auggie, we all got a shock tonight. Tell me what legend or dream or whatever you saw, what she did, or tried to do to you."

"She pretended to be Belle Morte, but she is not her." There was regret in that last word. Auggie, like all the vampires who were once part of her inner circle, always regretted her loss, even as she terrified them. "She tried to enter me. She tried to take me over, Anita. But she needed permission. I got the impression that if I'd said yes to the seduction by the false Belle, it would have given her the permission she needed to take me over. Then she was ripped away from me. I felt anger, fear, and that she needs a vampire who has big cats as their animal to call. She is weaker than she was, or she wouldn't need permission, she'd just rape her way inside one of us."

"It took Mommie Dearest a year to do this to the council. I think she's been hanging around like a shadow or ghost of herself until she was strong enough to strike at them. The bombing hurt her, Auggie."

"But not enough," he said.

"Agreed," I said.

"What did she do to keep herself alive and how did she grow stronger? If we could figure that out, then we might be able to keep her from getting any stronger than she is at this moment. Just keeping her from growing stronger would be something."

"She has a toehold in Belle Morte and Padma. That's strong enough to give us some major problems," I said.

A phone rang, and this time it was just a nice, normal buzz; of course it wasn't my phone since I was still talking to Auggie. Domino took his cell phone out of his pocket.

I "felt" lion, and it wasn't Nicky. I sensed energy as if I were standing in the middle of the sun-burnt grass with that hot light beating down on me, and over all the scent of cat and fur; lions.

Domino spoke to Jean-Claude, who motioned him toward me. He came around the bed to stand in front of us. "Haven is here with most of his lions, the muscle anyway. He's demanding to be let inside. The guards at the door won't let him in with that much muscle."

"I can feel them." I shivered and Nicky held us tighter, growling in my ear, "If you would let me fight him I'd be your new Rex and he'd be dead."

Auggie was talking again. I put the phone closer so I could hear. "I feel the lions, Anita. You and Haven need to work things out."

"Tell that to him," I said.

"I did," he said.

"What the hell did you tell him to do?" I said.

"I didn't tell him to come with all his men and challenge you."

"What did you tell him?"

"That anything that undermines Jean-Claude's power base right now is a bad thing. That he had to find a peace between you and him and the new lion, Nick. But you have to tame Haven, Anita. You have to make sure the lions are under your control as their master vampire."

"I'm not a real vampire, Auggie, and I don't have all the mad skills that I need."

"You have them; you're just too human to want to use them."

"What's that supposed to mean?"

"It means you feel sorry for people. It means you let your heart get in the way of business."

"And you don't?" I said.

"I don't," he said.

"I'll remember that the next time you visit us," I said softly.

"Jean-Claude helped you roll me, Anita. Without him I would have rolled you, and our power structure would be reversed. You need him to help you control the cats."

"I think Haven would kill us both if we tried for shared sex with him."

"Have Jean-Claude try the new females that Haven's recruiting for his pride. They're not like the bimbo that he brought down there for his Regina; I think you and Jean-Claude will like them both better."

"Did you help shop for them?"

"Yes."

"And you were going to tell us when?"

I heard him take in a deep breath and then let it out, and I had that moment to sense how much hotter his energy could be than most vampires'. His energy could hold a warmer edge of his animal to call than any other master I'd ever met. "I feel her outside your door; just let her in. I helped shop for women I thought you might actually get along with, and women that Jean-Claude might actually like."

"You mean like-like?" I asked.

"Jean-Claude is more Belle's child than I am, Anita. Her power over her animals all came through sex. Let him try some of the cats and see if he gains the ability to call them. It would make him much more powerful, and it would mean he could help you control all the cat-based animal groups."

"Did you talk to him about this?"

"My word of honor that it will be as big a surprise to Jean-Claude as it is to you."

"Don't go all Machiavelli on me, Auggie, I don't like it."

"This isn't Machiavelli, more Cupid. Put Jean-Claude on and go tame your kittens before someone gets hurt."

"How do I tame him?" I asked.

"Let me fight him," Nicky growled.

Auggie said, "If you could win the fight it would tame Haven, but he's good in a fight."

"I can do it," Nicky said, rubbing his face against my hair.

"How else?" I asked.

"Sex would be a temporary solution. It would smooth things over tonight."

"So I reward his bad behavior," I said.

"What's your goal for tonight, Anita?"

"What do you mean?" I asked.

"What do you want to happen with the lions right this moment?"

"I want everyone to survive the night. No one dead." I thought about it. "I'd like to make us all into a cohesive whole. We need to get our shit in order here, especially after what just happened with Mommie Dearest."

"Then offer him sex if he sends most of the lions home. He's Rex, so he's entitled to keep a couple of bodyguards."

"You really think sex with me will make him send them home?"

"Remember who're you're talking to, Anita. It was all I could do after sex with you and Jean-Claude not to stay in St. Louis like some sort of pet. Trust me, he'll say yes."

"That was Jean-Claude in charge of the metaphysical head games, Auggie. Haven won't go for that."

"Ask Jean-Claude what he could do to help the head games with hands off Haven. Besides, you completely rolled the other werelion. He's a fucking Bride of Anita, or I guess Groom, but whatever, you can do this if you get out of your own way."

"What's that supposed to mean?"

"It means you feel bad about what you did to the other werelion."

"I took his free will, Auggie; no one has that right."

"I won't argue right and wrong with you, kiddo, but I will point out that if Haven was as enthralled with you as this Nick is, then you wouldn't have a horde of angry werelions about to storm your battlements."

I didn't know what to say to that as Nicky hugged us all tighter.

"Hell, Anita, if you had just taken him as your Rex the way you did your Nimir-Raj, he'd be more manageable. I wouldn't have sent him to you if I thought you were going to hesitate. He's too dangerous to keep waffling. You need to either keep him or kill him, Anita."

"Could I send him back home to you?"

"No, he's been a Rex; if you send him back my Rex will kill him." I heard cloth move on the phone as he shifted position. "Now if you want to send him here so we kill him for you, I can get behind that."

"No."

"It would be easier on that conscience of yours," he said.

"If you think that's true, then you don't understand my conscience at all, Auggie."

"It's been so many centuries since I had one of my own that I don't quite understand them in anyone."

"It would not make me feel better to send him home to certain death."

"Then what will you do?" he asked.

"I do my own killing."

"Then do it, Anita. Do it before he tears your house apart."

"I don't want to kill him."

"Kill him, fuck him, make him your Rex the way you did Micah, make him your animal to call like Nathaniel, make him your Groom like Nick, but you are going to have to do something."

Domino's phone rang again. He turned around to take it, but the set of his shoulders let me know that the news hadn't improved.

"Thanks for the pep talk, Auggie."

"You have to help Jean-Claude get his house in order, Anita, like yesterday. You have to do what needs doing or the Mother of All Darkness is going to eat us alive, and undead."

"That's pretty much what Bibiana said."

Domino said, "What do you want us to do? The lions say they're coming to your rescue. The guards can open the door or they can break it down, but they are coming inside."

"How many men?" I asked.

"Twenty-five."

"Shit, he doesn't have that many soldiers, which means he brought cannon fodder, too."

"If Jean-Claude has sex with one of the female lions at the same time you're doing the Rex, he might be able to bridge the powers without touching Haven," Auggie said.

"I'll be suspicious later that you and Jean-Claude set this up so he could fuck other women, but right now, I have to think what to tell the lions."

Auggie said, "I know to talk to you first."

I looked up at Domino. "Tell Haven we need time to clean up, then we'll meet him and some of his lions."

"How many of them you letting inside?" Domino asked.

I turned to look at Jean-Claude, Richard, and Micah near the door. "Jean-Claude, how many lions do you want in here?"

"As few as possible."

"Which is how many? I'm trying to get a feel for how many is a deal breaker, Jean-Claude."

He looked at me, head to one side as if he were thinking, then he turned to Domino. "How many guards do we have on hand?"

"You mean how many bodies?" he asked.

"Yes, that is what I mean."

"Twelve."

"How soon could we get more? I would like at least a two-to-one ratio."

"Let me ask Claudia. She knows the wererats' resources better than I do."

Asher rolled over in my lap so he could gaze up at Jean-Claude. "We have over a hundred werehyenas that can fight, and twenty-five that I would trust against Haven and his people."

I said, "I thought you were threatening to take your werehyenas and go play somewhere else."

He rolled his head and shoulders in my lap so that Nathaniel helped me keep him from sliding off. Asher gave me those pale blue eyes. "The Mother of All Darkness is after us all. I will not divide our strength, but you know why I was leaving, Anita. You know what I needed to stay, and now I have it." He smiled.

I smiled down at him, because I wasn't just seeing him through my eyes, but through that glow from decades of memories when Jean-Claude had truly loved him. "Then how long for your werehyenas to get here?"

"A half hour, forty-five minutes, depending on how armed you want them."

I looked up at Jean-Claude. "How armed do we want them?"

"Are we allowed to slaughter your lions, *ma petite*?"

I thought about that. "I don't want them hurt, but if they try to fight us, then they aren't my lions anymore. They're just a danger to us."

"You will miss your Cookie Monster if we slay him."

I smiled at his using my nickname for Haven, but shook my head. "I miss what he could have been to me, but he was never a boyfriend, barely a lover. Tonight either he toes the line, or he has to go. Auggie says if we send him home, the local Rex will kill him. I won't let someone else do my dirty work."

Jean-Claude touched my cheek, then turned me to look up at him. I hadn't even realized I'd looked down. "If you mean that, then we can finish this tonight before all the bad little vampires must be abed." Asher reached out, caressing Jean-Claude's thigh. He moved closer to us, so that Asher could run his hand up the back of his thigh.

I nodded. "I'll call him, if he has his phone on him. We'll clean up and we'll do this."

I didn't want to kill Haven. I didn't want to kill any of them. But he couldn't bring armed men to our house and demand to be let inside. We couldn't let that go, and he had to have known that. As I took a quick shower so that I wouldn't go into the meeting covered in shapeshifter goop, I realized that Haven had decided to end things tonight, too. He'd even brought his strongest people so that if we slaughtered them all the pride would be back to the way it was before he came. It would be weak, but it would be open to another Rex coming in and building what he wanted out of it.

Haven was doing his version of suicide by cop, and we were the cops.

15

AN HOUR LATER we were in Jean-Claude's living room waiting for the lions. Haven had agreed to almost everything I'd asked with almost no negotiating. He'd kept two guards, his two enforcers, which was typical for a shapeshifter leader. If he'd not asked for them to come down the long staircase with him I wouldn't have let him come at all, because to me that would have meant he was planning to force me to kill him. I was still hoping to save this from becoming a clusterfuck of mammoth proportions. Haven had suggested that he bring the two new female lions for us to meet, and thanks to Auggie's little talk with me, I said sure.

Jean-Claude sat beside me on the big white couch that faced the curtains and the outer door beyond. We'd showered, but we hadn't had time to do more than put hair goop in and go with our hair still in damp curls around our shoulders and down our backs. The hair being wet had precluded silk shirts, so Jean-Claude had opted for another pair of his omnipresent leather pants that looked painted on. His shirt was a long-sleeved black mesh T-shirt that covered all that pale chest yet let you see his skin like a ghost through the fabric. He'd chosen one of my favorite pairs of his boots, the ones that laced up the back of his leg from ankle to the tops of his thighs, so that the pants seemed almost redundant, as if the boots had been designed to be worn with very short shorts.

Richard was back in the jeans he'd begun the night in, but his red T-shirt had gotten stained beyond repair, so a leather vest that still fit over his more muscled upper body was shirt enough. His brown hair looked very dark, almost brunet, fresh from the water. He'd tied it back in a ponytail so that it gave the illusion he had short hair. I'd honestly expected him to leave before we met with the lions. He'd said, "The last time Haven was in this room he tried to seriously injure some of your other lions, and I had to beat the shit out of him to get him off them. I can't leave until I know everyone's going to be safe. Jean-Claude may need his triumvirate tonight."

I couldn't argue with his logic, but for the first time in a very long time Richard was sitting on the other side of Jean-Claude, so that our "master" was in the middle. Shang-Da and Jamil stood behind the couch at his back with Wicked and Truth behind Jean-Claude. Claudia and Domino were behind me. Fredo, two more wererats, and a werewolf were by the door. The wererats weren't an animal I could call, but they'd proved they were loyal to me more than once. They both took my orders before Jean-Claude's, and Claudia actively disliked Richard. She thought he was just another guy who wanted his girlfriend barefoot and pregnant. Since I felt that way part of the time, too, it was hard for me to talk her down about it.

Domino's black-and-white curls matched his black-on-black look. Normally he'd have worn a red T-shirt to show that he was willing to be a blood, or sex, donor, but Jean-Claude had wanted us to look like we were on the same side. I hadn't argued. Domino hadn't, either.

Crispin was down the hallway out of the fight. He wasn't trained with a gun. Hand to hand he did well enough, but if we had to kill the lions tonight it would come to guns. Anyone who wasn't a shooter on our side had to get the hell away from this meeting. Jason was in his room with J.J. I'd suggested he take her to a hotel for the night, but she'd refused to go. Cardinal was in Damian's room waiting for him. We were as civilian-free as we could manage.

Even after everything we'd done in bed together, Richard had still not wanted to put Jean-Claude in the middle of us, but Nathaniel was next to me with Damian beside him. Jean-Claude thought it was time that I take my own triumvirate out for a drive. He'd be there to help me, and I'd have what he'd just done with Richard and me to learn from, but Haven was my kitty to call, not Jean-Claude's. Auggie was right; the cats were mine. I had to make them behave; unless we could figure out a way for Jean-Claude to gain power over the lions it was up to me. I did think about him sleeping with one of the new female lions. I tried to wrap my head around the idea of him sleeping with another woman, and asked myself as honestly as I could how I'd feel about that. I wasn't sure, but having more than just me to control the lions directly would have been really good right that minute.

Nathaniel and I were both in regular black T-shirts made out of that soft jersey material. His was almost too snug for the muscles of his chest, so that the cloth covered and managed to give hints of all that lay underneath. Mine fit well, but thankfully not that tight, over the black seamless bra I was wearing. I was in black jeans and a pair of black over-the-ankle boots. They were a compromise between the jogging shoes I wanted to wear and the higher heels Jean-Claude had wanted. The boots were actually comfortable and I could move in them. Nathaniel had on a pair of blue jeans so washed they were almost white, with holes here and there. It was the kind of thing shapeshifters wore when they thought they might have to change fast and didn't want to ruin something nice. He was curled barefoot beside me on the couch, again in case he had to shift quickly. His hair was in a braid down his back. He was ready to fight, and I didn't like it. Richard was a much better fighter, and he'd almost lost to Haven. If it came down to hand to hand between the lion and Nathaniel, I'd just shoot Haven. I'd already made that decision.

I was wearing my Browning BDM in its custom-made shoulder holster and had my backup gun in a holster at the small of my back. The custom holster let me carry a silver-edged knife as long as my forearm down my spine. My hair hid the hilt. I even had my two wrist sheaths with their silver-edged blades. I'd thrown one of my black suit coats over it so I didn't look so well armed. The only concession to not killing Haven, really, was that the clip I had in my Browning was regular lead. It would hurt, and make his body have to heal, but it wouldn't kill him. My backup gun was all silver. If I used fourteen bullets on Haven and had to go for my backup, then I wouldn't be shooting to wound.

I'd left only one thing in the bedroom that I normally wore to a fight: my cross. Since I was going to try to make my own triumvirate come online and that was technically a vampire power, wearing a holy object that glowed when vampire powers were used seemed like a bad idea. It had never glowed when I did vampy stuff before, but it would be a bad time for that to change. The only thing around my neck on my gold chain was the small amulet with its multiheaded cat on it. Keeping out the Mother of All Darkness seemed like a really good idea; in fact, I'd be sleeping in it from now on, and just putting the cross in the bedside table. The amulet, charm, whatever, didn't seem to mind what kind of vampire shit happened around it.

Damian was on the other side of Nathaniel in black dress slacks with a

matching jacket, his white T-shirt very stark in all that black. His long, wet
red hair looked like red neon against the black jacket.

The two overstuffed chairs with their silver and gold cushions had been
drawn up to either end of the couch. Micah sat in the chair closest to
Damian . . . that is, my triumvirate. He was in a black suit, but with a deep
pine-green T-shirt that made his chartreuse eyes more green than yellow.
Normally the shirt made his eyes look very green, but Damian was sitting
too close to him and he had the greenest eyes I'd ever seen.

Asher sat in the big overstuffed chair on the end closest to Richard and
Jean-Claude. It was in front of the faux fireplace. In spite of the potential
disaster of the Mother of All Darkness rearing her scary head tonight,
Asher was the most happy and relaxed that I'd ever seen him. Well, me
personally. I had memories from Jean-Claude's long-gone past, but for this
time and place Asher was a very happy boy.

He was curled in the chair in that boneless comfortable way that Jean-
Claude could do, or Nathaniel. Asher wore a pair of leather pants as
painted on as Jean-Claude's, but his boots were plain midcalf black. Asher
had topped the outfit with a black T-shirt made of some shiny, clinging
material, so maybe *T-shirt* wasn't the right word for it.

His shoulder-length gold hair was browner wet from the shower, but
against the black of the shirt the gold shone through more. I knew the
contrast would grow as his hair dried.

The fact that he was willing to be seen so publicly with his hair wet
enough that he couldn't hide the scars on his face said more than almost
anything about how good he was feeling. It was nice to see. Jean-Claude
glanced at me, and I caught a smile. I wasn't the only one happy to see our
moody boy more upbeat. I fought not to glance across at the other moody
boy with his werewolf bodyguards. Funny, they were both behaving great.
Haven seemed to be trying to make up for both of them. Maybe we were
only allowed so much happy without moody to balance it? Someday I'd
like to try everyone being in a good mood at the same time, but it wouldn't
be today, or rather tonight.

Asher's two werehyenas were on one side of his chair, but he seemed
more interested in Jean-Claude and even Richard, who he'd asked if he
could touch outside the bedroom. Richard had wisely said, "Define touch."
Which was guy-speak for no. Jean-Claude had told Asher not to push it,
though in much more polite words, but it amounted to the same thing.
Asher hadn't even gotten upset, again a first.

I'd made Nicky go farther into the underground to the area where the wereanimals kept food for fresh changes. Food was livestock, most of it pretty small, or fresh meat. He hadn't wanted to leave my side, but since he was one of the major sore points for Haven, having him standing beside me in his half-lion form, especially all naked, was probably not going to help things.

Micah had two guards at his back, too, but like me he didn't have enough leopards to go around. He had Lisandro, tall, dark, and handsome with shoulder-length black hair pulled back in a ponytail. He was around six feet tall; only Claudia was taller, though the guard beside him gave Lisandro a run for his money. Abraham, Bram for short, was new to St. Louis. His hair was shaved close and tight to his head, leaving the high cheekbones and sculpted look of his face very bare. It managed to look both stark and like some walking piece of art, as if the bone structure were too perfect and hair would just have distracted from it. His skin was so close to black that it shone with blue and purple highlights in bright light. I'd never seen anyone so dark. In leopard form he was a blond. It turned out that it wasn't the genetics of the host human that dictated the color of the animal form. It was the genetics of the shapeshifter who'd infected them. Micah and Nathaniel were brought over by black leopards, so their animal form was black. Bram had been brought over by a yellow leopard, so he was yellow. The same held true for wolf fur, which was why Richard had the reddest fur of anyone in his pack; he'd contracted lycanthropy in a bad vaccine batch, and not from a pack member.

Micah had explained, "That's why some extinct subspecies still exist as strains of lycanthropy when the real animal is completely wiped out." Cool.

Bram still stood military straight. The haircut was from that, too. He hadn't been a civilian long, but once he couldn't pass a blood test without the lycanthropy showing, he was given a medical discharge. One of the new werehyenas, Ares, was on the lookouts at the top of the Circus along with wererats who were sniper trained. Asher had called him to come when we weren't sure if the other werelions would just go away and let their leader come inside without them.

Ares had been part of a group of snipers and their spotters who were sent in when the bad guys had a shapeshifter on their side. The snipers used silver-coated ammo to take out shapeshifters from a nice safe distance. Apparently, a werehyena had figured it out and gotten very not nice, not safe, and oh-so-close. Again, once Ares' blood test showed the lycan-thropy, it was policy to do a medical discharge even though he'd gotten the "disease" in the line of duty. Ares still had a golden tan from some-where hot and dry, his yellow hair buzzed as short as Bram's, but beyond a certain military bearing they weren't much alike. Bram had said, "Snipers think differently than my specialty."

"And what is your specialty?" I'd asked.

He'd given me a little smile and said, "Up-close work." And that was all he'd say.

Micah looked small with Lisandro and Bram looming over him, but I guess no smaller than I looked with Claudia and Domino behind me, or for that matter sitting with the two six-feet-and-over guys on either side of Nathaniel and me. Micah had a gun at the small of his back, too. One of the things I had liked about Micah from the very beginning was that he was a shooter. We both had spent years being the smallest person in the room, and when everyone in the room is more than human-strong, and either as trained a fighter as you are or better, you want the gun. And the rule is, if you carry a gun you must be willing to use it. If you hesitate with a gun you might as well not carry one, because hesitation will get you killed quicker than not having one at all. There are people every year who get their own gun taken away from them by a bad guy and then the bad guy shoots them with it. If you carry, you have got to be willing to pull the trigger; if you think you'll hesitate, then don't carry. Micah didn't hesitate, and neither did I. We liked that about each other.

I knew that everyone at my back was armed and would not hesitate. If Haven wanted to die tonight, he'd come to the right place. I felt that part of me that helped me look down the barrel of a gun and pull the trigger open up, or close down, inside me. I felt distant and empty. It was almost a clean feeling: no distractions, no doubts, just what had to be done. I wasn't quite to that white-static center where I pulled the trigger, but I was headed that way. The moment I felt myself go all distant and empty, I would know that part of me had decided to kill Haven. Part of me wanted to keep him alive, but it wasn't as big a part of me as I'd thought. I felt a little bad about that, but not a lot. A year ago, I'd have poked at the feeling, but not now. Now I waited to see if Haven would give me a reason to keep him alive or give me an excuse to kill him.

We'd actually gone to little earbud headsets for the guards, and for me and Jean-Claude. I had to green-light the shooters. A voice on the earbud made me jump; I still wasn't used to it. "Eagle here, darling." Bobby-Lee's southern drawl was almost startling after so many months without him. He'd been away on some hush-hush job for the wererats. They did mercenary work to bring in money for their group. Bobby Lee had been away for a long time. He'd come back more tanned than when he'd left, thinner, too, and worn around the edges. The old British saying was *You've been in the wars*. Probably closer to true than I wanted to know.

"Yeah," I said, my pulse in my throat from jumping, "I mean Black Queen here." Eagle was whoever was in charge of the guards overall on a shift. Black Queen was my call sign. No, it wasn't my idea, but until I thought of a better one I couldn't bitch too much. Yes, Jean-Claude was Black King. Like no one was going to figure that out.

"The lions are on their way down. It's the Rex, two bodyguards, the two new female lions, and two other males that Haven's okay with you feeding on, just like you negotiated, darlin', but the two feeders are a little worse for wear."

"Stop calling me darling, and what does that mean . . . Eagle?"

"Means someone has beat the shit out of them. They're being carried down to you all."

"What the fuck," I said.

"Are ya asking why he beat 'em to shit?" Bobby Lee asked.

"Yeah, I am," I said.

"White King seems to think you've fucked them more than you've fucked him. He didn't like that." White King wasn't the code for Haven, but for any VIP of a visiting vampire or animal group. You had to be more welcome here to have your own code sign.

"Jesus," I whispered, "I haven't fed on many . . . Oh, shit. No, he didn't."

"You'll have to finish a sentence there, Black Queen, before I can give you an answer," Bobby Lee said.

"Shit, I don't know how to do this and not say names." I looked at Jean-Claude.

He covered his earbud and spoke low. "Who do you fear it is?"

"Noel and Travis," I said. They were in college and were two that had survived from the old pride's leadership to Haven's new regime. I had used them to help me control my lion when Nicky wasn't available, but I hadn't fed the *ardeur* on them, because they were too young. They were legal, but young in experience. As far as I could discover, Noel was a virgin.

I was so not going to be his first. I had tried to persuade the old Rex, Joseph, that they were too tender to throw to the *ardeur*, but he hadn't understood. Apparently Haven hadn't understood, either. It was just a different misunderstanding.

Jean-Claude spoke to that invisible voice. "Joe College and Christmas are who the Black Queen is concerned about."

"The concern is well placed, Black King."

"Shit," I said.

"Yep," Bobby Lee said, "that about covers it, Black Queen."

I didn't want to have to deny I'd had sex with Travis and Noel over the open airwaves, as it were; besides, I'd learned a long time ago that you can't prove a negative. You can prove that you did something, but it's the devil to prove you didn't do something.

Nathaniel said it for me since he wasn't on the headset. "You haven't had sex with Noel and Travis."

"I know that, but apparently the White King doesn't believe that." I fumbled at the neckpiece, trying to turn it off for a minute, but I couldn't remember how. I was angry. I hadn't been angry until now. It gave me an idea.

"Eagle, how angry is White King?"

"Angry enough to fry your bacon from a distance."

"You know, you can give the quaint southernisms a rest, Eagle."

"Are you disparaging my heritage there, Black Queen?"

"No, just cranky." I turned to Jean-Claude. "Help me turn this off."

He pressed something and I was suddenly alone in my own head again; yea. "You've thought of something," he said.

I nodded. "I can feed on anger, remember?"

"I remember, *ma petite*."

"Haven is angry; I'll feed on it."

"If you feed on his anger, he may take that as a form of attack," Richard said.

I looked past Jean-Claude to him. "If he's hurt Noel and Travis as badly as Bobby Lee says, then I'm not sure I care if he thinks he's being attacked."

"If you kill him, fine, but make sure you kill him because he needs killing, Anita, not just because you're pissed at him," Richard said.

I started to say something angry back, but Nathaniel touched my arm, and Damian touched my shoulder a moment later. They were both calmer than I was, and some of that calm seeped into me. It helped me take a deep breath and let it out slow. I nodded. "Point taken, but I can't let him hurt them like this and get away unpunished. If I do, then we won't have control of the lions, and Haven will do something worse."

Micah said, "He's like a teenager acting out. He wants your attention even if it's negative attention."

"Are you blaming me for this?" I asked, and the anger was just there again. Damian's hand tightened on my shoulder. Nathaniel put his hand in mine. It helped me push the anger down again, but it was there and if I wasn't careful it could raise my beasts and then we would be in a mess.

"I'm just saying that Haven thinks like the fifteen-year-old he was when he joined the werelions. He's stuck there emotionally. It makes him react to things."

"What do I do?" I asked, and that I asked him was a mark of what we meant to each other. I didn't ask many people's opinion.

"Save Noel and Travis first; get them on this side of the room, then see if Haven is willing to be reasonable."

"Reasonable how?" I asked.

"Sex, maybe."

"I don't want to fuck him; I'm so mad at him I can't see straight."

"May I offer an opinion, *ma petite*?"

I turned back to the man at my side. "Please, at this point I'm taking suggestions. I am in over my head here." I said out loud what I'd thought earlier. "This would be easier if you had a tie to the lions, and not just me."

Jean-Claude looked at me. His face was unreadable, but it was a long, considering look. "Augustine said he spoke to you about the lions and certain possibilities."

"We don't have time for coy, Jean-Claude. He told me that there was a chance, if you slept with the women of some of the cat-based animal groups, that you might gain them as your animal to call, too. He thinks you might be able to gain an animal through me, instead of me always gaining through you."

"Are you saying you want us to sleep with the female cats?" Richard asked.

I looked at him. "No, I'm saying maybe Jean-Claude should sleep with them." I added, because he was looking at me, "Jean-Claude makes me feel secure. You don't yet, Richard. Jean-Claude has hung in there while I fucked a lot of other men. He's been a good sport, so maybe it's my turn to be a good sport."

"*Ma petite*, the lions will be here in moments; I want to be very clear between us. Are you saying that you would be open to me sleeping with the female lions while you sleep with the males?"

I fought not to cross my arms or look pouty. "I think so, oh, hell, I don't know. As a theory, I think it's got merit."

"Merit?" Jean-Claude said. "That is not a strong enough word to get me into another woman's bed, *ma petite*. I think merit would come back and, how would you say, bite me on the ass."

I couldn't blame him. "I need help, Jean-Claude. The leopards work because Micah is reasonable and wants to help me, and he's leopard king to my queen. The tigers work because so far the only males in town are mine. We don't have a tiger group to get pissy with me. The rats and swans work not because they're our animal to call but because their leaders value the order you've brought to the city and they want to help that along."

Jean-Claude spoke into the air, into his earpiece, whatever. "Give us a moment." He forgot all about code names as he turned to me. "The lions are outside the door, and making Haven wait will not help things. Do you want me to try to seduce one of the women into my bed? It must be yes or no."

"Can I think about it?" I asked.

"No. Yes or no."

"No sex for tonight, but make friends so that maybe another night soon you can."

"Not precise enough," he said. "I will not be punished for doing what you tell me to do. Tell me to seduce them, or tell me don't, and tell me now."

I stared at him and didn't know what to say. But he was right; I had to decide now. Fuck. "I don't know how I feel about you with another woman that I haven't met. Can I meet them first and then ask me again?"

He smiled at me. "You may." He spoke back to the headgear. "Let the White King through." Silence and then he said, "Yes, the Black Queen and the Black King are in agreement, bring them through."

I didn't bother to turn my own headset back on because I was pretty sure that I wouldn't want anything I said in the next few minutes on an open frequency, and I didn't have to worry about giving a green light to one of our snipers. The lions had all gone home except the ones pushing their way through the curtains now. All the dangerous things were in here with us.

16

Two of our guards came through first, holding the long drapes aside so that Haven and his lions could go through. He was around six feet tall, a little narrower through the shoulders than I liked, but what frame he had was muscled. He took his conditioning seriously, but lions are more prone to have fights for dominance at short notice. Staying in shape could be the difference between living or dying. Most lions took their exercise pretty seriously because of that.

He was wearing a long, pale trench coat over a nice suit. He was all tans and cream, as if the clothing were a preview of the lion inside him. His hair was still shades of blue, with highlights and lowlights as if blue were a natural color for human hair, so that the dye job was still one of the best unnatural shades I'd ever seen. The hair was shaved short on the sides and longer on top so he could gel it in little spikes. His eyes were still blue. My lioness sniffed the air as soon as I saw him, because primate that I was, I wanted to see him, but my lioness wanted to smell him.

His power crept over me as if warm breath had suddenly drifted over every inch of my skin. I shivered and my lioness began to pad up that long metaphysical path. She'd liked Haven from the moment we met him. I'd known bad news when I saw it. But nothing changed how much my body wanted him. I wanted to be naked and roll every inch of me over every inch of him the way a cat will luxuriate while it's scent-marking. He was mine and I was his the way that Micah and I had belonged to each other. My pulse sped.

Nathaniel's hand tightened in mine, and Damian scooted closer, putting his arm around us both. It helped me think, helped slow my pulse. Jean-Claude put his hand in my last free hand, and that helped even more. I didn't have to look to know that Richard had put his arm across the couch so that he was touching Jean-Claude, too. I knew we were all touching, and with every touch I was a little less the victim of the lion inside me, and the one walking into the room.

Haven's energy breathed harder against my skin. I smelled sun-burnt grass, dust, and the rich scent of lion. Once it would have been enough to bring my lioness crashing against the walls of my body; with everyone's hands on me it was tempting, but I didn't have to give in to it.

A low growl vibrated out from between those human lips. The sound of it seemed to vibrate along my spine, as if my body were a tuning fork and that one low sound hit just the right note. I tried to stand up and hands held me in my seat. I turned on them, snarling, my lioness loud in my head.

Haven strode across the carpet toward us, and I knew he meant to jerk me free of all that restraint. His power went before him like an advance attack. I could either stand up and go to him in this body, or my lioness could try to go to him in a different one. I actually got to my feet. Jean-Claude and Nathaniel still had my hands, but I was standing, wanting Haven to touch me. His energy seemed strong, and giving in to it a little had kept the lion from trying to tear her way out of me.

Bram was a dark blur just suddenly appearing in front of me, blocking Haven's way. I knew that Micah had told him to do it. A small logical part of me knew why he'd done it, and even agreed as Nimir-Ra, but the lioness didn't agree. She snarled at Bram's tall form between her and her Rex. She'd have had the same reaction if Bram had stood between her and prey. I pulled free of Nathaniel's hand. Only Jean-Claude kept me from either jumping Bram or just running around him. Truthfully, attacking from behind was the first plan. The visual was of me as a lion on his back, claws digging into his flesh, my teeth sinking into his scalp, his head, crushing his skull.

The visceral almost-memory helped me climb back into my head and push the lioness back. I was a person, not an animal. I could control this. I didn't want to hurt Bram.

When Haven felt my lion go cold, his energy was still there, still seeking lion. It found the lions he'd brought with him. Their energy flared. I could see it, not with my eyes, but with the back of my head. I knew it was Jesse, tall, dark, and handsome, and Payne, tall, pale, and handsome. Payne really was his last name, not a nickname since he was an enforcer. But I saw their lions around them like halos, one with a mane that was almost black and the other so pale it was ghostlike. But there were other lions behind them: a woman I didn't know, tall, strongly built, but all curves. I had an impression of short dark hair, but mostly her lioness was tawny with darker marks so that she looked almost spotted in places. The other woman was much shorter, with long yellow hair, but her lioness wasn't smaller. It was a huge golden form snarling around her human body as if it were a wick and the lion the flame.

Then I saw two more lions lying on the floor. They didn't burn bright. Their lions were red-orange glows like a fire that was fading. They were younger lions, with shorter manes, ragged compared to the other men. Their lions turned and looked at me, one with a halo of dark mane, the other paler, but the lions looked at me. They knew me.

I suddenly saw the world through a golden haze. I turned my head and I could see my lioness over me like a glow just behind my eyes. She, like the other short woman, wasn't a small lion. She was a great dark gold shape rearing over and around me. I'd seen Micah's leopard once like this around him, but never again. Now all I could see was lions.

One of the lions on the floor stirred and lifted his head, and I had the double image of Travis; it was his golden-brown curls with that darker mane around it like an overlay. He looked at me, and he fought to reach his hand out toward me. Injured, it was the closest he could come to the begging gesture that most of the lycanthropes had. It was a submissive's way of asking a dominant to forgive him, to help him.

Noel lay very still beside him. The image of his lion was a dark red shadow, growing dimmer. Some part of me knew what that meant. Noel was dying. In that moment the lioness and I were in agreement. You didn't kill what was ours. In the wild, lionesses will band together to keep a male intruder from taking over a pride. They'll fight beside their chosen males to keep their land, their cubs, safe.

I tried to go around Bram and Haven. I just wanted to get to Noel before that energy died completely. Bram let me walk around, but Haven grabbed for me, and he was faster than either Bram or I thought, because his hand was around my upper arm before Bram could react.

The moment he touched me, all that golden energy swirled together like some golden bonfire. So much power, so much energy. It felt so good. He kissed me while my eyes were still closed from the rush of power. I kissed him back and we opened our eyes and it was like we stood in the center of cool, golden fire.

He smiled down at me, and I had to smile back. Then I heard a voice. "Anita." The voice sounded broken, and I looked behind me. Travis was reaching for me and Noel . . .

I looked up at Haven. "We save Noel first, then we'll talk."

Haven's grip tightened around me. "Even now, feeling this power and you want him. Them?"

"He's dying."

"The weak die; it's the way of lions."

"With this power we can call his beast. We can save him."

His arms tightened further around me. "I don't want him saved."

"I do."

"Be with me and we can save him."

I'd kissed him without thinking, and now my arms were pinned down between our bodies with his arms wrapped around me. I couldn't reach either gun or the big knife down my back, but I could reach the wrist sheaths. I pretended to struggle ineffectually and knew Haven of all the men in my life would buy it. One of our problems was that he just couldn't see women as equal. Equally dangerous, that is.

I used the struggling to hide my drawing one of the slender silver blades, and only as he felt my arm tense to drive the blade home did he realize his danger.

He started to let me go, to get distance, but I had time to start the blade into his body. Had time to feel it sink home, the razor-sharp blade slicing through his shirt and the meat underneath, sinking home the way it had a hundred other times in big bad monsters. The only thing that saved him was that he had my arms pinned too low on his body for me to reach his heart, even if he hadn't moved.

He let me go, stumbling back from me. I had time to see the blood on my knife, the first bloom of red on his shirt, the surprise on his face. His two guards were frozen, not knowing what to do. It was as if they hadn't believed I'd hurt him.

I yelled to our guards, "Keep him off me until I've healed Noel." I didn't turn my back on the wounded werelion, but I backed up as fast as I could. Bram and the other guards were moving around Haven ready to do exactly what I'd said.

The taller female werelion was kneeling beside Noel. She was stroking his hair, and I realized the moment I'd stabbed Haven that the double vision of glowing lions overlaid on the human form had vanished, as if I'd done something to damage all that power.

The woman raised brown eyes to me. They were shiny with unshed tears. She whispered, "You're too late."

17

I LAID MY hand on Noel's back. I waited for his body to breathe, but it didn't come. "Shit," I said. "Get Dr. Lillian, get someone. Get some fucking medics down here now!"

I heard someone on their cell phone doing what I'd asked. *Please, God, don't let him die.* He was only twenty-four, a year older than Nathaniel. The brown-haired woman knelt by his head, tears beginning to trail down her face. "Don't cry, not yet," I said. She looked at me, startled. I realized she was wearing a red dress. It was as if I were only seeing things in pieces. The other female lion came to stand by us. Her long blond hair was tied back in a ponytail, and she was wearing almost as many weapons as I was. "This wasn't our choice."

I realized that the guards and the other three lions were fighting. Haven was trying to get to me, whether to hurt me back or try for another kiss I didn't know and I didn't give a fuck. I trusted the guards to keep him off me. Hell, I trusted Wicked and Truth alone to keep a small army of werelions off me. Three lions was nothing.

"If we had a real Regina or Rex, we could delay it," the blonde said.

I nodded, because to some part of me that sounded logical. I remembered the energy between Haven and me, and the ghosts of fire around the other werelions. I prayed, *Help me save him.* I visualized my lioness, but not inside me; I tried to call that shining, golden fire that had been around us all just minutes ago.

The blonde knelt by me. "Like this," she said, and suddenly I could see her lioness again, so much bigger than her human form, a wavering golden energy that looked at me with golden eyes while her blue eyes stared at me through a lion's mask.

I reached out, and the moment her hand came near enough mine it was as if I caught fire. My lioness blazed around us, golden, shining, burning bright. I turned dark gold eyes to the other woman and held out my hand. She reached out and the three of us knelt over Noel. We didn't touch hands, but it was as if that pulsing energy touched the fire of our lions.

"We put energy into him, force his beast," the blonde said.

"Do it," I said.

She reached down to Noel's still form, and our hands came with hers so that we all touched him at the same time. But it was like trying to heat stone; there was no answering spark. I knew how to work with the dead, but not like this.

"It's too late," the dark-haired woman said.

"No!" I said.

"Maybe," the blonde said.

I called out, "Jean-Claude!"

He came to me, kneeling beside me. "What would you have of me, *ma petite?*"

"He's too far gone. Help me."

He didn't say the obvious, that he didn't know how, or that we'd never attempted anything like this. He simply called, "Richard, Nathaniel, Damian, come."

Nathaniel and Damian came immediately. Nathaniel asked, "Where do you want us?"

"Touch your master," Jean-Claude said.

They laid a hand on each of my shoulders as they knelt, and the moment they touched me I felt my eyes go. Through the golden glow of the lions I knew my eyes burned like dark brown stars. Nathaniel and Damian cried out beside me and they turned purple and green glowing eyes to me. The lion's energy flowed over them both. Nathaniel's leopard sprang to life like some wavering black shape. Damian had no animal to flow and he was just covered in the gold of lions.

Jean-Claude knelt behind the three of us and laid his hands over theirs, so we all touched. The energy flowed over him, too, but I felt it spark, like a jolt of electricity through it all. I didn't have to see it to know that his eyes had sunk to midnight-blue fire.

Richard stood above us, hesitating. "What do I do?"

"Touch Jean-Claude," I said.

I wasn't sure he'd do it, but he did. He stayed on his feet so he loomed above us all, but laid his hands over Jean-Claude's and the power spread, flowed. I heard him say, "God!" Then I felt Jean-Claude move closer against my body. I moved my legs apart so he could press as much of himself against as much of me as possible. I knew that Richard, still standing, was pressed against the back of Jean-Claude.

The five of us knelt in a flickering bonfire of different-colored energy, but it didn't travel to the lions. Their power flowed to us, but not the other way. I realized that the blond woman's hand was just above mine, not touching.

I grabbed her hand. She startled and started to pull away, saying, "It doesn't work like that . . . ," but then our energy jumped the circuit. It flowed down my hand and into her. Her hand convulsed around mine and around the dark-haired woman. I saw the black flame of my leopard, the spark of Jean-Claude's eyes, and the emerald glow of Damian, and a reddish shine that had to be Richard's wolf flow into the lions.

The dark-haired woman laid her hand on Noel. His body jumped as the power shoved into him. His human body split, gushing thick, warm, liquid around our knees. Fur flowed over him until he lay in the shape of a huge lion. Its dark mane was not very thick, not very impressive, but I didn't give a damn. I just wanted him to breathe.

Micah was suddenly there. He knelt on the other side of Nathaniel and took his other hand. The power jumped another octave.

The woman touching him said, "Heartbeat, but he's not breathing."

I felt lion, more lion, running down the hallway toward us. I knew it was Nicky still in lionman form. He was coming for the fight, coming toward the energy we were raising. I knew that the lions more than the other animal groups gave off energy to attract, or warn off, other lions, but I hadn't understood until this moment that there were other things you could do with all that power.

Noel spat blood onto the floor, but he had to be breathing to do that. The blonde kept the energy concentrated on him as I turned to look at Nicky. The golden lionman burst through the curtains and started toward the fight, but I said, "Nicky, I need you."

He never hesitated. He simply turned toward us and said, "Where do I go?"

I said the first thing that came to mind. "Puppy pile, touch as much as you can." It was all I could think of; the kind of vampire we were worked better with touch, and more touch couldn't hurt. He laid all that golden lionman across Noel's lion, and put his arm around Travis, drawing the still form in with us. Nicky put one hand out and grabbed my belt, putting his big fingers inside it against my bare waist. My lioness flared into that bonfire of energy, and Nicky's rose with mine. It wasn't as bright as it had been with Haven, but it was bright, and it was power, and it joined all the other power seamlessly. I realized what we'd missed, what we'd needed, willingness without will of its own. Nicky gave himself to this as he'd given himself to everything I'd asked of him since he became mine.

Barriers broke that I hadn't even known were still there. Richard stopped holding back, Damian stopped being afraid, Jean-Claude stopped being so careful, the blond woman let go of some deep anger, the dark-haired one let go of love searching for love, there wasn't enough left of Travis to give up anything else, Nathaniel gave up the last of his fear that I'd grow tired of him, Micah gave up that hard, deep rage that I'd never even known was there, and I gave up my control. I wanted Noel alive more than I wanted to be in control.

The power flared around us in a dark rainbow of energy. It blazed toward the ceiling. If it had been real fire it would have burned the Circus to the ground. We took that power and shoved it into Noel. I'd worked with other animators when we needed to raise a lot of, or very old, dead. I'd been trained to share power with others with similar talents and work as a unit. One magic is surprisingly like another.

Travis grabbed hold of the nearest lioness. I thought he meant to be healed until I saw his own dim orange-gold lion flare and realized he was giving up his own energy to Noel. With all that energy he gave and did not keep for himself.

Nicky wrapped his furred arms around the two lions. His grip on me tightened and he gave everything to me, no holding back, no fear, no hesitation. He let me have anything, everything, and he helped the rest of us give up, give in, and feed it to Noel. Noel shuddered and then he began to breathe. His furred side rose and fell, and I could hear his heartbeat. I could feel the rush and flow of the blood in his veins, feel the rise and fall of his life that we'd fought so hard to give him, and on the heels of that was a desire to bite him. It was a desire to bury my teeth in that warm fur until I found blood, and I realized that we'd given up our control, all of it. I was kneeling in a pile of wereanimals and vampires who'd given up their controls. We wanted flesh and blood. We wanted to feed.

Richard's voice, strained, said, "Anita, change it. Change it to something else, don't let us."

Jean-Claude said, "Change the feeding to something we can survive, *ma petite*. Change it or we will tear the lion apart after saving him."

I was drowning in the scent of fur, the feel of flesh. I realized that Nicky was rubbing his face against Noel's side. We so wanted to take a bite. "Help me, help us not do this. Jean-Claude, help me!"

"The *ardeur, ma petite*, like this it will be . . ."

"Do it!"

I wasn't the only one that screamed it; Micah and Richard echoed me. We all valued our control above almost everything, but in this moment we were out of control. It was just a matter of what we lost. I wanted to sink fangs and claws into that soft, breathing form. It was as if the power had turned on itself and become about death instead of life.

I smelled flowers, jasmine. Oh, God. But it wasn't her or not her alone, and not her voice that echoed through my head. It was a male voice that I'd never heard before. "Feed and I will feast," and then he laughed, a manic, insane sound.

I heard Jean-Claude think it—"The Lover of Death, God help us all"— and I knew in the fast-forward way that he could communicate with his servants that the Lover of Death, Morte d'Amour, fed on death the way that Belle fed on lust. He was the creator of the vampires that rotted, but were the hardest to kill of all. He would feed on the energy of every life we took. He was the ultimate carrion crow, a psychic vulture.

Jean-Claude took that need to stab and tear and bite, to taste raw flesh and have fresh blood gush in our mouths and over our bodies, and turned it to the only other hunger we had. One moment I was kneeling there with the feel of him behind me. I knew where everyone was and what we were doing, and then the *ardeur* hit the energy we'd raised. Hit it and exploded all that power out into the room.

I had a moment to hear the Lover of Death wail, "No, I cannot feed on that." I smelled jasmine and disappointment, because the Mother of All Darkness could only feed on what her host could feed on. Belle had escaped somehow and no one else could feed on the feast we were about to give them.

I had a moment of fierce happiness about that, and then there was nothing but hands and bodies and things to do with teeth that didn't kill, but would leave a mark.

18

I DREAMED. I knew it was a dream, but I also knew I wasn't alone in the dream. I walked through a building I'd never been in, turning on lights, but just behind me each room went dark again. I couldn't turn the lights on fast enough and in the last room where I turned on the light, there was a moment of brightness and then darkness came.

I woke, pulse in my throat and the amulet around my neck glowing softly. The glow faded, but I knew it had been her. The Mother of All Darkness had hunted me in my dream. She wasn't strong enough to talk to me without another vampire's body or powers to help her. Alone she was just that shiver that makes you walk faster at night. You don't know why you do it, but some part of you remembers that the dark is never really empty.

As my pulse slowed, and the glow faded, I saw and felt where I was, and my pulse went right back up into my throat. There was a weight across my shoulders and something across my lower legs and I was staring into Wicked's face from inches away. What I could see of him seemed to be nude, and the only reason I couldn't see below the waist was that there was a woman collapsed face down across him. Her long yellow hair hid just how nude he might be, but she was nude.

I raised my head on the white carpet, knowing we were still in the living room of the Circus. Raising my head showed me that the drapes that made up this side of the "walls" had been torn down. There were more bodies in the twisted drapes, arms and legs, hair, a face that I recognized as one of the female vampires who worked at Danse Macabre. She'd been in the coffin room last night getting ready to bed down for the day, which meant that the *ardeur* had spread outside this room. Shit.

I was almost afraid to rise up more. Almost afraid to find out whose arm was across my shoulders, because I could feel it was probably male and the line of body touching mine seemed to be nude, just like I was. Fuck. The weight across my lower legs was someone else's legs, no, not just legs. Male, whoever it was. Crap.

Fuck this, I had to get up. I even had to see who it was, I couldn't hide. Nope, it was too late for that. I rose up on my elbows. The arm across my shoulders rolled limply down my body. I took a deep breath and turned to see who belonged to the arm.

People look different out of their clothes, especially facedown on carpet. Short dark hair, curly, broad shoulders, darker complected, tall . . . It was the pile of ripped clothes on the other side of me with the pale trench coat on top that let me know it was Jesse the werelion. I had no memory of how he got out of his clothes. Did that mean we hadn't had sex and he'd just collapsed here, or that I just wasn't going to remember what I'd done?

Asher was lying near the fireplace on his side, wrapped around Meng Die, who lay on her back. Her shoulder-length black hair was spread around her like a fan, her body pale and perfect, and if they'd had sex together then all bets were off. It hadn't been about who you were attracted to last night, apparently. There was someone else on the other side of the mound of clothes but I couldn't see enough to know who it was, and since they weren't touching me I stopped trying to look. I looked down my body and again nude I wouldn't have been sure, but I thought Lisandro's face was turned toward me. His long black hair had come undone from his ponytail and trailed across his shoulders, almost hiding scratch marks on his back. One of his legs was partially across mine, his groin still pressed against my hip. I'd had enough sex to be pretty sure he'd been doing me from behind and then collapsed beside me, and then the lights had gone out. That meant the scratch marks weren't mine. A small blessing. He wasn't one of the guards that willingly fed me. Something about a wife. Shit. *Oh, I'm sorry, dear, I had to have sex with my boss because there was this metaphysical explosion and it was either fuck or kill each other.* Yeah, that was a conversation disaster waiting to happen.

I debated on whether they'd wake if I tried to crawl out from between them. If they were vampires, I wouldn't have worried, but wereanimals are like people; they just wake up.

"I do not believe they will wake, *ma petite*, if you wish to move."

I turned my head, craning back over my shoulder. My neck hurt. I raised my hand to find a bite mark. Jean-Claude was sitting in one of the overstuffed chairs. He was nude, legs carefully crossed, his long black curls disarrayed on one side as if there were something in it that . . . I just stopped that thought in its tracks. I didn't want to think about it, any of it.

I explored the wound and knew it was a vampire bite. As I started to crawl out from between Jesse and Lisandro, there were other sharp little pains in different places. Some of them weren't in typical places for a vampire to take blood. What the fuck was that about?

There were bite marks over one nipple, and higher up the chest. I was on all fours, looking down the line of my body, debating whether my legs would hold me. There was dried blood between my thighs, but it didn't have the feel to it of someone too large and too vigorous. It felt like I had multiple bites along both sides of my thighs. This many bites, I shouldn't have woken up at all. That many bites should have bled me dry.

I had a moment of my skin running cold with fear, and then I suddenly felt a whole lot better about waking up nude, in the middle of what looked like a hell of an orgy. It was better than not waking up at all.

Jean-Claude was in front of me, his hands on my arms, helping me to my feet. I had a moment of looking into his face, unreadable, shut down, and then I wrapped my arms around him, put my head against his chest, and started to shake. He held me, kissed the top of my head, and murmured, "*Ma petite*, I am so sorry."

"Not to complain," I said in a voice that was a lot less solid than his, "but why didn't I bleed to death from all the vampire feedings? I've got at least eight. That's enough to drain me dry."

He stroked my hair, and answered me, "I am not certain. I believe the *ardeur* saved you. There are multiple bites on most of the wereanimals, but none are dead. The *ardeur* is about life. I turned the Lover of Death's urge to life. My last solid thought was that we would not feed on death; we fed on life, on love, and I would not have my people serve the dark. We would serve the light."

I turned my head so I could look up into his face. "You really thought all that? I didn't have time to think much of anything."

He smiled at me. "It was in French, but that is the gist of what I tried to do with the power."

I hugged him tighter. "Is it night again?"

"No."

I frowned up at him. "You're awake again. What time is it?"

"We all passed out from the *ardeur*, but I do not believe I died at dawn."

"Sometimes you don't die at dawn when you and I are touching, but we weren't, were we?"

"*Non*, but there was a great deal of power to feed on, *ma petite*."

I was almost afraid to look around, but I couldn't be a coward. I couldn't tolerate that, so . . . I turned in his arms and looked farther into the room. There were bodies everywhere. They lay so still that if Jean-Claude hadn't told me no one was dead I'd have wanted to start checking pulses. Micah was on the other side of the room, as if he hadn't moved far from where we'd all started with the werelions. There was a pile of bodies near him, like a prettier version of the plague engravings depicting wagonloads of bodies to dump. Micah lay partially on top of that pile. I thought at first that the body entwined with him, arms and legs, was one of the male guards, but realized that I had the only man with long, straight, dark hair by me. I looked at that muscular back, those shoulders, those arms, and suddenly could see that it was Claudia. Her head was on Micah's chest, his arms and one leg around her, his head back against someone else's back.

"Where's Nathaniel?" I asked.

"In the hallway with Jason, J.J., and a few others."

"Richard, Damian?"

Someone groaned, the bodies on the loveseat began to shift, and one tanned, muscular arm came out from all the paler bodies. Richard's face, his hair wild around him, rose from the other bodies as if he were struggling to the surface of thick water. He looked bleary-eyed and confused for a second, and then I watched comprehension fill his face. I wondered if I'd looked as shocked.

He looked at the woman in his lap, and I realized it was the blond vampire, Gretchen. She was completely limp as he stood with her in his arms. His moving made the others slide into the spot he'd emptied on the loveseat. I recognized Byron, one of the vampire strippers at Guilty Pleasures. The woman who collapsed against Byron had bright red hair. It had to be Cardinal. Richard put Gretchen gently on the floor since there was no more room on the loveseat. His back was covered in scratch marks, some of them bloody. Were some of them mine?

He turned and there was dried blood coming down one side of his neck, and his thighs. He had a bite at the bend of his elbow, too. He, like me, should have been dead from blood loss.

He had more scratches on his arms, and even down the sides of his body. Someone, or someones, had liked nails. He had to pick his way between the bodies. I realized the big glass coffee table was missing. I glanced around Jean-Claude and found the remains of the table in the tangle of torn draperies.

"I do not think I will buy another glass table." Jean-Claude said. "Metal, perhaps."

Richard was almost to us; he just had to concentrate on where his feet went in the labyrinth of body parts. "I don't remember anything after you turned the craving for death into the *ardeur*," he said, still looking at the floor as he finished the last few careful steps.

"Me, either," I said.

"Nor I," Jean-Claude said.

Richard caught his foot on a leg that had been hidden under the pile of clothes. Jean-Claude and I both caught his arm, an automatic gesture. I got a sudden flash of memory: Jean-Claude and Richard kissing passionately. Richard ripping Jean-Claude's black shirt away to show white skin through the tattered black, and then Richard's part was gone. I was suddenly thrown deeper into the sensory memory of Jean-Claude behind me, inside me, and Noel in human form in front of me. I was going down on him, and the blond female lion was coming in to kiss him.

I was suddenly standing by myself not touching anyone. I had to blink hard to see the here and now. "What was that?" I asked.

"Memory," Jean-Claude said.

"It stopped when I pulled away. I didn't want to see what happened next." Richard sounded so angry. What did he think had happened? Oh, and had it? All I remembered was them kissing and him helping me undress Jean-Claude, but I had a vague memory of other hands pulling at Richard, pulling him away.

"I don't think you did what you think you did," I said.

He glared at me, and I knew he was shielding as hard as he could so that his anger didn't touch us with heat, or raise my beast. I appreciated the control, but I also knew that if he thought he and Jean-Claude had had full-blown sex, it could ruin all the positive work he'd done. It could throw everything back the way it had been. I liked us getting along better, but I wasn't sure how to save it.

"We did not have sex, Richard," Jean-Claude said.

"I saw us," he said.

"You saw a kiss and a little petting, but it was Gretchen who touched you and pulled you away."

"I woke up with her in my lap. She loves you in a stalker, obsessed sort of way. Shouldn't her depth of love for you keep her safe from the *ardeur*? I thought love kept you safe."

"She was likely pulling you away from me, but once she touched you the *ardeur* spread to her, and she likes men well enough that she did not have enough defenses to leave you for me. She does not love me; she is obsessed with me. Obsession is not love, Richard, it is a type of possessing. Love is not about owning someone, but about loving them."

"If love makes us proof against it, then . . ." I couldn't bring myself to finish the sentence.

"Then does it mean that none of us love each other?" Jean-Claude said. "No, *ma petite*. This was not *ardeur* for feeding, but the feeding taking the place of the slaughter that the Lover of Death wanted us to perform. It was all the energy we had raised and more turning from the beast's hunger, or the vampire's thirst, to sex. It was a food that the Lover of Death could not stomach, so he was pushed away."

"I heard him and I got your memories of him," Richard said, and shuddered.

"I just got how dangerous he was and how he feeds on death the way Belle feeds on lust. Did you get something I didn't?" I asked.

Richard looked at Jean-Claude. He wasn't angry now. "Every time I think I've been abused, then I get another memory from your past and I realize that it could have been worse."

Jean-Claude looked away, which meant he wasn't sure he had control of his face. He almost always had control of his expression. He'd once told me that after a few hundred years of your facial expressions being used against you by bigger, badder vampires, you learned to hide your emotions so deep that sometimes it was hard to show them at all.

"What am I missing?" I asked.

Richard just looked at the other man. It made me look at Jean-Claude. I had a moment to think about it, then said, "The Lover of Death doesn't feed on sex."

"You met Yvette, his minion," Jean-Claude said.

"She was a sadist and enjoyed rotting on people especially during sex."

He nodded. "She wanted to do that to Jason because it frightened him so."

"But you wouldn't let her; we wouldn't let her. You protected him from her," I said.

He finally looked at me, and his face was empty, not charming, but just empty. "When I went back to Belle to save Asher's life, she ceased to protect me from anything for a time."

I just stared at him, and knew that my face showed the thought. "She gave you to . . ."

"He doesn't truly like sex, but he still is functional, and he does enjoy fear."

I went to him, going on tiptoe, and putting my arms around his shoulders, drawing his head down to me. In that moment I wasn't bothered by whatever was dried on the side of his hair. Nothing we'd done was as terrible as what he'd been through. "I'm so sorry," I whispered.

Then there were other arms around us, tentative at first, and then Richard hugged us both. "I'm not happy about what just happened, and it reminds me why I stay the hell away from you, but nothing we've ever done, including today, is as terrible as the glimpses I get of your past." Richard raised his head up, and it made me glance at his face. "Aren't most of your worst stories things the council did to you?"

"Most," he said softly.

"And now they're going to try to take us over," he said.

"It would seem so."

"No," Richard said, "whatever it takes, no."

Jean-Claude looked back at the other man. Their faces were close, and I remembered the kiss, not as some visceral memory, but just as a memory. "You do not know what might be required to fight them, Richard."

"You may be a manipulative bastard sometimes, but you're *our* manipulative bastard."

Jean-Claude actually smiled at that. "Such flattery will go to a man's head, *mon lupe*."

Richard smiled, but his eyes stayed serious. "Morte d'Amour is evil, Jean-Claude. I felt him in my head, I felt what he wanted us to do to Noel, and once we'd killed Noel it wouldn't have stopped with him. He'd have made us kill each other and fed on every death."

"That was his plan," Jean-Claude said.

"Sex is not worse than that," Richard said.

"What can we do to keep them away from us?" I asked.

"We can keep them away, I think, but I am worried for our poor country. There are weaker Masters of the City, *ma petite*. I am wondering how they fared this night."

"You mean when he couldn't roll us, he hunted for other prey?" I asked.

"The Mother wants us, but he has children of his own line in charge of cities here, not many, but a few, and more in Europe."

Richard said, "You want to try to protect the entire United States from the Vampire Council?"

"If we can, *oui*."

Richard and I exchanged a look, and then we looked back at Jean-Claude. Jean-Claude with all his fancy fetish yummy clothes, standing there nude and covered in more body fluids than a *CSI* episode. It should have seemed like whistling in the dark that he, that we, could figure out a way to keep the most powerful vampires in Europe out of the entire United States metaphysically, but we'd already chased out three of them, plus the remnant of the Darkness.

We looked again into each other's brown eyes and then back to the blue of Jean-Claude's. "I'm in," I said.

"What do we do?" Richard asked.

"I believe we have freed Belle of the Mother's influence for now, so all that is left them is death, terror, and violence. We will lose if we try to meet them on with their own strengths."

"Are you saying we make love, not war?" I asked.

He nodded.

"I'd rather just kill them, but the Darkness will just jump to a different body, won't she?"

"I fear so."

"Can we really keep her out of the United States?" Richard asked.

"If the other Masters of the City are willing, there is a chance."

"Why wouldn't they want to keep this out of here?" I asked.

"They will want that, *ma petite*, but they will not like my plan."

"Why not?" Richard asked.

"It would require that they give up much of their autonomy and run America more as Europe is run."

"Why, what will that help?" Richard asked.

"It isn't just political autonomy that they give up, is it?" I asked.

"*Non*, they would have to give us some of their power."

"You're talking about setting up a council here in America with you as its head," Richard said.

He nodded.

"Didn't some of the council try to kill us when they just thought we were trying to do that?" I asked.

"They're going to kill us anyway, *ma petite*, don't you understand that yet?" He looked at us, and his eyes held something I didn't see much: fear. "If we cannot be conquered, then they must destroy us."

"For fear that we'll do exactly what you're planning to do," Richard said.

Jean-Claude nodded again.

"It'll be a race to see if they can conquer us or kill us before we have enough power," I said.

"Yes," he said.

"The other Masters of the City aren't going to want to give up their power to you," I said. "If they haven't felt the council's power they won't believe you. They'll think it's just an excuse to take their power.

"*Exactement*," he said.

"Some of them will fight rather than give you their power," Richard said.

"Some."

"Are we about to start a vampire civil war here?" I asked.

"*Non, ma petite*, between us and our allies they will not be able to mount such a strong defense, nor will they band together. Most will live, or die, in their own territories."

"Are you planning to force them to give up power, even if they refuse?"

"To keep Morte d'Amour and the Mother of All Darkness from raping this country, oh yes."

"This will make you the bad guy," Richard said.

"I am aware of that."

"Are you planning on us metaphysically raping the reluctant masters?"

"If necessary."

"Isn't that exactly what we're fighting to keep the council from doing?" Richard asked.

"Yes, but we are not doing it for evil purposes."

"So they just have to trust that we mean well," Richard said.

"No," Jean-Claude said, "they just have to do what I tell them to do."

"If you do evil for a good reason, it doesn't become good," I said.

"Do you want Marmee Noir to possess other masters in this country?"

"You know I don't."

"Then one man's evil becomes another's necessity, *ma petite*. We must be as ruthless as ever you have been, and as persuasive as ever I have been."

"What am I supposed to be?" Richard asked.

"Be honest with yourself and with us; help us not become the monsters that the other American masters will fear we have already become."

Richard held out his hand, and after a moment of hesitation Jean-Claude took it. I laid my hand on top of theirs, and all I could think was, *Is this how revolutions begin?* Not with a proclamation or a riot, but with a few people in a room somewhere with their hands clasped and a purpose. We were trying to save our country. I was betting the other Masters of the City wouldn't believe we were saving anything but ourselves, and *patriot* wouldn't be what they called us. No, *motherfucking bastards*, more like.

19

THE GUEST BATHROOMS were all very white and modern and stark, but I stood in the white tiled shower and didn't care. The water was hot and felt both good and bad. Good because the hot water helped beat out the stiffness from lying on the cold stones for hours, bad in that the water found every ache and bruise. The bite marks were the only visible wounds, but from the feel of things I'd be bruised eventually. Or maybe I wouldn't be. Maybe the rapid healing would keep most of the bruising down just like the vampire bites did. Bruises are just blood capillaries bursting under the skin, so did I bruise as badly as I had before all the vampire marks? I stood under the rain of hot water and couldn't remember.

For some reason that bothered me, not being able to remember whether I'd bruised more before. Stupid, but true. I felt power glide over my skin. The water was suddenly too hot. I turned it down so that it ran cold. The heat wasn't in the water, it was from the power. I knew the taste of it— Haven. My lioness gazed up at me, and I had a moment to watch her raise her muzzle from a pool where she was drinking. It was as if putting my human body in water made me visualize my lioness in water, too. The weird double vision made me put my hand out. I touched the cool, smooth tile, and it helped steady me. I was here in a shower. I was human. I wasn't a lion drinking at some pool in the middle of some hot, baked grassland. Shit. It was almost as if the lion's world was more real than it had been, and that wasn't Haven's doing, that was the lions and the healing we'd done with them. Something about it had made my lioness more "real."

She growled low in her chest. We didn't like him as much as we had before. But liking him and wanting him weren't the same thing. His power trailed like a warm hand over my bare skin, and all the cold showers in the world weren't going to make his power anything but amazing. Almost any other man in my life would have knocked, but I heard the doorknob turn.

He'd just tried to walk in on me, but I'd locked the door. Old habits die hard.

He called from the other side, "Anita, it's Haven, unlock the door."

One of the reasons I was in the shower by myself was that once Nathaniel, Damian, and Micah woke up I didn't know who to shower with, so in some weird attempt at being fair I'd gone off by myself. Now that seemed like less of a good idea. I hadn't thought Haven would have woken this soon. After feeling his power last night I should have. Fuck.

"Anita, open the door."

"I just need to rinse my hair out and I'll be done. Give me a minute and you can have the shower."

"We can share the shower," he said.

I knew that was a bad idea. I finished my hair in record time and turned off the water. The silence seemed louder than it should have. I grabbed one of the soft, white towels and wrapped it around my hair. I started drying my body with another towel. I really wanted to get dressed, and I was really kicking myself that I'd given up so easily on finding my weapons in the living room, but it was a mess. So many of us had been armed that there were holsters and weapons scattered among the passed-out bodies like mercenary prizes in a fleshy Cracker Jack box.

The door rattled as if he'd leaned against it. "I guess you don't want to share the shower," he said.

"Not really," I said. I was dry enough. I reached for the clothes I'd left folded on the side of the sink, and cursed myself for getting clothes but not any backup weapons. Was I afraid of Haven? Not exactly, but I was smaller and not as strong. There was a difference between being afraid and being cautious. Or that's what I told myself as I scooted my still damp skin into underwear and jeans.

Auggie's warning was in my head. I needed to make Haven my lion. I needed to make him mine the way that Micah was mine, but would that make him behave? Was it my "magic" that made Micah so cooperative, or was it just Micah? I couldn't imagine Haven being as reasonable as my Nimir-Raj. Micah made everything better, easier. Haven did just the opposite. His being tied to me tighter metaphysically wouldn't change that. I could bind him to me like I had Nicky, and then he'd be mine in a way that wouldn't let him misbehave. But I believed what I'd done to Nicky was evil.

Haven saw himself as my king, but I already had a king in my life. He might have outweighed Micah by a hundred pounds, and in a fist fight he'd have won, but sometimes winning the girl isn't about fighting.

I thought about what he'd done to Noel and Travis. I thought about what he'd tried to do to Nathaniel and Micah that one morning after he'd slept over at my house, on one of the last nights we'd all stayed there. I thought about the fact that when I cut him last night I had tried for a kill. I'd made the decision that he was too dangerous to try to wound. It seemed like I shouldn't be sleeping with him if I really believed that. But sex was the only way I could control him. It was my only ace in this metaphysical power game. Fuck, or rather, not.

"If I wanted inside I could just break the door down," he said.

I slipped on my bra, turning it backward to fasten the hooks, twisting it back to slip my arms through the straps. "Yeah, me, too. They're interior doors. They're not meant to withstand that much force."

He slapped the door hard enough that it rattled. "You won't even give me that, will you?"

I had the black T-shirt on now. Just boots to tie on and I'd be dressed. "I don't know what you mean," I said.

He slapped the door one more time and then I felt him move away. For a second I wondered if he was backing up to kick it down, but nothing happened. It was quiet—as the old movie line goes, too quiet.

I might have thought he had gone, but I could feel him on the other side of the door. I could feel him like a thrumming energy in the air. He wasn't gone. We were going to talk. I couldn't think of anything pleasant to talk to him about. Fuck.

20

His energy had calmed some by the time I came out of the bathroom. He was sitting on the edge of the bed closest to the door. He'd finger-combed his blue-spiked hair, but without more gel, it had just taken the spikes out and showed me that his hair actually had a natural part to one side. It was really too long on top to part well, but it was there. His shoulders were rounded as if he were hunching in on himself. But it was only as he sat up straighter that I saw he had found his gun in its holster, because it was there on the bed beside him. Not good. But honestly he didn't need the gun to hurt me.

"You're never going to forgive me for what I did to your two pet lions, are you?" he said.

"You mean almost beating them to death?"

"Yeah, that." He sounded tired.

"You told me once that you think, *What would Anita think of me if I did this or that?* That you worried that if when you did bad things I'd think less of you. How the hell did you think I'd react to what you did to Noel and Travis?"

"I don't know," he said.

"Did you think I'd be happy?"

"I was pissed. I wasn't thinking that far ahead. I just wanted to hurt you, Anita. I wanted you to hurt the way I've been hurting, so I hurt someone you cared about."

"Oh, that makes it all better then," I said, and the first heat of anger was there. I took a deep breath and let it out slow. I had a right to be angry, but I wasn't sure what it would do to my lioness to get angry with him. I didn't have any other animals in the room to help distract my lion. I sure as hell did not want to turn into a werelion for real now.

"You make me crazy, Anita."

"I don't make you anything, Haven. You choose to lash out at people. You decide that you want to hurt me so you hurt Noel. Lashing out at people is what muscle does, not a leader. Kings don't let anger control them."

"You felt the power between us last night, Anita. You know I'm the most powerful lion in this city."

"It's not always about who's the most powerful, Haven."

"Then what is it about?" he asked.

"Control," I said.

"What, like your bleeding-heart Ulfric?"

"Richard stepped up tonight."

"And just like that you forgive him everything? All the shit he's done just wiped out because he finally tried."

"I give points for trying," I said.

"You forgive him because you love him," Haven said. He looked at the floor as he said it.

"I don't know if I love Richard, but I did love him once."

"You've never loved me, have you?"

I wasn't sure what to say to that. I waited too long to answer, because he said, "I guess not answering is an answer."

"Do I say I'm sorry?" I asked.

"You shouldn't have let me kill the old Rex, Anita. You never should have let me move here."

I looked at him, all that male pride hunched in on itself, and said the only thing I had left: the truth. "You're right. I should have said no."

He looked up at that. He looked startled and his face looked more real that way. I realized that most of the time he wore a cocky, nothing-bothers-me mask, but the face he turned up to me was naked of its mask. There was real pain there, and it made my chest tight to see it.

"Did you ever really want me?" he asked.

"Yes," I said.

"But you don't want me now," he said.

"Right this moment, no."

"Why not?" he asked, and his eyes were so angry when he looked up at me.

I stopped moving forward. "Nothing's changed, has it? The power last night and knowing that we have one of the scariest vampires ever hunting us doesn't make any difference to you."

"Why should it?" he asked, and his big hands were gripped in front of him.

"Because you're one of the leaders of this city. Because you're the Rex, the king, and you're supposed to care about things that could hurt or destroy your lions."

"I don't care about my lions. I don't care about anything but you. I tried to be a good boy for you. I tried to be the kind of man you needed, but no matter how good I am it's never enough for you. There's nothing I can do to be more important in your life."

"Yeah, there is, but you won't do it."

"What? Tell me. What do I have to do to be higher up on your list?"

"Share better," I said.

He glared at me, and that hot, trembling energy rose a notch so it felt like the air was pressing on my chest. It was hard to breathe through the heat of his power.

He stood up, and the energy radiated off of him like heat from a summer road. I could see it in the air around him. "I am Rex, and I don't share, because I don't have to share. It's my pride and I get to run it the way I want to run it, and that means I don't share my Regina with anyone."

"Then find a nice little subservient werelion to settle down with and you can be master of your little kingdom, but I don't work that way."

He gave a harsh laugh. "I thought I was God's gift to women before I got to St. Louis, and you. But I can't be nearly as good as I think I am, or you wouldn't have been able to kick me out of your bed for almost a year."

"You tried to slice up Nathaniel and Micah, Haven. What did you think I'd do?"

"I was trying to make a point."

"And that point would be?"

"That I can kick both their asses. You do know that I could have taken all three of you, but I didn't want to hurt you."

"I know you stopped fighting as hard when I joined the fight. I appreciate that, but you need to appreciate that I didn't get a gun and shoot you when you started cutting up the men I love."

"They aren't men, Anita. They're wereanimals, and in our world if you can't fight your way out, you don't lead, you don't win, you don't get to fuck the queen."

"So why do all the other wereanimal leaders listen to Micah?" I asked.

I was angry now, too, or just frustrated to a point where I didn't know what else to say but the truth.

His hands were flexing into fists at his sides. "They shouldn't."

"But they do. Why is that, Haven?"

All the energy, all the fight seemed to go out of him at once and he sat back down on the bed. "Because everything I was taught about what it means to be a man and a werelion doesn't work here. Rafael and his were-rats could eat your wereleopards for breakfast, but he bows to Micah, and to you. Physically he could take Micah. Hell, all the other leaders fought their way to be leader, but not Micah."

"Who told you how Micah became leader of his wereleopards?"

"Merle, the leader of their group before Micah. He's bigger than me, and he fights dirty. I wouldn't want to turn my back on Merle in a fight." That was high praise from Haven.

"Merle's a good guy in a fight, and he's a lot happier being able to go back to a regular job than just be muscle to the new Nimir-Raj," I said.

"Yeah, he loves working on the motorcycles."

"Harleys. He always reminds us he's a Harley mechanic," I said.

Haven gave a small smile. "Yeah." The smile vanished as he looked at me. "Wereanimals from the group that Chimera brought to St. Louis still talk about him. I'm a bad man, Anita, and I've done bad things, but I've never heard of anyone doing some of the shit he did."

"He was crazy and evil," I said.

"And you killed him personally and saved everybody," he said.

I shrugged. "Someone had to do it."

"Yeah, but most people couldn't have done it." He looked at me as if he'd never seen me before, and I knew that wasn't true. He'd seen me a lot.

"What?" I asked.

"I was pretty pissed at Micah, because I didn't understand why everyone followed him. It went against everything I knew about wereanimals until Merle told me the story."

"Micah told me," I said.

Haven kept talking as if I hadn't said anything, as if he were talking more to repeat the words to himself than to me. "Chimera liked to force the wereanimals into their animal forms and keep them like that. He was going to force one of Merle's least powerful leopards into animal form for a long time. Sometimes the weakest of us never come back from that. They get trapped as animals. Not like the wolfman that's knocked up Gina, but full animal form. They can't speak, can't write, they're just trapped as big animals. I've seen it done twice. You can watch them go crazy. They just lose it after awhile, and you end up having to kill them to keep them from hurting people."

"I thought only Chimera did shit like that," I said.

He shook his head. "No, not just him, but the only other leaders I know did it as punishment. Chimera didn't do it as punishment, not according to Merle. He just did it to hurt. Chimera offered that Merle could take the punishment for the other wereleopard. Chimera shamed him in front of all of them, because Merle wouldn't offer himself up in the place of that other leopard. Micah did it. Micah offered himself up for a punishment he didn't deserve."

I knew the story. Micah had told me and Nathaniel on the same night while we held him and he relived it. But he'd also told us how afraid he'd been after awhile, and how his human mind began to slip away. There was a lot more fear in the story when Micah told it. "I know the story," I said softly.

Haven looked up at me. His eyes were filled with some emotion I couldn't read. "But you don't understand what he was risking, Anita. Micah didn't know if Chimera would keep him in full leopard form so long that he'd never be human again. He risked everything for one of his weakest wereleopards." He looked down at his clasped hands again. "When he came back with his eyes frozen as a leopard, Merle stepped down. He just gave the leadership of his pard to Micah, and everyone else with Chimera saw him as their leader after that. You divided Chimera's people up after he was dead. You sent them to their animal groups here in St. Louis. They were already following Micah, and they still do."

"I hadn't thought about it like that, but I guess you're right. But Rafael and Reece of the swanmanes wouldn't follow him if he wasn't worth following. They weren't part of Chimera's people. Even that kind of bravery and self-sacrifice wouldn't cut it with them."

"No, Micah's a good leader in a mainstream kind of way. He makes good decisions and he's good at human politics."

He was being so reasonable. It made me hopeful. "He is."

"I'm not a good man, Anita, not like that."

"Most people aren't that good," I said.

"Is he as good in bed as he is as a person?"

"What?" I asked.

"Is he better in bed than I am, is that it?"

I just blinked at him. "Don't do this."

"Is he?"

"Haven, don't . . ."

He yelled, "Is he?"

I so didn't want to do this, but . . . "Yes."

"Because he's bigger."

"No, it's not size. He's not that much bigger than you are. It's that he listens in bed. You act like anytime I ask for you to change something, it's a criticism. It's not, it's just that some nights I want it gentle, some nights I want rougher. I don't want the same thing every time I make love."

"I've never been with a woman who wants so many different things in bed."

I shrugged. "Sex is my only hobby, or so friends tell me."

"It's not your hobby, Anita, it's your passion. You like sex, really like sex, more than any woman I've ever been with. I think back now and wonder how many of the strippers and other women were faking it in bed with me just like they do on stage. They all wanted something from me. Pay their rent, buy them clothes, jewelry, but you don't want anything from me. There's nothing I can buy you that you can't buy yourself."

"It's not about buying me things, Haven."

"Jean-Claude gives you roses every week."

"I buy him presents, too," I said.

"You've given most of the men flowers, jewelry. You date like a guy, Anita."

I thought about that, shrugged again. "I guess so, I don't know. I've never understood why all the presents are supposed to be just one way."

"You don't let a guy be a guy, Anita. You take that away from us."

"I don't even know what that means," I said, and I didn't.

"I could live with the other men, but not the other lions, Anita. Do you understand how weak that makes me look to the other males? I could even live with you fucking Payne, or Jesse, but Noel and Travis?" He stood up and his power spilled through the room as if someone had turned the thermostat to broil.

"Last night was the first time with Noel, Haven, I swear."

"I don't believe you."

"You should be able to tell truth from lie, Haven."

He shook his head. "I can't tell anymore. It's like my own anger is blinding me."

"The only lion besides you that I'm sleeping with is Nicky."

"Why won't you let us fight? Are you afraid I'll kill him?"

"I'm afraid one of you will kill the other and it will be my fault."

"We're lions, Anita, not people. You need to let us be lions."

"What does that mean?" I asked.

"It means a pride only has one Rex and one Regina. You can't keep Nick and me. You can't fuck the weakest lions in my pride and not fuck me at all."

I gave up trying to explain that I hadn't touched Noel and Travis before last night. I'd learned a long time ago that it's almost impossible to prove you didn't do something, especially if someone is determined that you did it. Innocent until proven guilty only works in court, and even then every jury has its prejudices. We all judge.

"What would it take to get me back in your bed?"

The change in topic was too fast for me. "I thought we were fighting."

"Yeah, but you don't do makeup sex. If you're mad at someone you stay mad. Everything I thought I knew about women and dating them doesn't work with you. So tell me what does work. Tell me how to win this one."

I took in a lot of air and let it out slow. "It's not about winning, Haven. I'm not a prize to be won. I'm not the princess that needs rescuing from the dragon. I'm the prince and I kill my own monsters. You need to be okay with that."

"I got that the day you fought beside the other men against me. I got that last night when you cut me with a silver blade. If you and Jean-Claude hadn't put so much energy out I'd still be hurt." He studied my face, and something about the seriousness of that look made me want to look away, but I didn't. I could look at it if he could feel it. "Would you really have killed me last night to keep Noel alive?"

"We're supposed to protect those weaker than us," I said.

"Is that a yes, you would have killed me to save Noel?"

"Fine, yes," I said.

"Is he better in bed than I am?"

"I'll say this one more time. I don't know. I didn't have intercourse with him last night so I still don't know. I doubt if he'd be as good; he's too soft. I prefer my men with more life experience."

"I hear Nathaniel had plenty of experience."

"Are you going to throw Nathaniel's past in my face?"

"If you were a guy, I'd tell you the love of your life was a whore."

"I know what he was and how he earned his money when I met him," I said.

"See, a guy would be pissed even if he knew. You won't let me be the guy, but in the end, you're not the guy, either."

"Fuck this," I said, and moved toward the door. I didn't turn my back on him, but I was done.

Haven suddenly moved toward me. I had enough time, or speed, to be out of most of his reach, but he grabbed my wrist. We ended with me crouched back away from him, and him with one hand on my wrist. His power trembled down my skin in a hot wash that closed off my throat and made my lioness gaze up with dark, amber eyes. She growled, and it trickled up my throat and out between my lips.

He closed his eyes and a shudder passed through him from top to bottom. He opened his eyes and they were already lion amber. "Fuck me," he said.

I shook my head. "No."

He tightened his hand enough to let me feel how very strong he was. "No weapons, no guards, no boyfriends, you can't stop me."

I waited for my pulse to speed up, to be afraid, because he was probably right. I'd fight, but in the end in a fair fight there was nothing fair about someone outweighing me by over a hundred pounds of muscle and dwarfing me by nearly a foot of height. I'd seen him fight, and one on one he'd win unless I got very, very lucky. But the lion in me growled again. She wasn't afraid of him. Why? Then I had a thought.

I stopped pulling against his hand and just stood up. He moved back half a step as if he hadn't expected it. "I can't stop you doing what? You don't want just my body, Haven. You want me. You want me to want and love you. You can't win that by rape."

"Why can't I just want your body?" he asked.

I took a deep breath and let it out slow. "You're the one who keeps pushing for more of a relationship, not me."

I watched his lion eyes slide back to blue. "You've turned me into the girl." He let go of my wrist and stepped back. "Get out, get out, Anita, before I change my mind."

I backed up until I felt the door under my hands. I had to glance back to find the doorknob, and suddenly he was standing in front of me. He pressed his body against mine, pinning me against the door, his hand on one arm, and only my moving fast kept him from grabbing the other arm.

My pulse was in my throat, and I couldn't hide that he'd scared me. He leaned his face in over my hair and sniffed the air. "You smell like fear and sex and food. You smell good."

My voice was a little shaky as I said, "You smell like sweat and other people's sex."

He pulled me to him, pinning my arm between us. He let me keep the other arm as if it didn't matter. "Then you should feel right at home." His body pressed me close. My physical options were vanishing, but there were other options.

"Do you know why I haven't rolled you the way I did Nicky?" I asked.

I felt his whole body hesitate. I'd surprised him. Good. "You like Nicky better," he said.

"No, I like you better. I stole Nicky's free will. He lives to please me. I think that's kind of creepy actually. Auggie told me I should roll you, but I liked you too much to steal you away from yourself."

"Why tell me this now?" He whispered it against my hair, and I could feel that his body wasn't entirely unhappy to be pressed up against me.

"Don't make what I did to Nicky my only option, Haven."

"I'm a Rex. You couldn't roll me like that," he said.

"Are you sure? Are you sure enough to bet everything you are that I can't make you into my bride?"

He went very still against me, and then he was halfway across the room in a blur of speed that was breathtaking. I leaned against the door for a heartbeat and then groped for the doorknob without looking away from him. I opened it and stepped through, still keeping my gaze on him as if that would keep him from coming for me again.

The cool air of the hallway seemed to help chase some of that hot energy back. "I'm going to clean up," he said, and he didn't look at me.

"You do that," I said, and I closed the door slowly but firmly between us.

21

I WAS SEARCHING through the debris for my weapons and cell phone. I'd found a lot of guns, none of them mine. Haven barging in on me had really, really made me want my weapons back. But I wasn't the only one who had lost weapons in the rush to strip, and I was finding a lot of dangerous toys. Nathaniel helped me look, his hair freshly washed and trailing down his body in a dark wet mass. He'd put on a pair of cutoffs that looked like they'd begun life as a pair of jeans. Micah was in the shower now. We were cleaning up in order of who woke up. The six of us in triumvirates had woken first, and then it seemed to go by dominance and power level. I wondered what order Haven had woken in, but hadn't asked anyone. He hadn't hurt me, so I hadn't mentioned our encounter to anyone yet. We had to do something about Haven, but I wasn't sure exactly what.

Jean-Claude was making phone calls to find out which Masters of the City were alive and how early they were up. Just by leaving messages this early in the day, Jean-Claude was letting them know that he had woken first. It was a subtle type of one-upmanship among vampires. The earlier you woke, the more powerful you were, as a general rule. Though today in St. Louis there were a lot of early wakeups that had nothing to do with the individual vampire's power, but everything to do with Jean-Claude. He'd shoved some of the power to all his vampires, because the power had to go somewhere. If I'd been in charge of the power I'd have probably raised an army of zombies in the closest cemetery.

Some of the debris we were searching through was still tangled up with passed-out vampires and wereanimals. It was unnervingly like a crime scene with a lot of dead, since the vampires didn't breathe. I'd found my Browning and the big knife, but one of the wrist sheaths and my backup gun were still nowhere. I hadn't found my cell phone, either, but I wasn't as worried about that. Cell phones couldn't kill people. I wanted all the killing things back under my control. I'd check phone messages later.

I was starting to wonder if the gun and knife were hidden under someone when a hand grabbed my wrist. I jumped like I'd been slapped and don't know what I might have done, but I had a flashback, like the one I'd had with Jean-Claude and Richard.

I remembered the feel of Noel in my mouth, the look on his face as his body released, how he'd cried out. I had all that in my head before I even saw the face that went with the hand that had touched me.

He said, "Oh my God, what was that?"

"A flashback," I said, my own voice a little shaky. I knelt beside him. He was still holding on to me, but the memory had retreated. The flashbacks seemed to happen only for a moment and only with people that I'd fucked last night. Jean-Claude had no idea why it was happening, and if he didn't know, I sure as hell didn't.

Noel had lost his glasses, so his eyes looked bigger, darker. He looked younger, more unfinished without the gold frames around his eyes.

Nathaniel had moved past us, still looking for my things. I think he'd actually given us some privacy. "How are you feeling?" I asked.

"I thought I was dead. Was I dead?"

"Almost," I said. His hand was still around my wrist, tight, tension singing up his arm as if he were afraid to let go.

"You saved me."

"With some help, yes."

"How?"

"How much do you remember?" I asked.

"I remember the sex, but not much else."

"Can you sit up?" I asked.

He seemed to think about that for a minute. "I think so." He started to sit up, and I flexed my arm to help pull him up. He sat there for a moment as if he weren't sure sitting up was a good idea, and then he said, "I don't hurt. Why don't I hurt?"

"You're a shapeshifter. You guys heal quick."

"I don't," he said. I helped him to stand and as he moved, the torn cushions fell away and he was as nude as in the memory. It bothered me a little, because I'd put Noel in the protect category; no, let's be honest, I thought of him as too innocent for me. I kept very serious eye contact as he swayed on his feet, holding on to my arm.

There was a muffled voice. "Noel heals slow, almost human-slow." Travis dug enough of himself out from under torn clothes and unconscious vampires to get to his knees, and then stayed there for a moment. "Ow." He touched his inner thigh and came away with dried blood. "What's with all the vampire bites, and not to complain, but why don't I feel worse with three bites on me?"

"Richard and I had eight apiece."

Noel and Travis both looked at me with wide eyes, and I had that moment to think how young they were. In age they were only five or six years younger than me, but it's not always about chronological age. They just both hit my radar as very inexperienced.

"You should both be dead," Noel said, "with that much blood loss."

"Not diplomatic," Travis said, and used the back of the loveseat to get to his feet.

Noel looked uncomfortable and mumbled, "Sorry, I didn't mean to . . ."

"It's all right; we should have bled out."

"Why didn't we?" This from Nathaniel, who had wandered back to us. He'd had six bites of his own. "I had one night where I had this many vampires feed from me. I felt awful and was sick for over a day. But not only do I not feel sick, I feel good, better."

"The Lover of Death kept trying to force the power into eating each other, killing each other. Jean-Claude kept the power going to sex and healing."

"So it was meant to bleed us to death?" Nathaniel said.

I nodded, then winced, because whoever had bitten my neck hadn't been gentle. Apparently the major healing had gone into the two werelions in front of me, because the bites still hurt. I had bandages on the inner-thigh ones to keep them from rubbing on my jeans.

Noel's hand had moved from my wrist and I realized I'd been holding his hand for a little while, or he was holding mine. I had one of those moments where I debated: Did I let go of his hand or keep holding it? I'd had metaphysical sex with him and saved his life; how much hand holding did I owe him?

Nathaniel held out my phone to me. "I'll keep looking for the gun and the last knife, but at least we found your phone."

I took the phone, which gave me an excuse to stop holding Noel's hand. Travis asked, "What are you looking for?" Nathaniel explained, and the two of them started searching the far side of the room. Noel stayed by me as if he didn't know why, but he didn't want to leave me, either. I didn't know if he was afraid to leave my side, or if there was some metaphysical reason for it. I'd ask Jean-Claude later and hope he had an answer.

Noel stroked his fingers down my arm. "Is everything all right?"

I didn't like that he kept touching me. It wasn't that it felt bad, in fact it felt nice, but I did not need to have adopted another lion. I had too many lions already.

As if on cue, Haven came striding back into the room. He was nude, as all the wereanimals preferred to be, but he had his gun in its holster in one hand and a towel in the other. He was still rubbing at his short blue hair with it. Was he handsome? Yes. But all the muscles and being well-endowed didn't make up for faults of character. Sometimes you've just got to say no.

Noel moved closer to me, and behind me. He wasn't being subtle; he was hiding behind me. He touched me and I moved back, closing the small distance between us. He took that as the invitation it was and put his arm around my waist. I could feel him shaking, and even though he was nude, there was nothing sexy about it. He was terrified of the handsome man, and just the feel of Noel's fear made Haven less handsome to me. Pretty is as pretty does, and what he'd done to Noel and Travis hadn't been pretty.

Haven scowled at us. His blue eyes, made even bluer by the wet, richer blues of his hair, were instantly angry. "I thought I made myself clear, but I guess not. That's okay, I can be more clear."

My pulse and breathing rate sped. I could feel Noel's heart pounding against my back. Travis came to stand near us; he wouldn't hide behind me like Noel, but he came closer to me. I was the only other dominant in the room. The guards were either still unconscious or in the many showers and baths deeper underground.

I'd found the Browning but it had lead in it, not silver, which meant I could wound him, but I couldn't kill him. I had one wrist sheath blade and the big knife. They were silver, but if I had to start using blades on Haven I had few illusions. I'd seen him fight and he was trained. His arm reach was nearly twice mine and his legs more than doubled my reach. He'd demonstrated his incredible speed in the spare room.

I heard Nathaniel moving things around behind me. He said, "I'll find it." He was looking for my other gun with the silver bullets because he'd done the same math that I had. He'd find it if he could.

"I can't let you hurt them, Haven," I said, and my voice was clear and even.

He threw the towel on the ground, and stood there nude and beautiful, and deadly. "I am Rex in this city, not you, Anita. You tried to mind-fuck me last night, and the sex is a-fucking-mazing when we have it, but even for that I won't let you pussy-whip me. I can't."

"Then we have a problem," I said. Noel hid his face against my hair. I knew in that moment that the only way he was hurting Noel was after hurting me first. With the decision my pulse and breathing slowed. I was at peace with my decision. I would take a beating before I let him hurt them again. Sometimes it's not about winning; sometimes it's just about doing the right thing even if it hurts.

"They said you hadn't fucked them, but I knew they lied."

"I protect a lot of people that I don't fuck," I said.

He shook his head. He kept his gun wrapped in its holster, but then he didn't need a gun to hurt us. I had seconds to decide what I'd do next. If I shot him with lead, would he shoot me back with silver?

"Let go, Noel. I need room."

Travis came and backed him up. I drew both the knives and let the gun and holster fall to the floor. I set my stance and held them both backward so the blades went along my arms. Once I'd thought knives were held out from the body like swords, but it depended on the blade and the type of fight.

He stopped moving forward, studying me. "What—I'm supposed to throw my gun away and come at you bare-handed?"

"Your reach is twice mine, and you'll have claws, I won't. I think the blades help make it a little more even."

"Do you think I won't hurt you? Do you think you've already cut off my balls? That I'm just another big house cat for your collection?"

"No, Haven, I think you will hurt me if you can."

"Are they that good in bed? Are they better than me?"

"I've told you I hadn't touched them before last night."

"Lying bitch!"

"You're good at fucking, Haven, but that's not a good enough reason to like you."

"What the fuck does that mean?"

"You almost killed the two of them last night; are you going to try to finish the job?"

"They're male lions of my pride. If they can't defend themselves, then they die. It's the way the lions run their business."

"Now who's lying?" It was a woman's voice from behind him: the short blond werelion. She was as nude as Haven. Her body was lean and muscled, small breasts high and tight to her body, the swell of hips as slender as the rest of her. It wasn't the slender of starvation diets; it was weights and running and work that had honed her down. I knew it because though I had more curves, my body had the same look to it. Like we'd both carved ourselves down into something small and hard and dangerous.

"Stay out of this," he said, and there was the first hint of growl to his voice.

She walked wide past him, moving toward us. "The pride I came from was run by the women. A lot of prides are run by the women, because the men just want to fuck and fight."

"We're not all like that," Travis said, and his voice was more angry than afraid; good for him.

She smiled, but kept her attention on Haven as she came toward us. "No, you're not."

"They're the weakest lions in our pride," Haven said.

"I need a lover; I'm my own fighter," she said. She was almost beside me now. "I'm Kelly, Kelly Reeder," she said.

"You know my name," I said, "but I'm glad to meet you, Kelly Reeder."

She gave a quick smile. "I wasn't there when they started beating Noel, but Payne told me later that Noel was meant to be the only one. Travis wasn't in trouble until he stepped in to try to keep Noel from being beaten to death."

"Travis wanted a piece; he got what he wanted. Do you want a piece, too, Kelly?"

"If Anita is going to fight you, then yes."

"Count me in." It was the second new werelion female. Her short brown hair had been blow-dried and styled so it framed her face, but she hadn't bothered with clothes. Even if she'd asked, none of my clothes would have fit her. She was close to six feet tall, and she hadn't hit the gym for muscles. She'd exercised to be in shape, but she was all curves, breasts and hips. There was just something softer, more feminine about her, so that it would have seemed wrong for her to muscle herself down like Kelly and me.

"Stay out of this, Rosamond. You're not a fighter," Haven growled.

Rosamond—it was a name for a princess in a fairy tale or a romance novel heroine. She walked wide around him as Kelly had done. She didn't move like a fighter, but she still had that grace that all the shapeshifters could have. She moved cautiously, and well.

"I didn't stop you when you were hurting Noel, because I was afraid of you. Then Travis put himself between you and Noel. Travis isn't a fighter either, but he did it. He did it knowing you'd hurt him. But I think if he hadn't done it you'd have beaten Noel to death right then."

"Do you want me to hurt you?" he asked.

"No, I don't, I really don't, but I can't stand by a second time and let you hurt them. I didn't like myself very much last night, watching you beat them." She made her carefully manicured nails into fists. "But our Regina is standing against you, and I'll stand with her."

"She is not my Regina," Haven said.

"She helped me heal two of our lions with the power of her lion," Kelly said. "Any werelion can hurt and maim, but healing is rare. My mother could do it, and I'll take a Regina who can raise power and share it to heal us over one who can beat us to death. We can always bring over more werelions for muscle, Haven, but healing and magic, that's hard to find."

"She can't even free her beast. It's trapped inside her human body," Haven said.

"Her beast is real. It rose above us like a bonfire of magic and power."

"I smelled her lioness last night," Rosamond said, and I understood enough about wereanimals to know that meant that something was real. If they could smell it, it was real. She came to stand beside Kelly.

"A pride is supposed to be a family," Kelly said. "You've made it into an armed camp."

"Do you really think I can't defeat you all?"

"I don't know," she said, "but I'm willing to find out."

I didn't know what to say. I'd never had anyone come to my side of the fence like this; I was always the only girl with all the men, with rare exceptions like Claudia. What did I say to the two women who I barely knew?

"It's good not to be the only girl in the fight for once," I said.

Kelly gave me a fierce grin, more a baring of teeth, and it reminded me of a snarl, but that was okay; it was what we needed right now.

"This is Kelly's idea of female bonding," Rosamond said.

Kelly nodded and shrugged, but the shrug turned into her loosening her shoulders. I readjusted my stance because you couldn't hold any one stance forever, and besides, I had to make room for her being next to me. It was a different kind of fighting, knowing there were people on your side who would help.

"Is this a private fight, or can anyone join?" Claudia walked out of the hallway dressed in a black T-shirt and jeans. She lived here part time, so she had clothes. Her long black hair was back in a wet ponytail. She was taller than Haven by inches, and broader through the shoulders. I realized that even her biceps were bigger, as they strained against the T-shirt.

"This is lion business," Haven growled, but he made sure to keep an eye on her as she moved around him. It meant that he saw her as a more of a threat individually than any of the rest of us. I think I was insulted.

"I'm Anita's bodyguard. I wouldn't be very good at my job if I let you hurt her, would I?" Just the tone of her voice let me know that she liked Haven even less than she liked Richard.

"You think together you can beat me?" he asked.

I'd never seen Kelly fight, and Rosamond was going to be less than useful, but Claudia I knew. I said, "I think we can."

"Maybe, but I'll fuck you up before I go down."

"Knock your bad self out."

"What?" he said.

I felt myself smile, and it wasn't a nice smile. It was a cold, anticipatory smile. It went with what I said next. "You think you can win this fight, then come over here and prove it."

One moment he was just standing there, and the next he was a blur of movement. I had time for one thought—*He's too fast!*—and then the fight was on.

22

ROSAMOND WENT DOWN in the first few blows. She lay on the ground bleeding and dazed. I sliced Haven twice before one of his long legs swept mine out from under me and I hit the floor. With the knives in my hands I couldn't slap the floor and take the energy of the fall. I had to just fall. There's always something about hitting a surface abruptly that dazes you for a heartbeat. I didn't have a heartbeat to spare. He was above me and then he wasn't. It was like a magic trick, so fast, so powerful, but not his power. Claudia had kicked him away from me and into the fireplace. The force of it shook the room. I got a glimpse of her long jean-clad legs as she sailed over me, still moving from the momentum of her own kick.

I rolled to my feet in time to see Haven block her next kick and trap her leg with his arm, his elbow coming down toward her leg. She dropped to the ground, leaving him holding her entire weight. He could hold it, but it took him a second to keep his balance. She used that second to kick out with her free leg, so that it started to form a circle to connect with his face. He couldn't block it and break her leg. He blocked it, but now he had both hands controlling her legs. She was trapped, but we weren't.

Kelly moved in a blur to his right, and I was moving in on his left, switching the big knife to a point hold so I'd have enough reach to stab him while he couldn't block with his arms. I didn't really expect to be fast enough to land the blow, but the knife tip was just suddenly sinking in between his ribs and training took over. You hit someone there from a downward angle; you push up and go for the heart.

I knew Kelly was doing something from her side, but I didn't have time to see it. Then Haven used Claudia like a club and threw her into me. We ended in a heap on the floor with her on top of me. It was all I could do to hold on to both knives and keep them from cutting Claudia. At least this time an unconscious body broke my fall. But Claudia on top of me meant I wasn't getting up right away.

She rolled off me and got to her feet. I was slower, but I got up. Kelly and Haven were trading blows, each of them fast enough to block the other, in blurring movements that my eyes could barely follow. But she was my size and he kept her back from him with those long, long legs. She kept trying to get inside that punishing swing of legs, but couldn't. Neither of them could land the blow they wanted, but they were landing plenty of blows on each other's arms and legs. Whoever tired first, or whoever could break someone's arm or leg by sheer repetitive strength, would decide the fight, if it was just between Kelly and Haven.

Claudia moved in from his other side. He kicked out one last time, Kelly blocked with her arm, and I heard the sharp pencil snap of bone breaking. She had a moment where the pain and shock of the injury took her focus. His other foot snapped around and hit the side of her face. She went down and didn't get back up.

Claudia had her stance, arms and fists up ready to block, long legs loose and ready, almost bouncing in place.

His arms were up, his feet planted. The two shallow slashes I'd gotten in early were dripping scarlet down his stomach and one arm. The last deep blow over the rib cage was narrow but bleeding freely. The more he moved, the faster he'd bleed. Then I saw it, a tiny bubbling of blood at the wound. Had I nicked a lung?

Haven's voice was breathy as he said, "No woman can beat me one on one. That's why I'm king, and you have to cheat."

"I underestimated you; I won't do it again," she said.

"You think you can take me?"

"Yes," she said.

"Claudia," I said, "don't make this about some macho guy crap."

"I've wanted to beat the shit out of a couple of men in your life for a while now, Anita. It's not macho crap. It's a relief."

"Bring it, bitch," he said.

"Claudia . . . ," I started to say.

She brought it.

23

I HADN'T REALLY understood that it wasn't just me being a girl that kept me from volunteering for slugfests with wereanimals and vampires. It was that I was a small girl. Claudia wasn't.

She was taller than Haven. Her legs were longer. His arms were longer, but the legs are what give you reach in martial arts. She had the reach. She used it to force him to block again and again. The only way I was able to be certain which blow belonged to which was that her arms and legs were darker and his were paler, their skin tones turned into a visual Doppler effect by the unbelievable speed.

I climbed back over the fallen couch to get farther away from the fight. Keeping an eye on them so I didn't get someone else thrown on top of me made me trip. I fell into a little heap of clothes and found the only hard metal to land on in all that softness. I put the wrist-sheath blade back in its sheath as I dug another stray gun out from under me. It was a .357 Magnum. Who the hell was big enough to carry that concealed?

Nathaniel and Travis were kneeling by Rosamond and Kelly. Kelly was just unconscious, but Rosamond should have gotten up by now. Could a wereanimal die of a broken neck, or a cracked skull? I'd have said no, but I really didn't know. I was so used to the really powerful shifters who could survive nearly anything that I just didn't know about someone at Rosamond's lower power level. I didn't know where Noel was, but as long as he was far away from Haven, it had to be better.

There was a moment of clarity in the fight. A moment where I saw Claudia's foot connect with Haven's body and he was airborne. I felt the air as he went past. The sound of him hitting the far wall was a thick, meaty crash. Claudia rushed past me over the ruins of the couch to finish it.

A gunshot thundered through the room, echoing off the bare stone walls. I was turning toward the sound, the .357 in my hand. I had time to see Haven crumpled against the wall coughing blood. Claudia was on the ground. Her left arm hung useless; blood was pulsing out. It was one of those moments where the world slows down as if everything is caught in crystal. Things are hard-edged, as if your eyes will cut the images into your brain forever. Haven brought the gun up again to aim at Claudia on the floor. I was aiming at him but didn't have the shot yet. I screamed his name: "Haven!"

It made him hesitate for a fraction of a second. His eyes flicked to me, and then the world sped up and everything happened at once. He pulled the trigger and so did I. The force of the big gun's recoil made me end up pointing it at the ceiling before I could bring it back down to aim again.

His chest had a hole in it, but he was still bringing his gun around to aim at me. Whoever shot first would win. I didn't even have time to be scared or worried; all my concentration narrowed down to aiming, breath held, and I pulled the trigger. His gun exploded just behind mine. I heard the whine of the bullet and flinched as it hit the couch next to my head. Haven's chest blossomed crimson like an evil flower. Incredibly, his arm came back around one more time to point at me. I wasn't going to be able to aim the .357 again, not in time. I let the recoil of the gun take me up, come back down, and was trying to aim, even as I knew I wasn't going to be fast enough.

His gun fired wide and I got off that third shot, but my shoulder went numb, and I thought, *Oh, I'm hit*, but I made my shot and other guns echoed mine. I didn't bother to turn around. If they were shooting at me, I was dead; if they were shooting at Haven, great. I focused on making my shot count. My shoulder wasn't working quite right, but I could use it. I'd worry about it later.

Haven's body jerked as bullets hit him. I wasn't sure which hit was mine and which wasn't. We all aimed at center body, and that beautiful muscled chest and stomach became a red ruin.

I couldn't hear anything. My ears were ringing from all the shots. When someone touched my shoulder I jumped and started to bring the gun around. Wicked pinned my arm and the gun in his big hand. His mouth was moving. I couldn't hear what he was saying, but when he took the gun out of my hand, I let him do it.

I looked at my left shoulder but there was no blood. It hurt, but I couldn't see a wound. Wicked was still talking to me, and I still couldn't understand him, as he helped me to my feet. There were people rushing past us with drawn guns, headed toward Haven. Fredo was kneeling by Claudia. I asked, "Claudia—is she all right?" I had no idea how loud or soft I was talking. I couldn't tell.

Wicked shook his head, his wet blond hair clinging to his face as if he hadn't bothered to dry it. He was dressed. He was turning me away from Claudia, and I fought his grip to go check on her, but he tightened his grip. Did he not want me to see her? How bad was she hurt? Then he turned me enough for me to see that Noel was lying on his back, his chest covered in blood. I started forward, and then the crowd moved enough for me to realize they were kneeling by another body. Long auburn hair trailed out from between them. I knew now why my shoulder hurt, but there was no wound.

I was moving forward, shaking Wicked's hand away. In that moment if someone had wanted to shoot me, they could have, because I forgot everything but Nathaniel.

24

I PUSHED THROUGH the kneeling people, not even seeing who was there, to fall to my knees beside him. He looked up at me, lavender eyes wide. Jason was holding his hand. Lisandro was putting pressure on the wound in his shoulder. I touched my shoulder, where it hurt exactly where his wound was, but I'd felt pain when Richard and Jean-Claude had been hurt and that had been worse. This wasn't bad. I'd seen him survive worse. I knew that, but I still needed to touch him. I was crying and hadn't meant to, but Jason was crying, too, so I didn't feel so bad.

I touched Nathaniel's face and he smiled at me. My hearing was coming back in pieces. I heard yelling. "He's gone! He's gone!" I turned to find Jesse and Kelly kneeling on either side of Noel. I could feel their energy, their lions reaching out. "Go," Nathaniel said, "help Noel."

I laid my hand over his heart, as if I needed to feel the thick beat of it before I left him, and then I moved the few feet to Noel. It was Kelly who was yelling at Jesse, "He's gone! It's too late!" She was cradling her arm.

I looked down at Noel, and the moment I saw him I knew she was right. Brains don't belong on the outside. I stared down at the inside of his head spilling out into the floor. He'd been getting his master's in literature. All that studying, all that effort, was leaking out of his broken head and spreading in a thick, bloody mass on the floor. Even a powerful wereanimal couldn't have healed that. Almost everything else, but not this.

Truth was there, his hair black from the shower. "He was hiding in the hallway. We were running for the sound of fighting, and then he darted out. He tackled Nathaniel, saved him. We would all have been too late."

I knelt beside the body, because that's what it was now. It wasn't Noel anymore, it was his body, and that was it. There'd be no miracle to save him this time.

I heard yelling from the far side of the room. I said, "Claudia?"

"She'll live," Wicked said. He'd come back from that direction. "And looks like so will your Rex."

I stared up at him and Truth. "What?" I asked.

"He's healing the damage. The doctor thinks he'll pull through," Wicked said.

Jesse said, "Haven is just that strong."

I shook my head and stood up from Noel's body. I walked toward the guards clustered around Haven. Wicked and Truth trailed me. I wasn't sure if they were trying to keep me safe, or if they'd try and stop me. Dr. Lillian, our main medic, was kneeling over Haven. She must have come while I was in the shower. But it was a distant thought; I didn't really care when she'd come or how she'd known we needed her.

I moved up through the guards. I heard myself say, "It's okay, Lillian, you don't have to do anything for him."

"He's more badly hurt than Claudia. I need to stabilize him," she said.

"Will he live?" I asked.

"I think so."

"No," I said.

Lillian looked up at me, and I saw something in her face, her eyes. "Anita, you don't have to do this."

I nodded. "Yes, I do."

She tried to stop me, and I said, "Get her out of here. Let her save someone else."

Hands pulled her away. Haven looked up at me, his eyes terribly, amazingly blue against the blood on his lower mouth. Fresh blood poured out of his mouth as he tried to say something.

I aimed the .357 at his face. He stared up at me with those eyes. His voice was thick with things that shouldn't be in a living person's throat. He coughed, spraying blood, and said, "I'll heal."

I shook my head. "No, you won't."

"Did I kill your leopard?" he asked.

"Did you aim for him?" I asked.

He smiled, his teeth red with his own blood. "Yes."

"Why?" I asked.

"Because you love them all more than you love me." He coughed so hard that something thick and meaty fell onto the floor as if he'd coughed up some lung. Anyone who could heal from this much silver damage was so very powerful.

"Good-bye, Haven."

He snarled up at me and started to shapeshift. His power washed over my skin in a wash of electric heat. My lioness snarled. His blue eyes filled with lion amber. I pulled the trigger. The amber slid away and I pulled the trigger the second time, staring into the same blue eyes I'd watched in bed above me more than once. The second shot made it impossible to look into his eyes. I dropped to my knees and put the barrel against his face for the third shot. At such close range, it blew the back of his head out. Like Noel, just like Noel. I was left blinking blood and thicker things out of my eyes. Too close. Blowback, it was blowback.

I dry-fired twice before I realized the revolver was empty. I got to my feet and let the empty gun fall to the floor. Without bullets it was just a heavy rock, and that wouldn't help me against anyone in this room.

Everyone moved out of my way. No one tried to touch me, or comfort me, or talk to me. They just moved and watched me. I walked back to Nathaniel. Micah was there now, holding his hand. Nathaniel smiled up at me. I smiled back.

"I love you," he said.

"I love you, too," I said.

Micah took my hand, but I shook my head and got to my feet. I told him, "Stay with Nathaniel."

"He didn't leave you a choice," Micah said.

I nodded. "I know." Then I started walking back toward the hallway. I just kept walking. I had a vague idea I needed to clean up again. I kept walking. Jason was in the hallway with J.J. She stared at me with wide eyes. Jason tried to get her back in his bedroom, away from all the blood and death.

I walked until I found the new showers that Jean-Claude had put in when we realized just how many people were living in the underground of the Circus. It was a big open shower like at a gym. I turned on the nearest shower head and stepped under it. I hadn't taken off any clothes, that seemed wrong, but I just grabbed for the soap in the wall dispensers. I washed Nathaniel's blood off my hands. I washed Haven's blood out of my hair and off my face. Noel's blood had soaked into my jeans from the knee down and was all over my shoes. I couldn't get it out. I took off the jogging shoes and threw them across the room. I took off the pants and tried to scrub the knees clean.

"Anita, Anita."

I kept scrubbing at my jeans. "I can't get it out. I can't get the blood out."

"Anita!" Richard grabbed my arms, turned me to look at him while the water poured down my face and onto the front of his body. He was tall enough that the water didn't touch higher than his chest. His brown eyes held pity, sorrow, things I couldn't decipher.

I held the jeans up to him. "I can't get the blood out."

He took the jeans out of my hands. "It's okay," he said.

I shook my head. "It's not."

He drew me in against his chest while the water beat on my back. "No, it's not. I'm so sorry, Anita, so sorry."

I was stiff in his arms, and he just kept holding me tight and close, and gradually my arms unclenched and I wrapped them around his waist. I buried my face against the wet T-shirt and the muscled strength of his chest. He was just the right height so that my ear was against his chest. I held on to him, listening to the thick, strong beat of his heart.

He stroked my hair and murmured, "I'm here, I'm here. I'm so sorry, but I'm here."

I managed to say, "I'm glad you're here." And then I was crying. I cried until my legs fell out from under me and he had to catch me. He lifted me up into his arms, holding me close, putting his face against mine and whispering, "I'm here, I'm here." And sometimes, that's all you can say. Sometimes that's all the comfort you have to offer and all you can expect.

25

I SAT ON the edge of Jean-Claude's bed. Even after a year of living here almost every day of the week I still didn't think of it as our bed. I was wrapped in a soft navy blue blanket because one, my hair was wet again, and two, all my robes were silk. Jean-Claude knelt behind me in his black velvet robe with the fur lapels that were as black as the rest of the robe. I usually liked him in that robe a lot, but today I didn't seem to care. He held a bunch of my curls in his hand and rested them on the big, toothy-looking head of the diffuser on the dryer. I usually let my hair dry naturally, but I'd been shivering, so he'd asked to dry my hair. Fine with me, I didn't care. The best thing about the dryer besides the warmth was it was too loud for anyone to talk around me. Talking felt very overrated.

Jean-Claude picked up another bunch of my curls and laid it over the blow dryer. I sat there and let the hot air bathe my scalp, let him play with my hair. He'd rubbed some kind of leave-in conditioner into it, gently, so the dryer didn't dry out my hair. He'd asked first, and my answer had been what it had been for the last hour: "Fine."

To the question, "Are you all right?" my answer had been, "I'm fine." If it was a lie, I didn't know the truth yet. I was fine.

He turned the dryer off and laid it on the bed beside him. He bunched my curls in his hands, settling them in some order that made him happy. I sat and blinked. I had seldom cared less about what my hair looked like than right now.

I heard the door open behind us. I didn't turn around. It didn't seem important enough. Then I smelled coffee. My pulse sped a little, and I sat up and realized just how much I'd been huddling in on myself. I forced myself to sit straighter, shoulders back, spine straight. I would not hunch like a dog that had been kicked once too often; the fact that that described how parts of me were feeling was neither here nor there. My emotions felt kicked to hell, but I could not let it make me look like I'd been kicked.

Richard was in front of me shirtless, in a pair of jeans so faded they had white patches here and there, as if there'd been some sort of bleach accident. Richard threw out jeans when they looked like that. He was barefoot, too.

"Sorry all your clothes got wet," I said. My voice didn't sound right, as if there were an echo between what I was saying and the inside of my head.

He held a red coffee mug down to me. It was one of the new mugs that went with the new dishes that Nathaniel had picked out for here. Just like back at our house, he had picked two contrasting colors of plain, heavy dinnerware. For our house it was green and blue, but for the Circus he'd picked red and black. The dishes sat in the newly installed kitchen that had gone in at the same time as all the new bathrooms. Good thing nothing went this wrong when we'd had all the workmen in here.

Richard knelt in front of me and held out the mug. "Coffee. You need it."

I nodded but made no move to take it. All I could think of was that Nathaniel was down the hall with doctors and Micah to hold his hand. I was waiting to get my shit together before I went down to see him. There was a quiet part of me that kept repeating, "Haven tried to kill Nathaniel. He meant it to be Nathaniel lying there with his brains all over the floor." Then I'd shove the thoughts away and try to stop thinking about anything.

"Do you not want the coffee?" he asked.

"It smells good," I said, and my voice sounded as numb as I felt.

Richard touched my hand where it showed around the edge of the blanket and wrapped my fingers around the handle of the mug. "Drink it."

My hand started to shake as I raised the mug, so I had to use my other hand to steady it. Two hands were better. I took a moment to smell the aroma: rich, dark, good coffee. Nathaniel had been doing my coffee shopping for me. He was the only one who always got what I wanted.

"How's Nathaniel?" I asked.

"As I've answered before, *ma petite*, he is fine. He will be fine. He is hurt, but it is not permanent."

"Drink the coffee while it's hot, Anita," Richard said.

I sipped the coffee and it was good. There wasn't quite the right amount of sugar in it, but Richard didn't know that I'd started putting in more sugar. He hadn't been around enough to know that I'd changed anything.

"How do we keep everyone safe?" I asked, and I wasn't sure who I was asking.

"We will meet with the tigers when you are ready," Jean-Claude said.

I shook my head. "I don't mean from Marmee Noir, I mean from things like what just happened. I thought Haven and I had worked things out. I thought it was safe."

"We all did," Richard said.

Jean-Claude sat down behind me, so he could curl his body against my back. His arms slid carefully around my shoulders so that he didn't jostle the coffee, but he could still hold me. "You could not have known, *ma petite.*"

"That Haven was a bad guy? I knew that, and him beating them almost to death showed he hadn't changed."

He laid his head against my hair. "There are bad men among Rafael's rats, but they would never have behaved so. It is not his past that made this happen. It is not that he spent most of his life on the wrong side of the law that made this happen."

"Then what? Why?"

"Do not ask this now, *ma petite.* Please, let it rest until you have had more time."

"No," I said, "if you know why this happened, then tell me, because I don't understand it."

"Take the coffee, Richard," he said.

Richard took it and sat back on the floor, his hand finding my fresh jeans under the blanket. I had clothes to change into no matter how many times I ruined them. I had my whole damn wardrobe here. So I could keep changing after every bloodbath. Richard rubbed my leg through the jeans. I let him.

"Jean-Claude, tell me," I said.

He wrapped his arms around my shoulders, his face next to mine. "I believe that he had never been in love before, perhaps not truly loved anyone ever before in his life before you, *ma petite.*"

I frowned, putting my hands on his arms. "So what does that mean? If I was the first love he'd ever had, why did he try to kill one of the other people I love most?"

He held me tighter, and I knew whatever he was going to say I wouldn't like, but I needed to hear it. I needed to try to understand what the fuck had gone wrong.

"I am told he answered the question of why he had done it, *ma petite*."

I nodded. "He said, because I loved all the other men more than I loved him."

"A certain type of man, when he loves for the first time, his love is not really love, it is possession. Possessions don't have rights or feelings; they are something to be owned and controlled. He had spent more than a year trying to do just that, and failing."

"So when he attacked Micah and Nathaniel the last time we were all at my house, that was sort of a last-ditch effort to try to, what, own me?"

"When you fought on their side against him, he couldn't understand it," Richard said quietly.

"He hurt people I loved. I don't let that happen."

"But he was stronger than they were; he could have won the fight if you hadn't sided with them. I think if he'd been willing to really hurt you physically, you might not have won then."

I nodded, holding on to Jean-Claude's arms, leaning in against the solidness of him. Richard kept rubbing my leg over and over. "He was willing to hurt me today."

"Maybe," Richard said, "but it wasn't you he wanted to bloody. Even in the fight he didn't actually bloody you, did he?"

I stared down at him. "What do you mean?"

"He didn't want to hurt you physically, even at the end."

"Is that supposed to make me feel better?" I asked.

"No, I mean, yes. Shit."

"Are you saying Haven wouldn't have hurt me? That I didn't have to kill him?" My voice was rising, almost yelling.

"No," Richard said, "no, he had to die. He was too dangerous."

"Then what are you saying?"

Richard put the coffee mug carefully on the bedside table and knelt in front of me, his hands on my knees under the blanket. "I'm saying he didn't want to hurt you physically, but he wanted to hurt you, Anita. He just wanted to hurt you the way you'd hurt him."

"What does that mean?" I asked.

Jean-Claude spoke with his face next to mine. "It means, *ma petite*, that he knew who to kill to break your heart the most."

I turned so I could see his face. "What?"

"You love me, I know that," he said, "but the thought of Nathaniel dead and gone, the thought of how close you came to losing him today, that is the thought that turns your skin cold and makes you unwilling to feel."

I opened my mouth to tell him he was crazy, but I closed my mouth and tried to think. I shook my head. "I don't know what to say to that. I'd feel just as bad if it were one of you wounded in the other room."

Richard laid his head on my lap. My hand came down automatically to touch the foamy waves of his hair. "I know you care for me, Anita, and maybe if I stop being such an ass you'll love me again, but I had my own bad moments watching you fall in love with Nathaniel and Micah. Micah I got. He's Nimir-Raj. He might be too small to win a fistfight with me or one of the larger dominants, but he's a good leader, better than me, better than Haven was. We both recognized that, and respected it, but Nathaniel—it took me a long time to understand why you loved him." He spoke with his head in my lap, his tall, bare upper body bowed so he could fit his head and some of those broad shoulders in my lap. I could only see the side of his face as he talked, and he couldn't see mine at all. Was that on purpose?

"I didn't mean to hurt you, or anyone," I said.

"I know that," he said, "and sometimes I did mean to hurt you, Anita. I'm very sorry about that now, but Nathaniel offended that macho part of me. Haven had a lot more macho to live up to, partly because the lions are just that way, and partly because he'd been in the mob since he was a teenager. He just couldn't share you with someone he saw as weak." Richard wrapped his arms around my legs, hugging me. "He couldn't bear seeing that you loved someone who was weaker, less dominant, submissive in every way, but you loved him more."

I thought about that. "Is that why he was convinced I'd had sex with Travis and Noel? They're weak, submissive, or Noel was, not sure about Travis. I don't think he's sure about himself yet."

Richard nodded his head against my lap. "I think that was part of it. He looked at the men you loved most and the ones you seemed to fall in love with easiest, and it's usually less dominant men. Micah is Nimir-Raj, but he doesn't fight you about ruling the leopards. He doesn't argue with you the way I do."

Jean-Claude went very still against me. I looked down at the man in my lap, and finally said, "No, he doesn't."

He raised his head up so he could look into my face. "I thought you killed because it didn't bother you. I didn't understand until today how much it costs you." He swallowed, and his eyes were shiny. "I've let you do my killing for me for years. I've forced you to do terrible things because I'm too squeamish. I comforted myself at one point by saying that it didn't bother you, it didn't mean anything to you, to do the wolf pack's dirty business, but that was just to make me feel better. Everything you've done to keep us safe, and make other shapeshifters and vampires think twice before attacking St. Louis, had a price. I told myself that you didn't pay that price, that you were cold about it. Today I saw your face when you realized Noel was dead. I saw your face after you'd killed Haven. I saw the pain. I saw the price, and I am so sorry that you've had to pay that price on your own."

I looked into those brown eyes and didn't know whether to pinch myself or him. "What are you saying? That you'll help me kill people now?"

He shook his head. "I'll defend the wolves with violence when it's needed, but I'll never be a shooter, Anita. I don't regret that, but I am sorry that you have to pay more of the price for our safety than I do, because I'll never be . . ." He stopped as if he didn't know what to say.

"You'll never be a killer like me?" I said.

He looked up and shook his head. "I did not say that, I wouldn't have said that. Haven had to die. He was too dangerous, too unpredictable to be allowed to stay as Rex."

"I didn't kill him because of that," I said.

Richard studied my face. "I don't understand."

"I killed him because Noel did a brave thing. Noel pushed Nathaniel out of the way of the shot. Noel who was one of the weakest of all of you guys, but he was brave when it counted, and he should have lived through that. He should have lived and gotten to be brave and get his master's degree and have a life. He was only twenty-four and now he's dead, and we can't even tell his parents that he died a hero, because we can't tell them the truth about what happened. They'll never know that he died brave, and he died well, and he died saving the man I love, and all I could do was walk across the room and shoot his killer in the face until he died, too." I was crying and didn't mean to. "I didn't kill Haven because it was the best thing for the city, or for the lions, Richard. I killed him because if Noel had to die, it was the least I could do for him. I killed Haven because he tried to kill Nathaniel, and that is not allowed. For that he had to die, because I looked into his eyes and knew that while he was alive, Nathaniel wasn't safe, and I'd do anything to keep him safe."

Jean-Claude held me tight, murmuring comforting words in French. Richard buried his face against my legs again and wrapped his arms around them. They held me close, and I let myself cry for Noel, and for Nathaniel, and for the knowledge that I'd killed one of my own lovers, killed him with the taste of his body still on my lips, the feel of him still like a memory inside me, and I'd looked him in the same eyes that had looked up at me in bed while we made love, and blown his face into so much meat and bones.

And in the end, that last was what made the crying build to screams.

26

I FINALLY WENT to relieve Micah at Nathaniel's bedside. We had a series of rooms that had been made into hospital rooms so that when our people were hurt they didn't all have to go to the lycanthrope hospital that the wererats had set up years ago for the local shapeshifters. Human hospitals didn't always like treating lycanthropes. The room was smallish with a twin hospital bed, subdued lighting at the moment, but I knew that the brightest lights in the entire underground were in these rooms. It had been yet another remodeling project when we did everything else. Jean-Claude was really trying to make this our home. I missed windows.

I'd gotten my hysterics out of the way. I sat there holding the hand that wasn't attached to a freshly shot shoulder. Nathaniel smiled at me, and that was enough. I regretted having to kill Haven the way I did, but I couldn't regret him being dead. He'd shot Nathaniel. He'd meant to take that smile, those eyes, and the hand in mine away from me forever. No, I didn't regret Haven being dead. If Noel hadn't been dead, I think I'd have felt a lot better than I did about all of it.

"I'm sorry that you had to kill Haven," Nathaniel said.

I blinked and realized I wasn't sure what my face had been showing in the last few minutes. I smiled at him. "It's okay."

"No," he said, "it's not."

I shrugged, the spare shoulder rig a little tight. The old one was going to have to be repaired, again. At least I hadn't had it cut off me in an emergency room. "It is what it is."

"Do you want me to let you be all macho about this?" he asked.

I nodded. "Please. I had my breakdown earlier."

He squeezed my hand. "I'm sorry I wasn't there to help."

That made me smile again. "Jean-Claude and Richard handled me."

There was a soft knock at the door, and I didn't know who it was until

Damian came through. I was still numb from Marmee Noir and the Lover of Death, and from everything else. I realized this was the most alone in my head and emotions I'd been in a very long time. I used to crave being separate; now it felt weird, as if a piece of me had gone AWOL.

Damian had changed into his favorite robe. It looked like a Victorian smoking jacket except it came down to his ankles. The robe's velvet had rubbed almost away at the elbows and other places. I'd never asked, but I was pretty certain that the robe wasn't a reproduction. He'd worn this robe for over a hundred years. It had become a comfort object for him, but I didn't begrudge it to him; I might be sleeping with a certain toy penguin if I ever got to sleep again.

His red hair was dry and shining over the dark of the robe. Straight hair dried so much faster than curly. He had a small covered tray. The rich scent of coffee was mixed in with other scents. I smelled mainly coffee but was pretty sure there was food underneath the cover. I fought not to frown. I so wasn't hungry.

"Don't give me that look," he said. "You have to eat."

"I so don't want food, Damian."

He walked to the little sliding table/tray by the bed and sat the food on it. He lifted the cover and the perfume of the coffee filled the room. I had to admit it smelled good. The tray was heaped with croissants, various cheeses, and fruit. It looked like enough food for all of us, if Damian could eat solid food. "Coffee, then," I said.

He shook his head. "Nathaniel is drawing on us to heal himself. If you want him to heal quickly, and with no scar, we need the energy to feed him. You and I will have to eat more so Nathaniel doesn't drain us." He put a croissant, a small piece of cheese, and some fruit on a little plate.

I slumped in the chair and fought not to scowl. Nathaniel squeezed my hand. It made me look at him. "I can try to stop taking so much energy from the two of you."

I shook my head. "No, that's one of the benefits of the triumvirate." I made myself sit up straight. "I want you healed as fast as possible. I'll eat, but I'd really like the coffee first."

Damian held the plate out to me. "One whole croissant, one piece of cheese, or two pieces of fruit and then you can have the coffee."

"Yes, Daddy," I said, frowning as I took the food.

"I could have brought sausage. Protein will help him heal the fastest and give us the most energy. I was nice, bringing something light."

The thought of meat made me vaguely ill. I took the food he offered a little more gratefully. "Thank you, Damian."

He frowned at me, almost suspicious. "You're welcome."

His expression made me laugh. "Don't look so suspicious. You're right and I'm admitting it."

He smiled, but his green eyes held just a hint of mistrust. "You don't usually give in this fast."

I glanced at Nathaniel and then at the food. "I just want everyone well, that's all." I picked up a strawberry and took a bite of it. It was juicy and sweet and so ripe that another day would have seen it too ripe. It tasted good enough that I knew I was a lot hungrier than I'd realized. Two strawberries and half a croissant later, I asked, "Can I have the coffee now, please?"

He smiled and handed me the cup. It was actually a big travel mug with penguins on it. The words around the penguins were *Wake up and smell the coffee*. Micah had found it for me on one of his business trips. Everyone who could drink coffee had their travel mugs, or used the generic ones that matched the red and black plates. The kitchen was too far away from some of the rooms, so ways to keep hot things hot were important.

I sipped the coffee, closing my eyes so the smell and taste of it could have their way with me. I'd finally convinced everyone that good coffee was a necessity, not a luxury.

"That's better," Damian said. I heard sounds and opened my eyes to find he'd pulled up the room's second chair. His robe gaped a little, showing a lot of pale naked chest. He had that peaches-and-cream complexion of most redheads, but the complexion hadn't seen sunlight for hundreds of years. His skin was so white it almost seemed to glow against the dark of the robe.

"I've already taken blood again," he said. "Your job is to eat solid food, since I can't."

I nodded, sipping the coffee again, and went back to holding Nathaniel's hand. Damian reached out and laid a hand on Nathaniel's leg where it lay under the covers. The moment he touched him, it was as if the circuit completed. Power breathed over us, through us, so the warm rush of Nathaniel, the cool energy of Damian, and my own power that seemed to be a mixture of both just suddenly flooded over us like three different streams of water intermingling until I couldn't tell where one energy left off and the other began. My shoulder hurt, a lot. The pain was sharp and dull at the same time, and I knew that whatever the doctors had done to fix the wound had cost Nathaniel other pain.

Then it was gone, stopped. My shoulder was just a dull aching memory. I opened my eyes without realizing that I'd closed them. Damian was standing, not touching anyone. His taking his hand away had stopped it.

"You're our master, Anita; you have to get better at controlling this," he said from the far side of the room, as he rubbed his shoulder where Nathaniel's wound would have been.

"I'm sorry," I said. "It was like all the lights came on at once."

"I know bad things have happened, Anita. I'm sorry about Haven, and Noel, but you can't afford to retreat from your psychic abilities like this."

I stood up, ready to be angry. "I'm doing the best I can."

"We know that," Nathaniel said, voice low.

It made me look at him. Just seeing him hurt and lying there was enough to calm the anger. Nothing could be bad today. Nathaniel was alive, and he would heal. That alone made it a really good day.

"I'm sorry, Nathaniel." I looked at Damian. "I'm sorry, Damian." I shook my head. "I'm just tired, but I shouldn't be. We were passed out for hours."

"Passed out is not the same thing as sleeping, Anita. You're more than just tired," Damian said, and came back across the room, though he didn't try to touch either of us again.

"What do you mean?" I asked.

"You need to eat more food and then sleep for a couple of hours."

I shook my head. "Last I checked we're trying to stay ahead of some of the most powerful vampires in the world. I don't have time for a nap."

"If you push yourself, not only will Nathaniel not heal as well, or as fast, but you'll begin to drain me, too. You can't do your usual, Anita. Not eating, not sleeping, just pushing."

Nathaniel gave a soft laugh.

I glared at him. "What?"

"It's just I've heard this conversation a lot over the last year. You'll argue, Damian or I will push, and you'll finally take care of yourself. Can't you, just this once, give in now?" He closed his eyes, and a look of pain crossed over his face. I remembered the pain I'd felt from that one big connection between us. I sighed and slumped back into the chair. I picked up the plate I'd put on the bedside table. "I'll finish my food, and then what do you want me to do?"

Damian and Nathaniel exchanged a look. Damian said, "Wow, I'm not used to you giving in this soon; I was just supposed to get you to eat and then ask the doctor what she wanted us to do next. You eat, and I'll be right back with doctor's instructions." He went for the door.

"Am I really that big a pain in the ass?" I asked.

They spoke at the same time. Damian said, "Yes." Nathaniel said, "You can be."

"You know, the Vegas tigers should be on the ground by now," I said.

"They are," Damian said, "but Jean-Claude filled them in on what's been happening. They're calling the other tiger clans to try to get as many to St. Louis as quickly as possible. Get some rest for a couple of hours, before you have to start working with the tigers."

"What does that mean?" I asked, croissant in hand.

"It means I'll talk to the doctor and you don't have to worry about it right now. Eat, help Nathaniel get better, and stop being such a pain in the ass." With that he left.

I thought of a lot of things to say, but they all sounded petty, so I ate my food and tried not to be a pain in the ass. I think every man in my life, and most of the women, would say it wasn't one of my best things.

27

DOCTOR'S ORDERS WERE to curl up next to Nathaniel and share energy with him while we slept. As doctor's orders went I'd had worse. Micah had lain next to him while I got my shit together. Now it was my turn. We'd have shift changes of lycanthropes sleeping next to the wounded until they were healed. There was something about just the closeness of the beasts' different energy that sped healing for the shapeshifters. They usually put two shapeshifters per wounded, but we didn't have enough of them at the Circus to guard the building and put two apiece on Nathaniel *and* Claudia, who was just down the hallway. I'd checked on her, but she'd been deeply asleep. I'd been assured she'd be fine and she already had her bunk buddy, so I did what I was told for a change. I stripped down and cuddled with Nathaniel.

I let myself sink in against his side, one leg over his thigh so my thigh touched just the edge of his groin, not for sex, but because it comforted us both. One arm went around his waist. The rest of me snuggled in against his body until we fit like two puzzle pieces shaped and molded to form the corner of the picture. It was a place to begin, so that the other pieces could fit in around us, and eventually if there were enough pieces the picture would be whole, and everything would be fine.

I drank in the smoothness of his skin, the sweet vanilla scent of him, but under it all was another sweet smell. Sweet copper pennies, blood, meat, his body opened up and hurt. I snuggled lower on his body to bury my face deeper against his skin until all I could smell was his skin, whole and sweet.

Nathaniel fell asleep first, and I lay in the darkened room feeling his body rise and fall under my arm. I listened to his soft breath as it deepened. He usually fell asleep before I did, but I fought sleep so I could feel him beside me just a few minutes longer. I knew how close I'd come to never having him beside me again. The thought made me wrap myself tighter around him, and eventually I slept beside him.

I was back in the living room staring down into Haven's blue eyes. I raised the gun and started to pull the trigger, but it wasn't Haven anymore, it was Jason. I had a moment to raise the gun ceilingward and not fire into his blue eyes, and then it was Haven again and he was shooting me.

I came awake gasping, and only Nathaniel's body beside me let me know it was just a dream, just a dream. I lay there with my pulse thudding on my tongue, chest painful with the beat of my own heart. I heard the door open softly, and my hand went under the pillow automatically for the gun I'd placed there, but it was Nicky, back in human form, and armed. Apparently he'd been on guard outside the door. He closed the door softly behind him and walked toward us. I started to take my hand out from under the pillow and then didn't. I liked the weight of the gun in my hand while the werelion walked toward me. Nicky was mine in a way that no one else was, mine to the point where there was almost not anything left of who he'd been, but I'd thought Haven had been tamed, too. Be a bitch to be wrong twice in the same day.

He held his hands out to his sides, showing that he was unarmed. Something about how I lay on the bed, or maybe even my hand under the pillow, had let him know I was spooked.

He whispered, "You cried out in your sleep. Are you all right?" He stayed where he was, hands still out.

I let out a breath I hadn't realized I was holding, and nodded.

"Can I come closer?"

I nodded again and tried to force myself to let go of the gun under the pillow. I circled my hand around it a little more firmly as he moved toward the bed. He smiled down at me and started to reach out to touch my arm.

I whispered, "Don't."

He stopped moving, frowning. "What's wrong?"

"Bad dreams."

"About me?"

"No."

"Then why can't I touch you?" he whispered. It was a good question. I thought about it and finally realized I had to stop being this spooked. I couldn't function like this. Either I trusted Nicky or I didn't. We'd never trusted Haven enough to put him on guard duty here, even if he'd have done it. In fact, Nicky was the only werelion we trusted that much. That had to change. Anyone we couldn't trust had to leave St. Louis. With that decision, a little tension eased.

Then there was the sound of church bells, melodious and sweet, but it would wake Nathaniel. Nicky got my cell phone off my piled clothes and handed it to me without being asked. I'd forgotten to turn off the ringer.

I took the phone from him, forcing myself to let go of the gun so I could prop myself up better. Was it a bad sign that I felt less secure without the gun actually in my hand? I felt Nathaniel shift behind me and knew the phone had woken him. I answered the phone without checking to see who it was, just wanting the noise to stop. "I'm here." And I knew it was more a snarl than a greeting.

"Blake, is that you?"

I didn't recognize the man's voice at first. "It's me. Who is this?"

"You fuck me and my people over that completely and you don't remember me. Perfect."

I had a moment to try and think. The clue was, he said *me and my people*. "Jacob?"

"Yeah."

Nicky looked down at me with his one eye and his spill of bangs halfway down his face. He was watching more intently now, like a cat that sees movement.

I tried to picture Nicky's tall ex-Rex. He had blond hair going gray around the edges, but the face and body that went with the hair were still muscular and firm. When you're a werelion Rex, you have to stay in shape. Besides, all the shapeshifters age slower than normal humans, something about shapeshifting repairing their cell structure. "What do you want?"

"You always this friendly on the phone?" he asked.

"Yeah, when I've just been woken up."

"It's daylight where you are." Which implied that where he was, it was night. Since he and his pride were international assassins and kidnappers, among other things, he could have been anywhere in the world.

"I work nights, Jacob. What do you want?"

"Maybe I don't want anything. Maybe I'll just hang up and let you take care of your own mess."

"Jacob, it has been one of my harder days, after an even harder night. Tell me what you called to tell me."

"I got offered a contract on you and your boyfriends, Blake."

"What kind of contract?" I asked.

"They didn't want us to kidnap anyone this time," he said, voice quiet.

"Assassination," I said. My voice sounded bored.

"You don't sound surprised. Did you already know that it was happening?"

"No, I didn't know." Nathaniel put an arm around my waist, drawing me more firmly against his side.

"But you aren't surprised," he said.

"Let's just say that my surprise is all used up for a while. I'll assume that if you were taking the contract you wouldn't have called."

"I turned it down. I told the person calling that no one should take it, that if they did you'd find a way to fuck them up."

"Thanks for that, Jacob, but I take it you don't think they'll take your warning to heart." I tried to feel something about the idea that they'd tried to hire people to kill us, but I didn't feel anything, not really.

He didn't answer my question, but asked one of his own. "How's Nicky?"

I thought about a lot of answers but finally said, "Ask him yourself." I handed the phone to Nicky, who said, "A little wired, but good."

He was quiet for a few seconds. "No, really, Jacob, I'm good. I've never been this relaxed." He laughed. "Yeah, I guess you're always happy when you're on the drugs, but I don't come down, Jacob." He laid his hand on my bare shoulder. The moment he did, I felt a little better, a little warmer. Nathaniel cuddled closer, and it was better still. "All I have to do is touch her and it's just an upper," Nicky said.

He handed me the phone. "He wants to talk to you."

I took it and made room on the bed for him to sit down. The moment I had both of them on either side, it was better. I'd begun to realize that I might be Nicky's drug of choice, but the men that were connected to me metaphysically were mine, too.

Jacob said, "He sounds happy."

"I do my best."

"I buy that, but Blake, it's too much money. Someone will take it."

"Thanks for the warning."

"It's my fault you got your hooks into Nick. The least I can do is keep him alive."

"So you called not to help me, but to help Nicky?"

"Yeah, because honestly I'm not sure I didn't call you because I had to.

You rolled me a little, Blake, and I'm not sure I'm free of you. Did I call you to help Nick, or because at some level you're my master, too, and I had to protect you? I tried just to not take the job, but I had to call you. I had to warn you, Blake, do you understand?"

"I think so."

"Do you?" He was angry now.

"You kidnapped me, remember? You threatened to kill the men I love. Don't go all victim on me, Jacob. You started the bad stuff, not me. I just protected myself and the people I love."

"I know that, damn you. I know that I'm the bad guy here, but I still hate you, and it still scares me that I couldn't not call you, couldn't not warn you as if I were your lion to call, or something worse."

"If I told you to come to St. Louis and help protect us, would you?"

I heard his breathing on the other end of the phone, fast, hard. "You said *if*; please, Blake . . ." He stopped and I heard his breathing go out in a shaky line. "I know you don't owe me anything. Even this call, this warning, is probably because I can't help myself, but please, don't ask me again. Don't take the *if* off that question. Don't make it an outright request, please."

"We're looking for a new Rex, Jacob."

"Not last I checked, Blake. You've got a stone-cold killer as your Rex."

"Not anymore," I said softly.

Nicky stroked his hand down my arm. Nathaniel hugged me tighter. It all helped, but . . . I still didn't feel anything.

"Whoever beat him is your new Rex, Blake."

"My dance card is a little full, Jacob. I don't think I can add another job."

"You did not beat him in a fair fight."

"He cheated first," I said.

He was quiet for a second or two. "So one dead Rex, but none of his lions won the job?"

"Yep."

"You do complicate your life, Blake."

"Things just go weird with the lions; why is that?"

"Our culture is harsher than most."

"Maybe," I said, "but we still need a Rex now. You're a Rex with a pride and no territory of your own. We're a territory with a pride and no Rex."

Nicky had gone very still beside me, his hand still on my arm. He was concentrating like hell on the conversation now.

"Don't ask me, Blake. Please, you don't owe me this, but . . . don't ask me." His voice held pain.

"Do you really believe that if I asked you outright to come here and be our Rex, you couldn't refuse me?"

"I don't know, but I do know I don't want to find out."

I thought about it, but Jacob and his people were professional bad guys; we didn't need more killers in St. Louis. "How long ago did they ask you to come kill us?"

He let out a shaking breath, as if he'd been holding his breath waiting for me to ask, or not. "It's not enough money for me and my people, or anyone close to our talent. That's what they'll need to take you and yours out, Blake, but even amateurs get lucky."

"How long do we have before they hit town?"

"It's been forty-eight hours, so maybe no time."

"So you waited two days to warn us? Thanks."

"I knew you wouldn't like that. I tried not to warn you. The contract is just on you, your master, and his wolf. I thought maybe Nick wouldn't get in the line of fire, but I had to warn you. I couldn't resist the urge to call you."

"Next time call immediately, okay?"

He swallowed hard enough for me to hear it. "Okay."

"Give me a number where I'll always be able to reach you."

"Don't do this."

"You waited forty-eight hours to warn me until the compulsion got too strong. I may not like you, but you and your people are good at your jobs. You'd make good muscle. If your delay makes things worse I'll call. If your waiting gets us in trouble, I'll ask you to help us out of it. If it makes no difference, I leave you alone."

I heard him swallow again. "That's fair, I guess." He gave me a number.

"If you cancel the phone and I can't reach you . . ."

"I don't know if I could hide from you, Blake. I don't know if whatever you've done to me would let me hide."

"Then don't try, Jacob. I'll play fair as long as I can."

"What's that mean?"

"It means some bad shit is going to be hitting the fan soon, and we may need more muscle. I'll try to leave you and your people out of it, because frankly I may have rolled you but I haven't even met all your people. I'm not sure I want to bring that many wild cards into my town."

"I hope you mean that."

"I don't usually say things unless I mean them, Jacob."

"That I do believe," he said.

"Thanks for the heads-up," I said.

"Don't thank me; I'd have let you die if I had a choice."

"Aw, Jacob, you'll hurt a girl's feelings that way. I thought you liked me."

"I do like you, that's what scares me."

"Good-bye, Jacob."

"Good-bye, Blake." He hung up.

I lay back against the bed for a minute while Nicky watched me in the dimness and Nathaniel lay quiet at my back. It still felt good to have them touch me, and I still wasn't afraid, or even worried, and that, of course, was the problem. Too much fear will paralyze you, but too little fear will make you careless. I held Nathaniel's arm against my body and knew that afraid or not, I'd do whatever it took to keep him safe, to keep the people I cared about safe. I'd said that before; last night felt like I'd proved it.

"What do we do now?" Nicky asked. He'd started petting my arm again.

"We tell the others and we prepare."

"For what?" Nathaniel asked softly.

"Kill them, before they kill us." I said it with my voice firm, sure, and devoid of almost any emotion. For once I wasn't being brave; I sounded like I felt. I wondered how long I would feel numb, and what it would feel like when I stopped. I pushed the thought away, made Nicky move, and reached for my clothes. Assassins were either on their way or already in town. Eventually I'd be afraid, and before that hit I wanted a plan.

28

WHEN I OPENED the door, Nicky right behind me, I saw that he'd been sharing guard duty with Graham. Tall, broad-shouldered, he wore his straight black hair cut a little too long through the bangs, so that his eyes stared out through the hair like a cat watching from the grass. Though *cat* wasn't accurate. He was a werewolf. Other than a little uptilt at the edges of his eyes and the straight black hair, his mother's Japanese heritage seemed to have passed him by; most of him came from his tall, Nordic father. His parents were still the only ones to ever come down to Guilty Pleasures to visit their bouncer son at work. Graham had missed the orgy because he lived off-site and he was usually being a bouncer at the strip club rather than muscle here. He was wearing a bright red T-shirt, which meant he was available for blood donations or sex. So far I'd managed to keep him off my menu, and I was planning to keep it that way.

He grinned at me. "I can't believe I missed last night."

"Be happy you did," I said.

He looked stricken and way younger than his early twenties. "It was an orgy. You fucked people that you've never touched."

I glanced at Nicky, who was at my side. "Does he know everything that happened last night?"

Nicky nodded.

"You guard this door, and if anything happens to Nathaniel because you failed at your job I will kill you." My voice had just a little inflection at the end, but only a little.

Graham looked at me. "What'd I say to piss you off?"

"That you have to ask that question, Graham, is why I don't sleep with you."

He still looked totally lost. It was Nicky who said, "She feels bad about Noel and Haven being dead." His voice was pleasant as he said it, and I realized that his inflection never changed, either, but it wasn't numb, just pleasant like nothing he had just said moved him.

"We need another wereanimal to bunk with Nathaniel."

"You told me to stay on the door," Graham said.

"Sorry, just thinking out loud." My head felt buzzy and full of static. The shock was beginning to wear off, which was both good and bad, apparently.

"If you want more people to sleep with Nathaniel while he heals, the infirmary is the best place. People are on rotating shifts."

I opened that part of me that was connected to so many people. I just threw it wide to see who was close. Nicky hit the radar first because he was right beside me, but the energy went out and out. I knew that Jean-Claude was here, and he felt my urgency and my confusion and started walking this way. I found Jason, and felt sorrow from him. I wondered what was wrong. I found Damian still up, still awake. Apparently none of the vampires who woke early were going to sleep at all today. Crispin's and Domino's energy came and with that one brush I knew there were more tigers here. They flared brighter in my head. They shouldn't have been brighter on my metaphysical radar than the shapeshifters I was closest to. I narrowed down my search, leaving that bright energy out of my search pattern. I brushed a lot of people's energy inside the Circus, but one person I didn't find was Richard. He wasn't here. Crap.

I started dialing his number. Inside the Circus was like an underground bunker, almost impenetrable, but outside it all bets were off, and Richard was the least capable of the three of us to watch for this kind of danger. He was still too trusting, and too tied to trying to be "normal."

Stephen came down the hallway. He should have been at the apartment he shared with Vivian. No, wait, it was daylight out and since he worked nights he often spent the day here being snack food for vampires among other things. He wasn't on my food list. Stephen was cute enough but just not that kind of friend. He was wearing jeans and a T-shirt. His curly blond hair was loose around his shoulders. He always looked younger in his street clothes. He took one look at my face and asked, "What's wrong?"

The phone went to voice mail. "Shit." I waited for the beep. "Richard, it's Anita. Come back to the Circus. We have assassins in town with a contract to kill you, me, and Jean-Claude. You aren't safe. Call me back, damn it." I hung up.

"Text him," Graham said.

"What?" I asked.

"Text him. Some people check their texts a lot more than they do their voice mail."

I hadn't had the phone that long. I handed it to him. "I don't know how to text. Help me."

Normally, he'd have said something smart, but wisely he just started working the phone. "What do you want me to tell him?"

"Assassins in town. You're in danger. Come back to the Circus."

"How do you spell *assassins*?"

"Let me, faster if I type and spell," Stephen said, and took the phone. He typed in what I said. "Sent." He put that cornflower-blue gaze on me. "Now back up and tell me, why are there assassins in town and how do you know?"

I shook my head. "I don't have time to explain. I need to find Richard and get him back here."

"I'm supposed to be your replacement for Nathaniel's healing, but if you need me . . ."

I started to dismiss him. I didn't think of him as a fighter, but the first time I'd met him he had waded into a giant snake gone amok in the Circus of the Damned. He'd risked his life to help kill it. Funny how I'd begun to think of him as someone who helped me do my hair and makeup for Jean-Claude's fancy events, but not as a fighter. He was about my size, as delicate in his own way as Vivian, but he was also a werewolf and that meant something.

"Thanks, Stephen, but I think staying with Nathaniel will be great. I need to find Richard and bring him back here; after that we'll have a meeting or something." I was already moving down the hallway. Nicky followed me. I almost told him to stay at the door, but truthfully I would eventually have to go outside the Circus, and of our guards he wasn't a bad choice. He might be creepily overattached to me, but his fighting skills were excellent and the only thing that kept his killing in check was my conscience. He didn't seem to have one of his own. I couldn't stay in here forever. I had a job. I'd taken last night off, but I had clients to see this afternoon. Of course, all it would take was one of the assassins signing up as a client and they'd get to be alone with me. Or would have; now I'd need guards with me. Shit.

A small screaming part of me was saying something in my head that I was trying really hard not to listen to. *Richard is in danger.* The only comfort about him not answering his phone was that if he was really hurt I'd know it, the same way I'd known that Nathaniel got shot in the shoulder. I'd feel it. Richard was okay. He was safe, for now.

Then I realized I was being slow. I hit the phone screen and got my contacts list back up. I'd call Jamil, or Shang-Da. They were his main bodyguards, his Sköll and Hatí. One of the three would pick up their damn phone.

Nicky was already on his own phone. I heard him talking to Bobby Lee about the assassins. He was right. I should have told our men first. I had to pull myself together and work this emergency. I'd fall apart later.

Jamil's number was first alphabetically, so I hit it. He picked up on the second ring. "Anita, what's up?"

"You need to bring Richard back to the Circus, now."

I heard his voice twice, like a weird echo, as he said, "That's going to be a problem."

I turned to find him coming down the hallway with Shang-Da by his side. "Why aren't you with your Ulfric?" I asked.

"He's on a late lunch date. We don't go on the dates."

I pushed the whole date thing away. I'd worry about it later, if at all. I told them what was happening. "Well, shit," Jamil said.

"That about covers it," I said.

"If he's with the doc, he won't answer his phone," Jamil said. I wanted to say, *Richard is dating a doctor?* but it didn't matter. It wasn't like we were monogamous.

"Contact him mind-to-mind," Shang-Da said.

"I'll try. He's been keeping me out the last few months."

"Maybe, or maybe you both quit trying," he said.

I didn't try to argue. We'd decide who was right and wrong once I knew Richard was safe. I felt Jean-Claude coming toward me. He didn't try to shut me out. I pushed the thought away. I opened that link between Richard and me. Shang-Da was right; I'd stopped trying a while back. It was just easier that way.

I smelled trees, leaves, pine, forest. It was how I always found him by scent, as if wherever he was he smelled of the wolf pack's land. I felt him behind the wheel of his four-by-four. I saw him glance up, as if somehow I were hovering near the roof of his truck. We always looked up to see each other—the way we had for the council, come to think of it. That made me lose focus for a moment, and I had to fight to see him. I knew he was already close to his house, because of the trees by the road. I had a moment of seeing him looking up at me, and of seeing the road through his eyes.

He pushed me out a little, so that he was driving with only himself in his head. "Sorry," he said to the empty air, "but hard to drive that way."

"Sorry, but there's a contract killer out for you, me, and Jean-Claude."

"The council works fast."

"Maybe, but it doesn't matter who ordered it, Richard, just come back. We stay underground until we have a plan."

"I can't hide forever."

"Just for now, please, Richard. I've had enough emergencies for one day."

He started to do the turn to the last road. He caught a flash in the trees. I had a moment to feel him see it, and then the windshield cracked in front of him, and he was fighting the truck not to go into the ditch.

I screamed, "Gun!"

The second shot hit him, and I fell to my knees in the hallway. It didn't exactly hurt; in fact, my shoulder and half my chest felt numb. I couldn't catch my breath. It did hurt to breathe. Nicky was holding me. His face was frantic. "Anita!"

"Shot." I gasped it out, there was no air. They'd hit his lung, but his heart still beat, strong and thick in my head. I could see sunlight through the trees as the truck went over the side of the road, and there were trees, and we were falling, and there was no air.

29

JEAN-CLAUDE'S FACE ABOVE me. "*Ma petite*, what have you done?" He looked into my eyes and he saw it, felt it, but he dragged me away from it. He shut the link down. He left Richard bleeding and alone.

I gasped air in with lungs that worked, and said, "No! They'll kill him. They'll drag him out of the truck and kill him." I dug my hands into his white shirt.

"If he dies, I can keep us from dying with him, but if I open the link between us all to feed him enough energy to heal in time, if it does not work, one or both of us will die with him."

"We can't let him die knowing we didn't even try. Let me feed the energy; you pull me back if it doesn't work."

I watched the struggle in his eyes.

"Jean-Claude," I said.

He nodded. "What energy will be enough to get him up and moving in time? Nathaniel is still hurt; you cannot give the energy of your own triumvirate. It could kill them both."

"He is our Ulfric and we are sworn to protect him with our lives," Shang-Da said, kneeling all that long, dangerous body down next to us. "If by my life, or my death, I can save him . . ."

"Do it," Jamil said, and he was kneeling closer to my face.

"There isn't time for sex," I said.

"We saw what you did to Chimera. We felt the power you took from that feeding. Do it," he said.

There should have been time to look into his handsome face, admire the cornrowed hair and all that he offered, but the one thing we didn't have was time. I said, "I'm sorry."

"I know," he said.

I put my hands on his arms, bare skin to bare skin, and just as when I'd done it the one and only time to Chimera, there was no time to find the power, or worry over morals, it was a moment of do or die. To raise zombies I put energy into the dead; the more energy the better the zombie, the more completely the dead will rise. This power was almost a polar opposite to that. One second it was just Jamil's warm skin under my hands, and the next my necromancy spilled down my hands and onto that dark, muscled skin.

Jamil's brown eyes widened. His lips parted. He whispered, "God, it hurts." Then his smooth dark skin began to run with fine lines. I was taking back whatever it was that let me fill out a corpse so it was plump and smooth and rosy-cheeked. I took that from Jamil, and he stayed on his knees and let me do it. The first time I'd done it I'd thought it was watching decades catch up with the man, but watching Jamil's skin collapse around his bones, I realized it wasn't time I took from it, but literally life. I fed on the very essence of what made his body move and function. I fed on him, and the rush of power was as strong as and felt better than I remembered it. I think I'd been afraid to remember how good it felt. Afraid that if I remembered, I'd crave it.

The power poured down my skin and into my body. It spilled into Jean-Claude where his body touched mine, so that rush of life and energy, and everything Jamil was, filled us both. It was as if every fiber of my body filled with his essence, and I spilled that into Jean-Claude, until it felt as if our bodies should have glowed like stars with it. Jean-Claude opened that window inside me, inside us, and I was suddenly back in the truck with half my upper body not working, and one lung gone to a painful emptiness inside me. I could hear the men, at least two of them, crashing through the trees toward the truck. Jean-Claude helped me feed the power into Richard. His body convulsed on the seat of the truck, the energy almost too much for his wounded body to take in. He coughed blood, and so did I, spilling it around Jamil's withered skin. That spark that was Jamil's beast reacted to the scent of fresh blood and gave a surge of heat. I felt the balance of it. I could drain all of his life, or I could leave something behind to save later. It made me hesitate.

Richard opened the passenger door and fell out into the bushes. We had to get away from the truck before they got here. I felt him crawling through the underbrush, fighting to get farther away, but we could use both arms now. I realized I was afraid to take all I could from Jamil. I knew how to put it back, theoretically, but I'd never done it.

Jamil was suddenly gone, pulled away, and Shang-Da laid his hands against mine. I didn't have time to think it was brave of him, I just fed. I fed on him without hesitating. I fed on all that strength and warmth and life, and Richard was on his knees, and then on his feet and moving farther into the trees. If he could get far enough away he could shapeshift and heal the rest of the damage. He was willing to do that, but there would be moments during the shift where he would be helpless, and we couldn't afford that.

The power needed to go somewhere, and I found Nathaniel still in his bed, still cuddled with Stephen, and I poured the energy into him. Poured it in until his body ran with fur, and the last of the injury was washed away in a roll of muscle and skin and leopard. The power was so much, so much, as if the two of them together made the same kind of energy that I'd taken that first time. It had been enough to heal so many. I found the lions lying in their beds. Rosamond was very still, with Jesse curled beside her. The power filled her, making her body flow with fur until a great lion filled the bed and chased Jesse out of it. Kelly sat up in bed with Payne naked beside her, her arm in a cast, which meant it was badly broken. I spilled the energy into her and watched her body become the lioness I'd seen in my head, the huge paw cracking the now-useless cast.

I thought of Claudia and the power found her. I shoved the power into her, too, and her skin ran to black fur, and she cried out as the energy forced her broken body to heal almost too fast. I knew even as it felt good, it also hurt. I was losing the ability to be gentle with it. So much power, so much energy. Jean-Claude helped me reach out for Richard again. He was far into the woods now. Far enough he couldn't hear or smell them now. He took the energy we offered and his body shifted into a huge, shaggy wolf. I'd always seen him in wolfman form, never this, and I felt him think that in this form he'd be less likely to be reported to the police as a stray werewolf. He'd be able to hunt in the woods and not frighten people. He didn't say any of it, he thought it, and I thought it, too.

One minute I was padding through the leaves on all fours, the world alive with smells that I'd forgotten, the next I was in Jean-Claude's arms. He held me close, rocking me. *"Ma petite, ma petite."* And just from the level of emotion in him I knew that what we'd done hadn't been without risk, that there had been a moment, or two, when he'd felt both of us going.

I pushed at him, so that I could turn in his arms to see what I'd done to

Jamil and Shang-Da. They looked like mummies, shriveled and dead, corpses desiccated in some dry desert, but they weren't dead. Jamil was making a high keening noise.

"God," Nicky said, "they aren't dead." He was pressed against the far wall, as if he weren't sure he wanted to be near me right that moment. Maybe there were things terrible enough that even my hold on him couldn't make him see it as all right. I found that oddly comforting.

"No," I said, "they're not dead." I crawled toward Jamil.

"*Ma petite*, you gained a great deal of power, but we cannot afford to lose more vitality, or you will kill one of us."

"There's power in raising the dead, Jean-Claude. You should know that by now." Obsidian Butterfly, the vampire that I'd learned this nasty, useful piece of information from, had thought she was a goddess, for real, and part of what made her think that was that she gained power from taking life and from giving it back. Jamil's eyes were dried and blind, but as I leaned over him, he screamed, high and buzzy, but louder. Maybe he smelled that it was me, and he was afraid of me now. I didn't blame him for being afraid, because I could have killed him with this second touch just as easily as helped him. Both would be energy. Both would feel good.

I prayed. I prayed that I could give this back and gain energy through it. I'd never actually reversed the process. I'd only seen it done. I touched his face, and it felt like dried leather; the strong bones of his face felt fragile like sticks, as if I could have broken his bones if I held his face too tight. I was as gentle as I knew how to be, as I called my necromancy. This was a type of that energy, and it hadn't occurred to me at the time, but Obsidian Butterfly was the first vampire I'd ever met who could work with this kind of energy.

There was a rush of warm wind as if early summer suddenly filled my skin and the man underneath my hands. It was like watching one of those films where flowers bloom, except this was his skin, his flesh, his very bones filling back out, blooming into the strong, muscled, handsome man I'd known. He came to himself, eyes wide, and screaming. When he could move, he pushed me away and scrambled on hands and feet backward, away, until he hit the wall, and then he screamed again. He held his hands out in front of him as if to ward me off.

I should have felt bad that he was that afraid of me, but the energy felt too good to feel bad. I laid my hands on Shang-Da's shriveled face, his shiny black hair reduced to straw. That warm wind raced over my skin and into him. The energy filled him, plumbed him, like water returning after a horrible drought. He gasped back to himself, coughing and staring up at me with his brown eyes wide and panic-filled. I'd never seen him panic over anything.

"Your eyes," he whispered, "they're black and full of stars."

They weren't my eyes. They were Obsidian Butterfly's eyes. All power comes with a price. I turned to Jean-Claude and found his eyes filled with a night sky that had spilled over South America when the conquistadors had conquered the New World. I felt Richard's wolf in the woods miles away, and I knew that his eyes weren't wolf amber, they were night-sky black.

Damian staggered around the corner, wiping the blood of a fresh feeding from his mouth. His eyes were filled with blackness and stars.

30

SOME OF THE other shapeshifters took Jamil and Shang-Da to a back room to lie down. Jamil wouldn't look at me. Shang-Da did, but it wasn't a good look. It was more as if he were considering how he would kill me if he had to, and considering for the first time that he might not be able to. One of them dealt with his fear by being afraid, the other by estimating his chances. Either way, I'd damaged what relationship I had with the two werewolves. I could have pointed out that they'd volunteered, and that it did save Richard's life, but I wasn't comfortable enough with what I'd just done to be that logical.

I let them be led away like children lost in the mall when security finally finds them and takes them back to Mommy and Daddy.

The black-star vision did what it had last time: It helped me see things more clearly, as if everything were sharp-edged like it can be in an emergency. You see everything, and you notice things you might not have noticed otherwise—like I knew that Nicky had a knife tucked into his boot on the right side, because his jeans didn't lie quite right. It was a small knife; normally I wouldn't have noticed the slight rise along the seam of his pants.

I rose up to look at his face, and he wasn't afraid now. His face wasn't calm, though; it was considering. "What?" I asked him.

"The energy rush you shared felt amazing. Did it feel even better to you?"

"I don't know."

"Yeah, you do. It felt good the way killing something with teeth and claws feels good. It feels good to feed."

Jean-Claude stepped between us, took me by the shoulders, and made me look at him. "*Ma petite*, you have saved our Ulfric. You saved Richard's life. You have done no lasting harm to the other wolves."

I looked up at him, wondering if I'd see through some illusion with the new vision. He looked the same as he always did; amazing. "You really don't use any vampire wiles to make yourself this beautiful," I said.

He smiled. "I told you long ago, *ma petite*, that I do not try to appear to you as other than I am."

I nodded.

Damian came to stand beside us. The black eyes looked even more startling in his face, I think because he didn't have black hair to balance it. It was just pools of darkness in all that white skin and red hair.

"It was almost better than blood," he said, and his voice was distant. That was the real danger to some of these powers; it wasn't that it felt bad. It felt so good, good enough that if you weren't careful you might crave that power rush. If I craved it and gave in to it, I would be the monster. I didn't want to be the monster. I didn't want Jamil and Shang-Da to be afraid of me, not like that. But if the choice had been Richard dead or them afraid, I chose them afraid. Was that monstrous? No, not yet, but I was beginning to understand that the only difference between being the monster and being powerful was choosing not to be the monster. Not today. But there would always be tomorrow, and another chance to choose.

My cell phone rang. This time it was the peal of church bells, so I knew it wasn't a regular caller, or Nathaniel would have figured out a ring tone for them. I reached for it without thinking. Jean-Claude and Damian just watched me reach for it. I think they were being cautious, and I just needed something ordinary. "Blake here."

"Is this Marshal Anita Blake?" a man's voice asked.

"Yes, and you are?"

"Marshal Finnegan."

I stood up a little straighter. Shit, please don't let the Marshals Service need me now. Black glowy eyes and hit men out to get me, how would I explain it? "What can I do for you, Marshal Finnegan?" My voice sounded even and unemotional, business as usual. Good for me.

"I'd like you to take a look at some crime scene video."

There was a little spurt of relief. Usually I could do that sort of thing from a distance. Distance was good right now. "Be glad to. You want to email it to me, or give me an address and password for a site?"

"Got pen and paper?" he asked. Which meant it was going to be a password and one use of his site.

"Not on me. Hang on a minute." I pantomimed writing in the air, and Nicky handed me his iPhone with the screen set to notebook. I kept forgetting it did that. I used my shoulder to hold my phone and had my fingers poised to hit the itty-bitty keyboard. "Ready when you are."

He gave me a web address and a password. "This will let you view it for today. We'll change the password later today. Just standard protocol."

"It's okay, Finnegan. I wouldn't want someone I didn't know personally having full access to my stuff, either."

"Yeah, but I'm asking for your help, not the other way around."

He had a point. "Fine, I'll stop trying to play well with others."

"Rumor has it that all you preternatural branch marshals aren't team players."

"Being the Lone Ranger doesn't teach you good group skills," I said.

"He was a Texas Ranger actually, not a U.S. Marshal," he said.

"I know, just trying to make my point that being on our own didn't teach us to play well with others."

"Point taken," he said.

"When do you need me to get back to you?" I asked.

"ASAP," he said.

"Look, Finnegan, everyone says that. I need some kind of time frame."

"Watch the video, then you decide how quick you need to get back to me. I think you'll be calling ASAP."

"That bad?" I asked.

"Yeah, actually."

"I'll watch it and get back to you as soon as I can," I said.

"Ben Carter says good things about you."

"I only looked at some surveillance tapes for Marshal Carter."

"Yeah, but he says that you saw things on it that none of their people caught."

"Actually, I saw what everyone else saw; I just understood what it meant."

"None of the rest of us knew enough about vampires to catch it."

"But I'd suck on a forgery case. We all have our expertise."

"You know, Blake, I think you play just fine with others."

"Thanks, Finnegan, but you haven't told me what I'm supposed to be looking for."

"We're looking for reasons, Blake."

"Reasons? Reasons for what?" I asked.

"When you see the video you'll understand. We just want to know what the fuck happened, excuse my language."

"It's okay, Finnegan, I cuss like a sailor."

"I heard that about you, but my mother raised me that you don't curse in front of a lady."

I was both flattered that he'd called me a lady, and wondering if it would make him treat me as less of a marshal because of it. You had problems if they thought women were ladies, or whores; it was just different problems. "I appreciate that, but just wanted you to know it's not necessary."

"I think it is, but I'll try not to apologize to you again."

"Hey, I'm okay either way." Then I had a thought, and something about the weirdness of the day made me say it out loud. "You know, it's never occurred to me that my cussing could offend other women. Elderly women, yes, but, huh, I never thought about it."

He laughed. "I don't know if women are offended when other women cuss."

"Me, either, but it's worth a thought."

"That it is, Blake, that it is."

"I'll look at the video and get back to you."

"We'll be looking forward to any insights you can give us."

"Finnegan, I just realized, I didn't ask where you were? I mean, what city did this crime happen in?"

"Sorry, Blake, I thought I said. Atlanta. Atlanta, Georgia."

"Okay, I'll get to a computer and look at it."

"I'm on a landline, but here's my cell. You'll get me any time."

I wrote the number down on Nicky's iPhone. "Got it."

"I hope you come up with something."

"Me, too."

We hung up. I held the phone out to Nicky. "Make those notes appear on my phone and delete them from your phone."

He took it and began to do what I'd asked. Jean-Claude touched my arm, turned me to him and Damian. "Are you truly going to take the time to look at this video, *ma petite*?"

"I am."

"Our guests from Las Vegas have been very patient."

"Look, I don't want to see them while our eyes are still all black sky and stars."

"Why not?" Damian asked.

I thought about a lot of things but finally said the truth. "It felt good to feed on Jamil and Shang-Da, didn't it?"

Damian nodded.

"I don't want to be around wereanimals that I'm attracted to while this power is still riding me."

"You are afraid your hungers will not stop at the *ardeur*," Jean-Claude said.

I looked up at him, and his eyes were still a swimming sea of night. "Yeah."

"I believe your control is better than that, *ma petite*," he said.

"Maybe, but let me look at the video, and by that time I should be ready to meet our visitors."

He studied my face, and I wondered if he saw me differently with the power riding him. I almost asked, and then I thought better of it. I'd had enough shocks to the system for one day. I wasn't going to fish for any more.

"I need someone to help me get on the computer and then leave me alone to watch."

"I do not want any of us in the triumvirates to be alone, *ma petite*."

"You're afraid that the council or Mommie Dearest will try something else."

"Aren't you?" he asked.

I thought about it and could only nod. He smiled and touched my face. "Then I will watch with you."

I shook my head. "No, it's an ongoing police investigation. I can't share it with civilians."

He gave me a look. "I hardly think I qualify as a civilian."

"But you aren't a cop, either."

"I can spell our so-helpful Micah with the weretigers, but you can't be alone. If the council tried for you when you had no one to touch, I am not sure what would happen."

We debated, not quite argued, but in the end we compromised. Nicky stayed with me, because if I ordered him not to tell anyone what he saw, he'd have to do what I said. Damian got to stay with me for the same reason. Something about him being a vampire servant made it almost impossible for him to refuse a direct order from me. I tried not to give him orders much, but I seemed to have a lot more control over him than I did over Nathaniel, and for that matter a lot more control over Damian than

Jean-Claude did over either Richard or me. Since I was the first necro-mancer in vampire history to have a vampire servant, none of us knew why Damian had to obey me when the rest of us didn't have to obey anyone. It was just another mystery. Anyone who might know the answer to it was trying to kill us right now, or on the run from the Mother of All Darkness. We'd figure it out later, but right now I had a crime scene to look at.

I realized that I was glad to have something else to concentrate on be-sides our personal or metaphysical problems. Police work wasn't always simple, but it had clear-cut goals. You figured out who did it, or what did it, and you caught them, or killed them. Problem solved. When crime busting is easier than your personal life, something has gone seriously wrong.

The fact that the underground of the Circus of the Damned had a computer room still seemed weird to me. Most vampires weren't big on technology, or modern inventions that hadn't been around when they were "alive," but Jean-Claude was an early adapter and he was insisting that all his people know the basics. Hell, he had some of the dancers tak-ing turns with online blogs. They were on Facebook, MySpace, and even Twitter, whatever that was. It was getting to where I was the least tech-savvy person we had. That seemed weird, too. I was the human being, sort of; wasn't I supposed to be better with this kind of stuff than the vampires?

The only light in the computer room was the soft glow of monitors. Valentina was at one of the terminals with the chair cranked as high as it would go, so her five-year-old body could reach the keyboard. She was dressed in a pink dress that was all lace and bows down to white tights and patent leather shoes. No one made her dress like the proverbial little girl. It was actually a step forward from the centuries-old clothing that she'd come to us with. The delicate triangle of her face was painted ghostly by the monitor's glow. She was staring at something on the screen so intently that she didn't seem to hear us.

I had a horrible thought. She and Bartolome, who was stuck at twelve, had both been in the underground when the *ardeur* hit everyone. What had happened to them?

"Valentina," I said.

She startled visibly and hit some buttons. The screen flickered, and then there were pictures of little cartoon animals floating over it. She began to move the mouse as if she were concentrating on the children's game. She might actually enjoy the game, but whatever she'd been doing moments before hadn't been a screen full of big-eyed cartoons. She only looked five. In reality she was older than Jean-Claude. Actually both she and Bartolome were two of the oldest vampires in St. Louis. They were trapped in children's bodies, but they weren't children.

She glanced behind her, smiling, the intensity that I'd seen on her face when I first came through the door gone. She turned a perfectly good little girl's face to me. She could even make her eyes fill with that naïve light, but it was a lie. She'd been turned into a vampire too young for sex, but she had some of the drives of an adult. Those urges had been translated into pain. She was a sexual sadist and had been a professional torturer for centuries. It had been both a calling and a hobby. I wondered if that was what the *ardeur* would translate into for her.

She smiled sweetly at me. "Anita, do you want to play a game with me?"

"Sorry, I have police work to do."

She pouted at me. "No one ever wants to play."

I didn't want to ask the question, but the very thought that I had forgotten her in all this made me have to ask. "What happened to you and Bartolome last night?"

She crossed her arms over her thin child's chest and pouted harder. There was an edge of anger to it now. "He locked me in my coffin for hours."

I let out a breath I hadn't known I was holding. I fought not to look as relieved as I felt. But she noticed. She'd had centuries to watch adults and to manipulate them.

"I'm sorry for that," I said.

"No, you're not."

"I'm not sorry you were locked away while the *ardeur* went through us, no," I said.

"At Belle Morte's court, when the *ardeur* was unleashed they'd give me someone to play with while they had sex."

I blinked at her, not sure what to say to that.

"She doesn't mean *play*, Anita," Damian said.

I turned to him. "What does she mean?"

"They would give her someone to torture in a private area where no one could reach her, or her victim."

"I thought you only visited the courts once," I said.

"Once was enough," he said. He was looking at the little vampire, and even through the black eyes and the blankness of the very old vampires there was still something.

"You weren't her victim," I said.

"No, I wasn't."

"His friend was, though," Valentina said. "I heard your master shoved him into sunlight and burned him all up later."

Damian stiffened beside me, and I touched his hand. The death of his best friend and brother in arms was one of his worst memories.

"We need to use the room, Valentina."

She hopped off the chair, fluffing out the skirt of her pink dress. She came to us, her dark curls framing that forever face. She stopped looking up at Damian. "I liked your friend. It was a waste to kill him like that. I would have kept him safer than that."

Damian's hand tightened in mine. I said, "What did Bartolome do after he locked you in your coffin?"

She looked at me, narrowing her eyes. "Why are your eyes all dark?"

"New power," I said.

Either that satisfied her or she didn't really care. "Bartolome did what he always used to do. He went to find a woman." She rolled her eyes, which was more teenager than the rest of the act. "He's with her now. She seems quite besotted with him."

"Who is it?" I asked.

"Oh, I don't know her name, and I don't care. She won't play with me." She wrapped her tiny hand around one of Nicky's fingers. "You don't play with me anymore, either."

"That's because you cheated," he said.

"But we could have such fun," she said, pulling on his hand and swinging a little the way children will.

"Did I miss something?" I asked.

"You knew the rules, and you broke them." He held her shoulder so he could take his hand out of hers without her falling.

She stomped her little foot, hands on hips; it might have been cute, except that her eyes drowned in brown fire like any vampire's when their power comes on them or they lose their control. "There are plenty of wereanimals that enjoy pain. You could help me do it."

"They enjoy pain for pleasure, but you don't get off on that. You need them to really hurt before you're satisfied."

I looked from one to the other of them. It must have shown on my face, because she said, "If I'd known you hadn't tattled to Mommie, I wouldn't have said anything."

"Now I will have to tell her," he said.

"Someone tell me," I said.

"You know she was Belle Morte's torturer," Nicky said.

"I know," I said.

"She found out that I was an interrogator before I came here. She wanted to compare notes."

"*Interrogator* is a euphemism for *torturer*, right?"

"Right, but I saw it as more of a job. For Little V here, it's a passion. Her only passion." Just saying it showed that he understood her more than most people did. He got the true brokenness of her.

"Yeah," I said.

"She wanted me to help her by seducing some of the other wereanimals into some bondage sex and then she'd help me play with them, but her idea of play is something that even a pain slut wouldn't be able to enjoy."

"They'll heal, Nicky. They'll heal if I don't use silver metal," she said, hands still on her waist, face in that perfect little-girl scowl.

"When she found out I wouldn't help her lure the wereanimals in for torture, she tried to mind-fuck me."

"I take it that she couldn't roll you."

"There's too much of you in him," Valentina said. She stamped her foot again. "There's no room for anyone else in his mind, or in most of their minds. You're like Belle Morte was, Anita. You fill them up so that they think of only you, but she would give them to me when they disobeyed her or made her mad. I had more fun there."

"I didn't make you stay here," I said.

"No, we have to help Stephen and Gregory. We have to make up for scaring them." Her face went from pouting to serious. She and Bartolome had tried to take blood from the twins, but feeding for Belle's line is a kind of sex, and the thought of the child vampires feeding on them had terrified Stephen and Gregory. It had been too close to their past with their sexually abusive father. When they'd discovered why the twins were so frightened of them, they'd stopped tormenting them and stayed in St. Louis to make it up to the men somehow. We were going on two years and the child vampires were still trying to find a way to cleanse their honor with the brothers. Now, of course, they couldn't go back to Belle's court, because she was on the run with her court.

"If you would just let us kill their father," she said.

"Stephen's therapist says that he needs to handle his father personally. That you killing him might actually cause more damage."

"I know"—she sighed—"and so we are trapped here. At least Bartolome will have a lover now and I still have nothing."

"I never know what to say to you, Valentina. I can't give you people to torture."

"You could, but you won't," she said. She threw her tiny hands in the air in a gesture years beyond her size and stomped to the door. Her hands were a little small for the door handle, but she opened it hard enough for it to slam the wall.

"Nicky, find out what she was hiding on the computer."

He walked over and started hitting keys as the fat cartoon sheep bobbed around the screen.

Damian hugged me, burying his face in my hair. I hugged him back, my face pressed against chest. Nicky made a soft whistle. I turned in Damian's arms so I could see the screen.

"What is that?" I asked.

"Just keep looking at it, your eyes will make sense of it."

Damian put his hand in front of my face so I couldn't see. "And then you'll never be able to not see it."

"Damian, move your hand."

"I have to do it, because you ordered me, but don't look, Anita." He moved his hand, and I looked.

Nicky was right, my mind did see it eventually, and Damian was right, too. It was one of those images that once you see it you'll remember it. I'd seen cut-up bodies in person, but it was still gruesome even by my standards.

"Does she have a file of this kind of thing?" I asked.

He hit more buttons. He started opening files and all the pictures were like that. Images from actual war casualties, crime scene photos that had made it onto the World Wide Web, bondage images, but only ones that were serial-killer bad. Image after image flickered across the screen.

"It's all like this," Nicky said. "Even I have pictures of other things; women, weapons, online cartoons. There's nothing but this on here."

"You should kill her," Damian said.

We were both standing behind Nicky, staring at the screen. I noticed that Damian's eyes had gone back to their normal green. Mine felt back to normal, too.

"She hasn't done anything here to earn an execution, Damian."

"I didn't say execute her, I said kill her. The baby vampires always go mad, Anita. I don't know any as young as her that didn't have to be put down."

"*Put down?* You make her sound like a rabid dog. She's not an animal."

He motioned at the screen. "Yes, she is. She looks like a little girl, but that's what's inside her head. That's all that's inside her head. Eventually, she's going to find a way to make what's inside her come outside, and then people are going to get hurt."

"I like Little V, but he's right, Anita. The fact that she's been able to control herself this long is impressive, but the pressure is building up. Eventually, she won't be able to stop herself."

"So you agree with Damian we should kill her?"

He nodded. "You can do it now, or you can do it after she's cut someone up, but eventually one of us will have to do it. She talked to me about what she wanted to do to someone, and trust me, it's all she really thinks about. I think the longer she can't act on the urge in smaller ways, the bigger the urge gets, the more it's going to take to quench her . . . bloodlust."

"I can't kill her for something she hasn't done," I said.

"Like you couldn't let me kill Haven for you, because you felt sorry for mind-fucking me and not fucking Haven enough."

I glared at him. "Thanks, that makes me feel so much better."

"Either you need to send Little V to another master who will let her hurt people, or you need to kill her to make sure she doesn't hurt any of your people. But either with permission or without, eventually she's going to do this to someone."

"I saw what she could do to people, Anita," Damian said.

"We can't kill her for what she might do," I said.

Nicky hit some more buttons and the images began to cycle on the screen one bloody mess, one frightened tied-up person after another. "She was sitting in the dark looking at this, Anita. The only real question is, was she just watching, or was she masturbating to it?"

I stared at him instead of the computer. "That's . . . that's sick. That's . . . I did not want to think that, or know that. Fuck, Nicky, why . . ."

"I want you to understand, Anita, this is her passion. I wasn't joking. This is either sex for her, or as close as she comes."

"Turn it off," I said.

"You're not going to kill her because you feel sorry for her. Nathaniel talks to her, too, Anita. They don't talk about the same things. He's a bottom to her top, but he lets her talk about hurting him. He lets her talk some of her fantasies out with him, because he understands that she only looks like a kid. What would you do if she got Nathaniel alone? What would you do if she did that to him?"

"Don't do this," I said.

"I like Nathaniel, and it would kill you if something happened to him. Regrets are about decisions that you know you should have done different. Don't make this one of them."

"I can't kill her for what she might do, Nicky."

"I could," he said.

"You like her," I said.

"Yeah, and I understand her better than you do. Anita, if you hadn't mind-fucked me into a Bride I wouldn't be trustworthy around your people, either. I'm not a sexual sadist. I don't need pain or fear to enjoy sex, but I enjoyed having power over people. The hurting was more about taking pride in my skill at it and getting information out of people. I got off on breaking the strong until they were weak. That was my kick, but everyone breaks, Anita. If you have the skills and enough time there's no such thing as someone who won't break."

"And you had the skills," I said.

He shrugged as much as the muscles of his upper body would let him. "Yeah, I did, but she's better. Do you understand me, Anita? Little V is better, because she's spent the last eight hundred years practicing."

"Anita," Damian said, and he touched my shoulders, making me look at him, as Jean-Claude had earlier, "you know how they say practice makes perfect?"

"Yes," I said, but that one word was barely a whisper.

"Valentina is perfect."

31

I MADE THEM shut up about Valentina, but the thought that Nathaniel had been letting her whisper serial-killer fantasies in his ear to let off some of her pressure was almost more than I could handle for the day. I wanted to scream at them both that I didn't need this today. That we had enough problems without borrowing. If Valentina hurt him, I would kill her, but killing her after the damage was done would be cold comfort.

But once the video started, none of us were worried about what Valentina might do in the future. We were too worried about what some other vampires had done last night. We sat in the three computer chairs we dragged up in front of the big flat-screen monitor and watched the horror show in nice HD color. Some things are not meant for high-definition detail. It just makes it worse. The vampire's lair was underground, down a short flight of stone steps. There seemed to be moisture seeping down some of the walls. The first body was at the foot of the stairs with some natural sunlight filtering down from higher up the stairs. The first bodies were obvious vampire victims with neat bite marks at both sides of the throat, wrist, bend of the elbow, inner thigh, bend of the knee. The only thing that made the bites bad was that there were too many of them. No human being could feed that many vampires in one night and live.

"It's the same number of bites as you and some of the other wereanimals have," Nicky said. "Why aren't we dead?"

"Wereanimals are harder to kill, for one thing," I said, as we watched more bodies simply lying against the walls or in the middle of the tunnel. They lay as they'd fallen. No one had taken any time to reposition the bodies. They'd killed them and left them for the next victim.

"They meant to drain these people dry," Damian said. He'd gone very still beside me. I wasn't sure if he wasn't sure how I'd feel about him touching me while we watched this, or if the sight of all the bites excited him and he didn't want me to know.

"Why aren't we dead, again?" Nicky asked.

"Jean-Claude used the *ardeur* to keep feeding us all energy so that the Lover of Death couldn't feed off our deaths," I said.

"The bites are getting messier," Damian said in a voice as still as his body in the chair beside mine.

He was right. The bites weren't neat little puncture wounds anymore. There was tearing of the skin around the bites. The next man's neck was torn open on the side; blood had poured out of him. There was a pattern in the dried blood.

"Pause it here, Nicky."

He used the mouse to pause it.

"They didn't even try to feed on him," Damian said.

I leaned forward and pointed at the screen. "Are those the marks of knees, as if whoever tore his throat out knelt and let the blood pour over him?"

"I think so," Damian said.

"Could be," Nicky said.

"Start it up again."

"You mean from the beginning?"

"No, I mean just make it go again."

The images began to march down the corridor again. Someone's inner thigh was torn out, blood pooling between the body's legs in a terrible parody of birth. So much blood, and then the camera moved and I saw the second woman with her own torn neck and thigh so that the blood of both adult women had pooled together in the narrow corridor. There was no way for the police or the crime scene people to avoid stepping in the blood. It was either step in it or stop moving forward.

I watched the camera operator hesitate. The camera pointed downward, then up the corridor where the camera light picked up more pale, naked bodies as far as the light could touch. He, or she, picked their way through the mix of blood and bodies and found more of the same until the corridor went into a wider opening.

I let out a breath I hadn't realized I was holding. I didn't really want to see the devolution of the vampires' kills, because that was what we were seeing. It wasn't going to get any better inside the next room. The only comfort I had was that I wasn't there in person. As bad as the film was, in person would have been worse. It was nice that the marshals had enough vampire executioners that I was called in for consults rather than being the main shooter. I was very happy to delegate some of this shit.

The camera went through the opening, and it was like a mix of *Dracula: Prince of Darkness* meets torture porn, slasher flick. There was so many bodies that it was just a mass of dark shapes at first, as my mind couldn't make sense of it. It was like Valentina's pictures; the mind didn't want to see it. The human mind is pretty good at protecting itself and will sometimes just refuse to compute all the data in a vain effort to save the rest of the mind from what the eyes are seeing. But it was my job to look.

Nicky said a soft, "Wow."

Damian got up from his chair and walked away from the screen. I couldn't blame him; if I could have walked away before my mind made sense of it all, I might have. But I kept watching until I could see body after body scattered like broken dolls on the dirt floor. The bodies were torn apart, not by claws and fangs, but strength. The vampires had torn them limb from limb, spraying blood and internal organs like some meaty, bloody jigsaw puzzle. I was happy not to be able to smell it. Because once you perforate the lower digestive system it's not just blood and that thick hamburger smell, but also the outhouse smell. Death, this kind of death, has no romance to it. It was slaughter.

There were more bodies piled around a central coffin that was on a raised dais between two huge candelabras that were still burning, though the wax was low. They'd set up lights in the corners of the room. The light was pitiless, shining off the blood that was still drying, showing the internal organs in huge bloody strands.

The bodies were piled in pieces almost to the lip of the open coffin. There were bodies lying on the body parts as if they'd been placed there. "Pause it," I said.

Nicky did what I'd asked. He and I both leaned toward the screen, trying to make sense of it all. "God, I think those are the vampires."

"How can you tell?" he asked.

I understood why he asked; the intact bodies were covered in as much blood and gore as the pieces. "They're not torn apart, and see there, one of them has fangs showing in her mouth. It's like they bedded down on the mound of their dead. Also, if they were victims that intact, they'd have been moved for medical attention just in case they weren't dead."

"Have you ever seen anything like this?" Nicky asked.

"No," I said.

"You want me to hit play again?"

"No, but do it anyway."

He didn't even ask me to explain. I think my newest pet sociopath wasn't enjoying the show, either.

The camera rose and aimed at the figure in the coffin. Blood pooled around it as if the body were floating in the blood. How had they even gotten that much blood in the coffin? It was if they'd hung the dead over it and drained them, but nothing in that room had been thinking enough to do anything that organized.

"Gives a new meaning to *disorganized killer*," Nicky said, and his voice held a note I hadn't heard in the year he'd been with us: impressed, and scared.

The corpse in the coffin looked old, like they'd found a badly decayed body to put in the blood. Then I saw the fangs in the gaping skull and knew this was the master. He'd been blown apart with a shotgun so that the top of his head was missing, but the jaws were still intact. His chest had been shot up, too, so that the thickening blood pooled into the ruin of his heart.

"I didn't think vampires decayed like that just from being shot up, even when they die," Nicky said.

"Most don't," I said.

Damian was behind us. He said, "Only the descendants of the Lover of Death rot like that."

"When they're dead," Nicky said.

Then I had a bad, bad thought. I scrambled my phone out of my back pocket and dialed Marshal Finnegan's number. He answered on the first ring. "Blake, that was fast."

"I know that you have to film evidence before you torch the place, but tell me the vampire executioner did torch the place already."

"Morgan killed the Master of the City. Took his head, took his heart. We're already hearing complaints from the vampire lobby lawyers that we may have condemned all low-level vampires to certain death. Apparently without their master they may not wake up at dark, but we've found out that the lesser vampires that do wake up are usually fine. When the Master of the City goes crazy like this, kill him, or her, and the crazy goes with him. We try to spare most of the murdering vampires, and we're still hearing from their daytime lawyers."

"All potentially true, but, Finnegan, the Master of the City is a rotting vampire. Taking just their heart and head with a shotgun doesn't kill them, ever. The only reason he didn't get up and eat your executioner is that it was daylight and he couldn't rise from the grave, but if he's as old as most rotters he will rise in late afternoon underground, and definitely at full dark. Worse yet, some of the intact vampires might not rot unless shot up, so you may have an entire crypt of rotters."

"You make that sound bad."

"Finnegan, get your people out of there."

"You helped write the new law that makes us leave the lesser vampires alive when we can prove that it's the Master of the City gone apeshit," he said. "Now you're telling me that it's going to get my people killed."

"I'm saying the apeshit Master of the City is still alive, and when it gets dark enough he'll rise and all his vampires will rise with him and keep slaughtering people. The new law only works if the Master of the City is really, truly dead."

"I'll try to clear the scene. I hope you're wrong." He hung up.

"Fuck," I said. "Who'd he say was the executioner on this?"

"Morgan," Nicky said.

"I've worked with him once, unless we have two of them." I flipped through my contacts praying that the name was in there. I found it and hit the screen. I was praying as the phone dialed. *Please, pick up, please pick up.*

"Blake, I take it you saw the tape."

"Morgan, where are you?"

"Atlanta," he said.

"No, where are you standing."

"I'm outside the crypt in case some of the little vampires wake up still crazy."

"Are there still techs down there?"

"For another hour and then we'll clear it, except for me."

"Get them out. Get them out, now!"

"I took care of it, Blake. He ain't getting up."

"He's a rotting vampire, Morgan. They don't die when you destroy the brain and heart. Even sunlight may not do it. Fire is the only certainty and then the ashes need to be scattered over different bodies of flowing water."

"He didn't rot until I shot him, Blake. Once they look like a corpse, they're dead."

"He didn't turn into a corpse, Morgan, he rotted. It's different. Please, just trust me on this. Get your people out of there and flamethrower everything in the crypt."

"We're still dragging bodies out of there, Blake. I can't fry the evidence. We haven't even started to identify the dead."

I fought the urge to scream. "Morgan, just humor me. Just pretend I'm right, and at least clear the crypt of personnel, okay? Just do that and we'll debate the whole flame thing later. Please, God, please, just do this one thing for me."

"You really think he's a genuine rotting vampire. Those are really rare in the United States," he said.

"They are, but just in case, Morgan. It doesn't hurt to clear out the techs and the cops."

"All right, but unlike you, I don't carry a flamethrower as part of my usual vampire-hunting kit, Blake."

Truth was, neither did I. "Just clear the crypt and call an extermination team."

"You mean a bug squad." That was one name for the exterminators who did everything from cockroaches to rogue wererat infestations and ghouls. They were who you called if you found a zombie just wandering down the street, since fire would destroy it and most animators couldn't put the zombie back without knowing the grave it came from.

"Yeah," I said.

"I'll ask my superiors if I can call them as backup, but they aren't going to let me burn everything down there. The lesser vampires may wake up sane and fine now that he's dead."

"He's not dead, Morgan."

"How do you know that?"

I almost said, *Because the Lover of Death was looking for his bloodline last night*, but I couldn't share that without explaining things I couldn't explain to the cops at all.

"If you're asking me am I a hundred percent sure, I'm not, but I'm ninety-eight percent sure and I wouldn't have my people down in that hole this late in the day."

"Rotting vampires rise earlier than most, though they can't pass for human until full dark because they look like decayed corpses until then." He sounded like he was quoting. Morgan was one of the newer executioners who had been recruited for the job, and not grandfathered in like most of us. He was part of a new breed of vampire hunter, trained in classrooms with books and guest lectures. It wasn't a bad way to learn, and you probably had less death in the learning curve, but in this moment I'd have taken an old-fashioned shoot-first-and-ask-questions-later vampire hunter.

"I'll clear the crypt, Blake, but that's all I can do until I clear this with someone."

"I'll take what I can get, Morgan. Just get your people out of there."

"I will."

"Now," I said.

"I'm walking toward the entrance to the crypt as we speak. Good enough?"

"Yeah."

"Shit . . ." The phone fell against something loud enough I had to take it away from my ear.

"Morgan, Morgan, you all right?" I heard him moving as if he were standing on gravel and the phone were on the ground. "Morgan, are you still there?"

I heard noises on the phone as if he'd picked it up. "Morgan, talk to me."

I heard someone swallow as if his throat hurt. It was a wet sound. "I'm afraid Marshal Morgan can't come to the phone. To whom am I speaking?" The voice was male and thick, as if he had a speech impediment or injury to his mouth.

"Marshal Blake," I said.

"Anita Blake." The voice coughed as if to clear something.

"Yes. Who is this?" But my speeding pulse already knew the answer, before he said, "I am Clayton, Master of the City of Atlanta, Georgia, but my true masters have filled me with purpose. Do you know what that purpose is, Ms. Blake?"

"To slaughter as many people as you can so that your true masters can feed off the death."

"You do know what's happening." He hung up.

I screamed wordlessly into the dead phone. It took everything I had not to fling the phone across the room. I dialed Finnegan's number. He picked up, voice rushed. "Morgan isn't picking up his phone."

"He's probably dead," I said.

"How do you know that?"

I told him how I knew.

"Clayton isn't supposed to be a rotting vampire. He's never shown any sign of it."

"He was hiding, Finnegan. People may want to be vampires, but not if they think they'll be spending eternity looking like decayed corpses. That's not sexy enough for people to volunteer."

"How many others are hiding in plain sight, Blake?"

"I don't know."

I heard sirens, lots of sirens. "I'm almost there. I'll call you, let you know how bad."

"Finnegan, wait, you need an extermination team with flamethrowers. He walked out in daylight; only fire will kill him."

"That's not standard issue to cops," he said.

"I know that."

"Fuck," he said, and this time he didn't apologize. "If we all live through this I'll call you back." He hung up.

We were hundreds of miles away with no way to help them. "Motherfucker." Or were we? I reached out for Jean-Claude down that metaphysical pipeline and he was there. He looked up and whispered, *"Ma petite."* I didn't try to tell him everything, I simply opened my mind and he knew what I knew.

I asked out loud to the room, "Is there anything we can do from here? Can you help me control him from here?"

"I am sorry, *ma petite*, but no. He is a Master of the City, as am I. His ties to the land and the vampires there will keep us from interfering."

"Damn it!"

"I am sorry, *ma petite*."

My phone rang. I hit the screen almost yelling. "Finnegan, what's happening?"

"I'm sorry, I'm not Finnegan," a male voice said.

"Who is this?"

"Sorry to catch you on a bad day, Anita, but this is Jake. I gave you some jewelry once."

I think I stopped breathing for a moment. The turn of events was too fast. My hand went to the charm around my neck. "I'm wearing it now," I said.

"You do remember, then," he said.

"Yeah, though an amazing number of our people don't seem to."

"We need to stay secret, Anita."

Jake was the wolf to call of one of the Harlequin. They were the closest thing to police that the vampire world had. They were supposed to be some of the finest warriors to ever live, or unlive.

"If you'd come to kill us you wouldn't be calling, so why are you calling?" Jesus, didn't I have enough disasters on my plate without the Harlequin? Some days it doesn't rain, it fucking drowns you.

"Your Nimir-Raj put out the word that he's wanting clanless weretigers. He wants to honor all the weretigers and not just the clans."

"Micah's very fair-minded."

"He is," Jake said.

"You just want to bring us some tigers," I said.

"I'd also want to come back to work as security for you."

"Why?" I asked.

"Are you saying you can't use another guard?"

"No, extra manpower is going to come in handy."

"I want the kittens safe, Anita, and things are getting very dangerous out here."

"Kittens?" I made it a question.

"The weretigers, someone's hunting and killing them. It started in Europe, but I'm afraid it will spread to here."

"Funny coincidence that we're calling for weretigers and someone else is killing them."

"Do you really believe in coincidence?" he asked.

"No. How soon can you get here?"

"I'm in your parking lot in a van being watched by your guards. If you'll ask them to allow us inside, I would beg an audience with you alone before you meet my tigers."

"Just me?"

"I think at first, yes."

"Jean-Claude won't let me see you alone."

"Fine, choose the guard you would most want to stake your life on, but the fewer who know the truth the better."

"What truth?" I asked.

"Please, Anita, let us inside where it will be safer, and I will tell you everything."

I wasn't sure I believed that last part, but there was nothing I could do for the cops in Atlanta. Hell, I couldn't even leave the Circus until we had a plan for the hit men who had almost killed Richard. I wasn't sure that he and Jean-Claude would be as good at healing me, and there was always the chance that I'd take Nathaniel and Damian to their graves. It wasn't just my life anymore, in a very real way.

"Fine, I'll tell the guards to let you in, but you don't get into the underground with your tigers until I know what's going on."

"If you insist, but if not the underground, then where do you wish to meet?"

"Do you know where Asher's office is in the Circus?"

"Of course, I did work security here once."

"I'll see you there," I said. I got off the phone and started trying to find a number for one of the wererats who wasn't wounded and could plausibly be in charge. I guess we were down to Bobby Lee, who was finally back from parts unknown after a lengthy job out of town. I didn't know details, and with some of the business that the wererats did around the world I probably didn't want to know. Plausible deniability is good when you play with criminals but carry a badge.

"Anita," Damian said, "it isn't safe to meet Jake like this."

"He saved my life."

"He's also an assassin."

"Who is this guy?" Nicky asked.

"Jake is what he calls himself."

"But who is he?"

"Since you get to sit in on the conversation, you'll find out. Just stand in the corner and look intimidating unless he does something bad."

"Then what?" he asked.

"If he tries to hurt me, then kill him."

He widened his one good eye. "You're usually all about taking 'em in alive."

"Not this one. If he's on our side we are going to be very happy, but if he's not, then he's too dangerous for anything but killing."

"He must have hurt you bad last time he was in town."

"Actually he saved my life and gave me this." I touched the charm again.

"But you'll let me just kill him if he tries anything."

I nodded.

"I'm missing part of the story, aren't I?"

"Yep, and you can't repeat anything you hear in the room unless he kills me, in which case, tell everyone."

"If he's this dangerous, why meet with him at all?" Nicky asked.

"Because if he really wants to be on our side, maybe he isn't the only one."

"Anita, don't do this," Damian said.

"If he meant us harm he wouldn't have called," I said.

"Unless the council ordered him to lure you into a false sense of security."

He had a point, but . . . "They weren't too happy with Mommie Darkest last time Jake was in town. I'm thinking that everything that's happened won't have improved that."

"You're honestly thinking that they might join with us?" Damian asked.

"It's a thought."

"Who are *they*?" Nicky asked.

I dialed Bobby Lee as I said, "You'll find out." Bobby Lee wasn't thrilled that I wanted to meet Jake with just Nicky as backup. He'd been out of town the last time Jake was here, but I was the boss, or the Black Queen, since we were back to using code names even on the phone. I pointed out, "You know, me being the Black Queen isn't hard to figure out."

"Then come up with a better code name." And that was the theme of the day. Me bitching and the people I was complaining to throwing it back in my face and saying, *If you can do better, then do it.* I'd try.

32

I WOULDN'T LET Damian come with me. I didn't really think Jake would try to hurt me, but just in case I wouldn't put both Damian and me within reach of one of the finest close-in assassins in the world. Nathaniel might survive my death, but there was no way he'd survive both Damian and me dying. I'd almost lost Nathaniel just hours ago. I wouldn't risk it. Jean-Claude wasn't coming for the same reason. I knew that the guards had picked up Richard still in wolf form. Some of them were waiting for a tow truck and doing their best to keep it from being reported to the police. It would be hard to explain all the blood on the front seats without Richard being hurt. Again, playing Clark Kent was a problem for our furry Superman.

But right that moment I was more concerned with the werewolf sitting across the desk from me than the one down in the underground. Asher's office was at the top of the seats in the one permanent circus tent inside the Circus of the Damned. The office was set up almost like a press box for a ball game, but there were drapes over all the glass windows and the door in the back wall led into a bedroom. The outer office was still very plain: a desk and chair, two client chairs, and a small loveseat against one wall. The drapes at the back of the desk hid the door to the back room. It looked the same as when I'd first entered it years ago, when it was Jean-Claude's office. Asher had added nothing of himself to it. That seemed sad.

Nicky leaned against the wall, closer to me than to Jake, so that the other man would have to get past him to reach me. Jake looked like I remembered him: short dark hair, medium complexion, and brown eyes, attractive in a manly-man kind of way, but even there he was almost too ordinary. He was nondescript. He was even an average height. He would blend in, and since the Harlequin were supposed to be spies that was probably right for the job. The weretigers who had come with him were the opposite: eye-catching blonds, tall, and beautiful, or handsome, and somehow unworldly, as if they'd only recently been let out of their cages.

Jake slumped down in one of the client chairs, looking at everything and nothing with his brown eyes. "Are you sure about talking in front of him?" he asked.

"Nicky's okay," I said. I didn't feel the need to explain that he was my Bride and couldn't repeat anything we said unless I told him he could.

Jake shrugged. "I have to trust your judgment since I trust you with the pretty kittens."

"You're a werewolf. How did you end up with so many weretigers?"

"I've known these kittens their whole lives. I think they'd be safer here with you."

"I don't know, Jake, you may be bringing your lambs to the slaughter." I told him about the assassination attempt on Richard.

"Amateurs," he said.

"I agree, but they almost killed him. If they'd hit his heart with that second bullet, I don't think we could have saved him."

"I think Jean-Claude could have kept the rest of you alive, but you would have been down a wolf."

I frowned at him. "You say that like it's no big deal."

"I don't mean it that way, Anita." He rubbed his eyes as if he were tired, and I realized that there were lines around his eyes that I didn't remember from last time.

"Why are you here, Jake? Why did you bring me weretigers? The truth."

"I do think they're safer here with you, but ask me why I think they're safer."

"Pretend I asked, now answer the question."

He smiled. "Direct. I like that after dealing with all the old vampires. They're almost never direct."

"Then be direct back, Jake," I said.

"They aren't survivors of an attack, Anita. They're pureblood tigers."

"You said they were clanless. The purebloods all have clans."

"One color doesn't have a clan."

I frowned. "We only have one blue tiger, so Cynric doesn't have his own clan, but other than that they all have clans."

He shook his head. "Yellow doesn't."

"Because the last yellow tiger died here in St. Louis after she killed one of our people and did her best to kill more."

"Including you," he said.

I nodded. "Including me."

"She belonged to one of the Harlequin," he said quietly.

I blinked. "Last I checked it was against the rules to say that word out loud unless we were contacted by them first. In fact, saying it out of school is a death sentence."

"But you know that I am the animal to call of one of the Harlequin."

I nodded. "Most people don't remember that you revealed that. Even some of the powerful shapeshifter guards act like ordinary humans, as if you mind-fucked them and made them forget."

"My master thought it would be better that way."

"Are you contacting us officially?"

"Yes, and no. I am here as an agent of some of the Harlequin, but I am not sanctioned by the council to be in St. Louis."

"I'm listening."

He gave a small smile. "Almost anyone else would ask questions, at least be astonished, that I'm telling you that the Vampire Council's own spies, police, and executioners have broken with them."

"Let's just say we had some remote-viewing visits from a few council members."

"Then you know what has happened," he said.

"You tell me what you know and I'll tell you what we know and we'll see how deep the shit really is."

He nodded, the smile fading. "The Mother of All Darkness isn't dead."

I nodded.

"She's visited you," he said, sitting up from his comfortable slump.

"Sort of."

"When she felt her body destroyed by the bomb, she sent her essence out in search of a home. She found fertile ground in some of the council. Once, so long ago that most do not remember, that was what the council was, Anita. They would come to sit in their great chairs, but the deep dark secret was, once they took their places on the council the Mother possessed them. She had more trouble possessing some than others, but she took them all. The council only pretended to vote and be fair; in truth they were all her puppets."

I took a deep breath, let it out slow, and nodded. "I'm not surprised."

"The Traveller seems free of her; he and his human servant are running for their lives. They are hiding somewhere; even we do not know where."

"Are some of the Harlequin on her side, still?"

He nodded. "We are at war with each other. It is a very quiet, deadly little war, more like a series of assassinations, but we are at odds with each other."

"Do you really think we can hide you from some of the greatest warriors and killers that ever lived? We're good, Jake, but I'm not sure anyone's that good."

"No, I come to offer my gun and my strength to help fortify your safety, not the other way around."

"You think the other Harlequin will come for us?"

"I know they will."

"When?" I asked.

"It depends on how fast we can kill the ones that want to kill you. If our side loses enough manpower, then they'll come for you. Right now they see the other Harlequin as their greatest threat. Once we are neutralized, then they will turn to you."

"So it behooves us to help you guys."

He smiled. "I didn't come here for that, Anita. We will live or die as we always have, by our own hands."

"Then what do you want from us?"

"Depending on how our private feud goes with the other Harlequin, others of us will come to your aid, or to spy on you. There are some who are more neutral, because they do not believe that you and Jean-Claude and your two triumvirates could be Master of Tigers."

I stared at him. "Did you guys bug our phones again?"

He grinned. "No, your wererats sweep very effectively for listening devices now."

"We may be a little slow, but once we learn something we don't forget it."

His voice was all serious, suddenly. "The last remaining tigers that are not red or white belong to the Harlequin as their animals to call. When Mother Dark took the power of Father of the Day, she gave some of that power to us. We gained the tigers through it. Your blue boy is not the last of the blue, there is one more, but she is busy fighting for her life alongside her master, so soon your Vegas teenager may be the only blue tiger left in the world."

"Are she and her master on our side?"

"They are," he said.

"So, you have a black tiger or two," I said.

"We have one. We had two, but when the Father of the Day regained some of his power, he called Sebastian away from us."

"Funny, Sebastian never mentioned he was one of you guys." I felt a little spurt of anger, because I had let him go when I could have turned him over to the police, or just kept him.

"Sebastian was and wasn't one of us. He had been, but the Father of the Day was truly his master, so the Mother of All Darkness didn't trust him. She allowed him to live, but he had no one. My master and I kept track of him, but he has been on his own for a very long time."

"Tell me who's on our side and who isn't, Jake."

"The remaining black tiger's master is not. We have one male gold tiger, and he and his master have agreed to be on your side if we can prove to them that you can be Master of Tigers."

"How do we do that?" I asked.

"Funny you should ask."

"One more oblique answer, or question, and I'm going to get pissed."

"I'm sorry." He sat up and almost shook himself like a bird settling its feathers. "When the Mother of All Darkness declared the gold clan to be destroyed, some of us hid a few of them. We helped them escape to various parts of the world, including the New World. We've been helping them to hide, waiting for another Master of Tigers. One who wasn't evil."

"Or a sexual sadist," I offered.

He gave a very small smile. "That, too."

"The other clans think the gold is destroyed and the strain of lycanthropy inside me is the last remnant of them," I said.

"They would be wrong."

"You've hidden the gold tigers since the first emperor of China; that's twenty-two hundred years. You've been planning this for that long?"

"We've been hoping for that long."

I raised eyebrows at him. "That's a long damn time to hope."

"When you live forever and don't age, it gives you the time to hope."

I didn't know what to say to that, so I shrugged. "So you're saying the tigers with you are gold, yellow, whatever."

He nodded.

"They are the purest of their line that we have been able to preserve. There are some who are like your Domino, of more than one clan. We have found that the tiger survivors mated with the gold breed mostly true."

"I'm an American, Jake. It means that pure blood is sort of overrated. We're a nation that's all about the melting pot."

"The tigers are not. It's important to them."

"So, I pick one and do what?"

"Bond with them, Anita. Pet them, fuck them, mind-fuck them, whatever it is you do when you gain a tiger to call."

"I can also make them my Brides."

"Like your werelion," Jake said.

I fought to keep my face neutral. "How did you find out?"

"Rumors that you've just confirmed. And I've seen other Brides over the centuries; they have a certain smell to them."

Nicky moved against the wall, as if he'd say something, but he just settled back like a good bodyguard, seen and not heard.

"I think we need one of the tigers to call you master in the way that your wolf and leopard call you master. I don't think making one of them a Bride would be as impressive."

"You left out my other lion," I said, and studied his face, though no matter how human he looked, I knew that after enough centuries you could get pretty good at keeping your thoughts off your face.

"No games, Anita. We heard what happened to your local Rex. We know that you need a new Rex, and you haven't chosen a lion to call, which was one of your old Rex's bones of contention."

"You have spies in with us," I said.

"We have spies everywhere, Anita; don't feel special."

"Oh, it's not special I feel, trust me."

"The Mother of All Darkness is trying to turn the council back into her puppets. We must stop her."

"How? How do you fight something with no body of its own? How do you fight something that can jump from body to body?" I asked.

"By being powerful enough to cut her off from each body in turn, until she is nothing but spirit and spite. We believe she will fade then."

"But you don't know," I said.

"If I said we were sure, you'd know I was lying."

"How do we cut her off from their bodies?"

"The way you cut her off from Belle Morte."

"No one in that room told you."

"Belle told us, Anita. She has turned to us to hide her."

I just stared at him.

"Why do you look surprised?"

"I'm not sure, but Jake, we used the powers of Belle Morte's own line to free her. We don't carry the power of anyone else."

"Now who's lying?"

"I'm not."

"Anita, you carry the power of every line that's attacked you. You collect vampire powers like butterflies. The Master of Beasts attacked you and now you can call all manner of wereanimals. The Dragon barely touched you from a distance and you can feed on anger. I heard you even did her nifty trick of using the vampire's own aura against them to cut like glass."

"Only once, and Jean-Claude was driving the metaphysical bus."

"We want him to gain the powers, too, Anita. We need him to be powerful enough."

"Enough for what?" I asked.

"To head the council in America."

I shook my head. "Damn, word does travel fast. You must have spies in every major city."

"Not every city, but the ones that are powerful enough to be helpful, yes."

"So I choose from the boys. Who's the girl tiger for?"

"You can choose anyone you want, but knowing your preferences the girl is more for Jean-Claude."

"More for—what does that mean?"

"It means this works better if you like everyone in your circle of power. Your line of power is based on sex, lust, even love, so your liking everyone who sleeps over is a good thing. Maybe even a necessary thing for you."

"So how does this work? I just go out there and pick the cutest one? It's not like picking kittens from a litter, Jake."

"If you could wrap your head around it, I think you and Jean-Claude taking them all back to your room and seeing which ones you like best would be the fastest and surest way."

I just looked at him. "So we go from *Hello, my name's Anita and this is Jean-Claude* to *Let's all go back to our room and fuck*? Aren't they related to each other, as in a little too closely related to screw each other?"

"We don't want them to screw each other. We want them to screw you and Jean-Claude, and your other men."

"You're a little short on girls then," I said.

"We can get more if they make it here alive."

"So someone is killing the clanless weretigers because they suspect what you've done."

"Someone, probably another Harlequin, has figured out that we saved the gold tigers, but they don't know how weak the bloodline has gotten. So they're just killing every weretiger they find."

"I haven't heard anything about it."

"They're only hitting the clanless. They know the bloodlines for the clans, and they know about Cynric. They aren't worried about them. Please, Anita, take Nathaniel to bed with them, or Micah, whoever you need to feel better about this, but we need you to bond with a gold tiger, as soon as possible."

"Why is that so important?"

"Because once you have all the colors under your control, you will gain an astronomical amount of power and so will the tigers."

"Bibiana said that, too."

"Once you have a gold tiger to call your own, the others will not be able to resist you."

"Then why didn't the gold tiger who tried to kill me and her master rule the tigers?"

"Because she was just gold."

"I thought gold automatically gave you all the other colors."

"No, if it's a one-off, it's just like all the other tigers."

"How are you so sure that giving me a gold tiger will give me all the tigers then?"

"Because you already have a white and black."

"I'm not sure whether they're my tigers to call, or closer to what Nicky is," I said.

"Doesn't matter, you have power over them and the blue."

"Cynric was sixteen and I was his first sex. Any sixteen-year-old boy would have bonded with me."

Jake laughed. "I think you underestimate yourself, but it's a good point. What I mean is that you call to all the colors you've met, including the red.

You were little queen enough to put out a countrywide call to all unmated males. You damn near caused a riot with our gold males. They were ready to get on a bus, or a plane, whatever it took, and come to you. We had a hell of time stopping them. Soledad's mistress couldn't call all the males, and neither could Soledad."

I thought about it, then said, "We help you with the tigers, and you help us with the assassins."

"Rafael's rats are on it now. If your Ulfric didn't insist on playing human, he'd have had guards with him."

"He likes being a normal person, but I think he'll be willing to have guards until this is fixed."

"It may not be fixed by autumn, Anita."

"Jake, if people keep trying to kill us for another two, three months solid, the problem will be fixed, because eventually one of us will be dead."

"You're really calm when you say that. Most people would be afraid."

I shrugged. "I'll be afraid when I have to be."

"So, you and Jean-Claude and whoever else you wish to include will take the gold tigers?"

"If we're fighting the council and the Mother of All Darkness, we need all the power we can get."

"I remember you as arguing more the last time I was in town."

I shrugged again. "Maybe even I get tired of arguing."

"Or maybe circumstances have worn you down," he said.

It was my turn to give a little smile. "That, too. If you were going to offer the tigers to Jean-Claude, too, why not include him in the talk?"

"He's your master, Anita; if you wanted to include him you would. If you want to share information with him, you simply think it and let him hear your thoughts. This way he was able to talk to more of the American Masters of the City while I told you all this."

"Labor division at its best," I said. I stood up. He stood up. "Introduce me to your tigers, Jake."

"They aren't mine," he said.

"You've known them since they were born. Don't you feel anything for them?"

"I've watched them grow up; of course I do."

"Then how can you just offer them to us like they're not really people with their own free will?"

"They were raised for this moment, Anita."

"You make them sound like farm animals."

"I don't mean to, but we didn't keep them hidden and protected for thousands of years out of the goodness of our hearts, Anita. We did it because we needed them. We needed them so we could give them to you, and you could make them food."

"My animals to call aren't food," I said.

"Pretty to think so, but food is just energy that you eat, and they are energy that feeds your and Jean-Claude's power base."

"You do think of them like livestock," I said.

"We have married them, bred them, and watched over them like our special little flock of sheep for over a thousand years, Anita. When the new Master of Tigers emerged, there was no guarantee that he, or she, would be a kind master. We had to stay detached because when the moment came to give them to someone, we had to be willing to do that. If I loved them the way you love children, I might not have been able to do that. Do you understand that?"

"I understand that the big bad wolf has been watching the flock, when they thought you were the sheepdog."

"You're right. They call me Uncle Jake."

"And if I'd been an honorable but cruel person, you'd have still offered them up like lambs to slaughter."

He looked at me. Brown is supposed to be a warm color of eye, but in that moment there was nothing warm in his gaze. It was as cold and pitiless a look as any I'd ever seen, and I'd seen some good ones. "Yes," he said, "I would have."

"Evil old Uncle Jake," I said.

He nodded. "Yes."

"I couldn't be evil Aunt Anita," I said.

"Even to keep the Mother of All Darkness from spreading across the entire world like an evil, death-spreading plague?"

I wanted to look away then, but I forced myself to keep meeting his eyes. I finally said the only truth I had. "I don't know."

"Yes, you do," he said. "You just don't like that your answer would be the same as mine."

"If we do evil in the name of good, it's still evil, Jake."

"Lucky for me, you are a good person at heart, Anita Blake. You will do your best not to hurt them, so I can do my duty and not be evil this time.

But I never lie to myself. I know the only thing that keeps giving those kids to you from being evil is your own innate goodness. But if you were the most evil bastard on the planet and it would save the rest of us, I would give you all my golden kittens, and that is evil." He offered me his hand. I took it, expecting him to shake it, but he raised it to his mouth and laid a brief kiss on my knuckles. "Thank you for letting me do my duty, and not be the motherfucking bastard I feared I'd have to be."

He rose and turned away, but not before I saw the shine of tears in his eyes. He said he never lied to himself, but he did. He said he didn't love them like children, and I knew in that moment that he did.

33

WE WERE OUT the door and going down the steps when my phone rang again, that peal of church bells. I said a little prayer and picked up. "Blake, here."

"Check your email, Marshal." It was Clayton.

"What did you send me?"

"A video. I do love these new gadgets, don't you?" He hung up.

I sighed. "Go talk to your tigers. I've got to see what the bad guy sent me."

"What bad guy?" Jake asked.

I shook my head and handed the phone to Nicky. "Help me play the video he sent me."

"You know we do have spies in almost every major city, Anita. We have us in every major city."

I turned and looked at him. "What are you offering?"

He glanced back at his tigers with their circle of our guards around them. "Tell me what's happening, and I'll tell you if we have anyone or anything that can help."

"I've got it open, Anita," Nicky cut in.

"Hold that thought," I said to Jake, and turned to Nicky. He handed me the phone but stayed close so he could look over my shoulder. I didn't complain. If I needed to pause it or run it back, I'd need his help anyway. I really had to learn to work this damn thing.

The screen was surprisingly clear, like a little TV. There was a figure in white crime scene scrubs top to bottom, even with a hood on, and a face mask. She was crawling on the ground in front of the camera. I knew it was a she, because she was crying out, "No, please, no!"

A decayed hand with bones showing through the putrid flesh reached past the camera. She screamed, scrambling faster on her arms and one good leg. The other leg was covered in blood, the coverall torn so we could see the spurt of blood timed to the beat of her heart in the back of her knee. Something had attacked her down in the crypt. The other vampires were alive and still crazed, and once daylight stopped they'd come out. Only their master could brave the daylight.

He grabbed her by her wounded leg and dragged her back to him, while she screamed. He sat on her waist, pinning her to the ground. She just screamed, one long ragged scream after another as he jerked her hood down, spilling long brown hair, and tore her mask off with his rotting hand so her face was bare to the camera. He wanted me to see how afraid she was.

I was whispering something under my breath over and over as he reached for her throat. He gripped the front of her throat and squeezed until her face turned dark, purplish with lack of air, and then he let her go. He let her breathe, and then he reached for her throat again.

"Don't," I whispered.

"He killed her before he sent this, Anita. It's not happening now. You can't save her," Nicky said.

"How do you know?"

"He'd need both hands to send the video," he said.

It was such a practical reason for the woman to be dead that it calmed me a little. It helped me watch, but he didn't strangle her this time; he dug his thick, decaying fingers into the front of her throat and tore it out like you'd rip open a ripe piece of fruit. Blood gushed up and out. Her eyes rolled, and she made sounds, horrible, wet, choking sounds.

The camera stayed on her until her eyes glazed and the only movement was involuntary twitches. She was dead; she just hadn't stopped moving yet.

He put the camera on his face so I could see the Halloween mask that was all he could have for a face in the daylight. Even the rotting vampires that could brave the light couldn't pass for human in the day, but it didn't matter now, because Clayton wasn't trying to pass anymore. The face that stared back at me was a monster and happy with it.

"Come and get me, Anita Blake. Come and get me, because I and my vampires will kill as many as we can for as long as we can." His cheek was collapsed on one side, and I could see his tongue working in his mouth. It shouldn't have bothered me, but it did. With everything he'd done, that sickened me. You never know what will push you over the edge until you see it.

A gunshot exploded over the speakers and his body jerked. He moved the phone so I saw the second shot go through his chest. "Oh, look, more police to kill." He turned and the camera swung so that I saw the uniformed officer shooting into him as the vampire strode toward him, no hesitating, as if the bullets meant nothing. A shotgun roared off camera, and the vampire's body rocked and turned to an older uniform aiming at him over the hood of their car. The vampire laughed at them both and said, "Bullets can't hurt me while I'm like this." He laughed again, and the screen went dead as more gunshots sounded.

I stared at the screen. "Fuck, fuck, fuck!"

Jake came back to me. "What has happened now?"

I dialed Finnegan's phone number, wondering if he was alive to pick up. It went to voice mail and my stomach fell into my feet. When the phone rang I made a little squeak. Fuck. "Blake," I said.

"Returning your call." It was Finnegan.

"Is the vampire still at the cemetery?" I asked.

"No. He broke through the officers and he's gone. He's a rotting corpse and he just disappeared. How can we not find him?" He was almost yelling.

"He sent me a video," I said.

"What?"

"I think he used Morgan's phone to send me a video."

"Send it to me."

"You don't want to see it."

"Send it."

"It's him killing one of your techs and about to kill some uniforms. While he's in rotted corpse form he's almost invincible to bullets. Once he looks solid, human, then bullets will work again."

"Why?" Finnegan asked.

"I don't know. I just know that's how this kind of vampire works."

"How do we find him, Blake? And what the fuck do we do when we find him?"

"Burn him. Flamethrowers."

"We've got an extermination crew on its way. We'll burn the vampires in the crypt. Why did he leave them behind?"

"I think he's insane. Vampires go crazy just like living people. Think of him as serial killer who's devolved into a spree killer."

"So he'll just kill everything he sees."

"Probably," I said.

"How do we find him?"

"Follow the trail of bodies. If he hides, then use dogs. He's a decayed corpse, Finnegan. Right now that's what he is; get some dogs and track the son of a bitch."

"Cadaver dogs?" He made it a question.

"Yeah."

"That's the best idea I've heard from anyone. I'll get them."

"Bullets won't hurt him until after dark. Only fire, so every team of dogs needs a flamer with them."

"We don't have that many cadaver dogs, or that many flamethrower teams."

"No city does. Like Morgan said, this type of vampire is very rare in the U.S."

"I'll call for the dogs. Send me the video, Blake."

"Will do. I could be on the ground in a couple of hours."

"In a couple of hours it'll be over."

"Finnegan," I said.

"No, the dogs are a great idea. You couldn't do anything but follow the dogs and the flamethrower crew around like the rest of us." He hung up.

I thought, *Actually I might be able to track the vampire.* I was a necromancer, but the other marshals weren't always comfortable with my psychic abilities, so I let it lie. Besides, it was a trap. If I went to Atlanta the vampire would either try to kill me or try to open me for the Mother of All Darkness. Without my people to touch and get all metaphysical with, I wouldn't be as safe against Mommie Darkest. I knew it was too dangerous to go, even if there hadn't been assassins out to get us.

"You know it's a trap," Nicky said.

"I know."

"Would you really go if they asked you?"

"I don't know." I handed him my phone. "Send the video to Marshal Finnegan."

Jake asked, "What is it?"

I told him, because there was no way to keep this out of the media. Too much death, too much sensationalism, and they had to warn everyone. It probably wouldn't do anything but make the entire city panic, but if the police didn't warn the general populace and people died, they'd get sued, because everyone would believe that if they'd known they would have been able to keep themselves safe. I knew better, but sometimes the illusion of safety is all people have. I didn't even have that, and hadn't had it for years.

34

"TONIGHT MORTE D'AMOUR hit Atlanta. Tomorrow night he'll hit another city," Jake said.

"How many other Masters of the City are descended from his bloodline?" I asked.

"A few."

"Either share your information, Jake, or get out of my face."

"We can save the other descendants of Morte d'Amour in this country, Anita."

"How?" I asked.

"Pick one of my kittens," he said.

"You know, you calling them kittens doesn't help."

He smiled. "Sorry. Does it help to know that they're all older than Cynric from Vegas?"

"He's legal," I said, deciding that a frontal assault was the best defense.

"I heard through the grapevine that you were bothered doing anyone under eighteen. If I heard wrong, I'm sorry."

I sighed. "No, you're right. It's not just the age. It's the level of innocence. My life isn't about innocence. I prefer someone who knows his way around."

"A sadder-but-wiser girl for you, huh?" Nicky said.

We both looked at him. "Are you quoting *The Music Man* at me?"

If it had been anyone else I'd have said he looked embarrassed. He gave that shallow shrug around all that muscle again. "What, I can't like musicals?"

I blinked at him. "I sort of had you pegged for death metal, or club mixes."

He grinned. "I like club mixes, but you can't dance to most death metal. Silas was into that."

"You've been with us a year. I didn't know you liked to dance."

"You don't like to dance. You will dance for Nathaniel, Micah, and Jean-Claude, even Jason or Asher, but you don't enjoy it. My primary emotions seem to be about pleasing you. It makes me anxious if I feel like you're unhappy with me. Asking you to dance would make you uncomfortable, which would make me anxious. It's so not worth it."

I didn't know what to say to that. I looked at Jake. "Do you know much about this whole Bride phenomenon?"

"I've seen it. It's really rare. It only shows up in bloodlines descended from the Father of the Day, like Belle Morte or the Dragon."

"So it's a power that Mommie Dark doesn't have?" I asked.

He nodded. "The Sweet Dark isn't into long-term relationships, really. Brides can be treated pretty badly by their grooms, but often the vampire who makes them feels responsible for them and it does become more like a group marriage, albeit with a one-sided power structure."

"Is there a limit to how many Brides I can make?" I asked.

"It's usually limited only by resources. How much blood you can harvest in an area determines how many vampires you can have before they begin to starve."

"What's the biggest number you've seen?"

"Twelve," he said.

I gave him wide eyes. He studied my face. "You're delaying meeting the weretigers; why?"

"I know this is going to sound churlish, or childish, or just stupid, but I don't know how to go down to your tigers and pick one to sleep with when I haven't even introduced myself."

"There's a reason that most vampires who have Brides are men," he said.

"And that would be?" I asked.

"Women complicate things."

Nicky made a sound that he turned into a cough, but I was pretty sure it started as a laugh. "You got something to say, Nicky?" I asked.

He caught his breath, face shining a little too much with his "cough." "Nope."

"Fine, if I were a guy I'd just march down there and pick someone. I get it."

"Why don't you have Jean-Claude help you pick?" Jake suggested.

It wasn't a bad idea. I tended to pick low-power wereanimals and vampires to bond with, with a few rare exceptions like Micah. Jean-Claude could always be trusted to pick the wereanimal or necromancer most likely to up his power level, and if we were going to add someone else to our bed then it might as well pack a power punch to offset the embarrassment. My embarrassment, never Jean-Claude's.

35

THE WERETIGERS WERE in the living room, but the rest of us were in Jean-Claude's bedroom. I was sitting in one of the chairs by the fireplace. I was drinking coffee and watching the men in my life discuss how to pick the next man. Jean-Claude was in the other chair. Nathaniel was sitting curled by the fireplace, sipping tea and watching everything. Damian, Asher, and Micah were moving around the room as they talked.

Richard was still in wolf form, so his part of the discussion was sitting beside the chair and watching. I kept the coffee mug in one hand, but the other was on the ruff of his neck fur. He was warm and alive under my hand. His cinnamon fur was rougher than most dogs', but the pulse and beat of him seemed closer to his skin than it would in a dog. Most wolves are about the size of a German shepherd, but Richard was like most were-wolves; his wolf form was somewhere between a mastiff and a Great Dane in bulk and height. No modern-day wolf was ever this big. It should have been comforting to touch him the way it was comforting to touch a dog, but it wasn't. Because this "dog" watched the other men talk, his bright amber eyes moving back and forth following the conversation in a way that no dog, or wolf, would, could, or would want to. Dog just wouldn't care.

"Anita." It was Micah leaning over me.

I stared up into his chartreuse eyes, blinking. "I'm sorry, what?"

He touched my face. "Your skin is cooler than it should be. You're shocky." He laid the back of his hand on my forehead. "Did something happen with Jake that you aren't telling us?"

"Not with Jake, no," I said, and my voice sounded distant.

He knelt and looked at me. The wolf turned and looked at me with too much "person" in his eyes. With Micah kneeling and the wolf sitting, the wolf was taller, but neither set of eyes was human.

Jean-Claude looked past us to someone behind my chair. "Nicky, did Anita do more with the police than talk to them on the phone?"

"I don't know how to answer that," Nicky said.

"Just answer it," Micah said, gazing past me to the other man.

"Anita has to tell me to answer it," he said.

"*Ma petite*, did you forbid Nicky to tell us something?"

Micah took the hand in my lap in both his hands. I didn't remember when I'd stopped touching the wolf's fur. Richard put that huge head next to mine and sniffed above my skin. "Anita, did you tell Nicky not to tell us something?"

I shook my head.

"Nicky," Jean-Claude said, "is she lying?"

"Yes," he said.

I turned too fast and Micah had to grab my coffee or I'd have spilled it. I glared at Nicky. "I didn't tell you not to tell them."

"You told me not to mention the police work to anyone, that it was an ongoing investigation and that I couldn't share the information with anyone."

I thought about it. "I didn't mean . . . it is . . . I mean." I couldn't seem to organize my thoughts.

Micah touched my face and made me look at him. "Tell Nicky he can tell us anything we need to know."

I nodded.

"You have to say it out loud," Micah said.

"You can tell the people in this room what happened," I said.

Nicky and Damian both told about the crime scene video, because when I had said Nicky could tell everyone, I hadn't included his name so it freed them both up to talk. But it was when Nicky started talking about everything that had happened on the phone that Micah held my hand tighter, and Richard laid his head on my lap, eyes rolled up like a dog will do, though there was too much in those eyes. I laid my free hand on top of his big furry skull, but I realized that dogs weren't comforting just because of the fur and the cuteness, but because there was no demand to them. The eyes in Richard's wolf face demanded too much.

Jean-Claude cupped my face in his hands, raising me up so I gazed into those blue eyes. "And you were going to flirt with the new weretigers and take one to your bed with no time between these horrible events?"

I just looked up at him.

He kissed my forehead and laid his face against mine. "*Ma petite, ma petite*, you give yourself no time."

I drew back so I could look into his face. "There isn't any time to give. We need to do this now, right?" I started getting angry and I wasn't even sure why. I stood up, pulling free of all of them. I strode to the middle of the room and stared at them all, and in that moment I hated them. I wanted to lash out. I wanted to hurt something. I knew it wasn't rational. I knew it wasn't fair. But the anger needed to go somewhere.

Nathaniel stood up, holding his hands out empty as if to prove he was unarmed. He'd put on a pair of jogging shorts, shoes, and a muscle tank top. His hair was back in a tight braid. It was what he wore when he worked out.

"You need to run, or hit the heavy bag. You need to get this out, not keep it in."

"One workout isn't going to fix this!" I yelled it at him.

"No, but it will help. The anger has to go somewhere. I'd rather it not go into a fight with us, and until you get it worked out somehow we can't put you in a room with new wereanimals." His face was so gentle as he moved toward me. He moved cautiously, the way you do with jumpers on ledges and wild animals when you don't have a gun. Was I that horrible? Had I taught him to be that afraid of me? The answer, obviously, was yes.

My eyes burned and my throat was tight, but I didn't want to cry again. I'd already cried and it had helped, but not enough. I'd cried for Haven, for Noel, for what I had to do. For almost losing the man who was walking toward me so carefully. I was nodding over and over.

Nathaniel took my hand and started leading me toward the door. "I'll take her to work out. You guys choose which of the tigers you like best, but I think Micah should choose."

"Why, because he's your lover, or because he's your Nimir-Raj?" Asher asked.

"No, because Jean-Claude seems to be attracted to difficult people—powerful, but with heavy issues. We don't have time, or energy, to add another heavy-issue person to our group. I'd just pick the most dominant; it's what I'm mostly attracted to. Damian just wants another girl so badly. He's weirded out by how many guys Anita already has in her bed, so he'd pick the only girl. Asher said it earlier, that he'd like another man who isn't so heterosexual, but a man who likes mostly men won't move Anita. Nicky will be with us guarding, and his biggest thing is pleasing Anita anyway, so his opinion is her opinion. Even if Richard were in human form he and Anita don't seem to like the same people, or don't want to admit that they do. So he won't want anyone. Anita's last two choices have both been sociopaths or close to it." He squeezed my hand as he said it, but I couldn't argue with him, so I didn't try. "Micah is the only one of us who seems to pick well, and with less agenda. He's never brought anyone into our pard who was crazy or bad, or difficult. He makes sure that every new member works with us. That's what we need. Someone who works with us, not against us. So you guys meet with the new weretigers; Anita doesn't need to be there, and neither do I. I give my vote and Anita's vote to Micah, if she agrees."

He looked at me, and I nodded. "I trust Micah."

Nicky said, "I'll go with them, but Nathaniel's right. My vote, if I get one, goes to Micah. He doesn't let his issues get in his way like the rest of us do."

"Jason gave his vote to me," Jean-Claude said, "because he cares about nothing today as much as J.J. and her new attraction with the swanmane."

I'd forgotten about Jason and his sweetie in all this. I said, "Are they all right?"

"J.J. and Bianca are besotted with each other from the *ardeur* last night. I believe it will pass in time, but for now Jason is not entirely welcome in his own bed."

"If it had been any of the swanmanes besides Bianca," Nathaniel said, "they'd have shared with Jason just fine, but Bianca was treated badly by the old swan king. It's left her afraid to have sex with a man."

I sighed and moved in against his body, so he held me. "I didn't mean to fuck up Jason's chance at happiness."

Nathaniel hugged me and said, "You didn't do anything wrong."

"You helped keep us alive," Asher said, "you and Jean-Claude and all your magic. The blame goes to the Mother of All Darkness and Morte d'Amour, and to no one else."

I pressed my face against the sweet warmth of Nathaniel's neck and said, "I'll try to believe that." I pulled away and started for the door, his hand still in mine. "Get me out of here."

Micah called after me, "I love you. I love you both."

Nathaniel flashed him that brilliant smile and said, "I love you, too." I said the words, but I didn't feel them. The anger was fading and the only thing left behind was numbness. I wanted to be in exercise clothes and sweating before the numbness changed to something more painful.

We went out the door with Nicky behind us. Fredo and Bram were on the door. "How's Claudia?"

"We felt your energy, Anita. You healed her, all of them."

"We're going to work out," Nathaniel said.

"You want to work on your knife fighting again, Anita?" he said.

"Sure," I said.

"After she's run and hit the heavy bag," Nathaniel said.

"After all that, she'll be too tired to fight well."

"Yeah," I said.

Nathaniel looked at me. "And if you fight before the run and the bag work, what will happen to the practice fight?"

I looked away, frowned, and then met that lavender gaze. It was very direct. "I'll turn it into a real fight."

Nathaniel nodded. "Sweat first, fight later, then."

"Yes, sir," I said.

"Just yes, sir," said Fredo, "no arguing?"

"Not today," I said.

"Okay, now I'm glad we didn't fight first."

I looked at him. "Why?"

"Because if you don't want to argue, the anger will have to go somewhere, and I'd really prefer it not be carved into my skin."

"You think I've gotten good enough to win a knife fight with you?" I asked.

"No, but I won't want to hurt you, and if you don't have the same restraint with me, you are good enough to cut me."

"Do I say thanks for the compliment, or get pissed that you think I'd lose it enough to cut you for real?"

"Take the compliment," Nicky said. "I've never heard Fredo admit that anyone else could hurt him with a blade."

I took the compliment. "Thanks, Fredo."

"No problem. You've got a real talent for blade work, Anita."

"I like edged weapons."

"Most people are afraid of them."

"I'm not most people," I said.

"And that is the fucking truth," Nicky said. Normally, I'd have gotten mad about that last comment, but today I just let it stand. If it was true, why should it make me mad?

36

ONE OF THE larger caverns had been turned into a gym, complete with an indoor track and weights and other toys in the middle. There was even a locker area. I had a pair of black jogging shorts, black sports bra, and running socks and shoes. Nicky came out of his locker area in shorts and a T-shirt that looked like it was straining to hold all his muscles into one tight packet. Fredo had changed to black workout pants and T-shirt, but he wasn't going to jog. He was going for weights and then he'd see who he could get to fight with him. We'd all locked our weapons in the lockers. The idea was that here we were all safe enough that we didn't need to be armed, and honestly if anyone tried to take me here with all the guards, my money was on us, armed or unarmed.

Nathaniel, Nicky, and I were stretching out when I heard the crowd coming down the hallway. There was that sound of boisterous male energy. The guards spilled out of the hallway around us, laughing, and full of that energy that big, athletic men have. Some women mistake it for aggression, but it's not. It's a sort of awareness of their bodies, an eagerness to use them, almost an animal anticipation of it. Their being wereanimals just upped the ante for it.

Ares was in front with Lisandro and Graham. I went back to stretching, touching my forehead to my knee on the floor. This was my first time seeing Lisandro since we'd broken his prohibition on sex. I wasn't sure what to say to him, so I would ignore it if he'd let me.

"Hey, Anita." I rose from the stretch to find Gregory and Stephen settling down by us. They had both put their long blond curls in ponytails. Their eyes were cornflower blue and their faces beautiful; they were girl-delicate, and I'd seen enough pictures to know that they looked like their mother. She'd died when they were little, like mine. They were my height, give an inch here and there. When we were here we ran together.

"Hey, I didn't think you were staying with us, Gregory," I said.

"I heard I missed an orgy." He made a pouty face at me.

"Don't start," I said.

He opened his mouth to say something, but Nathaniel said, "No, really, not today."

Gregory looked at him and something passed between them, because Gregory just gave in, which wasn't his usual. "Fine, I'll leave it alone."

"Thanks," Nathaniel said.

Normally I'd have wanted to know what Nathaniel did to get the other man to behave, but today I didn't care. I was just glad he'd let it go.

They joined us in the stretching. I saw Clay and Bram, near the back. Socrates, who was a werehyena and an ex-cop with skin the color of coffee with a touch of cream, was there as well; his hair looked almost long compared to Ares' and Bram's military buzz. Most of the rest were wererats, then werehyenas. Clay and Graham were the only werewolf guards there. Stephen was a werewolf, but he wasn't a guard. Bram, Gregory, and Nathaniel were the only wereleopards. Again, only one was a guard. Did we depend too much on the rats and the hyenas? Yes. Should we change it? Probably. I pushed the thought away. I was here to work out, that was all. It was all about moving the body. I'd found that exercise helped with the anger, and even helped tire the energy that made it harder to control the beasts.

I knew everyone by name, all the rats. Emmanuel was one of the few blue-gray-eyed Hispanics I'd ever met. His skin was almost a gold color, so that he had the same kind of exotic vibe going that Vivian, Stephen's fiancée, had. The fact that Stephen was still here and hadn't gone home wasn't a good sign for them. I let that go, too. I couldn't even fix my own love life—what the hell could I do for anyone else?

Dino was as dark as Emmanuel was light, but where the other man was five-eight and just nicely muscular, Dino was big. Not just six feet, but almost as wide as he was tall. He ran like a lumbering elephant, but I'd seen him fight and one of my goals was never, ever to have Dino hit me in the face for real. He was one of the few fighters we had who had exploded one of the new heavy bags designed to stand up to preternatural strength.

God's full name was Godofredo. He was actually Fredo's nephew, which made me speculate that Fredo might be short for the same name, but when asked Fredo had given a flat look that made everyone drop the subject. Fredo was slender, not that tall, and honed down to lanky muscle like the slender blades he favored. God was inches taller, broader, and packed on muscle so that the nickname didn't seem funny when you saw him step into the practice ring.

"Hey, old man, aren't you going to run with us?" God called.

Fredo paused in his weight lifting with a barbell packed with the body weight of most of the smaller men here. He didn't put it back on the rack; he held it partway lifted and answered in a voice without any hint of strain. "When you can beat me in the practice ring, then you can call me old; until then, shut the fuck up." He started doing reps with the bar.

God chuckled, and the sound matched the big chest. They liked each other, but it was guy liking, so there was a lot of cussing and good-natured jibes exchanged. Until I'd hung out with enough men I'd never realized that *fuck you* could be an endearment of the highest order.

I was stretched out. I stood up and everyone around me got up with me. Part of me wondered if they did it consciously or if there was some meta-physical reason for it. I let the thought go. I was here to run.

The guards who had come a little behind us didn't stretch out as much as I did, but then they were less likely to pull a muscle, so we were all ready to run at the same time.

Ares said, "You're running with us?" He made it sound doubtful.

"I'm using the track at the same time," I said. I looked up all that height to meet his pale eyes in their desert tan.

He had that guy smile, the one I'd gotten most of my life because I was small and usually the only girl. "You can't keep up with us, Anita."

"If I were human, no," I said.

"It's not that." He came to stand next to me. He pointed at where my hip hit his thigh. "Most of us have a much longer stride. We're just going to be faster on the track."

"I'm not trying to race, Ares, just sweat some shit out."

He shrugged. "Just saying."

I felt the anger like a warm wave flowing over my skin. It hit that place where the beasts lived, and I had to take deep, even breaths to still it all.

"I didn't mean anything by it," he said. His voice sounded odd.

I looked up and found that the hairs on his arm were standing up. His face wasn't teasing now. "Its okay, Ares, but just so you know, my control and my mood, not so good today."

He stepped back, nodding. "Sorry, ma'am."

I didn't argue about the *ma'am* part. I just turned and stepped out on the track. I started at a slow jog. Stephen, Gregory, and Nathaniel fell into pace with me. Nicky started with us, but his natural stride wouldn't keep him with us. The thud of feet sounded behind us, and the crowd of guards spilled around us. I picked up my pace just a touch so we'd all have a good warm-up lap, but I had no illusions about what the pace would be.

We began to split up into two groups. Those six feet and more were ahead in a long-legged pack. The rest of us stayed a little behind them at a pace that worked for us. The tallest person who stayed with us was Dino. Like I said, he ran like a lumbering elephant and would eventually fall behind all of us, but under that layer of hard-looking fat was nothing but muscle. He was built like an old-time linebacker.

I wasn't fast, but I was relentless and I had stamina. When I'd been merely human I'd done a six-minute mile. Now I was faster, but then so was everyone on the track.

I didn't speed up. I didn't try to stay ahead of anyone. When Ares and some others lapped us in a full-out race I just kept running. Nathaniel, Stephen, Gregory, and Dino stayed with me. Somewhere on the fourth mile Dino faded a little so he was behind us, but not much behind us. Running with us as opposed to the other guards had helped him increase his stamina; at least with us he didn't get as discouraged, and we didn't give him a hard time about not being the fastest man on the track.

I concentrated on putting one foot ahead of the other. I concentrated on placement of my body in space on the track. I let the world narrow down to my body working on the track, arms going back and forth, legs moving, all of it just moving. I was aware of Nathaniel on one side and Stephen on the other. I knew Gregory was on the other side of him. I could hear Dino's breathing behind us, but it was all peripheral. I ran, and let everything else go away.

I ran until my hair streamed out behind me, no need to tie it because it wasn't touching my back. I ran until I had no air for talking, or anything else. I ran until sweat trickled down my spine and I heard Nathaniel's longer legs stretch out to stay at my side. Everyone else was bunched near me.

I found enough air to say, "Nathaniel, do it."

He didn't argue, he just stretched out and ran. He was five-seven, and at least half of that was leg. I had a moment of seeing his braid bouncing ahead of me, and then I kicked it up. I pulled beside him, stretching to stay there. Stephen and Gregory pounded up beside me, and the four of us ran. Dino wouldn't try to keep up now.

We raced around the track and found the taller men on the edge of it regaining their breath. We ran past them and it was all about running. It was all about staying with Nathaniel, keeping that pace. We passed the other men where they rested a second time.

I managed to say, "Kick it!"

Nathaniel kicked it, and we ran. We ran so fast that the gym blurred around me. We ran faster than I'd ever tried to before. We ran and I didn't question that I could do it. That I could keep up, that I could push us all. When we passed the men a third time, I gasped, "Slow it."

He did, and we did a cool-down lap so that we ended with the other men who were still sitting, standing, and watching us. "Not bad," Ares said.

"Not bad?" God said. "Fuck you, Ares."

I was still gasping a little as I said, "It's okay, God. Ares is just mad that he's fast out of the gate but doesn't have the stamina to keep up."

The men made appreciative noises at the comment. I watched Ares think about getting upset about it, and then he laughed. "I guess I deserved that."

"Damn straight," Emmanuel said.

Gregory, panting beside me, said, "I've never seen you run like that, Anita."

I bent back, stretching out the stitch in my side. "Me, either."

"You needed it," Nathaniel said. There was a sheen of sweat on his face. I'd never seen the three of them so winded from running with me. I'd always felt before that they held back because I was with them, but not today.

Nicky came over to us. He didn't say anything, just came to stand with us instead of the other guards.

"I need some tape, some gloves, and a bag," I said.

Nicky turned and went in search of what I'd asked. Was it arrogance to assume that, or had he just taught me that he did exactly what I asked?

"You want to work the heavy bag after that run?" Ares said.

I laughed, still waiting for my pulse to find a normal rhythm. "See, no stamina."

"If you can do the bag after this, so can I."

"Have you seen her hit a heavy bag?" Lisandro asked.

Ares looked puzzled. "No."

"Are you going to try to keep up with her?" Lisandro asked.

"If I say yes, then what?"

"We'll start taking bets." That Lisandro would say it, and not God, or Dino, or Graham, said that Ares had been snotty with more than just me. It wasn't just me being a girl and small, it was him.

"How do we score it?" I asked.

"Stamina," Lisandro said. "Loser quits first."

Ares looked at Lisandro and then to me. He was frowning as if trying to see something that he was missing. "You've never seen me work the heavy bag."

"No," Lisandro said, "but I've seen her."

Again, Ares looked at me. "She can run; that doesn't mean she can hit."

Lisandro shrugged. "If you think you can outlast our *negra gatita*, put your money where your mouth is."

"What does that mean? *Negra* is black, but I don't know the second word."

"It means *black kitten*," I said, with my pulse almost even again.

Ares studied me. "And you're okay with them calling you their black kitten?"

"They're wererats, Ares," I said.

He frowned at me.

"They're not calling me their little black rat. Think it through," I said. I went to find some tape for my wrists and some gloves.

37

THE BAGS WERE in a smaller room off the main area. Ares and I were taped up and gloved, and I had pads on my feet and shins, too. We had a heavy bag apiece, close to each other, but not too close. We weren't just going to be using our upper body on the bag, or I wasn't. If you're going to kick a bag, you need more room.

Ares made fun of the fact that I was wearing padding on my legs and feet. I ignored him and started hitting the bag. I punched like I'd been taught: Lead with your shoulder, your whole body turning into it and that twist of the wrist at the end, and aiming not to hit the bag, but to hit through the bag to the other side. You always visualized whatever blow, throw, or any force as a few inches deeper. The goal was always through your target, not on top of it.

Ares worked the bag the way he'd run, fast out of the box, heavy hitting, trying to make the bag move. I started slower, getting a feel for it, hitting fists, arms, working in close, then out. I started kicking, trying to kick through the bag. The last time I'd worked on the bag, Haven had been on the other bag. I pushed the thought away and kicked using the side of my leg, the front, switching legs.

Ares was flashy. I was punishing. He made his bag move more, but mine moved. His combinations were faster, but it wasn't about fast, it was about lasting. I let the world narrow down to the bag, to my fists, my feet, my legs, my arms, my body getting up close with the bag and hitting those short jabs, the knee work you needed to use if you had to fight your way clear of a grapple.

My pulse was in my throat, sweat running down my body, and it wasn't enough. It wasn't enough. I started fumbling at the pads on my legs.

Ares said, "Pay up," in a triumphant voice.

"I'm not quitting," I said. "I just want the pads off my legs."

"Why?" he asked.

"Because I need it," I said.

Nicky helped me unfasten the leg protection without a word, or a question. Without the padding, every blow of my leg on the bag jolted more, scraped more. I tucked my arms in close to my body and kicked, first one leg and then the other, over and over. I picked one leg and kicked over and over until the bag moved for me and my leg felt bruised, and then I changed legs. When my legs started to hurt through all the endorphins, I moved in and used my hands and the gloves. I punched, hit, threw elbows and every other part of me into the bag. I forgot about Ares, I forgot about the bet, I forgot about everything but the bag in front of me and hitting the shit out of it.

The world started graying out, my vision going in starbursts. Exhaustion miasma ate the edges of the world. I grabbed the bag with both arms and leaned so I didn't fall down. All I could hear was my blood thundering in my head. I blinked, trying to clear my vision. I blinked and through the stars and gray I saw that the other bag was empty. Ares was sitting against the wall. I'd won.

I let myself slide down the bag to my knees and put my head down. The world was still gray with white starbursts. I needed water, or something with more electrolytes. Or maybe I just needed to pass out. I put my head between my legs to see if I could keep that from happening.

I felt a hand on my back and knew it was Nathaniel before I heard him say, "You okay?"

"Yeah," I heard myself say, and it was mostly true. I got to all fours, my head still down. Nathaniel started to take my arm and I just looked at him.

He sat back on his knees and said, "No one here would think less of you if I helped you stand."

"I would," I said.

He sighed but didn't try to help me as I debated on whether I could stand.

"You won't be in the practice ring with me today. You won't be able to lift your arms enough to use a knife."

I turned slowly to find Fredo in the doorway. I had to fight to focus on him through the gray and white. "Rain check," I said.

He smiled. "You're on."

I heard Lisandro say, "See, *negra gatita*."

Ares said, "I get it. Cats eat rats, and you're calling her a cat."

"We're calling her *our* cat," Lisandro said.

I crawled to the wall and put my back against it while I waited for my vision to clear and fought not to throw up. People with nifty nicknames like *negra gatita* didn't puke from exhaustion and dehydration, or we tried not to.

38

FRESHLY SHOWERED, FRESHLY dressed, with guns and knives back in place, I was ready to meet the gold weretigers. Or as ready as I was going to be, because honestly, I still didn't want to. I had enough men in my life. I didn't want more. I wasn't monogamous, that was okay, but there's not being monogamous and there's having so many men in your life that you can't possibly do justice to any of them. I was either at that point, or perilously close, and now we were going to add more. It just sounded like a bad idea to me.

Nathaniel had made me drink a Powerade from the cooler near the locker rooms, but he'd also insisted on stopping at the kitchen so he could make me a protein shake. They were designed to replace things a hard workout would take out of you, and the interesting thing was if you didn't need the shake, it tasted bad, but if your body needed it, chocolate tasted like chocolate. It tasted very good today.

I sat at the small kitchen table while Nathaniel and Nicky made shakes for all of us, including Stephen and Gregory. Dino had dressed and come with us, leaving Fredo to do knife practice with the other guards. He was our teacher for short-blade work. For sword work it was Wicked and Truth. The sword training wasn't mandatory for the wereanimal guards, but it was for the vampires, because it was still possible to be called out in an old-fashioned duel. Besides, Fredo was right, most people were afraid of knives, and a sword is just a damned big knife. Truth had told me once that the only thing people fear more than a sword is an axe. He'd actually offered to teach the guards axe work, but there weren't enough takers for a regular class.

I sat and sipped my shake and thought nothing. It was like a roaring emptiness in my head. It reminded me almost of the place my head went when I killed. It told me better than anything else that whatever was wrong with me wasn't fixed. I was warm and showered and stretched and even achy from the heavy bag, but I wasn't all right. I was better, but that's not the same thing as being all right. I thought the thought, and then I let it go. I used to hold on to thoughts like that, like hiding dirty clothes under the bed, but now I just let the thought go. I didn't judge it or worry at it; I just thought it and let it drift away.

My phone was ringing. I knew it was my phone because it was vibrating in my back pocket, but it was playing "Cat Scratch Fever" by Ted Nugent. When I slid the phone open it turned out to be Micah's ring tone.

"Hey, Micah," I said.

"Are you feeling any better?"

That was an easy answer. "Better, yes."

"Nathaniel let us know that you were done with your workout. I'm sorry I missed it."

"You were busy shopping for weretigers," I said, and my voice was oddly uninflected, so that what I'd meant to be humorous wasn't.

"We've narrowed it down," he said.

"How narrow?" I asked, and still I didn't really care.

"Three."

"The girl is one of them," I said.

"Yes, do you mind?"

I shrugged, realized he couldn't see it, and said, "It's fair, and God knows we have enough men."

"Okay, we're in the living room when you can get here."

"We're getting a protein shake in the kitchen, then we'll be there."

"You don't seem to care, Anita."

"I don't."

"You should feel something about this. We are shopping to keep one or more of them."

"We're keeping them all here at the Circus for their own safety. You're just picking which ones we're going to try to sleep with," I said.

"Usually, you get angry about this, or embarrassed, but I'm not sensing anything from you."

"There isn't much to sense right now," I said.

"Have the Atlanta police called back?" he asked.

"Not yet."

"We'll be waiting for you."

"We'll be there."

"You and Nathaniel?"

"And Dino and Nicky," I said.

"Anita, I love you."

"I love you, too," I said, but even that didn't have much feeling to it. I felt like something had died inside me, something that let me feel was just gone.

We hung up, but a few minutes later Nathaniel's phone rang with the same song, and since he had put the ring tone on my phone I was pretty sure Micah was calling him to check up on me. Once upon a time it would have annoyed me, but I was being difficult. Maybe in a different way from my normal difficult, but this attitude wouldn't exactly win over the weretigers. But honestly, I was all out of wanting to impress anyone.

Nathaniel went to the edge of the kitchen and spoke low, and again, I just didn't care.

The chocolate shake thingie was down to the slurpy dregs. I went to the sink, unscrewed the top, and started rinsing it out. We'd discovered that if you left the drink in the screw-top cups that helped stir them up, you never really got the cups clean. The remains of the protein powder solidified in the cracks and crevices, and you just had to throw out the cup. I cleaned it, then put it on the draining board beside the sink. The movements felt automatic. It let me know that my arms were still a little shaky from trying to beat the heavy bag into submission. I should have felt good about outlasting Ares on the bag. I should have been excited about the run and my all-time personal best on the track, but I wasn't. I wasn't unhappy with it, but I wasn't happy, either.

Nathaniel said, "I'll clean it for you."

"It's done," I said.

He touched my arm, then turned me to look at him. "Anita, what do you want to do?"

I blinked at him. "I don't understand the question."

"What would make you feel better?" He leaned his butt against the sink, and looked nifty in his black jeans and black T-shirt. I realized that from the boots to the clothes, we were both dressed like we'd started the night in the same closet. We matched. He'd probably laid out my clothes for me today, so I shouldn't have been surprised. I stared down at the shirt and realized it was low-necked, not as much as some I owned, but enough that there was a lot of creamy goodness going on in the front of my shirt. The moment I realized I hadn't really seen what I was wearing all day, that sort of scared me.

"Am I in shock?" I asked.

He laid his hand over mine where I was gripping the sink. "I'm not sure, but I think it hurt you to have to . . . kill Haven." He wrapped his arms around me, pulling me into a hug. I kept gripping the sink and stayed stiff in his arms. He laid his head against my hair. "Anita, please, talk to me."

I let go of the sink and wrapped my arms around his waist. I held on and didn't know what to say. I said the truth. "I don't know what to say."

"Say how you feel."

"I don't feel anything."

He held me tighter, kissing my hair, pressing me against him. "He had to die, Anita."

"I know that."

"But you didn't have to do it. Any of the guards would have done it."

I pushed against him, until he let me go. I backed away, shaking my head. "I did have to do it. It was my fault. I thought I'd tamed him. I thought it would all be all right and I was wrong. I was so wrong, Nathaniel, so wrong."

"He wasn't willing to share," Nathaniel said.

"It was more than that and you know it. The signs were all there. He attacked you and Micah and got pissed because I helped you win the fight. He kept wanting me to put him first in my bed if not in my heart."

"You told him that wasn't going to happen," Nathaniel said.

"I know that. I didn't lie to him. So how did we end up with him trying to kill you and Travis, and killing Noel? How did we end up with Haven dead? How could I have let it get that out of hand, Nathaniel?"

"You did not make Haven do any of this," he said.

"But I'm supposed to be this uber-dominant of all the wereanimals, and I've just finished failing the lions so badly. How can I add more were-anything? I can't handle what we have already. How can I add more when I don't know what went wrong with the lions?"

"Haven went wrong with the lions," Nicky said.

I looked at him. "You told me just a couple of hours ago that if I'd let you fight him, you'd have killed him, and Noel would be alive and Nathaniel wouldn't have gotten hurt."

"I didn't say that," Nicky said.

"You said that I felt guilty about mind-fucking you and that made me not want to let you and Haven work things out, or something like that."

"But it shouldn't have been necessary for me to fight Haven. If he'd had his pride well organized I would have just been more muscle, but he let his personal feelings get in the way of being a good Rex. He let his obsession with you ruin everything else."

"Gee, Nicky, that makes me feel so much better."

He sighed, frowning. "I don't mean it like that. I mean that Haven wasn't a good Rex, you know that. The fact that he tried to beat Noel and Travis to death for having sex with you when they hadn't had sex with you says that he was letting his feelings blind him."

"I didn't have sex with them, not until last night anyway. I still don't remember everything I did last night, but I know I did something with Noel."

"A strong wereanimal can tell when someone is lying, Anita. We can smell it, taste the pulse speeding, like a furry lie detector."

"I know that," I said.

"But Haven couldn't tell that Travis and Noel were telling the truth about not sleeping with you."

I looked at Nicky. "Say that again."

"Haven was a powerful werelion. He should have known that Travis and Noel were telling the truth, Anita."

"Yes," I said, "he should have. Why didn't he know?"

"He let his emotions overwhelm what he smelled, or tasted," Nicky said, and that was an insult among the wereanimals. To say someone was nose-blind, or couldn't taste his way out of a wet paper bag, meant essentially that he was doing the human equivalent of refusing to see the truth.

Gregory said, "Some men don't want to believe that it's them you don't want. If they want a woman badly enough and she doesn't want them, then they want another man to blame." He said that very smart thing and took another sip of his protein shake. The twins together sipping on their shakes looked like an ad for a sexy malt shop.

"As long as there's another man who stole you away," Nicky said, "then the man doesn't have to look at himself."

"There's nothing wrong with him," Stephen said from the table. "It's that you prefer the other man, not that there's anything wrong with him."

"I could see that if he picked a fight with Nicky, but why Travis and Noel?"

"He knew I'd kick his ass."

I looked at Nicky.

"I think I would have, but more than that, Haven thought so, too."

"I forbade you to fight him," I said.

"You gave me the option that if he or his lions attacked me, I could fight back."

"I was afraid you'd let them kill you if I didn't give you the option."

He gave that half-shrug. "I don't know, maybe; you had told me not to fight him, but the last time Haven got up in my face in the gym I told him what you'd said. I told him that if he attacked me in the practice ring I'd be able to fight him. That if he attacked me first we could settle it."

"What did he say?" I asked.

"Nothing, and that's my point. If he thought he could win against me he'd have pushed it, but he didn't."

"I was there that day," Dino said.

I looked at the big man. "Do you think that Haven was afraid of Nicky?"

"Haven was a good fighter, but so is Nicky. There's more than one reason that none of the werelions but Nicky are on guard duty here, Anita."

"I thought we just didn't trust them," I said.

"That, but Bobby Lee, Fredo, and Claudia looked them over. They didn't like what they saw."

"How so?"

"They were muscle, and they were ruthless, but for one-on-one fair fighting we didn't see them in the same league with us."

"With the wererats?" I asked.

"No, with the level of training that Rafael demands from his people. Any of the guards here have to keep up those standards regardless of their animal group."

I raised eyebrows at that. "Graham and Clay meet standards."

Dino smiled. "They aren't our best hand-to-hand fighters, and Clay seems weirdly awkward with anything but a gun, but they do the training. They hit the gym just like the rest of us. Rafael wouldn't trust the safety of Jean-Claude and you to any guard he didn't trust."

I thought about that. "Of the other werelions, who's the best? Who do you guys like?"

"Payne is too much like Haven," Dino said. "He's a thug and not a deep thinker."

"Jesse is okay," Nathaniel said.

"I think he'd be softer if he were in a pride that let him," Dino said.

"I agree," Nicky said.

"What about the women?"

"We haven't seen them," Dino said.

"Haven ran his pride like some of the ultramale prides do," Nicky said. "The women are second-class citizens, almost cloistered away from any other wereanimals. Most werelions take a lot of pride in the fact that their lionesses don't want or need to go outside the pride for sex."

"Most animal groups stay within their own animal, right?" I asked.

Everyone agreed.

"There's a reason for that," Stephen said quietly. "If we go outside our animal groups, we can have misunderstandings just based on being different beasts."

I almost let it go, but in the end I did the girl thing and said, "You and Vivian aren't having troubles because you're a wolf and she's a leopard."

He looked away. "I know that." His tone, his body language all said, *Leave it alone.* I did the guy thing; I left it alone.

"So the fact that so many of the St. Louis wereanimals interdate is unusual?" I asked.

"Very," Dino said.

"Haven saw your rejection of him for Nathaniel and Micah, and all the rest of us, as a direct challenge to both his maleness and his lion," Nicky said.

"I couldn't make him my one and only, and he didn't share well enough to sleep in big kitty piles with us."

"No, he didn't," Nicky said.

"Am I missing something here?"

"Anita, you can't save everyone," Nathaniel said.

"I'm a cop, I know that."

"Do you?" He took my hand in his, and I let him this time. "You're blaming yourself for Haven and Noel, but the only thing you could have done differently would be to have killed Haven sooner."

I met those serious lavender eyes. I studied his face. "You believe that, don't you?"

"Even if you'd let Nicky fight him, Haven would still be dead."

"But Noel wouldn't be," I said.

Pity, sorrow filled his face as he took both my hands in his. "Anita, how do you think I feel? Noel died saving me. If it had been one of the guards, I'd be sad, but it's their job. It wasn't Noel's job to die for me."

"God, Nathaniel, I hadn't thought . . ." I hugged him. "I'm sorry; I'm being a selfish bastard. It wasn't your fault. You didn't ask Noel to do it."

Nathaniel pulled me away from him enough to see my face. "It isn't your fault, either, and you didn't ask Noel to give his life for mine."

We stared at each other, inches away, our hands on each other's arms. There was pain in both our faces.

"I don't mean to be callous," Nicky said, "but whatever you're feeling, get over it. We need both of you to meet the tigers and be charming and sexy. Guilt is not sexy."

I gave him an unfriendly look, but Nathaniel said, "He's right."

I looked back at him. "How can you just . . ."

"Forget?"

I nodded.

"I won't forget, but we need to make this city, this territory, as safe as possible. That means we need the tigers, Anita. We need for you and Jean-Claude to be the Master of Tigers."

"I don't know if I can do this, be this."

"Just go make nice with the tigers that Micah picked, that's all, don't worry about more."

"I could have sex with them, I think, but it's the idea of keeping them. They're strangers and suddenly they get to be in the bed with us, too. I'm not getting enough alone time with you and Micah now."

He smiled then and drew me into his arms. "I miss it just being the three of us, too."

"Should my feelings be hurt?" Nicky asked.

I looked at him, but he was smiling. "Yes, they should be," I said, "but they aren't, are they?"

"No, because my primary drive is for you to be happy. Micah and Nathaniel make you happy."

"Aren't you allowed to work for your own happiness?" I asked.

"I don't think that's what a vampire's Bride is for," he said, and he sounded so calm about it.

"What are they for?" I asked.

"Cannon fodder, unquestioning obedience, I don't know."

"You were afraid of what I did to Jamil and Shang-Da in the hallway."

He frowned and looked uncomfortable. "Yeah, that scared me."

"But if you have to obey me, then if I asked, you couldn't refuse me, could you?"

He frowned, thinking about it. "I think I'd let you do anything you wanted to me, but I'd rather not. That was so much power and it felt so good when you shared, but I wouldn't want to be the wereanimal you were sucking energy off of."

"Is that where all that energy came from?" Dino asked.

The three of us nodded.

"It was more powerful than the *ardeur* when you share that," Stephen said.

"I wasn't feeding off their sex. I was feeding off their lives, their energy. It's more power because I'm taking more away, I think."

"Did they understand what they were volunteering for?" Nicky asked.

"They offered it to save their Ulfric," Nathaniel said.

"They're his Sköll and Hatí; they're supposed to be willing to give their lives for their Ulfric," Stephen said.

"After seeing the looks on their faces afterward, I don't think they'll want me to feed from them again."

"They were scared of you," Nicky said.

I nodded. "My allies shouldn't be afraid of me."

"It's better to be loved than feared, but if you can't be loved, then fear will do," Dino said. "I'm butchering the quote, but I like what it says."

We all looked at him, and we must have looked surprised because he said, "Hey, I read."

"I didn't know you read Machiavelli," I said.

"He was an interesting guy," Dino said.

"That's one way of putting it. But honestly, Dino, even though I do it myself, I worry that when you start quoting Machiavelli to justify your actions, you have ceased to be one of the good guys."

"No, quoting Nietzsche does that. Machiavelli is just cool."

Nathaniel said, "Just go meet the weretigers, Anita, no strings, no expectations. Just meet them and we'll go from there."

"Sounds fair," I said.

"But . . . ," he said, smiling.

I shrugged. "Let's do this."

"You're feeling all monster because you killed Haven," Dino said.

"I hadn't thought that, exactly."

"Yeah, you had," he said, and that big, dark face had way too much going on in the eyes. He was so big and so much muscle that sometimes you forgot that there was a good mind in all that heavy packaging.

"It's not that I killed Haven. It's that I was able to look him dead in the eyes, the same eyes that I'd looked at during sex, and I looked into those eyes and pulled the trigger. I stared him in the eyes and turned his brains to mush. How could I do that? How could anyone do that and not be a monster?"

Nathaniel put his arms around me, and I let him. I held on, because I believed what I'd said.

"I would say, I could have done it, but we all know without your control I'm a sociopath," Nicky said, "so that isn't comforting."

"If it was a woman I might hesitate," Dino said, "but if she had a gun I could do it."

"Don't look at us," Gregory said. "Guns are not our thing."

Stephen just nodded.

"I couldn't kill someone I loved," Nathaniel said, "but I'd kill to protect someone I loved, and that's what you did, Anita." He kissed my forehead and put his hands on my face, sliding his fingers into my hair so he could make me look at him. "You protected me."

"There were guards all over the place, from what I hear," Dino said, "and any of them would have done it for you. It wouldn't have cost them this kind of pain."

I turned from Nathaniel, his hands still in my hair, so I could see Dino. "That's why it had to be me. It was supposed to matter. It was supposed to hurt."

"You were raised Catholic, right?" Dino asked.

"Yeah, why?"

He shook his head. "Nothing. One more quote, and this is Nietzsche: 'Is it better to outmonster the monster or to be quietly devoured?'"

"What?" I asked.

"You heard the question, now answer it," he said.

I took a deep breath in and let it out slow, laying my head against Nathaniel's chest with his hands still cradling my head. I hugged him once and then pushed away so I was standing on my own. "I won't be quietly devoured."

"So you vote monster," he said.

I thought about it. "If there are only two choices, yeah."

"Me, too," he said.

"Me, three," Nathaniel said.

We went around the room and everyone voted to be a monster. "Haven picked on Travis and Noel because they let him devour them slowly," Dino said.

"They weren't good enough monsters," Nicky said.

"Travis is still alive; don't talk about him in past tense," I said.

"If he wants to stay that way, he needs to get better at fighting back," Dino said.

"Can I order him to start going to the training sessions?" I asked.

"You're the local Regina, Anita, and they're fresh out of kings; you can order Travis to do anything," Nicky said.

And there it was again, being in charge of someone's life to a point that I didn't want. But Dino and Nicky were right; Travis had to learn how to defend himself better or find a pride that was a little less lionlike.

Nathaniel took my hand and started leading me toward the door. "Travis is safe here, so worry about him later."

"You really are okay with me adding more people to our bed," I said.

He grinned at me. "I like making new friends."

I frowned at him.

He kissed me, soft and sudden. I couldn't frown while he kissed me; I couldn't do anything but kiss him back. When he drew back I was left staring up into those eyes. "You really are a little excited to meet them, aren't you?"

He put his forehead against mine and whispered, "I like watching you with other people, and you know that."

"Does Micah like watching?" I asked.

"He likes watching us together, and he likes Jean-Claude. He likes Jason."

I closed my eyes and leaned in against him. "I just want to sleep between the two of you for like a couple of days."

"We get through this, and we will."

I moved back enough so I could see his face. "Promise," I asked.

His face went very serious and he said, "Promise."

I nodded and stepped away. I stood up straight, because I'd been huddling in on myself. I could do this. We could do this. And then when this was over we'd find a bed for just the three of us and sleep until I wasn't tired anymore. It felt like I'd need about a hundred years to catch up, but I'd settle for eight uninterrupted hours. Sometimes you take what you can get.

39

THE DRAPES HAD been stripped around the living room so that the carpeted area looked like an island in the middle of the bare rock walls and the uncarpeted floor that led farther into the underground. The light and warmth of the area looked like a stage set surrounded by all that naked rock.

I must have hesitated, because Nathaniel's hand tightened on mine and he kept us moving forward. I glanced at him and found a welcoming smile just appearing on his face, but then his day job as a stripper had taught him how to smile and be charming when he really didn't feel like it. None of my jobs taught me how to be charming, strangely.

Nicky and Dino were at our backs. Stephen and Gregory had stayed back in the kitchen, but with both Nicky's and Dino's shoulders behind us there really wasn't room for anyone else.

Micah came to us. It almost looked odd to see him in nice black jeans and a T-shirt. He wore suits for work and relaxed in faded jeans and colorful T-shirts. He really wasn't that fond of black outside his suits. The black shirt tucked into the black jeans with a black belt and silver buckle made his waist look tiny. In fact the whole outfit emphasized how almost delicate he was, especially for a man. The saving grace was the way the tight T-shirt showed off the muscled upper body, but it looked all done in miniature, especially after just exercising with so many of the guards. Most of the time I didn't think of Micah as that small, because we were the same size, but as he walked toward us, smiling, hand out, his long, dark brown hair curling free past his shoulders, framing that triangular face, with those startling eyes, he was simply beautiful in a very girl way. I understood why he wore suits most of the time; it helped make him look like a grown-up. The same for keeping his hair back from his face. Why had he picked now to dress so unlike himself? It being Micah, I knew he'd have a reason.

He kissed me, light but good. It made me smile. He smiled back, and with his hand still on my arm he leaned up and kissed Nathaniel. He stiffened for a second, startled I think, because other than the kiss at the dance recital they didn't kiss in public. But Nathaniel recovered almost instantly and kissed him back, even putting a hand on the other man's shoulder. Maybe Micah had just gotten more comfortable with it, but I was betting that like the clothes he had done it on purpose. I knew that later I'd ask and he'd explain, but not now, not in front of company. Since they were most likely the very people he was doing it all for.

He took Nathaniel's hand to lead us forward, because to take mine he'd have had to take my gun hand. I'd taught them both that I didn't like that. Now I would have preferred his hand in mine rather than the gun hand free, because what was waiting for us wasn't a matter of guns.

Micah led us toward the carpeted area, but I couldn't resist looking toward the corner where Haven had died. I noticed Nathaniel looking at the floor where he and Noel had lain. As far as I could tell the blood was cleaned up, though as we passed the place where Noel had bled out I caught the sharp scent of bleach. I knew if I could smell it that all the wereanimals would smell it more. Our guests would know there was blood underneath all that bleach, but there was nothing we could do about it.

Jake stood on the far side of the room with Claudia beside him. He'd already adopted the black T-shirt that was the unofficial uniform for our guards. Claudia looked like her normal self, with her muscles smooth and her hair in a tight braid. If I hadn't seen her shot I wouldn't have known that she'd even been hurt. The fact that she'd healed this completely this fast said just how powerful a wererat she was. She gave a small nod at me, and I gave one back.

Wicked and Truth were near the fireplace because the loveseat had been put close to it at an angle, and that's where Jean-Claude was sitting. Unlike Micah, he'd gone for his normal look: tight pants and tall black boots, both made of intricately sewn leather, so that his lower body looked like it was bound in thin leather strips, and where the boots left off and the pants began was hard to see. His white shirt had a lacy front tucked into all that leather. His jacket was black and velvet, cut short enough that it hit barely at his waist. He'd pinned the lace in place with the antique cameo pin that I'd gotten him for one of the first Christmases we exchanged gifts. Asher was beside him on the loveseat with his unbound golden hair spilled along one side of his face so it hid the scars. Asher had dressed to match

Jean-Claude, so he was also in leather pants and boots, but his were smooth leather, so smooth that it looked painted on. His white shirt was a tuxedo shirt with the collar unfastened at the neck, but beyond that it fit his upper body tight. To my eyes you could see the difference in skin from one side of his chest to the other as he rose from the loveseat and glided toward us, smiling. But I knew that smile; it wasn't a real one. It was a smile that could either be happy or turn to harsh cruelty. There was something about our guests that Asher didn't like.

The big cinnamon-brown wolf trotted at Asher's side. I had a moment of not knowing how to greet Richard in wolf form. Asher took my free hand, my gun hand, and raised it for a kiss, but as he rose from it he let me see his eyes. They were unhappy. I wanted to ask what was wrong, but since Asher and I weren't able to talk mind-to-mind I'd have to wait for privacy.

The big wolf bumped my leg with his head. I wasn't ready for it, and it staggered me a little. I reached both hands down to pet him. He stared up at me with wolf eyes, but the look in them was human. He wasn't happy, either. What the hell could have put Asher and Richard on the same side of unhappy? Other than both being pissy, they didn't have a lot of the same issue buttons.

I had to fight the urge to ask him, *What's wrong, boy?* like he was Lassie or something. Asher offered me his arm and I slid my hand through his; if I had to go for a gun I was screwed, but with Wicked, Truth, and Claudia in the room, if my gun was the one that saved us, then things would have gone too wrong for one more gun to make a difference. The wolf walked ahead of us and lay down beside the loveseat at Jean-Claude's side like a good dog.

There were two men I didn't know in the overstuffed chairs, which had been moved to the side of the room where the loveseat normally sat. That put Jake and Claudia at their backs. They had to be the gold tigers.

Since I still had Nathaniel's hand and he still had Micah by the hand, Asher led us all to Jean-Claude, as if the tigers weren't sitting there. Nathaniel took some cue because he let go of my hand and Asher twirled me onto the loveseat beside Jean-Claude. Asher kissed my hand again and moved away, as Micah sat down on the other side of me. Maybe that was what was upsetting Asher, that he had to move off the loveseat. Maybe, but his and Richard's mood had made me tense, looking for something wrong. There better really be something wrong and not just the two of them being pissy, because for my tension level to rise this way there better be a damn good reason. I didn't have the energy to spare for anything but good reasons.

Jean-Claude put an arm across my shoulders, drawing me into the curve of his body. His voice whispered through my mind, spreading shivers down my skin. Mind-to-mind communication wasn't always this titillating with Jean-Claude. What was up?

"*Ma petite*, these tigers are not like the others. I do not know what is different about them, but something."

I mind-talked back to him. "You're afraid of them."

"Tiger is not my, or Asher's, animal to call. Perhaps you can tell us what is wrong with them."

Micah sat down on the other side of me, putting his hand on my thigh so he wasn't holding my gun hand. Nathaniel sat down at our feet with only Jean-Claude's legs between him and Richard's wolf.

Dino and Nicky took up posts on the other side of the two new men so that they were flanked by four of our guards, though honestly I wasn't sure Jake would help us against them if the shit hit the fan. He could pretend not to care about them, but it was a lie.

I looked at the two men and they looked back at me. They were both tall and athletic looking. They had that sense of energy contained that some of the wereanimals had even at rest, as if the difference between sitting quietly and furious action was only a thought.

One had curly yellow hair that fell around his ears, longish, but not long by my standards. The same was true of the other one, though his longish hair was straight with only the slightest wave to it, as if it got longer the ends would flip under or up. They both had strong faces; one was a little more triangular through the jaw, and the other more square, but they looked alike, down to the arrogant expression on their handsome faces. They looked at me with pale eyes. Curly Hair with his soft triangular chin had the palest brown eyes I'd ever seen, until I wanted to give it another color, but had no word for it. Brown eyes shouldn't look pale in a golden-tanned face, but these did. The other's eyes were pale blue and gold, or brown, as if blue eyes could be hazel. His skin held a soft gold tan, too, until the longer I looked at it the more I wasn't sure it was a tan at all, but just their skin color. But no one, not even clan tigers, had skin that was pale gold, almost yellow, as if their skin were warmed by the sun even inside.

"I'm Anita," I said, finally.

Straight Hair with his blue-hazel eyes said, "Mephistopheles."

I blinked at him. "What do you go by?" I asked.

"Mephistopheles," he said.

I looked at him, waiting for him to crack a smile, but he just gave me serious arrogant handsome. There was no smile coming.

I turned to Curly Hair. "And you are?"

"Pride," he said.

I frowned at them. "Come again."

"My name is Pride," he said. His voice was a touch apologetic as if he weren't too happy with it, either. I wondered if Mephistopheles was so adamant about his name because only a bold front would make it work at all.

I wanted to ask if their mother hadn't liked them, but resisted. I turned to Micah. I gave him a look that I hoped said clearly, *These are the best of the five?*

"One of the other gold tigers is named Envy," Micah said, face as empty as he could make it.

I wanted to ask if he was joking, but knew he wasn't. "Elementary school must have been interesting," I said, finally.

"We were homeschooled," Pride said.

"I'll just bet you were," I said.

Jean-Claude breathed through my mind, "Do you sense it?"

I sensed they were arrogant and way too full of themselves, but suspected that part of it was bravado. Bravado always hides fear, or at least uncertainty.

"Sense what?" I asked him.

"Something," he said.

Out loud I said, "You were homeschooled."

"I just said so," Pride said.

"Okeydoke, have you ever been this far from home?"

They looked at each other, and Mephistopheles glanced back at Jake and then quickly back at me. "No," Pride said.

"Why does that matter?" Mephistopheles said, and his arrogance went up a notch to almost angry. He was hiding it well, but he wasn't comfortable.

"Just trying to get a feel for things," I said.

"Your Nimir-Raj picked us for you," Pride said.

"And I'm going to be talking to him about that later," I said.

Micah leaned in and whispered a bare brush of air against my ear. "The others were more scared, or angrier."

I put my hand on his thigh through the jeans. I wanted both to comfort him and be comforted, and touch did that. I didn't like these men. I sure as hell didn't want to keep them permanently.

Nathaniel leaned back against both our legs, letting his hand begin to play over my calf inside the knee-high boots he'd chosen for me. He didn't like them, either.

Asher moved to stand behind Jean-Claude, putting his hand on the other man's shoulder. I knew why Asher wasn't happy with them, and why Richard wasn't, either. None of us were happy with them. Jake and I would soooo be having words later.

"Do you guys want to stay with us?" I asked.

They looked at each other again, and Mephistopheles caught himself before he could look at Jake again. Pride said, "We were told we don't have a choice."

"I'm a big believer in choices," I said.

"If we leave here, they'll kill us," Mephistopheles said.

"If you want to stay here until it's safe to leave, that's one thing. But what I want to know is, do the two of you want to stay here with us and be our tigers?"

"What will you do if we say we don't?" Pride asked.

"I really don't like to force people to do anything."

They looked at each other again. "That's not what we heard," Mephistopheles said.

"What did you hear?" I asked, and that first thread of anger trickled into the words.

"Didn't you make him your Bride?" Pride asked. He nodded toward Nicky.

"Yes."

"That's force," he said.

I couldn't argue with that, and I didn't know them well enough to explain that I'd done it to save the two men sitting next to me, that Nicky had kidnapped me and I'd used the weapons I had at hand. I couldn't explain myself to them, so what could I say?

"Yes, it is."

"But you don't want to force us?" he asked.

"Let's say I'm not wanting to add to my list of sins today."

They frowned at me. "Sins?" Mephistopheles said. "What does that mean?"

"It means that taking someone's free will away forever seems sort of evil to me. I'd rather not do it again."

"What would cause you to do it again?" Pride asked.

"Self-preservation, or protecting the people I love."

He looked past me to Nicky. "Did you threaten Anita and her people?"

"Yes," Nicky said.

"How?"

"Can I tell them?" he asked.

I thought about it and then said, "Sure."

"I helped kidnap Anita, and we threatened to kill Micah and Nathaniel and Jason, who's Anita's wolf to call. We took her weapons, we used magic to make sure she couldn't call for help, and we injured her. She used the powers she had left to make me willing to do anything to protect her and the men she loved."

"You don't blame her?" Mephistopheles asked.

"No."

"Why not?"

"I don't think I can."

"What does that mean?"

"It means that I don't think I can blame Anita for anything. I just want to please her."

Pride looked back at me. "So he really is a Bride in the full sense of the term."

I shrugged. "Apparently."

"But you don't like it. It bothers you that he has no free will," he said.

"Yes."

"Why?" he asked.

"Wouldn't it bother you?" I asked.

He just shook his head, and his brother did the same. Though maybe I was jumping the gun on that one. "Are you brothers?"

"Cousins," Pride said.

"There's a strong family resemblance," I said.

"Not as strong as with Wicked and Truth," he said.

"True," I said. I looked at Jake. "They don't want to be charming and neither do I, so how do we do this?"

"Ask us?" Pride said.

I turned back to him. "Fine, you don't like me and I don't like you, apparently, but I'm supposed to find out how my inner tiger feels about yours, so how do you want to do this?"

"Jake said you were blunt."

"This isn't blunt, Pride, not yet."

He looked at me and there was something in his eyes now, interest maybe. "I look forward to seeing blunt, then."

I smiled, couldn't help it. "You say that now."

Voices sounded from farther down the hallway. Damian and Cardinal came in with her on his arm, very much the happy couple. She was talking excitedly with another woman who could only be the other weretiger. The family resemblance was too great for anything else. She had long yellow and white curls that spilled around her shoulders. Her eyes were the same blue and gold of Mephistopheles' eyes. She was tall and curvy, and gave off a roll of energy when she saw me sitting there. There was emotion to it; it was fear. Why was she afraid of me?

"The rooms are nice," she said, but even her voice held a thread of nervousness.

Jean-Claude said, "We're glad you like them. Anita, this is Envy."

"Envy?" I made it a question.

"Yes," he said.

"Pride and Envy, two of the deadly sins," I said.

"Yes," Pride said.

"Is she your sister?"

"Cousin."

"The seven deadly sins and Mephistopheles. What's the theme for your clan names, selling your soul to the devil?"

"*Dr. Faustus* by Christopher Marlowe," Pride said. "We're all named after characters in the play."

"Someone must be a serious Marlowe fan," I said.

"Jake's master is," Pride said.

I glanced at Jake. "It couldn't be Shakespeare?"

"He prefers Marlowe," Jake said.

"Are you making fun of our names?" Mephistopheles asked, with that arrogant pout to his lower lip.

"Trying hard not to, actually."

"What's that supposed to mean?" he asked.

"Fine, what do your girlfriends call you? I mean they can't call out

Mephistopheles in the heat of passion, it's too long. You've got to have a nickname."

He actually blushed.

I had an awful idea. I looked at Jake. "Please tell me that they aren't virgins."

"That's a question for them, Anita."

I took a deep breath, let it out, and turned to the men. "Well?"

"We're not," Pride said.

I looked at Mephistopheles, who didn't seem to want to make eye contact. "He seems awfully uncomfortable."

Mephistopheles stood up, and his power flowed through the room like someone had just turned on a hot bath. "We're trained to meet the needs of every bloodline, and that includes Belle Morte."

I had to think about it for a moment, then said, "So, trained in sex for Belle Morte. Combat for the Dragon. What did you train in for the Master of Beasts, and the Lover of Death?"

"The Lover of Death is combat, and the Master of Beasts is weak," Pride said. "We knew no one in his line would ever come for us. The Earthmover never made enough vampires to be a bloodline that would come for us. The Traveller's line is all but dead. He can't make more of his own bloodline unless he uses his original body, and he won't do that. He won't risk it being destroyed."

"What about the Mother of All Darkness?" I asked.

"She's not a bloodline," Pride said. "She's the enemy."

"So really you guys have been training your whole lives for just three bloodlines: the Dragon, the Lover of Death, and Belle Morte."

All three of them agreed with that.

"Which brings us back to our original problem: How do I find out if my tiger likes your tiger?"

Pride, who was the only one still sitting down, said, "A kiss may do it, but sex may be necessary." He said it as if he were talking about the difference between getting an inoculation or having to have surgery.

"Since you seem as thrilled with the whole idea as I am, why don't we just kiss and call it done."

Mephistopheles said, "You don't want to have sex with us?"

This was a tricky question from a man. I tried to answer it carefully. "You're both handsome. It's nothing personal, but you just seem to come with a lot of baggage and I don't want to mess with it."

"Baggage, what does that mean?"

"You're angry just from this. I have my own anger issues; I don't need yours."

He balled his hands into fists, and his power went up a level. Something moved inside me, a golden shadow among tall, dark trees. I caught a glimpse of the golden tiger, but she wasn't trying to walk down that long road. She was hiding in the shadows, her skin cream with stripes of yellow-gold.

Pride stood then and sniffed the air. "You don't smell like vampire."

"She smells like us," Envy said from the doorway. She took a few steps onto the white rug.

Mephistopheles came to stand in front of me. I thought he was going to try to kiss me, but his hand darted out in a movement so fast I wasn't sure what he was going for, but it wasn't a kiss. My gun was just suddenly in my hand and pressed against his chest. My pulse was trying to push out the side of my throat. "Don't move," I whispered, afraid to shout because my finger was on the trigger.

"No human, and few vampires, would have been able to see I was going for their gun, let alone gotten to it in time to turn it on me." He sounded impressed with me.

"If you have a death wish, you're messing with the right girl," I said.

"We're supposed to make sure whatever vampire tries to possess us is worthy of us." He was a little afraid, but not really. He didn't believe I'd shoot him. I'd passed his test.

"Are there any more tests that I should know about so I don't accidentally kill you?" I asked.

"Don't you want us to prove that we're worthy of you, too?" he asked.

"Hold that thought." I backed away from him, carefully, and began to take off my weapons. "If we end up killing these guys, let's not make it because we had a cultural misunderstanding."

"What do you mean?" Micah asked.

"He really believes I want him to prove he's a warrior. He really believes that I need to prove myself worthy of him. It's like they've been raised in a culture that I don't understand." I divided my weapons up between Micah and Nathaniel. When I was safe, or at least weaponless, I went back to the two men.

"Are we done with the warrior stuff?"

They looked at each other. Pride said, "If you were male we'd probably do hand-to-hand, but we outweigh you by a hundred pounds or more, and we're at least seven inches taller. Hand to hand, you won't win. It's not about training. It's about size, and you can't help that you're small. We won't hold that against you."

Again, I felt like I was missing something. "Glad to hear it, so who's up first?"

"Up first?"

"Kiss, a kiss, who's first?" I asked.

They looked at each other again. "When we go to the human clubs, the women are a little more eager," Pride said.

I pointed behind me. "They're my guys. It's not that you aren't cute, but when this is already waiting at home it makes a girl a little less eager to add new men."

They did that look again. Pride nodded. "That seems reasonable."

Reasonable, that was an interesting choice of words, but I let it go. "Fine, let's reason together. Who kisses me first?"

"See who smells the best," Pride said.

It was a perfectly reasonable wereanimal thing to say. Since I had no better suggestions to offer, it was as good as any other. I expected them to offer their wrists for me to smell, but they both slipped their shirts over their heads. I was suddenly looking at their bare chests from inches away. My head came to just below Pride's pectoral muscles, and a little lower down the ribs on Mephistopheles. Either way I was suddenly staring at a lot of muscled half-nakedness. You'd think I'd get used to that sort of thing.

They both moved in closer. I put a hand on both their stomachs to keep them from sandwiching me. It was a mistake to touch them. But it was like so many mistakes; it looks harmless until you do it, and then it's too late.

40

EACH OF THEM pressed one of my hands to his stomach. The tiger inside me looked up and growled. The other tigers all came out of the dark and sniffed the air. I'd never seen all the colors at once. The gold stood in the middle, with the other colors fanning out in a half circle. They didn't try to trot down that long metaphysical road and become real. They didn't do anything but stand there in a soft line and sniff the air.

I felt the men bend over me and sniff along my skin. I had to blink to clear my inner vision enough to see them and not just the tigers inside me.

"She smells of all the tigers," Mephistopheles said.

"It's not possible," Pride said, but his face was against my hair. He rubbed his cheek against me, and then seemed to catch himself and straightened up. "It's not possible," he repeated. He stepped away from me, rubbing his arms as if he were cold, but that wasn't it. He was rubbing at the line of goose bumps on his skin.

I stared up into Mephistopheles' blue-hazel eyes and knew he wouldn't move away. Hands on my shoulders turned me to find Envy at my back. She leaned over my upturned face and kissed me. She tasted of tiger and sweet lipstick. The fact that I didn't pull away encouraged her more than I knew what to do with, and I had a moment of thinking, loudly, "Jean-Claude."

He was there, his arms sliding around her waist, pulling her away from me and turning her to him. Auggie had asked me how I'd feel to see Jean-Claude with another woman; in that moment I felt relieved.

Mephistopheles bent over me, his arms sliding behind my back, drawing me into the warmth of him. "We're supposed to be proof against vampire powers, but I want to touch you, and I want you to touch me. Why?"

I answered him with his mouth inches from mine. "The other tigers are looking for someone who smells like home."

"I have a home," he said, and his lips moved against mine as he said, "I just want to put as much of my body against as much of your body as you'll let me."

I tried to be reasonable. I tried to think, but in that moment it sounded like such a good plan. I heard myself say, "Yes, please," before I'd finished thinking anything.

Envy made a bedroom sound, and out of the corner of my eye I saw her and Jean-Claude kissing. She was pushing his jacket off his shoulders, while she made small eager noises at his mouth.

Jean-Claude drew back enough to say, "*Ma petite*, the bedroom?"

"I don't know," I said, but I did, or I knew what I wanted to do.

Micah's voice. "The bed is more comfortable."

I turned and saw one of the loves of my life calmly urging me to take the bed. Nathaniel was on his feet. "I want to watch."

"Yes," I said.

Mephistopheles said, "Sure." He kissed me, and he tasted so good, so right. His hands lifted my shirt out of my pants, and the moment his hands slid around my bare waist it was my turn to make eager noises. It was the way I'd been with Micah from the beginning, and Haven. That thought helped me swim up through all that skin hunger.

I looked for Micah and found him watching with calm eyes.

Jean-Claude said, "*Ma petite*."

I turned in Mephistopheles' arms while he played with my hair and kissed down the side of my face. Envy was kissing her way down the side of Jean-Claude's neck. Her hands had managed to strip off his jacket, and her fingers were fumbling at his shirt. "The tigers seem eager," he managed to say.

"Do you want to touch her, like roll around naked on top of her?"

His eyes fluttered back into his head as he answered, "Eagerness can be contagious, *ma petite*."

That was a polite way of saying yes. Mephistopheles pulled my shirt over my head and dropped it to the floor. Whatever we were going to do, we needed to do it soon. He dropped to his knees so he could nuzzle my breasts above the black lace of my bra. Yeah, soon.

The big wolf got to his feet growling softly, but even soft it was like listening to the deep, bass growl of some dangerous motor. If you heard that sound in the dark, you'd be afraid.

"Don't make this harder, Richard," I said.

He gave me a look out of his wolf eyes that was all too human, and even through the fur and the wolf face I knew that look. He was back to pouting. I so didn't need this.

I turned to Micah as Mephistopheles bit into the mound of my breast. It made me gasp. I looked down to find his blue and gold-brown eyes staring up at me. His eyelashes were very long, very dark, and framed his pale eyes as if they'd been picked especially to make his eyes stand out, as if whoever shopped for him had paid extra for the pretty parts.

He rubbed his face against my hand, closing his eyes and luxuriating into it as only a cat can. He was gorgeous and I wanted him, but I didn't know him. I was tired of trusting my life and everything I loved to strangers, no matter how pretty they were. I held my other hand out to Micah. He put his head to one side, sending all those deep brown curls sliding across one shoulder, but he came to me without any questions. He simply took my hand, and the moment he did it was as if every beast inside me looked up at once. My skin ran hot with the brush of every beast I had. The hair on my body rose and made me shiver. I realized why I hadn't been able to bond with Haven, or any other animal king: because I was truly Nimir-Ra to Micah's Nimir-Raj. I had my king.

Mephistopheles opened his eyes, and I could see the hairs on his arms standing up in a golden shiver. "You smell like everything at once. What is that?"

"Micah is my Nimir-Raj. We are a true mated pair."

"Then there is no room for me," he said, and he sounded sad.

"There is always room," Micah said.

"But not for another king," I said. "You can be mine, but I already have a king."

"He's only leopard. You need a golden tiger." Pride said it, from the side where he was hugging his arms tight. I didn't know if he was getting the goose-bump run of energy, or if he was fighting not to touch one of us.

Envy gave a soft moan behind us. It made me turn to find that she had climbed Jean-Claude, wrapping her long legs around his waist. His hands were on her ass, holding her in place. The clothes were still in place, but if we didn't go to the bedroom soon he'd be doing her here.

"What do you think, Mephistopheles?" I asked the man kneeling at my feet.

"I don't know," he said, as if thinking were hard. He rubbed his face against my hand again. "As long as you touch me, I don't think I care what else happens."

I squeezed Micah's hand. He reached out and touched the other side of Mephistopheles' face. Our leopards rose and poured down our hands. Normally they would have slid into and out of each other as if we could be rubbed inside and out by warm, muscled fur, but our beasts poured down our hands and into Mephistopheles. It shouldn't have worked. He was tiger, and Micah and I as Nimir-Raj and Nimir-Ra were so not, but the muscled fur flowed into him and through him so that it was like a metaphysical ribbon flowing from us to him and tying in a soft, eager, silken knot inside him, around the golden tiger that looked up at us like a golden haze around his face.

"They're not going to make it to the bedroom," Claudia said, and she was walking away from us. "I'm sorry, but I can't do this again, not this soon."

I said, "It's not the *ardeur*."

"Not yet," she said and kept on walking. The other guards spread around the room so that Jake wasn't left alone, and Pride was a little closer to them.

There was a prickling rush of energy and the scent of pine and forest was thick on my tongue. Richard flowed from wolf to human, gentler and more instantaneously than I'd ever felt. He knelt on knees and one hand, nude and human, his hair spilling around his face. The look that had been in the wolf's eyes made me dread seeing his human eyes when he raised his face to the light. There was a moment of anger and resentment in his face, and then I watched him struggle to control himself. He succeeded. The effort showed, but that didn't make it any less good. He said, "I know that I was supposed to be your king, Anita."

I don't know what I would have said to that, but Richard looked away from us and to Jean-Claude and Envy. He went to the other man and left us to our own devices. I waited to be jealous, but I wasn't. Part of it was that he'd used up that part of me that wasted that kind of emotion on him. The other part was that look in his eyes made me remember why we weren't together, and why Micah was the one holding my hand.

Our beasts wove in and out of the three of us like some sinuous sea creature. It was as if someone had a fur glove and was caressing us all over and over, except it was warm and alive. I felt the weight building low in my body, and knew if we kept doing this it was going to work for me.

"If we're doing more than this, we need to do it soon," I said in a voice that was already breathy with anticipation.

"Do you need sex to make him your tiger to call?"

"I didn't with Domino or Haven."

Mephistopheles opened his eyes and said, "This is amazing, but God, please tell me I'm getting sex, too."

We stared down into those lovely eyes, that handsome face, and I remembered the last wereanimal who had said something similar to me over and over again: our dead Rex.

"Sex, *ma petite*, no more holding back. They are ours, or they are not."

"Ours," said a growling voice, and I knew it was Richard. Just the sound of his voice made me glance at them. Jean-Claude was still holding her, but Richard on his knees was sliding a pale silken thong down her thighs. Richard liked giving oral sex. The thought of it tightened things low in my body so sudden and sharp that Micah had to steady me.

The energy that had been so warm, so alive, suddenly spiked and Mephistopheles cried out. His hands reached out, clutching at the front of my belt and Micah's arm. His eyes were closed and I doubted he even knew what he'd grabbed. It was sexual because sex had caused him to reach out, but it was more about holding on so he didn't fall.

Micah steadied the other man, grabbing wrist to wrist. To me he said, "What made you react like that?" But he glanced behind as he asked it, and he turned back to me with an "Oh."

I glanced back too and found Richard kissing his way up her thighs while Jean-Claude peeled the party dress over her head to show that there was no bra to match the thong. She was just suddenly naked except for the silver spike heels. Jean-Claude grabbed a handful of her curls and laid his lips against the side of her neck. He'd wait for Richard to bring her, and then at that critical moment he'd bite her and because she wasn't tied to him as I was, it would be like a double orgasm. The only vampire in St. Louis who could roll me like that was Asher.

The thought made me search the room for him. He had moved back to the far corner, as far away from us as he could get and not step off the carpet. His hair spilled around his face, leaving it half in shadow, the other half in stark light, so that his beauty was the beauty in the painting above the fireplace. The illusion that all the sadness to come hadn't happened. He leaned against the wall, his hands behind him as if he didn't trust what he might do with them. Nathaniel liked to watch, but Asher only enjoyed it if he knew he could play later.

Micah saw where I was looking. "He looks lost again," he said.

Mephistopheles' hand convulsed on my belt so hard it almost pulled me over on him. Our faces were close and it just seemed natural to bend over and kiss. His lips were soft and warm, and he tasted of honey. Had that changed? He hadn't tasted this good a few minutes ago, had he?

He let go of Micah's arm and his hands went to my belt buckle. He started sliding the leather through the metal, his face uncertain, his eyes looking up at me, waiting for me to say no.

There were sounds from behind us that let me know without looking that Richard was making progress with Envy. I wanted to be doing something of our own before he hit that golden moment. He was new, and I wasn't good with new unless I raised the *ardeur*, but I was good with familiar.

I leaned over Mephistopheles and whispered against his lips, "I promise you sex. I promise you intercourse, but I don't know your body yet. I want to do what they're doing for foreplay."

His eyes flicked behind me and he frowned. "We're short a vampire," he said.

"Not for long," I said, and I called to Asher. There were more ways to gain power and solidarity than metaphysics and magic. Love mattered, in the end. A house without love would always fall, maybe not today or tomorrow, but in the end without love nothing could endure.

Asher pushed away from the wall with a smile on his face that lit my heart and made me smile back. Jean-Claude breathed through my mind, "Thank you, *ma petite*." I had a moment of feeling his hands on the other woman. Her body began to buck in small precursors to the orgasm from Richard's mouth between her legs. Was I jealous? Maybe a little, but I watched Asher walk toward us and the new tiger didn't protest it; I pushed the jealousy away. It wasn't who we were. There was enough love, enough sex, enough for everyone. When there's enough, you don't have to be jealous of anyone.

41

I REALIZED THAT without the *ardeur* I didn't want to have sex in the bare living room with the only main door from the upper areas forcing people to walk right by us. I'd gotten better at being nude in front of people, but it didn't do anything for me. I was just never going to be the exhibitionist that some of my boyfriends were, but since Micah wasn't an exhibitionist, and Asher had issues because of his scars, going to the bedroom worked for all of us. Mephistopheles was fine once I took him by the hand and made it clear we weren't stopping, just finding privacy.

It was too late for Jean-Claude and Richard even if they'd wanted privacy. Envy's face and body language as they held her between them said she was too far gone to stop. If I'd been the woman in the middle and they'd tried to make me stop, I'd have been pissed. I paused, unsure whether I needed to explain to Jean-Claude and Richard where we were going. Asher and Micah waited just ahead of me; Mephistopheles waited with his hand in mine. Nathaniel was just behind me. I had one of those Miss-Manners-doesn't-cover-it moments. Do you need to tell Boyfriend A and Boyfriend B that you're leaving not because you don't want to see them have sex with another woman, but because you'd rather not get all naked and fuck in front of anyone who might happen to walk through the door?

I'd never watched any of my men with another woman. I'd never really seen them this completely comfortable with anyone but me. I think Jean-Claude would have been more comfy with the other men, but he was always very careful with their comfort level; for the first time with Richard they were doing something that they could both just enjoy. No being careful was needed, and it showed. With the heels Envy was as tall as Jean-Claude, so he'd bent her body backward just a little; his hand cupped her chin, fingers tracing the long curve of her neck, her hair pushed to one side by his arm coming around her neck. His other arm was around her waist helping bow her body just that slight curve backward, tilting her lower body forward so that the long naked line of her was held out for Richard. He knelt at her feet, the summer brown of him looking even darker against all that pale skin. His mouth was pressed between her legs, his hair forward so I couldn't see exactly what he was doing, but I knew. One hand was between her thighs, and the other was curved around the outside of the other leg. Between the two of them they had her legs spread wide, so that she was unsteady on the tall silver stilettos. I realized that Jean-Claude was holding most of her weight, because between the two of them they had her completely off balance, but she wasn't complaining. Her eyes were closed, mouth half-parted, her breathing fast and faster, making her breasts rise and fall frantically.

She was a better height for them both. I'd have been too short to be stretched between them on my feet. There was something graceful in the curves of her body between them. She screamed, her body bucking. Richard pressed himself tighter against her, and Jean-Claude's mouth closed over the strained curve of her neck. Her body spasmed between them, and Jean-Claude rolled just his eyes up to look at me over the line of her neck. I looked into those dark blue eyes. His eyes bled to midnight fire as I watched. I gave a small wave and led the rest toward the bedroom. It looked like a lot of fun, but I wanted more privacy.

Nicky followed us, but Dino stayed. It was Wicked who fell in beside Nicky to guard us. I thought they meant to take up posts by the door like they did when I was with Jean-Claude and the rest, but they followed us into the bedroom. I turned and said, "If I'd wanted an audience I'd have stayed outside."

"He looks tame, but he's an unknown weretiger who's been trained in combat by some very good warriors. We can't let you be with him the first time with no one in here to guard you."

"What, I'm like royalty, I have to have witnesses to the bedding process?"

"They didn't insist on witnesses just because of some old-fashioned idea that if it wasn't witnessed it wasn't real, Anita. Sometimes they put witnesses in the room so that one half of the new royal couple couldn't accidentally injure or kill the other," Wicked said.

I looked at him, and my face must have asked for me.

"Not everyone was happy with their arranged marriages," he said.

I thought about that for a moment, then shook my head. "I don't know what to say to that."

"Don't say anything; just know that Nicky and I will be by the door keeping everyone safe. We'll just be on this side of the door."

"Yeah, we would suck as bodyguards if we let you get hurt because we were too pussy to watch," Nicky said.

I frowned at him.

He grinned. "But if you want me to do more than guard, you know all you have to do is ask. I'll be happy to lend an extra hand or mouth."

I frowned harder at him, but he knew I didn't mean it, not really, because his grin got wider. If he'd really thought I was mad at him he'd have reacted to it, because he had to. He was designed to make me happier, not unhappy. It was all very reasonable, the guards on this side, as I looked up at six feet of muscle that was still holding my hand. Even if he'd been just human, he would have outweighed me by a lot, but he wasn't human, and that made him potentially very dangerous. I agreed with their guarding us in principle, but in actuality something about the walk here and the talk with them had taken some of the shine off the mood for me.

Micah came to me. He hugged me, kissed my cheek, and whispered, "You're thinking too hard."

I turned with a frown, but staring into his face from this close I couldn't keep it. I felt my face soften, felt some of the strain slip away. I hugged him back, leaving Mephistopheles standing by himself while I wrapped myself around Micah and let him wrap himself around me. I held on, trying to decide why I was suddenly so tense.

Had it bothered me to see Jean-Claude and Richard with another woman? No. And then it hit me: What bothered me was that it hadn't bothered me, and I felt vaguely like it should have, and more than that I thought Envy looked beautiful stretched between them. The thought of them doing the same to one of the other men while I watched tightened things low in my body, so I found that more titillating, but I hadn't found Envy stretched between them unappealing. Was I having a homophobic moment? Was that really what was wrong? Or did I just think that I should have been jealous, and was surprised that I wasn't?

I whispered into the thick fall of his hair, "I think I'm bothered that I'm not bothered."

He drew away enough to see my face. "Two years of being with you and I actually understand that."

I frowned at him.

He laughed. "Anita, you've never seen any of us with another woman. You think you should be jealous, but you weren't."

I shrugged, and moved a little way away from him. I took a deep breath and said, "And I'd like to see that with one of you guys in the middle, and that bothers me, and she wasn't . . . she was beautiful." I frowned and looked at him.

He smiled and moved toward me. "You're bothered that you liked seeing another woman like that?"

"I think so, or I'm bothered that it didn't bother me. Oh, hell, I don't know."

"Being bothered about seeing same-sex fun and games, welcome to our world." He tried to hug me, but I stepped out of reach.

"Does it bother you?" I asked.

"No," Nathaniel said. He came up to both of us. "We are not going to do this tonight."

"What?" I asked.

He took me in his arms. "I love you," he said.

"I love you, too," I said, but I was studying his face, because I wasn't sure where we were going.

"But you are trying to talk yourself out of sex."

"I'm not," I said, but I looked away, because he was right.

"Are, too," he said.

I looked up and found him smiling at me. I didn't want him to smile at me. I didn't like the feeling that they were both more reasonable than I was. I didn't like being treated like the difficult one. Of course, if the shoe fits . . . but this particular size-seven stiletto pinched.

"I guess I am," I said.

"Please, don't," he said.

I hugged him, resting my head in the curve of his shoulder. "Something hit an issue," I said.

He kissed my head, stroking his hand over my hair. "I know, but we need to bring Mephistopheles over."

I raised my head and looked at him. "What do you mean, bring him over?"

"Make him yours, ours."

I narrowed my eyes.

"It's important, Anita."

"Why?"

"I'm not sure, but I know that for me and for Damian the sex was part of the binding. We needed it to complete it. Maybe because sex is how you feed your vampire. To make him yours, you need to feed on him."

"But . . . ," I started to say.

Micah came in behind me. He insinuated his body against the back of mine, his arms sliding around me and as far around Nathaniel as he could reach so that I was sandwiched between them. I felt myself relax almost immediately.

Micah whispered, "We need to make certain that any new wereanimals or vampires, especially powerful ones, are completely ours, Anita."

"Do you really think that if I'd fucked Haven sooner he wouldn't have gotten out of control?"

They both hugged me tighter, but it was Micah who said, "I don't know. Maybe he would have never been content with sharing you, but I know sex is the glue that binds Jean-Claude's line of vampires together. We need to play to our strengths, sweetheart. We don't have time to pretend we aren't what we are."

I tensed in their arms, started to try to push away from them, but forced myself not to. I made myself take a deep, slow breath, and another. I didn't relax, but I didn't fight, either.

"Tell me you don't want to have sex with us, and we won't have sex," he said softly.

"You know that would be a lie," I said, almost a whisper.

"Tell me you don't find the weretiger attractive, and you don't have to do anything you don't want to do. Tell me you don't want him, and this stops here, but if you want him the way I felt you want him, then don't lie to yourself, or to him. Want him or don't want him, but if you want him, let yourself want him."

I swallowed and it almost hurt, like I was trying to swallow something hard. I turned and looked at Mephistopheles. His upper body was smooth and muscled, and beautiful. He didn't have the muscle definition that some of the men in my life did, but the promise of it was all there in the muscled rise of his trapezius at the top of his shoulders by the wide, strong neck. He had the beginnings of a six-pack-like lines you could trace on his skin. His yellow hair was very straight, and I realized that the soft blond wasn't just blond but had streaks of cream and almost white in it so the yellow was even more subdued. Both Pride's and Envy's yellow had been brighter. Mephistopheles could have passed for human easily with a different name. The name sounded like something you'd pick as a teenager when you went through the wearing-black-and-writing-death-poetry stage. It didn't match someone who looked so college-normal.

Even his eyes with their circle of blue around the pupil and the ring of pale, pale, golden brown around the outer edge weren't that far outside human-normal. The biggest difference was his skin's pale gold color. It was probably permanent. But again it could be a pale summer tan.

He was one of those tall men who seem big; maybe it was the shoulders, or that wide chest, but he was someone you wouldn't forget was physically big. Nicky and Richard were broader through the shoulders, but they hit the weights more. Mephistopheles had the potential to be a really big guy.

"You look like you're making a list," he said.

I blinked. "I'm sorry, what?"

"You're looking at me, but you're not seeing me."

That was actually a smart thing to say. It made me think better of him, and of his chances of fitting in here. Smart was good, because a pretty package without it had never moved me much.

"I'm sorry, you're right. You are handsome, cute, whatever, but I just met you minutes ago and I'm not usually that quick without metaphysical interference."

"If the *ardeur* is what you need, then I'm okay with that." He walked toward us slowly, as if he didn't want to spook me. "Whatever you need, Anita. Whatever you want, just tell me."

I turned but couldn't see Micah with him at my back, and had to move out of their double hug, so I could see Micah's face. "What did you do?" I asked.

"I just wanted someone easy to deal with, someone who wants to fit in, who wants to be here."

"Were you thinking that while we put energy through him?"

"Yes."

Mephistopheles said, "You said that the rest of the tigers are looking for someone who smells like home."

I turned so I could see him. He was almost to us now. He reached out for me, again slowly, as if he were waiting for me to say, *Stop*. "But the gold tigers aren't looking for a home." His fingers traced the edge of my jaw, and when I didn't say no, his hand slid back around my neck. His hand was big enough that he encircled the back of it with inches to spare. He was so warm.

"What are you looking for?" I asked.

"A master." He began to bend over me, again slow, giving me plenty of time to protest.

"What does that mean?" I asked.

"Pride and some of the others said we should be our own master, that we're stronger than most vampires in power, and maybe we are." His face was so close that his hair spilled forward to tickle along my cheeks. "But I don't want to be stronger than you. I don't want to fight you. It feels like I've been waiting my whole life to belong." His mouth hovered over mine.

I whispered into his lips, "To belong to what?"

"To you," and he kissed me. He kissed me and his mouth tasted like honey.

42

WE STARTED OUT doing something similar to what Jean-Claude and Richard had done, but we used the bed. One, I was shorter than Asher by a lot. Two, I wasn't fast orally, and if you're going to stand and kneel on a stone floor, you want fast. I lay back, cradled against Asher's body. His leather pants were both soft and rough against the back of my body. He'd kept his clothes on, and technically Jean-Claude was still dressed through the foreplay we saw, but I hadn't meant Asher to keep his. But we had a new boy in bed with us, and he was tall, athletic, and physically imposing—a lot like Richard, and Asher liked that body type. He didn't discriminate, but his first choice was tall, athletic men. But the new guy was very interested in me. He didn't seem to mind the other men, and liked Micah, but he wasn't looking at the other men the way that Asher would have if we'd been without company. Richard had pegged Asher right; if he'd been more into girls he'd have been one of those men that loved to be a woman's first. But he liked his women knowledgeable, and his men knowledgeable with women, and he got off on being a man's first man. I had the memories to prove it. Mephistopheles was potentially exactly the kind of man Asher liked. Until he figured out what his chances were, he'd hide the scars.

It occurred to me as Micah and I helped ourselves out of our clothes that there might be another reason Asher stayed dressed. He'd had Jean-Claude the way he'd wanted him for so long, but Jean-Claude and Richard had both been enjoying the new girl, a lot. Did it bother Asher to see Jean-Claude showing such a strong preference for body parts that he didn't have, or was I overthinking it? Maybe, but considering it was Asher, maybe not.

I got Micah out of his shirt, and he got me out of my bra, so we were still on our knees on the bed when everything waist up was bare. I ran my hands up his arms, and he moved into me so that we could press our naked upper bodies against each other. The hug turned into a kiss that started innocently enough but grew into mouth and tongue and gentle teeth.

"I don't know where you want me," Mephistopheles said.

It made us come up from the kiss and turn to him almost as if we'd forgotten he was there, and for a moment maybe we had. "Sorry," I said, "don't know what your comfort level is."

"Comfort level about what?" he asked.

I looked at Micah and then back at Asher, who was still near the head of the bed just watching. What I could see of his face through all that shining hair was absolutely arrogantly handsome. It reminded me of the looks that Pride and Mephistopheles had been wearing earlier. Asher was hiding what he was feeling. He didn't want to spook the new guy.

I glanced at Nathaniel, who had brought up one of the chairs from the fireplace so that he had a good view of the bed. Nathaniel shrugged and smiled.

I looked back at Micah. He said, "You can join us, Mephistopheles, anytime you want."

He flashed a bright smile and climbed onto the bed. He was still wearing his jeans, but his shoes had gone. He crawled toward us and the bed was big enough that he had time to put a sinuous roll into it. It was graceful and lascivious, and promised sex like the air could promise rain. You just knew that anyone who could move like that would be good at it. I hadn't yet seen anyone move like that and not live up to the promise of it.

He stayed on all fours, pushing his face against my stomach and then sniffing and rubbing just his lips ever so lightly against my skin. He kissed my breasts as he moved up my body, but it was a light kiss, until he was kneeling in front of me. Then he looked down at me and there was that heat that all men seem to have in their eyes somewhere. He leaned down and I raised my face to him. He kissed me and this time it wasn't gentle. He kissed like Micah had kissed me, all lips and tongue and teeth. His big hands went behind my back not to hug, but to knead against my skin like a cat would. He broke from the kiss with a gasp as if he hadn't gotten enough air. I was a little breathless myself.

"You've got a scar on your back. Can I see it?"

I just turned so he could. "What caused that?" he asked, and his fingertips were already touching it, tracing it delicately.

"A broken wooden stake," I said.

"You fell on it?"

"No, a human under a vampire's control tried to stake me."

"I've got one, too, and mine's bigger."

"What?" I asked.

He turned around so I could see his back, and he did have a scar and it was longer, though mine was wider. Men, they're always more impressed with length than width. Because he seemed to expect it, I traced it with my fingertips. It was a thin curve of white scar tissue from the right side to the spine.

"How'd you get cut?" I asked.

He turned around. "My cousin Thorn did it in a practice match."

"You use real silver blades for practice matches?" I asked.

"If you don't use silver, then you don't know how you react to being hurt. Pain is all theory until you get hurt. You have to know how you'll react."

I studied his expression trying to read something behind that handsome, eager face.

Micah said, "Thorn is one of the weretigers we didn't bring down for you to meet."

I looked at him. "What was wrong with cousin Thorn?"

"He has a temper, and he tried treating me like I was small."

"Oh, so not winning points with me."

"I told Jake that Thorn could only stay if he didn't cause problems. If he caused trouble then he's not our problem, and he has to go," Micah said.

Mephistopheles touched the mound of scar tissue on my left arm. "Did a wereanimal do this?"

"Vampire, same as the collarbone scar."

He traced it with his fingertips. He touched my shoulder and the shiny flat scar there. "Gunshot," I said.

"Silver?"

"It was before I was Jean-Claude's human servant, so no."

He traced the cross-shaped burn scar with the claw marks that made it slightly off-center now. "And this?"

"A vampire's Renfield thought it would be funny to brand me."

He traced the claw marks with his fingertips. "That's a shapeshifter."

"Shapeshifted witch, not a lycanthrope."

"You mean like a magic belt made out of one of our skins?"

"Yes," I said.

"What happened to the witch?"

"Dead," I said.

"Are they all dead, everyone that hurt you?"

"Yes," I said.

He looked at Asher. "Jake told us what the Church did to you. Can I see?"

Asher went very still, that still that they can do after a few hundred years, but he moved his hair to one side, showing the scars on his face to the light.

Mephistopheles knee-walked to him and, without asking, touched Asher's face, traced the scars with his fingertips as he had mine. I knew how delicate the touch was, butterfly light. Asher showed nothing while the other man traced the scars.

"My cousin Martino is going to be so jealous."

Asher looked at me. I said, "Jealous about what?"

"Martino thinks he's the most beautiful man ever, but he isn't even close to Asher. Or to Jean-Claude, for that matter, but you are the most beautiful man I've ever seen."

Asher pulled away from him, letting his hair fall back beside his face. "You've just finished touching the scars; you know that's not true."

"The scars barely cover any of your face, just this little part." He reached out to touch the scars again. Asher turned his head so Mephistopheles couldn't touch them. But he was a persistent boy, and his thumb slid across Asher's lower lip.

Asher jerked back. "Why did you do that?"

"Because I wanted to," he said, as if that made perfect sense, and I guess it did.

"I am not beautiful," Asher said, and he started unbuttoning his shirt. He unbuttoned the tight white fabric and pulled it wide to expose both the smooth muscles and the deep runnels of scars, like a before-and-after shot.

Mephistopheles said, "Wow, that must have hurt."

"You have no idea," he said.

He reached out to touch it. Asher started to move back and it was Nathaniel who said, "You want him to touch you, don't you?"

Asher shot him a not entirely friendly look, but he let the weretiger run his delicate fingers over the scars and then move his hands to the untouched side. He ran a hand up and down both sides, exploring the difference in texture. "How far down do the scars go?"

"Are you trying to get me out of my clothes?" Asher asked.

Mephistopheles looked surprised and said, "Isn't that the idea? Aren't we all getting out of our clothes?"

"Yes," Nathaniel said, and he was looking at Asher. The look said clearly, *Don't blow this for yourself because you are a pain in the ass.*

"Then can I see?" he asked.

Asher looked at me. I don't know why, because I was totally out of my depth. It was Micah who said, "Don't you want to?"

Asher looked back at me and I understood the pleading now. I crawled to him, so that I was on one side and Mephistopheles on the other. "Want some help?" I asked.

Asher nodded. I realized that he was nervous. A man he was attracted to was trying to get him out of his clothes and had called him the most beautiful man he'd ever seen; I think Asher thought it was too good to be true, and it scared him. I couldn't blame him. I'd spent a few years watching him chase after men who didn't like men as much as he did, and the men who liked him best he was almost disdainful of. It had been a recipe for unhappiness.

"Lie back," I said.

Asher hesitated, and then he did what I asked, lying back against the pillows. His hair spilled out around his face and he didn't try to hide his face. He just lay back, and I agreed with Mephistopheles. He was one of the most beautiful men I'd ever seen.

Micah moved beside Asher's long, slender legs. "Boots first," he said.

Nathaniel climbed up on the bed so he was on my side but lower down so he mirrored Micah. "I thought you were going to watch," I said.

"I changed my mind, unless you don't want five of us?"

I smiled at him. "I'm fine with it if Mephistopheles is okay with it."

He was already stroking his fingers over the very edge of Asher's leather pants. He was feeling the texture of the leather, and very carefully not going lower on the other man, or maybe he was just feeling the more intricate texture of the leather at what would have been the belt area, where instead of a belt the pants had their own interwoven lacings.

Asher was watching him stroke the leather. The look of naked longing that he'd had earlier in this very room with Jean-Claude and Richard was missing. His face was very careful, but his eyes followed the other man's movements.

"I think he's okay with it," Nathaniel said.

The three of us exchanged a look and then I nodded. "Boots first," I said.

They each started to work one of the soft leather boots down his legs. I went to the top of his pants and undid the front lacings. Mephistopheles helped me ease the leather apart. "I like the pants."

"You'll be seeing a lot of leather here," I said. We had Asher's pants open enough that Mephistopheles could trace the scars where they went below the pants line. His touch was still delicate as his fingers slid down inside Asher's pants, tracing the trickling line of scars as if he weren't bothered at all that he was putting his hands down another man's pants.

Asher's eyes closed and I caught a look on his face. If Mephistopheles had groped him for real he'd have been a very happy vampire, but the other man said, "The scars stop." If he found it titillating, it didn't show in his voice or his reaction as his hand came back to light.

"Not exactly," I said, "but we'll have to get him out of the pants to show you what I mean."

Micah and Nathaniel got Asher's boots off and Nathaniel put them over the side of the bed. Mephistopheles cheerfully helped me peel the leather pants down Asher's body. He didn't react when he saw him nude. But when he saw that the scars continued on the side of Asher's thigh he started tracing the thin line of scars. Micah and Nathaniel took over pulling the leather down the rest of all those long legs, until the only thing Asher was wearing was the open shirt.

Mephistopheles went back to the scars on his chest and stomach. "These are a lot deeper." His fingers traced down the thigh and the thin line that crawled across the thigh toward the groin. "But this is light." He looked at Asher's face. "It's like they couldn't bear to ruin your face or your junk."

"They didn't do to my face what they did to my chest," he said, "but they didn't spare me elsewhere. I wasn't circumcised. The foreskin was horribly scarred. I was . . . ruined for more than a century."

"But the scars were all in the foreskin?" Mephistopheles asked.

"Yes," he said.

"Why would they do that?" he asked.

"They wanted to burn the devil out of me."

"There's a little more scarring," I said, and moved Asher's thigh so the thin scar on the inner thigh was visible.

Mephistopheles traced his fingertips over Asher's inner thigh just like he had everything else. He was all about the texture and didn't seem to differentiate between what he was touching, focused only on how it felt.

I glanced at Asher's face while he did it. He and I locked eyes for a moment. He gave me no clue, no encouragement, but he didn't discourage what I was thinking, either, and he had to know I was thinking it.

"There's one more scar," I said. I ran my hand over Asher's testicles, and he reacted to that with a small wriggle against the bed. Mephistopheles didn't react to it in any way that I could see. I moved my hand enough to show the thin white line that traced the loose skin.

His fingers traced along that scar as they had every other one. There was no moment of homophobic hesitation. I couldn't tell if he was moved by Asher's nudity or not. His reactions were odd, and that made it hard to judge, but he wasn't bothered by it, either. I knew from experience that the scar on Asher's balls was harder to touch, because the skin moved. To really feel it, you had to do more than just run your fingertips over it.

Mephistopheles figured that out, and took the skin gently between his fingers so he could trace the scar back and forth. Asher's body was starting to react to being touched. I ran my hand up the shaft of him and began to stroke over and around him while Mephistopheles played with his balls. He wasn't playing with them the way Asher liked, he was mostly playing with just that line of scar, but he didn't stop exploring when I started doing Asher by hand, either. But for the life of me I still couldn't tell if Mephistopheles was okay with touching another man, or if he was just after the texture in an almost nonsexual way.

Asher grew long and hard in my hand. Mephistopheles kept exploring lower. He wasn't just tracing the texture of the scar now, but the texture of the skin and the delicate bits inside. He'd actually closed his eyes so he could concentrate on just the touch.

I wasn't sure how to move us past this, or if I should. Asher was getting more touch from the new guy than he'd gotten from anyone else until just yesterday. I didn't want to spoil it for him, but . . . I looked at Micah for a clue, or an assist.

It was Nathaniel who said, "There are enough of us to do oral on two of us at the same time."

It made Mephistopheles open his eyes and his hand go still around Asher's body. "Who does who?" he asked.

"Do you want to go down on someone, or have someone go down on you?" Nathaniel asked. I realized that of the three of us he was the least fazed.

Mephistopheles grinned. His hand stopped playing with Asher and rested on his hip in a gesture that was very comfortable. "It's oral sex. I'd like someone to do me."

"If you go orally then you don't get to fuck anyone," Nathaniel said.

He frowned. "Hard choice."

"Are you good at giving oral?" Nathaniel asked.

He smiled and the look was enough. "No complaints."

"Any compliments?" I asked.

That seemed to puzzle him for a moment and then he said, "Some, yeah, but I mostly go on the whole screaming and eyes rolling back into their head as the compliment." He was back to being pleased with himself.

"Screaming, so girl," I said.

"Mostly," he said, "but oral sex is like kissing; close your eyes and you can't tell who's kissing you, only that it feels good." He made an unhappy face. "Except for facial hair, and I can't get past that."

"No one in the bed has facial hair," I said.

He smiled. "So it works out."

What I wanted to ask was, did he honestly not have a preference between guy or girl, but I was afraid if I asked the question that he'd suddenly decide he did; I figured if we just kept acting like it was no big deal, he would just go along with it. I'd never been with anyone like this, where there wasn't some strong preference one way or the other. It was a little unnerving.

Asher said, "Have you ever had a vampire go down on you?"

"No," he said.

"Do you like pain?"

"You mean with sex?"

"I do."

"Not that much."

Asher opened his mouth wide, flashing the delicate but very there fangs. "Then you don't want me going down on you."

"Good point," and then he laughed at his own accidental joke. "So, I go down on you?"

Asher blinked at him and then said with no change of expression, "That works for me."

43

NORMALLY I HAVE trouble getting naked in front of a stranger, but Mephistopheles was so unembarrassed, so totally at home with it all, that it was almost impossible to be uncomfortable around him. If he honestly had as few hangups as it seemed, he'd be damn near refreshing.

The clothes came off, and he made good on his offer. Some men, like some women, will go down on someone, but they do it as if it's a duty, something that's expected, not something they enjoy. The new man closed his eyes and treated Asher's body the way he'd treated touching our scars, like he wanted to feel every texture change in the other man's body. He sucked, rolled, lipped, kissed, and just enjoyed everything he could do with Asher.

It was only when Asher shuddered, spine bowing, head thrown back against the pillows that Mephistopheles raised his face up and looked up the long line of Asher's body. He drew his mouth off of him with a smile, hand still wrapped round the base of his penis. "You taste close."

Asher could only nod.

Mephistopheles looked at the three of us on the other side of the bed. "Why are you just watching?"

"I like to watch," Nathaniel said.

"I wanted to watch Asher's reactions to what you were doing," I said.

Micah said, "I knew they wanted to watch."

He grinned at all of us, his hands still playing around Asher's body so that he kept him long and hard, and didn't lose any ground. "Trade me," he said.

Micah and I blinked at him. I said, "What?"

Nathaniel said, "Okay." He moved from between us and crawled toward them. I was beginning to get the idea that maybe Nathaniel was more comfortable with a lot of things than we were, but without anyone else in the bed that comfortable, he'd been gentle with us.

Micah put me very firmly in front of his body. I got the distinct impression that it was one thing for Nathaniel to have crossed certain bridges after two years, but a different issue for a strange man. I would have said I was projecting, but the firm grip he had on my shoulders, and the fact that he stretched my body down the length of his as he lay back against the bed, both mirrored what Jean-Claude and Richard had been doing with Envy, and used my body as a happy shield.

I was caught between watching Mephistopheles crawling to us, nude and erect for the first time, and Nathaniel settling himself between Asher's legs. I watched Nathaniel's mouth slide over Asher, and felt the sight of it tighten things low and hard in my body. I'd enjoyed seeing Mephistopheles go down on Asher, but I'd enjoyed Asher's reactions to it more. But watching Nathaniel and Asher like that did more for me. It wasn't just watching men doing each other; it was watching the men I loved do each other.

Hands stroked my hips, then slid inside my thighs. It made me gaze down at the man who was settling between my legs. He slid his hands under my ass. "You are beautiful," he said, as he lowered his face toward me.

I'd never tried to be this intimate this quickly with a stranger without the *ardeur*. I'd never tried anything quite like this with just me in my head. I felt my body tense, and Micah's hands slid over my breasts, cupping them, kneading them. It made me put my face back next to his so he could kiss me, as Mephistopheles lowered his mouth to me. I got glimpses of Asher and Nathaniel as my eyes fluttered open and shut. Then I gave myself to the men touching me and lost track of all else. Micah put his hand under my chin, keeping my face upturned so he could kiss and explore my mouth with his lips and tongue. The kiss made me grind my body against the front of his, and I felt his body begin to swell against my back. Mephistopheles licked between my legs and it drew a small sound that Micah ate with his kisses. His other hand tightened on my breast the way he knew I liked it. Mephistopheles plunged his tongue between my legs, and it made me cry out again, pushing against Micah's body, his mouth pushing at mine. His tongue found the center between my legs and began to lick, long, slow strokes. I writhed against his mouth, Micah's body, Micah's mouth, and both their hands.

Mephistopheles began to shorten his strokes, licking around and over, up and down, over that sweet spot. He began to lick in short, quick flicks of his tongue, and I felt that warm, heavy, weight growing between my legs. I whimpered into Micah's mouth as he continued to kiss and explore me. He rolled my nipple between his fingers and pinched, knowing that little bit of pain would push the pleasure for me.

Quick flicks of Mephistopheles' tongue, fast and faster: One minute it was a building warmth, heavy and delicious, and the next lick he pushed me over that sweet edge. I screamed my orgasm into Micah's mouth, my body spasming between them. Mephistopheles set his mouth around me and sucked so that the orgasm grew and grew. He tightened his hands around my thighs to keep me from bucking too hard against him, and Micah held me with both arms to keep me still, or as still as he could. He finally let me tear my mouth away from his so I could scream my pleasure.

I felt Mephistopheles hesitate as if I'd startled him, and then he went back to sucking, until my eyes fluttered back into my head and my body was limp and twitching between them.

Micah whispered against my face, "Is that enough?"

I managed to tap my hand on the bed, which was one of our signals when we were rendered speechless with orgasm. Micah laughed and said, "She's done."

Mephistopheles gave one last long lick that made me cry out again and writhe against Micah's body. I could feel him hard and ready against my back, and I wanted that between my legs. I so wanted that.

I felt the bed move, and Mephistopheles wasn't between my legs anymore. If I could have opened my eyes I would have looked to see where he'd gone, but the next minute I didn't have to look, I could feel. The tip of him was pushing against my opening while I still lay back against Micah's body.

I struggled to make my eyes work enough to watch him above me, but about the time I tried the head of him slipped inside me and my eyes rolled farther back into my head, spasming my body against Micah. Mephistopheles began to push his way inside me, and he was big enough and wide enough that just that made the orgasm aftershocks of the oral sex continue. My body spasmed around his, and I felt him shudder above me.

I struggled to open my eyes and look at him. I managed to see his face above mine, his body held up on his arms, his lower body pressing in against me. His eyes were closed, his face turned away. I heard him mutter, "God, she's spasming around me, so tight."

Micah said, "The first time is amazing."

"Is she always like this?" he asked in a breathy voice.

"After oral sex, yes," Micah said.

Mephistopheles worked his way until I felt my body stop, before his did. It made me open my eyes, made me look down to find that he was buried as deep inside me as he could go, our bodies wedded to each other. Just seeing it made me cry out, my body pushing against his.

"God," he whispered, "I don't want to hurt her, but, God!"

"You won't hurt her," Micah said.

I found enough of myself for me to whisper, "Fuck me."

"What?"

"Fuck me," I said.

Mephistopheles looked behind me at Micah. He said, "Do it." Micah was so hard and so big pressed against my back, and the other man was big and hard and inside me. The combination made me scream and try to put my nails in someone's flesh. Micah pinned my arms against me, and being held even that little bit upped everything for me. I bucked between them and that was it. Mephistopheles drew himself out of me just enough and began to fuck me. He found a deep, pounding rhythm and with my body raised against Micah's he couldn't get deep enough to hurt me. It was just deep, thick, pounding fucking, but Micah had angled me so that Mephistopheles would have had to change position to hit hard at the end of each stroke. Micah's own body was pushed against me. Not in me, not even close, but I felt his body grow wet and I knew it was his own excitement lubricating against my back. It made me begin to move more for both of them.

Mephistopheles' body began to lose its rhythm, and I felt him fight to keep it, to last. He recovered the thick, stroking rhythm of his body into mine, and I felt that deep, heavy build of orgasm begin. I said in a voice gone breathless, "Close, I'm close."

"When she goes you won't last," Micah said, "trust me."

"I believe you," he said, and I felt his body shudder as he fought to keep stroking himself in and out of me, faster, harder, deeper, but never too deep, never too hard, as if he could feel that sweet spot inside me and knew he was stroking over and over and over it. Micah's body danced behind me as his body grew hard and wet against me. Then the next stroke of Mephistopheles' body filled me up and spilled me over so that I screamed and drove my body harder onto his, pushing my back harder against Micah. He kept my arms pinned to my body, and I fought and danced between them, my body bucking and writhing as the pleasure filled me, spilled me, and then Mephistopheles shoved himself into me one last time. I felt his body spasm above me and inside me. I felt his release, and it made me cry out again. I felt Micah's body spasm behind me and spill out in a hot wash of pleasure. I cried out again, at the feel of them both going at once in me and on me, and finally ended in a limp, twitching puddle of happy between the two of them. Micah lay behind me against the bed. I could hear him breathing hard, feel his heartbeat against my body.

Mephistopheles half collapsed, pulling himself out of me as he moved. That made me writhe more, and Micah cried out behind me as my body danced over him. Mephistopheles lay over my lower body and Micah's. His breathing was heavier, more labored than Micah's, but then he'd been working harder.

Asher cried out, and I turned to see his body bowed in a line of desire and release. Nathaniel was pressed as deep to his body as he could get. Nathaniel reduced him to eye-fluttering writhing and only then did he rise up from the other man's body. Nathaniel's eyes were soft focused, lips parted, as if he'd orgasmed, too.

"Devil," Mephistopheles gasped.

"What?" Micah asked.

"Anita . . . asked what to call me . . . Family calls me Devil."

I managed to focus my eyes enough to look at him where he lay half on us. "I know that Mephistopheles is the devil in the play, but why is it your nickname?"

"My twin sister's full name is Good Angel. When I was little I asked what my name meant. My mother told me it was the name of the devil in the play. My sister said, 'I'm the Angel, and you're the Devil.' It stuck. Besides, almost anything is better than Mephistopheles."

He had a point, but . . . "So your twin sister is Angel and you're Devil?"

"Yes."

"Did that give you a complex of some kind as a kid?" I asked.

It took him two tries to turn more on his side so he could look at me better. "Do you mean did we live up to our names?"

"Yeah."

He smiled, sudden and bright. "Are you asking if I'm the evil twin?"

It made me smile. "Yeah," I said.

The smile faded around the edges, and his eyes were all serious when he said, "You better hope not."

44

NEWS OF WHAT happened in Atlanta had spread through the vampire community faster than the human one. Those who had been reluctant to give up their power to Jean-Claude earlier were suddenly on board with the plan. The Lover of Death and his dark rider had done in hours what would have taken us days, or even weeks. They had frightened the vampires into turning to the only one who had a plan. When people are scared enough, they'll give up their freedom, their rights, everything, in a bid to be safe. Being undead didn't change that. Scratch them deep enough and vampires were just people, and people will follow a calm leader with a plan.

The first part of the plan was to introduce me and Jean-Claude to the tiger clans now that I had a gold tiger bound to us. It was an *us*. Micah and me, me and Jean-Claude, him and Richard, us and Asher, me and Nathaniel and Damian, none of it was solitary. It was as if the power and loneliness of the vampires' world had combined with the group-oriented puppy-pile world of the shapeshifters and made something new.

But as usual with Jean-Claude and the vampire world, the next step involved a party. All right, a big gathering, but if I have to get dressed up it's a party and not in a good happy way. We were in Jean-Claude's bedroom when the door opened and the guards let in the women who were going to help me dress to impress.

High heels clicked sharply over the stone floor. Cardinal strode toward us in four-inch spike sandals as if she were on a catwalk and photographers were snapping her picture. The dress looked like it had been inspired by a 1920s beaded flapper dress, but the colors were orange and yellow, in every shade they could come in; with her red curls spilling around her shoulders she looked like she was wearing fire. The dress was short enough that her bare, creamy legs went on forever. With the sandals she was well over six feet.

Meng Die was behind her in a dress just as short, but black, with a collar of clear faux gemstones catching the halter top of the dress. Her black high heels were spike-toed, with at least four inches of spike. Her straight black hair was shiny, bobbing as she moved. The hair caressed her bare white shoulders, the ends of the hair flipped under. They were both wearing distinctive but artful makeup, so that Meng Die's brown eyes looked huge and even more exotic than usual. Cardinal had gone for the fresh-faced, sexy girl-next-door look, which meant she was wearing more makeup than it looked, but most men wouldn't figure it out. Hell, even I didn't know everything she had on her face.

What really bothered me was that she had a clothing bag over one arm and her makeup case in the other. Meng Die was carrying a shopping bag.

"We don't have time for me to get dolled up," I said.

"We don't have time for you not to," Cardinal said. She held up the garment bag over her arm and started unzipping it as she towered over me.

"Don't be a baby about this, Anita," Meng Die said, as she knelt on the floor and started taking shoe boxes out of the bag.

"You have great skin. We won't need much makeup. You'll be ready in twenty minutes or less," Cardinal said as she shook the dress free of its bag. It was as short as I'd feared, but the real problem was that the black material was utterly sheer from the scoop neck to the hem. There were black sequins catching the light here and there sort of randomly around the hem and skirt and a little on the bodice.

"Oh, don't look so shocked," Meng Die said, and drew a black slip out of the bag of shoes as if it had been on the bottom of everything.

"Where are my weapons going to go in that?" I asked.

"If you need a gun today, then we've lost," Meng Die said as she held the slip up to Cardinal.

"I'm lost now," I said.

Meng Die looked up at me from where she knelt. "Anita, you need to go in there on Jean-Claude's arm and sell this dress, this attitude, all of it. I'd do it if I could, but I'm not his lady, you are." There was real bitterness to that last, as well as the implication that if she were, then this would all go so much smoother.

"Off with the clothes," Cardinal said.

"How much am I going to hate all of it?" I asked.

"You have no idea what we went through to get these. We had to send someone out shopping, because we can't go out in daylight," Cardinal said. "The guards may be good at guarding us, but they are not personal shoppers. You should see the crap they brought back. This is the best of the lot, Anita. Most of the dresses won't fit your curves. It would work for either of us, but once breasts pass a C cup they're just a real challenge for cocktail dresses."

"I have dresses," I protested.

"You have last season's dresses, or heaven help us, three seasons ago. You never get rid of anything as long as it fits you," Cardinal said.

"Why should I?"

The two women exchanged a look. "Wait until you see what the other women are wearing," Meng Die said. "You'll understand then."

I looked at Jean-Claude. "They came to impress, *ma petite*. They came to be pretty."

"How did they get new dresses this fast?" I asked.

"They had them," Cardinal said, and started tugging my shirt out of my jeans.

"I'll do it, I'll do it."

"Then do it," she said.

Meng Die started holding the shoes against the dress, which was hanging from her other hand. "Most women try to buy at least one nice dress per season so they'll have it, Anita. If you have the money that's what you do. Some women change out their entire wardrobes once or twice a year."

"I like my clothes, and sometimes what's in for the season is ugly." I stripped off my shoulder rig, started to hand it to Jean-Claude, thought better of it, and reluctantly handed it to Nicky. I had to push Cardinal's hands away from my shirt so I could pull it over my head myself.

"See, I told you she'd have nice underwear on," Cardinal said.

"Glad you approve," I said, and didn't try to keep the sarcasm out of my voice.

"You may dress like one of the boys, but you always have really nice underthings," Cardinal said. "We counted on that."

"The guards could not have shopped for lingerie," Meng Die said, standing up with the shoes in one hand and the dress in the other.

"Hurry, Anita," Cardinal said.

I didn't want to hurry. I didn't like the dress.

Micah kissed me on the cheek. He was dressed in a tailored black suit, except it was made of soft black leather. His shirt was white and made his summer tan look very dark. The collar of it was open to expose the bite marks on his neck. The idea was that we would all show the vampire bites to demonstrate that Jean-Claude kept the best stuff for himself. It was a way of emphasizing he was still master, even though a lot of the metaphysical stuff with the tigers would seem to come mostly from me.

"You're okay with this?" I asked.

"Anita, after last night and what happened in Atlanta, I'd wear the dress myself if it would help us be safe." Jean-Claude looked at me, and there was something of weight, and sorrow, and just him, that made me take his hand.

"If I really thought the dress would help us be safe, I wouldn't mind."

Micah kissed me. "Anita, have I ever asked you to just do something?"

I thought about it and shook my head.

"I'm asking now." He looked sad.

"Did I miss something? Has something else happened?"

"Anita, it's afternoon. We have about six hours until full dark. Whatever we are going to do with the tigers, we need it done before dark."

"But Europe isn't on the same daylight schedule," I said.

"If they are underground, *ma petite*, the council does not sleep much. They await our darkness, not their own," Jean-Claude said.

"Richard is in the other room wearing a hell of a lot less than I am. He's sucked it up and is playing host while the rest of us are in here holding your hand. You're about to throw a fit because the dress is sheer. Anita, honey"—and he took my hands in his—"Richard is doing what we need him to do; are you going to do less?"

I sighed. "I'm sorry, you're right. I'm just not the exhibitionist that—oh, hell, Micah. I'm just not comfortable mostly nude in front of a roomful of strangers."

"I'm sorry for that, but we need to play to our strengths. Those are sex, psychic ability so strong they won't know what hit them, and bluntness. The dress is sexy, and blunt." He smiled. "Honey, it's you. I'll go help the other men with our guests. Okay?"

I nodded. "Okay."

He kissed my cheek again, gave Jean-Claude a look I couldn't quite understand, and went back down the hallway to our guests. And just like that, I stopped protesting. Micah's attitude brought home more than anything else could have that modesty was no longer a virtue. It was the proverbial midnight, and the clock was striking. Whatever we were going to do before that last strike, we had about six hours to do it.

45

THE SLIP HADN'T worked with the dress, so I wore it with just the nice black bra and panties under it. The shoes were three-and-a-half-inch heels, a little wider than spikes, thank God, but with panels on the closed-toe heels that were silver, clear, clear black, and ended up being mostly clear like the dress, so that the silver heels were the thing you noticed most about the shoes. Meng Die had produced a pair of thigh-highs from her bag so that the shoes weren't rubbing as I walked. With the sheer dress, the sheer black hose just seemed to make it all lingerie, but it beat the hell out of having blisters before I'd walked a few yards, which was what the shoes promised without hose.

Cardinal had applied makeup in a record speed. She even had a mirror so I could see that she'd made my eyes large and exotic; the lipstick was a red so deep and rich that it was going to be distracting just to watch me talk. Of course, my breasts might distract any heterosexual man in the room from ever seeing my face. There was way too much yummy mounded goodness going on in front of me for me to be entirely comfortable meeting a roomful of strangers, but I hadn't protested anymore. Micah had made his point. I kept my mouth shut and just let the two women do their jobs. Besides, the dress didn't hide a damn thing, so my breasts being obvious should have been the least of my worries. One of the interesting side effects of the dress being see-through was that every vampire bite was very visible. So were the scars I'd gotten in the line of duty, but the bites were actually more attention-getting. They were fresh, after all. The fact that I'd started wearing thongs since I found some that were actually comfortable meant that my ass was bare, though at least the front was well covered with black lace. I had other thongs that were pretty much nudity with decoration. That would have been worse, or that's what I told myself.

I'd divided my weapons among Nicky, Wicked, and Truth. They'd rotate around me and Jean-Claude. The only jewelry I had left was the gold chain with the charm on it. I felt very underdressed without the weapons or my cross. But since Jean-Claude might have to pull out some serious vampire powers to help me tame the tigers, a holy object that would start to glow seemed like a bad idea.

The gold tigers and Jake himself were going to stay out of sight until we'd done the tigers, because we were pretty certain there'd be spies among them. Since even the Harlequin never saw all of them unmasked, not everyone knew what the others looked like, so Jake had a high-percentage chance of not knowing the bare face of the spies. It was one of the things that made the Harlequin so effective even to each other.

The big dining room had begun life as a speakeasy, back when Prohibition was the law of the land. It was a huge natural cavern with gas lamps in the walls, giving a soft, warm glow to everything. The big table had been moved to one side of the room and had candles on it, so that the only light in the big cave came from gas and candles. There was enough light to see everything, but it was soft-edged and there were lots of shadows, as if the flames that lit the room filled it with both light and darkness.

Except for the light and shadows it was a cocktail party, with everyone standing around sipping drinks, eating hors d'oeuvres, and chatting. I hated cocktail-party small talk mainly because I'd always sucked at it, but all the men in my life seemed really good at it. As long as Jean-Claude or Micah or Nathaniel or Asher or Jason was on my arm they took the conversation and I just smiled and nodded. That I could do.

Damian and I were both almost equally bad at this kind of thing, so he kept Cardinal on his arm, and we waved at each other.

I was on Jean-Claude's arm when we met Victor, weretiger and son of the Master of Las Vegas and the white tiger queen, Bibiana. Victor was still tall, broad-shouldered, and handsome with his short white hair carefully cut, looking as if someone styled it one hair at a time. His suit was expensive and tailored, and looked almost as good on him as Micah's had on him, but in very different ways. Victor was built more like Richard. Victor's tiger eyes were a rich, deep blue, bluer than Crispin's. I liked Victor's eyes; in fact my white tigress liked everything about him. He took my hand when I offered it, and the moment he touched me I wished he hadn't. His power breathed along my skin in a warm wash. It made it hard to breathe for a moment, and I watched his eyes go a little wider. His breath came out in a shaking line as he let go of my hand. It took visible effort for him to stop touching me.

He laughed, and that shook, too. "Is it my imagination or are you even more captivating now than you were a year ago?"

"Thank you, and I don't know." The white tiger inside me wanted to touch him. I took a step forward without realizing it. Victor actually backed up a step, before he caught himself.

"Aren't you going to introduce us?" A woman came to lean against him in a possessive way that some girlfriends have. My white tiger didn't like it, and I had a moment to fight the instinct to mark him as some sort of territory. I'd met him twice, and slept with him twice, and had sex only one of those times. I had no right to mark him as mine, but wasn't I supposed to do exactly that? Shit, I didn't know.

The woman had long pale curls, mostly white, but with edges of pale golden brown here and there, and I knew that meant her white tiger would have stripes the color of her darker curls. She had the same lush curves as Bibiana, but on a body that was nearly a foot taller. Part of it was silver stiletto heels, but her legs were almost longer than I was. Her dress was silver, too, and managed to both cling and billow as she moved. She, like me, had to be wearing a bra under the dress or things wouldn't have stayed put.

Her eyes were a blue so pale they were gray, but with a line of black around the iris so that it echoed the eyeliner around her large, uptilted eyes. The effect was startling, and beautiful, even to me.

"Julia, this is Anita Blake, Jean-Claude's lady."

She held out a perfectly manicured hand. The nails were French-tipped with white. Cardinal had buffed my nails and declared them hopeless. I didn't really care about nails, so I smiled sweetly and held out my hand.

She wrapped her hand around mine and sent a flash of power into me. My white tiger was just suddenly there, roaring up through my skin, not to tear me apart, but to spill around me like some white phantom.

Julia tried to take her hand back, but I held on, and my tiger spilled over and through her. I tasted her tiger, saw it in its pale stripes, and knew she was no queen. She tried to slap me, like a girl, but my other arm was there blocking hers.

"Let go," she said, but her voice was high, and afraid. Fear meant food. Fear meant weak.

I started to, honest, but Jean-Claude was at my side. He said, "She began this, *ma petite*. You must finish it."

I glanced at him, and my tiger seemed to look at him, too.

"She challenged you," he said. "Answer it."

I glanced past the woman to Victor, who had moved so he wasn't touching her. "You must answer her challenge, Anita. Either you are queen, or you are not."

It was as if some faint piece of resistance melted away. We were supposed to play to win.

"Let go," she said again.

"Make me," I said, and I knew that though human words were coming out of my mouth, the attitude wasn't human. The white tiger in me knew that Julia had tried my power with hers; it was something you did only if you thought the tiger in question was lesser. Julia was about to learn she'd made a mistake.

Victor and Jean-Claude had moved a little back from us. The other white tigers had formed a little circle around us. I could feel the rest of the tigers beyond the white like a distant hum, but in that moment the white tigers were what I wanted, needed. One color at a time.

She tried to use all that otherworldly strength to pull me off my feet, but my sport of choice was judo, and that was all about leverage and balance. She pulled, and I went with it, so that I was suddenly up against her, her hand still in mine, and my leg went behind hers at the same time that I pushed on her with my other hand, and down she went. She didn't know how to fall, so she hit hard. I was suddenly on top of her, straddling her waist, my hands in her hands. I wasn't holding her down. I couldn't by strength alone, but there are other ways to make someone stay on a floor.

I was leaning over her, my face above hers as she caught her breath. But it wasn't my face near hers that widened her eyes and made her scream. It was my tiger's. We thrust that white, hot energy into Julia. We plunged it between those beautiful eyes and we brought her tiger, as we'd, I'd, they'd, brought Rosamond's lion, in a gentle wash of fur spilling over her skin, so that there was barely any fluid, just one moment human, the next fur and muscle and the face that went with those gray and black eyes.

She lay underneath me, still in the silver dress, though the shoes had been split. She blinked up at me, and I leaned our foreheads together, while my hands were still in hers. I rubbed my cheek against the silky fur of her face. She was stiff under me for a moment, and then she rubbed back and that deep thundering purr began.

And one by one the other white tigers crowded around us and rubbed their human faces against me and against Julia. Victor was last. He didn't kneel. He picked me up in his arms while the white tigers rolled around his legs. I could see his tiger now, white and untouched by any stripe. The great white beast rolled through me, and my beast rose up to his, as white and untouched. It was as if he and I were the center of some warm, wonderful fire, and every tiger at our feet was fuel for it. His arms locked around me, so strong, so very strong, and the energy grew, thicker, richer, deeper, more, until his mouth touched mine and then we thrust our power into each other, and it was as if his beast and mine exchanged places, one sliding into the other so that they intermingled and became one, and then two, and then we were many. I could feel every tiger around us, and it was all fuel, all energy, all mine.

46

I THREW THAT energy into the other tigers. Cynric was already at the edge of the white, and when the power swept over him, my blue tiger knew he was already ours. He was such an easy mark that the power barely hesitated before it swept out to find harder prey.

Domino was half black and half white tiger, so that half of him was already prepared to bend to my—our—will. I had a moment to wonder whether this was how it felt to be a multiple personality, to lose yourself in the pronouns so that you weren't sure what you were doing and what the other was doing, or what you were doing together. I should have been afraid, but I wasn't. It felt too good to be afraid of it.

The black tiger filled Domino and he climbed the white tigers to lay a hand on my skin, and the moment he touched me the black tiger scented something else. Something that was hers, that was ours was here.

The power searched outward until it found the weretigers who had no clan, but were just survivors of attacks. The power eased through them like a warm wind, and they were tiger and they were tasty, but the black tiger was seeking something else, like calling to like.

We found her pressed against the far wall. She wasn't very tall, dainty like me, like Meng Die, with the same straight, shining black hair, except hers was long, sweeping past her waist to caress the swell of her ass. She was even wearing one of those short Oriental-style dresses, in bright royal blue. Her eyes looked brown and human from here, but the power knew better, the black tiger knew better. I told the power and the tiger about contact lenses, and we wanted to see her closer. We wanted to see her eyes.

I tried to sweep through her the way I had Domino and Cynric, but she stayed by the wall. I—we—concentrated on her, and still we could not make her come to us. I had Victor put me down, and I walked through a forest of hands and bodies, as I left the other tigers. I walked toward her. The other tigers had already parted like water when a fast boat slices it open, leaving the woman alone against the wall.

Her lips were painted as red as mine had started the night, though I'd left most of mine on Victor's mouth. Her lips were parted, her breathing faster, her heartbeat speeding, just from refusing the call of all that power. But the fact that she had been able to stand against us said more than anything else, that she was more powerful than any tiger I'd tried yet.

I walked toward her, the black tiger's energy riding on the strength of the white, and blue, so that each color grew and fed off the power of the others. The black tiger was like a dark image blurring and growing more solid around me, as if I, Anita, were somehow already inside it. My human hand reached out, encased in a huge, black, phantom paw.

"Don't," she whispered.

"You're a black tiger," I said in a voice that was almost an echo, as if my words were bouncing off the shape I could see around me.

"Yes," she whispered.

"You've been hiding in plain sight, pretending to be a survivor of an attack," I said.

"Yes."

I held my hand out to her. "Take my hand."

Her hands came out from behind her body where she'd been leaning on them, as if she'd needed the weight of her own body to remind her hands not to touch me. "I want to."

"Then do it. Touch us." I stretched my hand out toward her, with that shadow of black around it that I could see behind my eyes. Could she see it?

Her fingertips touched ours, and I wrapped my fingers through hers, drew her hand into mine, and my black tiger flowed over her skin, down her arm, and found her beast. It was as if I'd tried to pick up a stray kitten and found out I had a full-grown tiger on my hands. Her power didn't just pour into mine, it came like a tidal wave trying to drown me under the crushing burden of all that power.

I was on my knees, her hand still locked in mine. I'd thought Bibiana in Vegas was powerful, but she was nothing to this. I'd never dreamed of anything this powerful from a wereanimal. It felt more like vampire, and the moment I thought it, I knew. She belonged to someone. Someone old, and that someone was pushing power through her and into me.

I spoke through gritted teeth. "Cheat."

"Can you not tame me as you did all the others?" she said, and her voice was derisive.

My black tiger reached out and found Domino. He came to me and my tiger, and we felt him come like some vibrating thing, so full of energy.

The woman looked past me and said, "Do not help her, brother."

"You are not my sister," he said, and he knelt behind me. The moment his hands touched my shoulders, bare skin to bare skin, it was like touching a live wire. The power jumped and crackled through me and into her. She cried out and fell to her knees in front of me, and I used our joined hands to spill her in against me.

Her face was inches from mine, my hand in the back of all that silky hair. Her face was a mixture of fear and need. She'd been so lonely without another black tiger, so lonely. Others had their color, but she had no one. She drew in the scent of us, because we both smelled like home. We were what she had been mourning for more than a thousand years. That was the true strength of the *ardeur*, that it could see into your mind, your heart, your soul, to the thing you wanted most, and if I could I would give it to you, and it would be exactly what you wanted most. How many people can resist their heart's desire?

Domino's arms came around me so that we both held her, and drew her into me for a kiss. She whispered, "Master, help me." My lips touched hers before I realized she wasn't talking to me.

Her vampire master shoved his power into me, not like I was a necromancer, or another vampire, but as if I were just another black tiger to call, because that was his beast. Not just tiger, but this tiger. My tiger snarled at him, a huge, black beast, and he laughed at us. That laughter tried to spill out of her mouth and down my throat, but I kissed her. I kissed her because she was soft and fragile in my arms. I kissed her, because Domino was solid at my back, his strong arms folding over us both, so that he gave me not just the strength of his black tiger, but of his white, and the vampire on the other side of this tug-of-war wasn't ready for that. He faltered, a metaphysical stumble, and my two tigers spilled into her mouth, and down the long, shining curve of power that connected him to the woman in my arms.

I had a moment to see his face, upraised, startled. He was close by; he'd sent her to us like a Trojan horse. No, he hadn't believed that any of us could be a danger to the tie that bound them. His skin was both dark and pale; he looked as if he'd begun life as someone very dark, but vampires grow pale with age, as if the centuries try to lick them down to bone and blood. His eyes weren't brown, they were black, his hair short and tightly curled, his lips full and soft. I kissed the woman in my arms, but I thought of him as I did it, and he raised fingers to his own mouth as if he felt that distant kiss.

Her arms traced over me and Domino, her mouth feeding at mine, until small, eager noises fell from her lips and into mine. I pressed her to the floor; she wrapped her legs around my waist, while the kiss grew between us and her bright red lipstick smeared across our faces like blood. Her dress was pushed up around her ass, which was pale and bare. She proved she was wearing nothing under the dress as she ground herself against my body and the extra friction of my dress.

Normally that would have freaked me out, but Jean-Claude was there, and so were Richard, Nathaniel, Damian, and Micah, and they liked girls just fine. They helped calm me, and the black tiger inside me already saw her as beautiful.

I was in more control than I'd ever been of the *ardeur*. It was a weapon at last. Then two things happened that I hadn't expected. He drove his power into her so hard and sharp that it tore her mouth from mine, and spasmed her body underneath mine as if he meant to kill her if he could not keep her, but she was his animal to call; the death of one might mean the death of both. Then the power hit my black beast, and I realized he wasn't trying to kill her, he was trying to tame her, and me, but he'd used pain and sheer force to tame her once before, long ago. I offered something so much better than violence.

I ground my hips against hers, pinned her to the floor underneath me, thrust my beast into her not to harm, but to pleasure. Even then I think I would have kept control, but I wasn't used to other women. I didn't understand that some of them were easier to bring than I was. One moment I was riding the edge of sex, using it to push back the threat that the vampire had used on her for centuries, and the next her orgasm caught me. I was too tied to her, too far into that line of power that connected her to her master vampire. I couldn't pull out in time, couldn't separate us, so that I rode her pleasure and Domino's weight was suddenly on top of me, as the pleasure spread. His weight pressed me harder against the most intimate part of her, and her body began to dance under my body again.

I saw her master fall beside the bed, one hand holding desperately to the bedspread, as he tried not to feel what she was feeling. It wasn't just the pleasure; he was feeling her pleasure, a woman's pleasure. He tried to draw his power to hurt her again, but as pain had hurt her concentration, pleasure seemed to hurt his.

Domino went to his knees behind me. I had a moment to stare down into the woman's face. Her eyes were unfocused, body limp under mine. She saw something past my shoulder, and whispered, "Please."

I felt Domino slide my thong to one side, and knew before he pressed his weight against my body that he'd be nude, or nude enough. The vampire in his distant hotel room yelled, "No!"

The woman underneath me whispered, "Yes."

Domino angled himself against my body. I lifted my hips to help him find that magic angle, and felt the edge of sorrow that shadowed her face as I moved my body away from hers. I felt the triumph of the vampire in the distant room. Fuck that. I reached my hands down and lifted her hips in my hands. She smiled at me and angled her own hips upward, wrapping her legs more tightly around my waist, pressing herself against me. Domino began to push himself inside me. The feel of him entering me made me lose concentration on her for a moment, bowing my head, making me shudder as he worked himself inside me.

I had to put one hand on the floor to support myself against the push of his body. I kept one hand on her ass, pressing her against my body, helping her stay as tight as she wanted. Domino slid himself inside me, and I was already wet, tight, but wet. It helped him find a rhythm quicker, long, deep, thrusts, caressing that point inside my body. She put her arms on the floor and used them to lift her body and began to dance her hips against the front of my body as Domino did from behind.

I found my own rhythm, grinding myself between them, helping caress myself over and around him, and helping her rub herself against the front of me, and again she found her happy before anyone else did. Her body shivered underneath me, and I held her in place while Domino's rhythm grew faster, harder. I felt that warm weight building inside my body.

The vampire on the floor in the room tried one last time to take back the woman. I felt him gathering his power, and my tiger and I didn't like him. He'd offered the cat underneath us nothing but pain. We felt his power coming one last time. The woman's eyes went wide, face afraid, like she felt the blow coming. I meant to thrust the black tiger down that metaphysical link and beat him with his own game, but Domino made that one last stroke and I was suddenly bucking against his body, against hers, where I still held her against me, and it was enough for her to join us, so that we all screamed our orgasm at once in one long, warm spill of pleasure. I shoved all that pleasure at the vampire, and I felt the connection between her and him break. She was suddenly mine, so much mine. The three of us collapsed to the floor with her trapped underneath our double weight. Her mind floated in a wash of nearly liquid happiness. Her body, like mine, was limp and almost boneless with pleasure. I could feel our three heartbeats inside my head like three drums beating in unison. And from one moment to the next, her mind opened to me. She wanted me to know.

Her master was one of the Harlequin, and he would kill her before he let her go. She'd been sent to spy on us, because the Harlequin had broken with the Vampire Council. They were running from the Mother of All Darkness. The warm edge of pleasure began to fade under that revelation, and then came another.

One of the other tiger survivors was a golden tiger, and the animal to call of one of the other Harlequin. His master was kinder than hers. They'd been sent to see if Jean-Claude could really stand against the Darkness, and if I could really be Master of Tigers. She let me see his face in her mind. She betrayed him to me, because he and his master had done nothing to help her in all those long centuries. They'd respected the bond between servant and master, even knowing that her master had abused her for over a thousand years.

I whispered, "Bastards."

"Yes," she said.

I didn't have to say a word; I thought, "Jean-Claude." I just let him see what I knew. I felt his fear at the word *Harlequin*, but he directed Wicked and Truth and some of the wererats toward the huddled survivors. He knew which man they wanted, because she had given me the face, and I'd given it to him. I also knew her name. Yīyú. It meant Jade, Black Jade.

47

MINUTES LATER I was standing staring down at our other spy. His straight hair was cut short and was a pale, nondescript color. I was betting the hair was dyed. The eyes were a pale brown, almost lion amber. I remembered the eyes of the golden weretiger who had cut me up. Her eyes had been brown in human form, too. But in tiger form she'd had yellow and orange eyes like most tigers. Did only some goldens' eyes change with their shift, like humans'? The eyes were uptilted and there was something exotic to the bone structure, but he couldn't have passed for Chinese like Jade could.

I shook my head. "You're not as old as she is."

"How do you know?" he asked, and his voice, like the rest of him, seemed delicate. He was like most of the older weretigers, not very big. Taller than me, but then most men were.

"You feel younger," I said.

He shifted in the metal bindings. They were a new type of cuff that was being tried by law enforcement for the preternaturally strong. We'd had some of our people try them and so far, they'd held. Wicked touched the weretiger's shoulder with one hand; the other hand had a gun naked in it. The weretiger had given up, just let them capture him, but he was one of the Harlequin and that was supposed to mean something.

Truth had a short sword bare in his hand. The brothers were prepared. I felt pretty safe with them holding him. I knew his name was Topaz. I knew it matched the deep, golden yellow of his tiger color. Through Jade I knew a lot of things.

"He isn't a gold tiger," a woman's voice said. I stepped back from the kneeling man, and turned so I could see who the voice belonged to. It was one of the two female red tigers. This one had red hair cut just above her shoulders, so that the end edges of the hair framed her face. Her hair was a red so dark it was almost a kind of black. Humans didn't come with hair like that outside a dye bottle.

The woman's skin and hair were darker than any of the other tigers, including my memories of Alex's body, the first red tiger I'd met and accidently rolled. Whatever I did tonight, there'd be nothing accidental about it. Her eyebrows were black and blended with the dark red of her hair. Her eyes were the orange and yellow of fire, even at this distance. The white tigers could pass for human eyes if you didn't know what you were looking at, but nothing would make those fire eyes human.

"He is not a gold tiger," she repeated.

"Why not?" I asked.

She made a derisive sound, crossing her arms across the shining cloth of her own designer dress. I thought the dark red was an unfortunate choice for her coloring, but she hadn't asked me. "Because gold is supposed to control us all. If there were a true gold tiger in this room, we would all be bound to his will. I feel nothing. He's just a survivor with delusions."

She had a point. I didn't feel much of any energy from the kneeling weretiger. I believed Jade's memories, but I'd seen no proof beyond that. "If he's supposed to control all the tigers, are you really sure you want him flexing metaphysical muscle?" I asked.

"I enjoyed the floor show, though I thought the women were sent here for Jean-Claude, not you. I don't do women." She made it sound like doing them was somehow bad.

I caught movement and found Jade standing with Domino off to one side. She was looking away, down, her posture as if someone had struck her. Women weren't my normal cup of tea, but I couldn't regret anything I'd done with Jade. Even now I wanted to touch her, and I didn't fight the urge. I just held out my hand and thought of the smell of her skin.

She smiled at me, and that one shy, pleased smile made it worth noticing her pain. She came to my hand and tucked herself in against me. In the heels I was enough taller that she was able to cuddle in against my shoulder the way I did to some men.

The look of disgust on the red tigress's face made me smile. She didn't like that I smiled at her. "I felt your power over the other tigers, but the red clan is made of sterner stuff."

"Who are you?" I asked.

"She's Reba," Victor said, "daughter of the Red Queen."

"I expected your brother," I said.

"Alex is out of the country on some journalist assignment. He's catching a plane and disrupting all his plans because you and your master put out the call." She made it sound ridiculous.

I looked at the men with her. One of them had long red hair spilling over his shoulders. It wasn't as dark as Reba's, though there was a touch of black to its edge. Hunter, that was his name, had hair the color they tell you is red in school. Again, humans didn't have hair like that. His eyes were pure yellow and caught the candlelight as he looked at me. He raised his hand and gave a little wave and smile. I smiled back. I'd have rather had Alex, but I'd already slept with Hunter. He was one of the few in the room I could say that about.

"Don't flirt with her," Reba said, voice cutting like an angry whip across his smile. He stopped looking at me but said, "I thought that's why we were here."

"My mother made us come, but I'm the dominant red here, and that means if I say, no, it's no."

I hugged Jade and laid a soft kiss on her temple, then sent her back to Domino. I looked down at the weretiger in front of me. "I'll be right back."

I stepped out into the middle of the room, and I held my hand out. I understood now that it would have worked with everyone else I slept with in Vegas. I was ready for something a little less dramatic. "Hunter," I said, "come to me."

He smiled, and he started to do what I'd asked.

Reba told the other men to grab him. "Don't let her bewitch him, too."

My red tiger circled inside me, looking up, as if she'd have to climb to escape. She gave a low growl and sniffed the air. I echoed her and we both wanted the red tigers. We wanted people who smelled of home.

We, the tiger and I, looked at the other two men who had grabbed Hunter's arms. They both had shorter hair. One had waves that promised if he'd grow it longer it would be like the other woman with her soft waves that fell around her shoulders. She and the first man had skin that was closer to human redheads, all peaches and cream, and the red of their hair held an orange undertone to it rather than a black. Their eyes were both nearly solid yellow. Siblings maybe, or close cousins, down to the similarity of bone structure that made their faces a little long through the cheeks.

I realized that Hunter's face had that shape, too, and his eyes were strongly yellow. How intermarried was everyone in their clan?

The second man had more difference to him. His hair was the palest red of all, falling around his ears in unruly curls and waves as if he were growing it out from the shorter haircut of the first man. Curly hair was always a bitch to grow out. There was always a stage where you couldn't do anything with it. His eyes were gray with green in them if the light caught them right. Of them all I liked his face best. It was a little like trying to pick a kitten from a litter, except you aren't trying to decide which kitten you'd like to have sex with—well, not unless something's gone horribly wrong for both you and the kitten.

"You aren't our master, Anita Blake. You can't even make one of us cross this room to you. My mother sent us because all the other tigers urged her to, but she believes like I do that you are just another pretender to our throne." She pointed a finger at the white tigers. "It's your two males that are teaching our secrets to outsiders and giving her and her vampire master delusions of grandeur."

"You have not tasted her power yet," Victor said. "Taste it and then tell us that Crispin and Domino are still ours to command."

I decided not to choose. I'd call whichever one wanted to come the most. I held my hand out and felt the red tiger swelling up around me like a red mist. "Red tigers, red tigers, come to me." But it wasn't the words that called them, it was the energy. Once I'd accidentally called every color of unmated male tiger in the country when Marmee Noir had been trying to make me her perfect vessel, but I'd learned to narrow my focus. I narrowed the power down to that handful of people standing there.

Hunter pulled free of the other two men, and they didn't fight him. They just stood there, arms at their sides staring after him, at me.

"Hunter, no!" Reba yelled.

He ignored her and hurried to me. He took my hand in both of his and laid a kiss on it. He began to lay kisses up my arm, and at six feet he was tall enough that it was easier to drop to his knees to kiss his way up my lower arm than to bend over. Every kiss grew the energy between us, so that I saw a visual behind my eyes of little red sparks, as if every kiss warmed my skin. Sex didn't make tiger energy grow stronger; that was my little extra, Jean-Claude's *ardeur*, and my succubus.

The man with the pale red hair started across the room. Reba yelled, "Jared, come back here!"

Hunter had gotten to his feet so he could kiss up to my shoulder. He moved behind me, lifting my hair so he could kiss my neck. Jared touched my hand, and Hunter snarled at him over my shoulder, one arm around my waist drawing me in closer to his body. Jared dropped to his knees, which let me know that either Hunter was above him in the hierarchy of their clan, or Jared had already lost fights to him and didn't want to try it again.

The red tiger might have tried to choose, but I understood now that I didn't have to; we needed them all. "No fighting over me, Hunter; you know I share well."

I almost felt him pouting for a moment, body tense, and then he let it go. Even his body relaxed. The red warmth spilled down my hand and helped me draw the other weretiger closer. Jared stayed on his knees as if he didn't trust Hunter, but he kept my hand, rubbing his cheek against me, scent-marking me. The weight of Hunter at my back and Jared at my side helped spread that warm, red energy farther like a pool of water trickling closer, growing deeper.

The last man started toward me. Reba yelled, "No!" She had the other woman by the arm. She wasn't letting her last tiger get away; she'd hold this one herself.

The man stopped, obviously torn.

Hunter bent over my neck and suddenly bit me. Not hard, not to hurt, but it tipped the energy closer to sex. He set his teeth in my neck until I made small noises. A hand began to slide up my leg, tracing the edge of my hose. Somewhere in all of it I'd closed my eyes, so that when a third pair of hands started up the other leg, I had to open my eyes to see the last weretiger on his knees beside Jared. His fingers played in the hollow of my thigh, just at the edge of the cloth of the thong. Either it was a way of teasing me, or he was waiting for permission to cross that last lacy barrier.

I felt the energy spike, red tiger, hot and angry, and it wasn't us. Hunter stopped biting me to look across the room. Reba had a knife in her hand. The hem of her dress was still shifted so that I saw the thigh holster. She'd slashed the other woman's face open and was holding her by her wrist while she bled. Reba turned her tiger eyes to me and roared, "You can't have us!"

The nameless male stood up and started back toward them. "Lacey."

"She's his sister; his twin," Hunter said.

"You had to use a blade on her," I said. "You can't shift just your hands."

"She only has one form," Jared said.

I'd never seen a wereanything use a blade on another wereanimal before. Reba had just admitted that she was too weak to shapeshift fast enough to fight. She only changed into a big tiger, no half-human form for her. So weak.

She pulled the woman's arm up hard, meaning it to hurt. The woman made a small, hurt sound for her. It pissed me off, and better yet it pissed off the red tiger. She'd missed her own kind. They all smelled like home, and she didn't like them getting hurt.

"Let her go," I said, and my voice echoed as if the red mist were more solid than it looked behind my eyes.

"She's mine!"

"No," I said, "she's not!" And that last word growled out from between my lips. I could feel the rumble of it all the way down my chest. I didn't think what I'd do next, I was just moving toward them faster than I should have been able to move. It was as if I were there beside them before I'd had time to think. Reba tried to move the woman back with her, as she slashed at me. That one slash let me know that she didn't know how to fight with a knife.

I smiled; I couldn't help it.

"I will cut you."

I shook my head. "No, you won't." I moved into her, and she had the speed, but now so did I, and I had the training. She tried to keep the girl's arm in hers, like a hostage, and that put her off balance even more. I got close, and she did what I thought she would do, slashing at the air in front of her. It was more trying to keep me back than trying to cut me. I blocked her arm at the wrist, grabbed her elbow, applied pressure, and hooked my leg behind hers. I brought her to the ground with her arm and its knife still trapped in a joint lock, so that when she hit the floor I already had pressure on her elbow.

The woman that she'd cut ran toward the other red tigers. It was just Reba and me. "Drop the knife or I break the arm."

She didn't drop the knife, so I added a little more pressure to the elbow. She cried out, then sent the knife clanging to the floor. I kicked it out of reach and found Truth there to pick it up. So hard to bodyguard someone when they have to do their own fighting.

"It's against every rule for you to use a knife to discipline your people. If you aren't queen enough to shapeshift and do it right, then you aren't allowed to be queen at all," I said.

"Look who's talking, human!" She spat that last word at me.

I called out, "How bad is Lacey hurt?"

"The blade was silver," one of the men said.

"If she's scarred for life, Reba, I promise you, you will be, too."

Her eyes widened and she struggled. I leaned on the joint a little more, and it stopped her moving. I couldn't grow claws and discipline her like a real queen, but I could do something that most dominants couldn't do. It was a rarer gift, and depending on how you did it, it hurt more. I'd been gentle with the white tiger, Julia. I wouldn't be gentle with this one.

I gazed down at her, and I could almost see the red tiger over me like a hood. The energy of it called to her tiger. I whispered, "Change for me."

"I will not, and you can't make me. You are a survivor of an attack. You are not pureblood."

She was so angry, but anger was food, too. I drank her anger down through the feel of my hands on her skin and the pulse of her blood beating against my hands. There wasn't much anger; it was a thin disguise for her fear. She was so afraid, afraid of me, afraid of how weak she was, afraid that her mother had sent her here to die.

"Let go!"

I let go of the joint lock but not the arm. I rode that down so that I was straddling her waist, pinning both her arms to the floor.

Fear and anger fought in her eyes, down her skin, across the energy of the red tigress. She tried for bold, and said, "Are you going to fuck me, too? Is that all you know how to do here in St. Louis?"

I laughed, and felt my eyes go, not tiger, but vampire. My eyes if I'd been one for real. I felt the fear win out over the anger, as I moved her arm down, so that I could pin it under one knee. She could have fought me. She had the strength, but for all she tried to do she could have been human; hell, most people would have fought, but she didn't. I put my hand against the back of her neck. Her skin was warm; the small curls at the back of her neck, silky against my hand.

"What are you doing?" she whispered.

"Making my point," I said, as I leaned into her. I kissed her, and she froze against me, as if she didn't know what to do. I let my tiger spill into my mouth, and into hers. Not because I was about to change, or in danger, but because I needed her never to fight me again.

I tried to think, but the red tiger would have killed her, and distant behind that was a very practical thought, that if we did this there would be no more arguing. I looked up from the woman under me and found Jean-Claude standing by me. I knew it wasn't my thought. The problem was that I agreed with that very practical, very ruthless thought. It's hard to fight the bad thought when you agree with it.

I had a moment of choice, and then I closed my eyes and I kissed her. It wasn't just the red tiger that spilled through me, it was all the other colors, only gold held back, but the others spilled into my mouth and across my lips and into her. The energies tore her apart. I straightened up a second before a wave of clear, warm fluid and blood exploded across me. The violence of it tore screams from her, her body bucking underneath mine, until a tiger lay underneath me, shivering as if everything hurt. Her fur was so dark a red it was almost as black as her stripes. She stared up at me with the same eyes, but now they were full of pain, and very afraid.

I got up from her, a little shaky on my heels. Jean-Claude was there to take my hand, to steady me. I looked into his eyes and they were as blue and blind with power as mine were brown and black with it. I was covered in blood and fluid.

"The dress is ruined," I said.

He smiled. "We'll buy another." He led me until we stood in front of the gold tiger who was still kneeling between the guards. His eyes were a little wide, lips parted. He was afraid of us.

"Do I need to make my point again?" I asked.

"What point do you want to make?" he asked.

"That the tigers are ours. That we can be Master of Tigers. That's what you and the rest of your people came to St. Louis to find out, isn't it?"

"You read that from Jade's mind," he said.

"We did," Jean-Claude said. Jake had also told us that, but we let that slide. We were winning. Never overexplain when you're winning.

"My master knows what I know. He knows you only need gold to complete the tigers."

That was our cue, or rather Devil's and Envy's. We were keeping the other golden tigers hidden, but the two that were ours would get trotted out. The rest could stay hidden for now.

I didn't have to use a phone. I just thought of Dev, and Jean-Claude did the same for Envy. Micah had Dev by the hand and led him to me. His hand wrapped around mine and my skin was flushed and warm, like being wrapped in a blanket of comfortable power. Richard had Envy by the hand and handed her to Jean-Claude.

The other golden stared at them. "The young ones we cared for were massacred. Those of us who were hiding them never told the others, so that if one was destroyed the others would be safe. My master and I didn't know if you would have more of my kind here."

"Jade saw you with your master and was envious that you seemed to love one another," I said. "I wouldn't break a love that's survived thousands of years. That's got to be rare even among vampires."

"I did not want to give up our tie, but I did not know that we would find other golden tigers in time to help you."

"We could part you from your master," Jean-Claude said.

"If it is your will I don't think we can stop you." He seemed very calm about it.

"You really did come here to sacrifice yourself for the common good, didn't you?" I asked.

"The gold tigers have hidden for centuries. We learned from our earlier ignorance. Now there are more of us than the black or the blue clans. We want you to be Master of Tigers, Jean-Claude. We need you to be, because if we do this we break with the Darkness that made us, and if she ever gains power again she will make us long for true death long before she gives it to us."

"Why would you risk her anger to join with us?" I asked.

"She knows now what we did."

"That it was her own beloved Harlequin who put her into that long-ago sleep," Jean-Claude said.

He nodded.

"So the white tiger's myth is true," I said.

"It is," he said.

I raised eyebrows at that. Jade hadn't known that. I didn't think he read my mind, but he said, "We heard how you divided master from servant with the lion and the Master of Chicago, and the two Vegas tigers from their queen and master. We knew that there was a chance that you would divide at least one of us from our masters. It was always one of the gifts of the Mother, to break all bonds and bind only to her."

"Jade didn't know your whole plan," I said.

"No, because then her master would have known, and we considered him corrupt."

"Without Jade's energy to raise his level, you can kill him," I said.

"We could not trust him."

"You hoped we'd steal Jade from him and make him weak," I said.

"Yes," he said.

"And you wanted her free of him so that when he dies, she doesn't die with him," I said.

"She has endured enough at his hands. When we realized there was another vampire who could break her free of him, we moved to make it so."

"She thought you did not see her suffering," Jean-Claude said.

"We saw, but we could not free her from him."

"You waited for another vampire to be created who could free her," I said.

"Who could free us all," he said.

I gave him the look that deserved. "We're good, but we aren't the immortal Darkness."

"You don't have to be. You just have to be able to cut bonds between master and servant, all servants, and that you can do, you have proved that."

"What do you want of us?" Jean-Claude asked.

"So you would spare me and my master, even feeling the power you gain from each broken bond?"

"We have enough power," I said.

He studied us. "You have a great deal of power, but to do what we need, more would be better."

"We'll find more," Micah said.

He studied us all. "You would spare me and my master, because he and I love each other. You would spare us for love," he said.

I looked at Jean-Claude and my other men out of habit more than need. "What else is there?" I asked.

He smiled up at us. It was almost a beatific smile, his face shining with love close to adoration. I didn't think it was from looking at us. I thought he was more thinking of his master, his love. "That is the answer we hoped for."

"So you gambled centuries of happiness, your free will, and your very existence, on love?" I said.

He shrugged with his arms still bound behind his back, and the guards still heavy on his shoulders. "As you said, is there really anything else worth gambling everything for?"

What could I say but, "No, there isn't." And standing there holding everyone's hands, feeling the hum of the energy we'd raised between us, I believed that.

48

THE HARLEQUIN'S GOLD tiger went back to his master. Jake and Jade stayed with us. Jake joined us in the gym like all the good guards. Jade joined us in the gym, too, but she's not a guard. She can fight and she's fearsomely good, but the centuries of abuse have left her with a victim's mentality, and that doesn't make a good guard. Maybe I can introduce her to Richard's therapist?

Cynric, who wants to be called Cyn, pronounced *Sin*, stayed in St. Louis. He's the only blue tiger we have and we need him close to us. I'm still not sure how I feel about it, but unless I want to divide the female blue tiger from her master, who she also loves, Cyn is the only one we have to bind to us. He's hitting the gym, and we're looking at enrolling him in his last year of high school. When I realized he was a junior I was totally creeped, but he's legal, and his guardians Max and Bibiana did what they had to do to make his stay with us legally okay. I'm still working on my issues with it all. But one problem at a time.

They found the Master of Atlanta by using the cadaver dogs like I'd suggested. They fried him with an exterminator team and it made international news. He'd slaughtered another dozen people before they tracked him down. The few vampires that survived his death are in need of a new Master of the City. Jean-Claude and I are debating on who to send. Meng Die wants it to be her. She's friendlier to me since we helped her up her power level. What she actually said was, "When you dance with the devil, it might as well be a devil who can give you your own corner of hell to rule." Not a rousing endorsement, but it'll do.

Richard has continued to be okay. I learned that the three men who tried to kill him were dead. I'd assumed the guards that we sent to rescue him had killed them, but they'd only helped dispose of the bodies. Richard as his wolf had hunted them through the woods and killed them. Jean-

Claude and I held him one night while he cried about that. He didn't cry about killing them so much as about how much he enjoyed killing them. In our ways, all three of us worry that we will be the monster.

It turned out that the effects of the *ardeur* and some of the odd pairings wore off. We offered every woman not on birth control a morning-after pill. I was thankful once again that I was on the pill. Condoms for me were an extra protection—not my only one. J.J. is back in New York, but she's also back to being in love only with Jason. Bianca, the swanmane, is a little unhappy about that, but it's not the *ardeur* that makes her miss J.J. She just liked J.J., and who could blame her?

Jake helped us hunt Padma, Master of Beasts. It wasn't that hard to break the Mother's hold on him. Jake thinks it worked so well because my power is similar to his. I'm not so sure. It was too easy, as the old saying goes. But we took our victory, and the Dragon and the Traveller are sending people of their line to St. Louis, so if the Mother does try to take them over we can have a leg up on breaking them free. We can't find the Morte d'Amour. He still carries Marmee Noir inside him, but he's stopped trying to take us over. If I didn't know better I'd say he, and she, were afraid of us. He took over another of his descendants in Europe. The vampires killed nearly seventy people before they were stopped by the army. Countries where vampires are still illegal don't have legal vampire executioners. They usually call in what amounts to the National Guard.

Some tigers of every color stayed with us. We have enough blood donors that most of our vampires can feed on shapeshifters. We're the only vampire kiss in the country that can boast such rich food for all our bloodsuckers.

I still miss windows and light and air, but until we find and free the Lover of Death, the Circus of the Damned is the safest place to be. We're doing the best to make it home.

I've rearranged my schedule so that I have three afternoons a week free of clients, so I can train with the guards. Nathaniel tries to have coffee ready for me in the kitchen when I come home so we have a few minutes to visit. One afternoon Matthew was at the kitchen table drinking milk and eating a freshly made peanut butter and jelly sandwich.

"Hey, Matthew," I said, and made sure my suit jacket was lying flat over my gun so I wouldn't flash.

"Hey, 'Nita," he said, with a mouthful of sandwich. He stood up in his chair and raised his arms for me to pick him up. He puckered up for a kiss and I gave him one. He got lipstick and I got grape jelly.

I went to Nathaniel and started to kiss him, then remembered Matthew's comment at the dance recital: *All the big boys kiss you, 'Nita.*

Nathaniel gave me a puzzled look and then kissed me, and I kissed him back, because I didn't know what else to do. Besides, the smell of his skin made me feel better than the smell of the coffee he handed me.

Nathaniel sat down at the table near Matthew, and I did, too. "Monica's taking a deposition out of state. It's apparently a witness they've been searching for on a fraud case."

I sat down at the table and sniffed the coffee. It smelled good. "How long is she gone for?"

"Overnight. We drop him at preschool tomorrow, and she'll pick him up like normal."

The guards spilled into the kitchen. It was shift change. They'd get coffee and maybe a snack and then we'd all go work out. The guards called, "Hey, kiddo." Lisandro, who had two little ones of his own, ruffled Matthew's auburn curls. He chattered with them, excited, like it was all normal. I took off my jacket, because I wanted to and every guard was armed to the teeth and not hiding it. My little gun didn't seem so bad.

He called out to Devil. "Can I come watch you practice?"

"Sure," he said, and he leaned over and kissed me hi. So did Nicky. All the big boys kiss 'Nita.

When everyone had had coffee or water, or just a few minutes to decompress, we all got up and went for the gym. We moved surrounded by muscular armed and dangerous men. Matthew took my hand and Nathaniel's. "What are we reading tonight, Natty?" he asked.

"*Goodnight Moon?*"

"No, that's a little kid's book. I'm big now."

Nathaniel smiled and said, "How about *Peter Pan?*"

"You mean like the cartoon?"

He smiled wider. "Yeah, like the cartoon."

"I like Peter Pan, he can fly!"

Peter Pan was the first book Micah, Nathaniel, and I ever read to each other, and now we'd read it to Matthew. I wasn't sure I was comfortable with everything Matthew saw and learned with us, but his mother was okay with it. Who was I to bitch?

What bothers me most about keeping Matthew is that Nathaniel is starting to hint that maybe we could have a rug rat of our own. Me, a mom? So not happening. But if he keeps hinting about kids, he may talk me into that puppy he's been wanting.

I can see us with a puppy, but a baby? Not only no, but hell no. I'm a U.S. Marshal, a legal vampire executioner, and I raise the dead for a living. None of those jobs would work with a baby, and not even the thought of having Nathaniel's lavender eyes staring up at me from some curly-haired moppet is enough to change that. Besides, brown beats light-colored eyes genetically. I'd more likely be staring into a pair of my own dark brown, and I can see that every time I look in a mirror. I'm not fond enough of my own eyes to want to see them in someone else's face.